Amber and Danielle Brown both graduated from Rider University where they studied Communications/Journalism and sat on the editorial staff for the *On Fire!!* literary journal. They then pursued a career in fashion and spent five years in NYC working their way up, eventually managing their own popular fashion and lifestyle blog. Amber is also a screenwriter, so they live in LA, which works out perfectly so Danielle can spoil her plant babies with copious amount of sunshine.

SOMEONE HAD TO DO IT

AMBER & DANIELLE BROWN

PIATKUS

PIATKUS

First published in the US in 2022 by Graydon House,
An imprint of HarperCollins Publishers
First published in Great Britain in 2022 by Piatkus

1 3 5 7 9 10 8 6 4 2

A CIP catalogue record for this book
is available from the British Library.

ISBN 978-0-349-43321-9

Printed and bound in Great Britain
by Clays Ltd, Elcograf S.p.A.

Papers used by Piatkus are from well-managed forests
and other responsible sources.

Piatkus
An imprint of
Little, Brown Book Group
Carmelite House
50 Victoria Embankment
London EC4Y 0DZ

An Hachette UK Company
www.hachette.co.uk

www.littlebrown.co.uk

Mom and Dad,
Hope this makes you proud.
(Not the sex scenes, but you know what we mean.)

SOMEONE HAD TO DO IT

PROLOGUE

BRANDI

A stranger's hands have been all over me. Their touch invasive, like my body held no value to them at all, filthy and unworthy of decency and respect, and I had to take it all silently, standing there like a piece of cattle.

The last trace of Nate's cologne has been contaminated by a suffocating stench I'm not sure I'll ever be able to fully scrub from my skin. But I keep thinking about another man's scent.

It wasn't just that he smelled expensive; he had a kingly scent, like I should curtsy in his presence. His smile was as intimidating as it was inviting. At the party, which feels like forever ago now, he somehow made me feel like the only one in a room of hundreds, radiating power and vitality like no one I've ever met. It was impossible not to get fully swept up in his magnetism once we locked eyes.

And then he was dead.

1

BRANDI

I had a ton of illusions, vivid fantasies of what it would be like to score a coveted internship at Van Doren. Deluded old me thought I would be strutting around the stunning tri-story headquarters in single-soled heels, flitting from design concept meetings to on-location photo shoots, living my best fashion-girl life. Instead, I'm in the back corner of the two-thousand-square-foot ready-to-wear samples closet scrubbing fresh vomit from a slinky gown worth double my rent during my lunch hour.

Italian Vogue's current cover girl borrowed the hand-sewn dress for a red-carpet event last night, and apparently getting it back on a rack without ruining it was too much for one of the other interns to handle. She was so hungover when she came to the office this morning that she vomited all over the dress before making it out of the elevator. But of course this dress needs to be ready for another model to wear to some big extravaganza tonight, and since I'm the designated fuckover intern, I have to clean it by hand because the satin-blend fabric is too delicate to be dry-cleaned.

This is what it takes.

I chant this to remind myself why I'm here as the lactic acid builds up in my biceps. Working for Van Doren has been on my proverbial vision board ever since I reluctantly gave up the idea, in middle school, that I could be Beyoncé. It's a storm of hauling hundreds of pounds of runway samples around the city and sitting in on meetings with the sketch artists. A glorious, next-to-holy experience when I'm on duty at photo shoots and one of the stylists sends me to fetch *another* blazer, not a specific blazer, which means I get to use my own vestiary inclinations to make the selection. Which has only happened once, but still.

Just as I get the stain faded by at least seventy percent, I hear the sharp staccato of someone in stilettos approaching. I turn around and see Lexi. Lexi with her bimonthly touched-up white-blond hair and generous lip filler that she'll never admit to having injected. When she steps closer in her head-to-toe Reformation, I am grateful that I remembered to put on a few sprays of my Gypsy Water perfume. The one that smells like rich people. But the way she's staring at me right now, it's clear that no matter how much I try, I am still not on her level. I do not fit in here. She does not see me as her equal, despite the fact that we are both unpaid, unknown, disposable interns. It's become glaringly obvious that at Van Doren, it's not actually about what you contribute, but more about how blue your blood is. Lexi doesn't even know my name, though I've been here a solid nine weeks and I'm pretty sure I've told her at least a dozen times.

I'm already on edge because of my assignment, so I jump in before she can ask in her monotone voice. "Brandi."

"Right," she says, like she does every time yet still forgets. "Chloé wants the Instagram analytics report for last week. She said she asked you to put it together an hour ago."

Which is true, but completely unfair since Jenna from marketing also asked me to run to Starbucks to buy thirty-one-ounce cups of liquid crack for her and her entire department for a 9:00 a.m. meeting, an effort that took three trips total, and technically I'm still working on the data sheets I promised Eric from product development. Not to mention the obvious: getting rid of the puke from the dress.

"I'm still working on it," I tell her.

Lexi stares at me, her overly filled brows lifted, as if she's waiting for the rest of my excuse. I understand her, but also I'm wondering how she still hasn't realized this is not a case of Resting Bitch Face I have going on, that I am actually intolerant of her nagging.

Normally, I am not this terse. But nothing about today has been normal. Since this week is my period week, I'm retaining water in the most unflattering of places and the pencil dress I'm wearing has been cutting off the circulation in my thighs for the past couple of hours, and being that I've spent most of my break destroying the evidence of someone else's bad decisions, it is not my fault that I'm not handling this particularly well.

"I'll send it over as soon as I'm done," I say to Lexi so she can leave. But she doesn't.

"HR wants to see you," she says with what looks like a smirk.

My mouth opens. I have no idea what HR could want, and although I'm still new to this employee thing, I know this can't be good.

"Like, now," Lexi barks and pivots away in her strappy, open-toe stilts.

I hang the sample next to the door, and before I leave the room I pause to briefly take in the rest of the dresses stuffed on the racks, each one in that chic, elevated aesthetic that is the cornerstone of Van Doren. This is my favorite part of the day, the chaotic nature of this room a little overwhelming but also inspiring, and I can't wait for the day that this is *my* world, not just one I'm peeking my head into. A world in which I command respect.

I cross through the merchandising department, where everyone has their own private office with aerial views of Hell's Kitchen, Soho and the Garment District, and then move through the maze of the sprawling suite in a mild sort of panic until I remind myself that I have done nothing wrong. Ever since spring semester ended, I've been putting in more hours than the sun. I slip in at six-thirty when the building is dark and vaguely ominous, my eyes still puffy with sleep, and when I finally drag myself into the elevator at the end of the day, it's just as black and quiet outside. I religiously show up in current-season heels despite the blisters, albeit mass-produced renditions of the Fendi, Balenciaga and Bottega Venetas the other summer interns casually strut around in, and mostly stick to myself. I am careful about raising my voice, even if I vehemently disagree with my neurotic supervisor. I keep my tongue as puritanical as a nun's, even when *fucking incel* or *coddled narcissistic bitch* are on the tip of it. I'm not rude or combative. I stay away from gossip. I complete all my tasks with time to spare, which is usually when I check Twitter and help out some of the other interns, even though I'd rather FaceTime Nate in the upstairs bathroom with the magical lighting. I even entertain the gang of sartorially inclined Amy Coopers in the making who insist on obnoxiously complaining to me about all of their first-world, one-percenter problems. I've done nothing but consistently given them reasons to think I am a capable, qualified, talented intern who would make an exceptional employee.

I have nothing to worry about.

When I knock on the door to Lauren's office, she looks up from her desk and waves me in through the glass. I have

a feeling this will not go my way when I see that my supervisor, Chloé, one of the more amiable assistants, is also here,
fiddling with her six-carat engagement ring in the corner and
avoiding eye contact.

"Have a seat, Brandi," Lauren says, and I tell myself to ignore that her bright pink lipstick extends above her lip on
one side.

There is no small talk. No *hello* or *how's it going?* Under al-
ternate circumstances, I would feel slighted, but because I'm
growing more anxious by the second, I'm grateful for her
smugness.

As I sit down, Chloé shifts in her chair, and I speak before
she can. "I'm sorry. The Instagram report is at the top of my
task list. I'll definitely have it to you before I leave today. I
just—"

"That's not why you're here, Brandi," Lauren interjects.

"Oh." I pause, and as she glances down at her notes, I try
to make meaningful eye contact with my supervisor, but she
is still actively dodging my eyes.

Lauren begins by throwing out a few compliments. My
work ethic is admirable and I have great attention to detail,
she says, and the whole time my heart is pounding so loud,
I can barely make out most of her words. Chloé jumps in to
effusively agree, then Lauren finally stops beating around the
bush and looks me directly in the eyes.

"We just don't feel like you're fitting into the culture here
at Van Doren."

Every word feels like a backhanded slap across the face,
the kind that twists your neck and makes the world go still
and white for a few disconcerting moments, like an orgasm
but not like an orgasm. It's obvious what they mean, yet can't
quite bring themselves to say.

They just don't like that I'm black.

They don't like the way I wear my braids—long and un-apologetic, grazing my hips like a Nubian mermaid.

They don't like that I'm not the smile-and-nod type, willing to assimilate to their idea of what I should be, how I should act. *Culture.*

That's their code for we-can't-handle-your-individuality-but-since-we-don't-want-to-seem-racist-we'll-invent-this-little-loophole.

Black plus exceptional equals threat.

"If we don't see any improvement in the coming weeks, we're going to have to let you go," Lauren says with no irony, her mouth easing into a synthetic smile.

I blink. I cannot believe this is happening right now. It wasn't supposed to go like this, my internship at Van Doren, the *one* fashion company whose ethics align with mine. I wasn't just blowing smoke up Lauren's ass when I interviewed for this job, though I was looking at her sideways, wondering why she had not a stitch of Van Doren on. I'd splurged on a single-shouldered jumpsuit from this year's spring collection that I couldn't really afford just to impress her, while she hadn't even felt the need to represent the brand at all as she shot out all those futile questions interviewers love propelling at candidates, I'm convinced, just to see them squirm. Even minuscule amounts of power can be dangerous.

This is bullshit, being put on probation, and I'd give anything to have the balls to call them on it. As I sit here paralyzed, Lauren's words reverberate in my head and I rebuke them, want to suffocate and bury them.

We're going to have to let you go.

Her pert voice keeps echoing in my head, not just the words, but the detached, artificial concern in her tone, and every time it does I feel defenseless and betrayed all over again. That weird feeling you get when a nightmare becomes too hopeless to bear; that breathless moment right before you snap awake.

They both stare at me, waiting for my reaction. I tell myself to say something, to stand up for myself. But instead, I just nod in acquiescence and turn the edges of my mouth up into what I hope is at least some semblance of an assiduous smile— exactly what they want me to do. As if this is all *my* fault, *my* doing. As if I am taking full responsibility for their narrow view of what a future member of their team should look like.

Most girls like me, from the hood, from the other side of the Hudson, where the median household income is in the same bracket as the cost of a preloved Birkin, can't afford to participate in a three-month unpaid internship. And of course, it was set up this way by design, to keep a certain demographic out, to keep the new hires white and well-bred with plenty of generational wealth to subsidize a full season of free labor.

I want to say all this to her. I should. But that would be like trying to put out fire with a jug of diesel. So I nod again, robotically, and go back downstairs to finish my assignment, head tucked, a low-frequency hum muting most of the sounds in the suite.

Once I've gotten the dress to the point where I have to squint to see where the rust-hued stain used to be, I tap the screen of my iPhone for the time. Nate's plane should be landing in about an hour. I take an elevator back upstairs so I can grab my bag, and though I should probably check in with Chloé to remind her that I'm leaving early, which she approved over a week ago, I don't because I'm sweaty and hurt and still a little salty. Also, I do not want to be held accountable for what comes out of my mouth while I'm in this state.

Before I head out the door, I stop into the bathroom to pop a few Advil to keep my cramps at bay and check to see if my face is still intact. I end up bumping into Vanessa from PR, who is on her way out, and she asks me to stop by later to pick up her personal dry cleaning. While this isn't the first time this has happened, I can't help but feel degraded, especially since she doesn't even attempt to look up from her phone as she passes me. I politely tell her I can't because I'm actually leaving the office now, but let her know that I can come back for it first thing Monday morning. She stops so fast, it's like she's collided with an invisible wall.

"Well, you can pick them up now, can't you?" she asks, swinging around to face me.

But I can tell by her tone that it isn't actually a question. I should really say no since I'm already running late and I might not even be at Van Doren for much longer. But I have always been docile in the presence of authority figures and I really don't want word to get back to HR. So I nod and follow behind her as she leads the way to her bright corner office with her impossibly large Monstera. I lug her Theory and Zimmermann on the express R train with me, clutching them tight to my chest next to a guy who is aggressively watching hentai on his iPad and quietly masturbating under his dusty backpack with his free hand.

I make it to baggage claim just in time. Nate told me I didn't have to trek all the way to JFK this time, but it's been three weeks since we've seen each other in the flesh, no screen or satellite signals between us; way too long since I've felt his mouth on the darkest, sweetest parts of my body. And after the shitty day I've had, I want to soak up every minute I can with him. I wait next to an elderly couple, dressed in his favorite vibe: cropped FIT sweatshirt that I slashed myself slouched over one shoulder, high-waisted cutoffs and the Yeezys he got me for my last birthday. At first, I was on the fence about accepting them, but Nate was adamant about convincing me to separate the man's politics from his art. I still haven't quite managed to detangle the two, but they're hot, so I've somehow managed to work out this cognitive dissonance to the point of tolerance.

Just as I glance up from my phone, a slim Asian guy strapped with a heavy Nikon connected to a behemoth lens crashes into me. He's tall and dressed in a thin, crew-neck sweatshirt and jeans with busted-out knees, his black hair hanging past his shoulders. He apologizes briskly but doesn't stop moving. He's rushing to turn on his camera and adjust the overhead light panel. My eyes flick around. Someone's coming down the escalator and a crowd is forming.

Of course the paparazzi have beat me here. I roll my eyes and look away. Until Nikon guy bumps into me *again*, down on his knees now, trying to get a better angle of Nate heading through the crowd.

Nate must have spotted me first because he's already making a beeline for me, head down as he bypasses the guys with their cameras—there's three of them hovering now—but he slows for a few fans who ask for pictures with him, two girls in crop tops and a little boy with his father, and it's hard to tell which of the latter two is his biggest fan.

Sometimes I forget that other people look at him so differently than I do, that he's a frontrunner for the next NFL draft pick, the son of a Hall of Famer and even better than his four-time MVP father. But Nate isn't like most ballers.

I know, I know. They all say that. But it's true. Camera flashes give him anxiety, and he's into monogamy.

For Nate, the game is just the game, his passion, his EKG, but not a gateway to fame and above-the-law regard. When we first started hanging out, I didn't even know who he was. I knew he played football at Ohio State, a whole five hundred miles away, and honestly, that was enough to make me apprehensive about the whole thing. But after FaceTiming each other for a few weeks five hours at a time, peeling back the layers and witnessing how sweet and unassuming he is, I was blindsided when he showed me pics of him and his father, his dad wearing his black-and-yellow jersey in most of the shots. It quickly became obvious that he's basically like the first son of professional football. Nate thought it was cute, charming in a sort of pitiful way, how completely oblivious I was to the football world and its titans. Of course, I'd heard his name before, but Robinsons are almost as ubiquitous as Smiths and Browns, so it wasn't my fault that I hadn't made the connection.

I thought all celebrity kids were coddled, entitled, self-absorbed assholes, and maybe most of them are, but not Nate. He comes from money but never leads with it. It's only in the small, significant moments—like when a waiter accidentally brings out the wrong entrée and he says it's cool, orders another, pays for both and still tips twenty-five percent—that I remember he's rich and doesn't ever have to worry about a nebulous 401(k) or paying off student loans. Everything is always "cool" with Nate. Except when the suited security guards at high-end department stores are on us like bees on a snapdragon, or when he finds a "fuck you nigger" comment under one of his touchdown dance videos on Instagram. I remind him that their micro- and macroaggressions aren't personal and do whatever I can to make him laugh and forget the rest of the world on those nights. I hate how much it gets him down. He went to a thirty-grand-a-semester PWI in liberal Manhattan where his white peers treated him like a prince and created a warped perception that we live in a post-racial society.

Nate finally makes his way through the small but multiplying crowd, most of the people swarming now just to see what all the fuss is about, not because they actually recognize Nate, and our eyes meet. My heart flutters just the tiniest bit. Multiple cameras are still going off, the flashes almost blinding now, but I ignore them. He's got his backpack slung over one shoulder, and is wearing his usual uniform—a plain white tee, slouchy hoodie, sweatpants—and it's obvious what's underneath, or lack thereof, and maybe it's vainglorious of me, but I like it. I like the rest of the world knowing what my man's got because I know he's only giving it to me. My eyes want to linger, but I look up. He's smiling at me, white teeth framed by full lips, cheekbones high like mountains and deepset eyes. I want to sit on his face while he laughs and tells me he can't breathe.

I can't hold back my smile any longer because even after this clusterfuck of a day, I feel anew. "Hey, you."

"Hey, yourself. Thought you weren't coming?"

Not waiting for an answer, he leans down to kiss me. I stand on the tips of my toes and wrap my arms around his neck. He smells warm and clean, shea butter with hints of soap and water underneath. I love this place, right here in his arms. It feels safe, familiar and comfortable. Like nothing bad could ever happen here.

Shutters are still going off, closer now. I pull away, my eyes darting left to right, suddenly empathizing with every fish stuck in a bowl somewhere.

It wasn't always like this. Things did a one-eighty last year after one of Nate's teammates accidentally leaked naked footage of him in the locker room in an Instagram Live. Nate was in the frame for no more than three seconds, approaching his locker in the background—but of course, someone took a screenshot and posted it. It was trending on Twitter for two days straight. At first, it was entertaining, watching him squirm under the gale of sudden attention. But then there were so many Big Black Dick and anaconda memes going around, the dean at his school heard about it and his dad's publicist had to release an official statement asking for privacy. He gained almost a quarter million followers in twenty-four hours. It's been this way ever since, a maelstrom.

Of course, if it had been a girl caught on camera with everything exposed, it would have been a crime against humanity and all the #MeToo enthusiasts would have rallied around her. And for some, it wouldn't have been an accident. The media would have insisted that it was a scam, a cleverly planned stunt for attention and publicity.

"Come on," Nate says against my ear. I can barely hear him over the crowd, which is maybe two dozen people now. He takes my hand, and we head for the exit.

We barely make it past the threshold of his apartment before our hands are pulling at each other, clothes and shoes on the floor behind us as we slam into walls, knock over stacks of books, picture frames, tripping over ourselves and laughing as we back into doors, moving from corner to corner as if the place isn't big enough to hold the both of us. The AC isn't running and it is at least ninety degrees in this place, but neither of us stops to adjust it, and by the time we finally make it to the bed, we've both dissolved into a liquid state, nothing but sweat and soft moans between us. I'm panting before he's even inside me, and when he finally pushes through, slow and sure, it feels new and familiar at the same time.

Like finally coming home after being away for too long.

Like discovering your favorite song all over again.

"Hey," I say, rolling onto my side, and all I see is delectable brown skin. "You deleted those pics I sent you, right?"

Nate is on his back, sweat glistening down his broad chest and lean stomach, looking as if all the life has been drained from him. He'd sleep and fuck and football, football, fuck and sleep on repeat if it was up to him.

"Not yet," he mumbles with a lopsided smirk.

"Don't forget," I say as gently as I can.

I don't even know why this is on my mind right now. It's not like I haven't sent him nudes before. We weren't even together a full three months yet, that solid span of time after which you know if you can really trust a guy or not, when he sent me pics of himself in all his glory, face included, like a Mapplethorpe portrait. They were so beautiful, so uniquely vulnerable, and since we were coming up on six weeks of zero physical contact because his campus is in the middle of West Bumblefuck, USA, I felt obligated to send something of equal immodesty back. I made him delete them that weekend. And then last week I was at the laundromat, scrolling through Twitter, waiting for my clothes to dry, when I want to see your pussy popped up on my screen. Then: Send me a pic. It was so unexpected, so completely out of nowhere, that I felt like a slave to my own body, like embarrassingly, pubescent-level horny, so desperate to fuck I sent a few pictures as soon as I got home without even considering *not* sending them.

And it's not like I don't trust him. I *know* he won't show any of his boys or do anything nefarious with my pics—he's not like that, not at all—but there is also the voice in the back of my head that knows it's a risky situation no matter what. You never know. If a picture is worth a thousand words, nudes are priceless sagas that can be misinterpreted in more ways than the Bible.

Nate nods absently. "I'll do it later."

I know he will. I let it go. "So how long are you here for again?"

"Training starts back up in a few weeks. Supposed to take it easy until then, but I think I'm still gonna hit up the gym in the morning while I'm here. Maximize the momentum." His head turns on the pillow. "When do you find out if you got picked for that Milan gig?"

I pause, surprised that he even remembered. At the end of the spring internship, one of the interns at Van Doren will be selected to work from their showroom in Italy for three weeks, all expenses paid, to help prep the spring collection. It's a dreamy assignment with insane perks, especially for someone like me. I've never been outside the tristate area, let alone to one of the other major fashion capitals of the world.

I don't want to tell Nate about what happened today. What that woman said to me. I don't want to kill his mood. He seems genuinely happy, and it doesn't feel fair to dump all my bad news onto his lap when he's just touched ground.

"Interviews are next week," I say lazily. "But I'm not even gonna get my hopes up."

If life has taught me anything, it's to not go into shit with expectations. That's the only way to truly be disappointed, and sometimes disappointment is the most searing kind of pain because you have to grieve what never became, like a stillbirth. And then there's the whole on-the-edge-of-getting-fired thing.

Nate leans over, his body a pool of warmth against mine. "Why not? You're perfect for that gig. Isn't this the kind of thing you've been—"

"Yeah, but you know how it goes with jobs like this. It's who you know, not what you know or how hard you're willing to work. It's how melanin deficient you are and the kind of stock you come from." I shrug and hope my attempt at nonchalance doesn't look as forced as it feels. "Pretty sure my chances of getting it are lower than my chances of winning the Power Ball tonight and I didn't even buy a ticket."

Nate gives me a look. I know that look.

"What?" I ask anyway, but really I'm silently hoping he says *okay* and drops the conversation. I don't want to be vulnerable tonight, and this day has already been humiliating enough.

"You know I went to Regency Prep with Simon's daughter, right?"

That's probably the last thing I expected him to say.

I push up on my elbows. "Uh, no."

His eyes slip down to my exposed nipples as he shrugs with one shoulder. "I mean, it's been a while, but I can text her if you want. See if she can put in a good word or something."

He kisses my nipples, one by one, then draws back and lets out a contented sigh as the pillow absorbs the weight of his sculpted back again.

I haven't blinked yet. I can't tell if he's messing with me or not. "You're seriously cool with Taylor Van Doren?"

I don't know why I sound like this, why her name came off my tongue in practically a whisper. Like she's my idol or something. She's not. I'm one of the two million who follows her on Instagram; I just eat up her style, or at least the kind of fashion she can afford. I barely know anything else about the chick.

"We graduated the same year." He says it like it's nothing.

But then again, he doesn't know I've only been stalking her feed and the hyper-stylish crew she hangs with for almost two years. She's been on my radar since before I even started interning at Van Doren. The first snap I ever saw of her was a pap shot of her stepping out of the obligatory you-can't-sit-with-us, cool-girl spot, Mr. Chow's. She was rocking an emerald green Valentino statement coat, unbuttoned, with nothing but heels and a resplendently bitchy closemouthed smile. It was more than a fashion moment; it was everything I wanted to *be*. That amount of confidence, the undeniable but not in-your-face femininity, she was goals on so many levels. I had no choice but to stan. I instantly joined her legions of voy-eurs and voraciously scrolled through her entire three-year-old feed, obsessed with everything she wore, her incredible eye for styling even the most outlandish of pieces. The girl will wear a Chanel visor with a band T-shirt and over-the-top Versace heels and somehow pull it off. A pair of sequined Isabel Marant jeans with clear Yeezy boots.

I know Nate is friends with some cool people, but he's never mentioned her. He doesn't really talk about any of the famous or celebrity-adjacent people he knows; only tells a brief an-ecdote if they happen to come up, mostly stories from high school or people his dad knows. I usually appreciate this, but right now it kinda feels like I've been slighted.

So he and Taylor went to Regency Prep together.

I roll that around in my head for a minute, trying to imag-ine them as friends. The things they would talk about. It's hard to draw even a couple of parallels between them. But maybe I'm misjudging her. Maybe she's different in real life than the persona she portrays online. She wouldn't be the first.

"So you…you really think she'll talk to him for me?" I ask.

"I'm sure she won't mind. I'll hit her up later."

I can't help but smile, a real, flash-my-teeth kind of smile. "Thanks, babe. You always have my back."

He tilts his head down at me as if I should know better by now. "Get out of here with that. You know you don't have to thank me."

Nate kisses my forehead and I look up, then kiss his lips. I want to tell him I love him, how much I appreciate having him in my life, how I can't imagine my world without him.

I don't remember exactly when things got serious between us. It was…intense right from the start. We'd only known each other for a little over a month when Nate left New York for a few weeks. I didn't think it would be a big deal. I thought in the time we'd be apart, I could finally be objective and find something wrong with him. An annoying habit that I just couldn't deal with. A tic of some sort. Some fatal flaw. But no. I just missed him. His perpetually hoarse voice. His easy smile. His hand in my hair. Everything. Not just being with another person, being with *him*. That's when I knew he was different. *This* was different.

It makes sense that we met at an airport since Nate's always on a plane, and I'm always thinking about leaving, going somewhere new. I had a summer job at JFK then. Nate was flying out to California and came up to me asking about his flight, why it was delayed. He wasn't trying to pick me up. There were no cheesy lines. No forced, awkward laughter. We ended up talking for hours while he waited for his flight. It felt more like a conversation with an old friend than a stranger. There was something so disarming about how immediately familiar he felt that I inadvertently told him about my misophonia and my IBS. He didn't think I was weird, just laughed at each idiosyncrasy I shamelessly hurled at him, and that was when I knew I could fall in love with him.

The words sit like lead in my throat. *I love you.*

We haven't said those words to each other yet. It's sort of an unspoken thing. I know Nate cares about me just as much as I care about him. I trust him. He trusts me. And honestly, what we have feels like something more substantial than love. More important. More real.

And words are just words.

2

TAYLOR

I have no idea whose blood is staining my dress, or how long I've been curled up in this cold, empty tub. I instantly recognize the shoes, though—Saint Laurent Opyum sandals with the gold "YSL" heel.

I sit up and the fucking shooting pain in my head makes me check to see if I still have all my teeth. I do, and the relief is enough for me to muster up the courage to get myself to my feet. I'm terrified to see what I look like.

I slip climbing out and skin my knee. I don't know why it's so funny, but I can't stop laughing until I straighten out and get a glimpse of myself in the mirror. It's not as bad as I thought. The smudged eyeliner and faded lipstick look intentional, though I can see the clips holding up my extensions and there is a faint black line of mascara running down one side of my face.

The tiny toiletries neatly arranged on the vanity let me know I'm in a hotel room, but I can't remember anything from last night. Bits and pieces come back to me in sections. Thunderous EDM. Fireball shots at the bar. Someone whispering in my ear. But they're all too distorted to put together into anything solid.

I twist my hair into a knot and jump when my phone vibrates on the counter. I want to flush it down the toilet when I see my agent's name because I can't handle another lecture right now, but I tap to answer. I clear my throat so that it sounds like I've gotten at least six hours of sleep and have been meditating, but before I can say a word, she's freaking out, demanding to know why I've been off the grid all day. I don't answer and tell her that of course I didn't forget the step-and-repeat I agreed to attend tonight. She reminds me that I've been the designer's muse for the last three campaigns and have to show my face in forty minutes. Forty minutes.

Fuck.

I push through to the bedroom and am so busy texting my glam team, asking them to remind me where we decided to meet to do hair and makeup before the red carpet, that I almost miss the naked guy sprawled across the bed. I stop only to scrutinize his face, because even though he's lying on his back, I don't recognize him, and just as I start to wonder what the hell I was thinking coming up to his room, I see it. A faint veil of snow where his mustache would be if he wasn't clean-shaven. I flick my gaze to the nightstand. There's a half-smoked joint, some pills—whites, blues—and an empty baggie we must have spent all night working our way through.

Somehow I make it to our suite in the Hôtel Plaza Athénée with enough time for my glam team to get me HD-ready. I know they can smell last night on me, but I appreciate their silence as they pat, swipe, blend and slick. I practice my smile in the car and by the time I'm in front of the huddle of paparazzi, it's so effortless, no one can see how every flash is killing me, the sudden bursts of light exacerbating the banging in my head. I use the energy of the crowd to push through it, angle my face for each photographer as they call my name.

Taylor. Taylor. Taylor.

Everyone clicking and watching thinks I have it all. They think my life is perfect. They think I'm perfect.

They know nothing.

A shiny Benz brakes soundlessly at the crown of the runway as soon as I step out onto the tarmac. The impeccable timing briefly distracts me from the agony of my pulsing, blistered feet. I scoop the bottom half of my heavy gown into my arms midyawn and dump myself onto the creamy leather backseat. I should have put the one-of-a-kind, hand-beaded dress back on the rack after the step-and-repeat, but I was too worn out to peel it off before I rushed straight to the airport for my eight-hour flight back to New York. They will just have to deal with it until tomorrow. I'll ship the thirty-thousand-dollar dress back to the studio with an offensively expensive bottle of Cheval Blanc from my father's private cellar and everything will be fine.

As soon as my driver tucks himself behind the wheel, I meet his eyes in the rearview mirror. "Did you get the package?"

Without a word, he slips me a small, nondescript box. I hold down the small button until the partition creates a wall of privacy between us and lower my mask-like Celines to inspect the vial. The golden liquid is still warm in my hand.

I roll it around in my palm a few times, then tuck it into the inner slit of my bag.

A text comes in as soon as I get home, but I don't respond right away. I drag myself up the curved staircase to my room and strip immediately, the Dior a pool of couture around my ankles in one swift motion. I get the bulk of my makeup off with one of those premoistened wipes with the satisfying ridges, but it takes three sheets to actually see my skin again, pores and all. Then I slip into a pair of Balenciaga sweats that scream last season but match the low-key vibe I'm going for.

I grab the vial from my purse and tuck it into my bra so it can stay warm. I glance at my phone again and decide to reply to my father's text because he's impatient, and also, he is dying.

Are you upstairs? Let's talk.

My father does not want to talk. He wants to probe. Today is test day.

Every month I have to squat over a tiny plastic cup and until my piss comes back clean, not even a trace of cannabis in my veins, I don't get my trust, the money that's been waiting for me since before I was even brought home from the hospital. I should have gotten it back in April when I turned twenty-one, but the test came back positive. I went through the same humiliation last month to my father's delight, who has already cut off my allowance. There is no way I can fail this time. He gave me a six-month deadline to get clean or my five million goes to charity, and time is running out.

But I've handled it. The test *will* come back clean this time.

In my room, I finally send back, falling onto my bed. I take a deep breath and let it out slowly, staring at the ceiling.

Before I can stop her, my one-eyed calico leaps onto the bed next to me and rolls around on her side, gazing up at me like she wants me to rub her belly. She's not supposed to be in my room because the sheets and the carpet get covered in dander, which means I break out in hives and turn into a coughing, wheezing monster with puffy eyes no concealer can hide. But she's cute, and today has been so stressful that even though I haven't taken my allergy meds, I scoop her into my arms and let her rub her cheek into mine.

"Hi, Cindy. Missed you today," I whisper, staring into her dilated eyes, and I can't help but think of my mother. She adopted Cindy right before her cancer diagnosis, and now she is one of the only things that makes this cold house feel like a home. One of the only pieces of her I have left.

A soft rap comes from the other side of my bedroom door. I throw my legs over the edge of my bed and move across the suite to unlock it. My father smiles at me when I swing open the double doors, and even that feels wrong. It's like a rip in his face.

I make myself smile back. "Hey," I say as he steps in.

"Are you okay?" he asks as he glances around my room, trying to be discreet, but failing miserably.

I know exactly what he's looking for, but he won't find anything here. I got rid of my stash last week, every trace. I hid the joints, the powder and the pills in the lining of my Audi. I found a med school dropout from Craigslist who agreed to sew in a hidden compartment on the underside of the passenger seat, and he pulled it off with such surgical precision, sometimes even I struggle to find it.

"I'm fine," I say, following him inside.

He's still looking around, still being obvious. I ignore him and smother Cindy Crawford in kisses.

"I'm gonna book a room at the Gansevoort for tonight," I say after a few moments, carefully setting the cat on the floor, since she hates sudden movements. He doesn't stir, doesn't blink. Nothing. "I can't sleep in here tonight. Cindy was in here while I was at my—" I stop when I realize he's gone catatonic. "Dad?"

Still nothing.

As if on cue, I sneeze. It's a huge one, straight from the depths of my diaphragm, and I swear my heart stops beating for a moment. At least the explosive sound of my sternutation snaps my father out of his trance.

His eyes flutter and he looks at me as if he hasn't heard a word I said. "My doctor just phoned me."

I'm not sure what to do with that. More bad news. I swallow and do my best to shift gears. I ease closer to him, take his hand and add practiced concern to my voice, hoping he doesn't hear the effort. "Look, don't worry. We knew this would probably happen. I've already made calls. I'll make sure the funeral is—"

"No, it's gone. The surgery…" He shakes his head in disbelief. "I'm in full remission."

I'm so stunned that I stumble back a step. "Full…"

He's smiling now and my brain can't process what it means fast enough. "Can you believe it? It's a fucking miracle."

His words hang in the space between us like smoke after a fire, tainting the air, leaving a foul taste in my mouth.

I'm quiet for too long.

In my silence he steps forward, rests his face against my shoulder and wraps his arms around my back. I'm too startled to even move. It's so foreign, the feeling of him, the warmth of his body, his strength, that none of this makes sense to me at first. And then I realize what this is. A hug. I can't remember the last time I felt his touch, any touch, much less an embrace.

My instinct is to pull away, but I don't. Of course I don't.

"That's amazing, Dad," I finally croak, and my voice sounds hollow even to my own ears.

I don't know what to do with my hands.

Eventually, I manage to pat his back and even that small movement feels like a lie. When he looks up at me, his eyes are damp with tears, and I know I should be the one crying, but when I try to force it, nothing happens.

"Not to compete with your good news," I say, "but I chugged a gallon of water on the ride here."

"Right. Let's get this over with," he says, just as there's a knock on the door, a sleepy voice calling his name. He rushes over to open it.

"I'm not interrupting anything, am I?" she says. "Just letting you know I'm home."

I fold my arms. "Actually, we were in the middle of something."

Her eyes flick to me.

"I'll be right down," he says to her before she can say anything to me, stepping slightly outside the door. "Just give me a few minutes, hmm?"

His arms ease around her waist as he nestles his face into her neck. A soft laugh escapes her mouth, and then she is whispering into his ear.

I roll my eyes and look away. He never made Mom laugh like that. He was too busy making her cry.

I remember him in the oncology ward in the beginning, the few times he bothered to show up to see her on her deathbed, the way his face hung slackly around his sunburned nose. The way he cried softly as he held her limp hand and whispered sweet, meaningless words of encouragement, of hope. Emo as fuck.

I fell for the whole fucking act.

But his tears were paltry, forced. He couldn't wait to get out of there, run to the new bitch he was fucking behind my mom's back, the one he didn't know I knew about. His lover is a cliché. Barely older than me, unencumbered, quiet like a lamb but not as sweet. The kind of woman weak men use to boost their fragile egos, make them feel like the men they wish they were.

Just thinking about it makes me wince. Too many terrible memories crowd my head, overlap, crash into each other. I suddenly feel the weight of my father's hand tightening around my arm, can still see his expression as his heavy hand flew across my cheek. I remember hissing at him even though tears were in my eyes. And the blood. I'll never forget the blood, the way it leaked across the tile, thick and sticky, staining my knees as I knelt in it, clinging to my fingers as I picked Mom up, holding her, begging her to be okay. And then the last time, hanging in the bathroom, gone before I could get to her.

Everyone thinks my father is the perfect family man. I've even skimmed articles online that claim he's sensitive. Patient. Gentle.

They don't know about his new bitch. They don't know what he did to my mom. To me. Simon Van Doren is a businessman, a natural-born salesman. A liar. He could get the public to believe anything he wants them to believe; I've seen him do it. I've watched him lie straight through his shimmering white teeth and not one person batted an eye. Unlike them, I know the real man behind the facade. But I have to pretend, stay quiet and smile.

Like his new bitch.

I've been pretending for over two years, ever since I found the texts on his phone, the vintage-filtered nudes sent back and forth like they were teenagers in heat.

When my father is finally done making me wait, he follows me into the bathroom. He glances around, then steps in farther to properly scrutinize the space. He searches my hampers, opens drawers, and this time he even unfolds all my towels, which is so petty I can't even be offended. I don't bat an eye, just stand back and let him run through his little routine. When he's satisfied, he leaves the room for a moment and comes back with a small kit wrapped in plastic. I take it, and he steps out, gently shutting the door behind him.

When I come out, he's sitting on the edge of my velvet tufted sofa. I hand the cup to him and wait for the results to show on the paper stick he slides inside. After a few moments his face goes still, frustration mixed with surprise. When he gets up and stops in front of me, he's impassive and foreboding, his expression a dark mask of tension.

I study his uneven face, those squinty blue eyes and immaculately groomed brows that are sprinkled with gray. "What's wrong?"

He flashes me the paper stick.

I stop breathing.

This can't be happening. Not this time.

I snatch the test from his hand and check for myself. It's positive. I wave it, like that's somehow going to change the results.

Fuck. I'm *fucked*.

I don't even have to look at my father's face to know how stupid I look right now. He shakes his head and sighs, then looks at me like he wants to say something but never does.

He turns to leave, and I scramble after him. "But Dad, I'm *literally* broke. What am I supposed to do? Max out all my credit cards like poor people?"

"You know the deal." He doesn't slow down. "You're not getting a dime until you're clean. That's not up for negotiation."

I roll my eyes and fold my arms, stopping at the doorway as he marches into the hall. "You're such a dictator now that Mom's gone."

That finally stops him like I knew it would, and he glares at me like I'm a petulant child. I know he expects me to take back that last insult, but I avoid his eyes and refuse to retract it on the basis that it's the truth.

"September is right around the corner, you know." He speaks softly, but his voice is smug. The air between us is so different now. "If you don't sober up soon, there sure will be some happy tigers roaming around."

My eyes fall down the length of him, then back up. "You

won't really give all my money to charity," I say, calling his bluff.

He sets his jaw and turns to walk away without another word. And then he's gone, his footsteps loud on the floor as he descends to the first level.

I all but slam my door shut.

My heart goes into overdrive as I snatch my phone from my bed, beating against my chest like a warning. I find Mei's contact and start a new chain.

The test came back positive. Wtf? Call me ASAP.

By the time my phone rings, it is a whole twenty minutes later and I'm at the local drugstore heading straight to the medicine aisle. I click Mei over and hit FaceTime. I need to see her; I need to know if she's lying or not. Her face appears on screen after a few seconds of a bad connection. She's wearing no makeup and is dressed in a sleeveless black leotard, her hair tied up into a catastrophe of a bun, a cup of liquid crack in hand. Iced coffee isn't her only way of getting through the grind of being a soloist at the New York City Ballet, but definitely one of her tamer vices. She's that slightly gaunt, nineties-model thin, but it looks good on her.

I wait until she pushes into the bathroom to speak, but she's quicker. "This better be good, bitch. I was about to break my record."

I frown, noticing the line of sweat on her forehead. "For what? The number of corns accumulated on a single human foot?"

She flips me her featherless bird, then runs a hand over her dark hair. "How long I can balance in arabesque on pointe. Almost passed sixty seconds." Her voice is even, unaffected.

She never lets me bait her. "What's wrong? You didn't get the package?"

"Your piss wasn't clean, narco ballerina."

Mei frowns, confused. "The only pills I've popped in the last thirty days were vitamins and fish oil." A pause. Then she bites her lip like she's just realized something. "Oh, wait. Fuck, I forgot about those gummies I had at Sophia's party last week."

I roll my eyes. "You're useless."

She scoffs. "Then stop using me, bitch."

We both laugh at that. She knows I won't. And part of me thinks a part of her likes being used—a dark, damaged part of her. Mei can be weird like that. Extreme.

"Come on, you think I can be sober *and* broke at the same time? I'd go mental." I scan the shelves on both sides of the aisle as quickly as I can and hold in another sneeze.

"Welcome to the club." I hear the click of a lighter from Mei's end, then a sharp inhale as she lights up. "My dad only pays my rent and utilities now that I'm with NYCB. He says since I'm employed now, I should learn to manage my money like everyone else."

I scoff. *"Everyone else?"*

"Do you know how hard it is to live off a dancer's salary in this city?" She takes a drag of her cigarette, then I hear the flush of a toilet. "I haven't been to Fifth in over two weeks. I'm seriously starting to get the shakes."

I shrug. "Barneys is your therapy. He's depriving you of proper medical treatment. This is child abuse."

She laughs and sips her flat white, which, knowing her, has four shots of espresso inside, then immediately spits it out.

"What the fuck?" She wipes her mouth with the back of her hand and pours the entire cup down the sink. She looks like she wants to murder someone. "This bitch tried to poison me."

I finally find the Benadryl and grab a box, then head to the register. "Whole milk again?"

"I told her two times. *Oat* milk. Is that so fucking hard? Honestly?"

"You know how these people are. They can't do basic shit like take people's orders without messing them up, but they're always complaining about things not being fair." I take a breath. "But seriously. I only have ninety days to get clean now."

"Damn, that's right around the corner. Are you sure you can't milk him for more time?"

"I'm done playing his games," I snap, then remember where I am and lower my voice. "I want my money."

It doesn't matter what anyone else thinks of me: that money is mine. I've worked hard for it. I've earned it. People have no idea how exhausting it is to lie every day, to act like someone you're not, to pretend to love someone you hate. It's hell, a never-ending cycle of torture, something worse than pain.

Mei pushes out of the bathroom with a heavy sigh. "I have to cram in a physio session before rehearsal. Text you after the curtain goes down."

I want to be mad at her, and part of me is, but I let it go. It's not worth fighting over. She's my rock, my sanity. I need her. She's one of the only people who understands my pain, who knows what it's like to constantly be judged for the way you look, to have to constantly hear you're not thin, good, perfect enough.

It gets to you. Nobody thinks that. You can put on a brave face and say you don't care, but deep down you feel it; there's no way you can't. I'll never be pretty enough. I'll never be skinny enough. I'll never be enough.

When I was younger, people used to tell me I was beautiful. But they were liars. All of them. They didn't mean it; they were just trying to be nice. Placate me. I know that now. I'm not beautiful, not in that perfect, undeniable, universal way. I have the height, proportions and bone structure that lend well to catwalks and magazine covers. An interesting face. That's what my agent told me. And that was *after* the nose job.

Interesting.

Not beautiful, but not ugly, either. If I don't smile in photos, I look too harsh. Unapproachable. I've had to work on it; I've learned how to soften my face in front of the lens and in real life so that I come off as edgy, but not severe. Confident, but not intimidating.

Mei deals with the same shit, day in and day out, maybe even worse. We've been through so much together. We're soul sisters. Allies until the end.

As soon as I hang up, I delete the text I sent her.

In the car, I toss back two capsules too many of the Benadryl, then I think about it and swallow one more.

Just as I'm about to check my DMs, another text pops up. It's not Mei. The words on the screen freeze me.

Hey. What's up? It's Nate.

Just like that. Casual. As if it hasn't been three years since we've seen or talked to each other. As if he doesn't hate me.

My heart wants to leap from my chest, but I won't let it. Not yet. It might have been a mistake. He probably texted the wrong person.

Then.

Another message pops up. I know it's been a while. How u been?

It wasn't a mistake.

I allow myself a smile, a small one, and text him back.

3

BRANDI

"I talked to Taylor last night," Nate shouts over the sound of the running water.

I finish brushing my teeth and stare at my reflection in the mirror. "What'd she say?"

"She was cool. She said we should come to this ball at her house tonight. Her pops will be there. She said she'll introduce you."

Ah. Right. It was mentioned in one of the newsletters earlier this week. Every year Van Doren hosts a charity ball to fund the Save The Animals foundation. It's invitation-only and each plate costs five thousand dollars.

Five thousand dollars.

I almost forgot all about it.

I turn to Nate even though he can't see me with his head bent forward, the water pounding at the nape of his neck. "Do I look like Cinderella to you?"

There is no way I'm going to a *ball* tonight.

Nate turns around in the stall and I watch the water fall over his face through the frosted glass as he talks. "You will after we hit up Fifth Ave."

"No. I wouldn't even know how to act...what to say around those kinds of people. They're all rich. And important. And—"

"Brandi. This is your *one* chance at landing your dream job and you're gonna throw it away because you're scared? Since when do you care so much about what people think of you anyway?"

I open my mouth. Close it.

He's right. I know he's right. But—

"This is different. You want me to go to a ball. An actual *ball*."

I never go with Nate to parties. Every time he asks, I scavenge for an excuse, claim student-intern exhaustion or just tell him no. I hate the crowds, the energy, the performance of it all. It's not fun for me. I don't like to drink. I'd rather stay in and do something much more chill, much less...intense. And this time it's not just a party, it's a whole-ass ball.

Nate shuts off the water and reaches an arm out for a towel, and I'm suddenly distracted by his dripping-wet body. It's been so long since I've seen him like this.

I lick my lips. "Besides, I can't let you drop thousands of dollars on a dress I'll only wear once."

It's already enough that he's paying my rent. Well, technically, it's *his* rent, so it's *his* apartment because it's *his* name on the lease, but he never makes me feel like a visitor or freeloader. Nate wanted to go all out, get a two-bedroom apartment on the Lower West Side when I first started classes at FIT, but I insisted on a one-bedroom. The square footage is minuscule, but it's cool in that New York kind of way, everything two people need.

Nate lifts the towel to his face. "All right, I'm done negotiating. You already won't let me help you with your tuition." He steps out of the shower, knotting the towel around his waist, low enough for the creases in his pelvis to show, and I want to rip it right back off. "You know that independent-woman thing turns me on, but you're gonna let me do this one thing for you. You deserve this." He presses into me, and my breath catches. "That's it. It's a wrap."

His tone leaves no room for debate or negotiation. My eyes flick up to meet his.

"Really? I have no say?" I ask, biting my lip to hide the smile pulling the corners of my mouth.

He brushes a thumb across my lower lip, and my mouth falls apart like my conviction. "Nope."

Nate leans in close enough to breathe warmth against my neck and then our lips touch, two puzzle pieces pressing into place. It's barely a kiss, his lips brushing against mine in the most subtle way. He's so strong, so capable, that I never expect him to be this gentle, but by now I shouldn't be so surprised. And then his mouth is carnivorous against mine, warm and wet. Our breathing is loud in the small space between us. My hands find the counter as he lifts me onto the edge of the sink, my legs spreading like broken wings. I grip his hair and pull him back. I glance down at his swelling lips, stare up into those deep brown eyes.

"You're lucky I trust you," I say.

It almost slipped. The L word. But I caught myself just in time. Nate gives no warning before he slips a hand up the hem of my T-shirt and shoves aside my thong, or when he eases two fingers inside me. I suck in a sharp breath and stare at him, and he watches, fully aware of what he's doing to me. He knows my body, exactly what I like, what I need. I've taught him.

"Nate..." I say, but it's barely a murmur.

"Like that?" he asks, because he likes to do this; he likes to hear me say it.

I arch into his rough touch. "Yeah."

"That's right, babe," he whispers, his words falling into my ear, hot and dripping, and just like that, everything in life is right. I'm flying. I have the wings of a raptor. I want to stay inside this moment forever, but a small part of me, the part of me that I hate, fights its way to the surface, telling me it's all going to be over soon.

When Nate finds out about my past, what I've done.

I can't help but feel like an imposter, like I've cheated the universe somehow, stolen someone else's hand in this vicious game of life, and soon it's going to realize. I know how life works. Nothing good lasts forever. At least, in my world, it doesn't. I know this probably won't last, either. We're so young. We can grow apart as easily as we were drawn together. Lots of couples do, even the ones who truly love each other. We're all constantly learning, changing, evolving. I'm not afraid of change. It would just be nice to finally have something that's constant in my life for once.

I try to push that voice away, stay right here in this moment. But it's all-consuming.

I've been staring out the window for miles. After an hour-long drive to Long Island, and a subsequent ride down a seemingly never-ending winding road lined with hundred-year-old oak trees, we're outside the Van Doren mansion, a sprawling estate with enough acreage to rival the iconic homes from the Gold Coast era. It's all tall columns, black shutters and wisteria vines that look more like art than anything else, the greenery so thick it feels primordial. The entrance is swarmed with flashing lights. A handful of paparazzi is huddled around the step-and-repeat at the end of the red carpet. A platinum blonde twirls for the cameras in a Giambattista Valli gown like a music-box ballerina.

Nate takes my hand and helps me out of the backseat. His strong hand is on the small of my back, gently steering me the way I like once we get inside, and the views only get more un-real. Stark, fifteen-foot white walls outlined in ornate mold-ing and a stained-oak floor frame the hexagonal entrance hall. English pedestals topped with ferns are paired with a regency-style table where a woman sits, taking names. Her dress is vo-luminous, bright yellow and over-the-top. It's breathtaking, in that you-have-to-see-it-to-get-it kind of way. Behind her, a silk runner stretches off into a world of generational wealth.

I glance around at the guests shuffling in, the city's elite and beautiful, as Nate gives her our names. When we step beyond the threshold of the foyer, my eyes go up. The ceiling stretches two stories overhead, crossed with exposed wooden beams, a midcentury gold chandelier hanging in the center. The main party is taking place in a room just beyond that, a huge space with a wall of accordion-style doors that open to a terrace that offers a sublime view of the pool. At least a hun-dred people stand inside, talking, mingling, sipping.

After hours of shopping, breezing through endless slinky satin gowns and embellished jumpsuits, I finally settled on a quartz-pink Givenchy dress trimmed with faux feathers and tiny crystals affixed along the bodice. When I first stood in front of the mirror, it was too much, and it still felt wrong to let Nate spend this much money on me, even if we were just renting it. But he wouldn't take no for an answer.

I expected to feel confident, fierce. But I can barely walk in this dress. It's ten pounds heavier than it looks, limiting at least eighty percent of my mobility, and my shoes—strappy Gianvito Rossi heels—are making me feel like I'm on the edge of making a fool of myself.

I feel like an imposter.

I don't fit in with these people. They're all the same. Rich, thin and beautiful. I don't know how I let Nate talk me into crashing this homogenous crowd.

"You're good," Nate says, leaning down for the edge of my ear. The spike in my anxiety must be obvious. "Relax. Just smile and pretend you're having fun," he says, slipping behind me. His arms ease around my waist and even through the thick layers of my dress, I can feel his strength.

"Is that what you do?" I ask.

"That's what everybody is doing."

I laugh.

"Serious." He smiles and takes my hand in his. "Come on. Taylor's somewhere around here."

His hand grips mine, strong and steady, and I exhale my first full breath since we got here. He's right. I should try to enjoy tonight. Not overthink it. Get out of my own head. Whatever happens, happens. I wish I could be like him. Calm. Casual. Indifferent. Never says much because he doesn't have to. Funny without even trying.

It's not long before people start to recognize Nate and flock our way. I let go of his hand as a few people ask him for a selfie. He starts to pose for the photos and then glances at me with a glint of expectance in his eyes. I shake my head, but it's too late. He's already pulling me over to get in the shot with them. I want to opt out, but it'll probably cause a stir because everyone's already turned to look at me, so I just smile and pretend I'm having fun, like Nate said.

Just as I start to find my angle, I see a girl strutting over to us in a floor-length Van Doren slip dress with a narrow split just below the hip. I recognize the dress right away, then I recognize the tall, slim girl wearing it and I have to force my face not to betray me as the memory of the rancid smell of dried vomit slams into me like a freight train. She's statuesque in that mythical, Amazonian way, hip bones jutting out through the satin of her gown, which clings to every curve. Her dark, glossy hair hangs down to her waist in perfect, soft waves. Her skin is obscenely tanned, as if she's just come back from somewhere in the Pacific Islands, almost as brown as me.

We couldn't look more different.

Taylor floats right by me and leans straight for Nate. "Hey, stranger."

He smiles back at her; it's a generous smile. "Taylor. Long time no see."

She thrusts herself into his arms with no hesitation and lingers for a little longer than I'm comfortable with, that subtle few seconds that seems like more of a power move than legit affection. There is a familiarity in the way she rocks into him, in the way her arms lock around his neck, but I brush it off. Because why wouldn't there be? They're friends. They've known each other since high school.

"God, you're so big now. Look at these arms." Her voice is low and gravelly, nothing like the vocal fry modulation I expected. Obviously, she reaches out to squeeze his biceps.

Something small and petty flares inside me. I push it away before it metastasizes into something obsessive, before it breeds the kind of insecurity you can't ever really recover from. I am not that girl. I will *never* be that girl who—

But what if I am? What if this bothers me? What does that say about me? I just can't believe it. I was on my hands and knees breaking out in a sweat for this girl and now she's sweating my man right in front of my face. If I squint, I can still see the faintest remnants of the puke I scrubbed out, so at least there's that.

Nate chuckles softly, looking awkward in a way I've never seen him look, and I can tell his chill is a front. "Yeah, I was pretty scrawny back at RP."

Taylor shifts a little and my eyes drop to her tits. They're real and beautiful, slightly mismatched, which makes them that much more interesting. I want to slap them, rub my face between them, feel their weight in my hands. I glance over at Nate, but he doesn't seem to notice the way they sway every time she shifts with even the slightest movement. Not once does his glaze slip below her chin. It almost seems like a conscious thing; he obviously knows I'm watching, and I wonder if it is, but the thought is flimsy and ephemeral.

"Seriously, what have you been doing?" Taylor asks, her gaze still on his arms.

I feel my smile harden. She's going there. Right in front of my face.

"Just keeping up with training, you know. New season starts in a couple months." Nate laughs again, but this time it's nervous, and I don't know why. Then his eyes catch mine. "This is Brandi. My girlfriend."

His hand is on the small of my back again, easing me forward.

Taylor's eyes shift over to me as if she has just realized I'm here. As if I'm nothing but an insignificant addendum to their little nostalgic moment. When her gaze settles on me, I am sucking in my stomach, trying to ignore the fact that my mascara is clumping so much I can feel it and hoping my irritable bowels don't hold me responsible for the Chipotle Nate and I ravaged right before we left. Up close, it's clear that she is one of those fringe white people who understands the importance of daily sunscreen. Her face is striking, almost eerily symmetrical—strong cheekbones, angular jaw and a slender little nose that might as well be nothing. Thick black lashes frame blue eyes, a hue that could compete with the waters of Santorini. Her makeup is so flawless, she's literally glowing, and the diamonds dripping from her ears are bigger than all my hopes and dreams put together.

I don't know what to say to her.

"She's the one I told you about," Nate says, filling the silence.

Taylor's eyes flutter like she's trying to make sense of this. Of me. "Oh. You didn't say she was your..." Her eyes sweep over me, and I resist the urge to fidget with my— "Givenchy."

I look up at her, confused, then I realize what she means. The dress. Obviously. "Oh. Yeah. It's—"

"It looks better on you than it did on the runway." She's still staring. Not at my face. Not the dress. She's roving my body with her gaze.

I shake my head in dismissal of her flattery, but she's already flipping a hand.

"Trust me. I was the one wearing it." Her eyes flick up to mine, then move over me once again. "Your body is insane." She looks up and I almost feel afraid to look away. Something about the way her eyes hold mine makes me shrink into myself a little. "And you're so pretty. Like, beyond."

Her words flow so easily, they sound recycled, like she says this to everybody, rinse and reuse. And then she smiles, a second too late.

Once again, I'm at a loss for words. The right words. Any words. I don't know what I expected her to be like, but this isn't it, and regardless of whatever fantasies I had about coming here tonight, about this moment, our pussies do not immediately unite us. Taylor has an edge about her, the way she walks, the way her eyes seem to cut straight through you when she looks at you. She's so intense, you almost feel hypnotized in her presence. And there's something oddly calculating about her, something I can't quite place.

"Thanks," I finally say, disappointed with how lame that sounded given how long it took me to come up with it. Before I can think of anything else to say, Taylor leans into me. Her perfume is heady and sweet, like a bed of wet gardenia petals. I can taste it on my tongue. When she wraps her arms around me, our bodies barely touch. Except for her nipples. They press into my collarbone, hard and small, and I can't help but think she did this on purpose, as if to say, *look at what I got, bitch*, like it isn't already painfully obvious. I try to hug her back in the least awkward way I can, but I'm pretty sure it's still awkward. When she straightens, her smile is broad, and I still don't know if I trust it. The smile I give in return is perfunctory, but I hope she can't see the effort in my eyes.

Nate leans for Taylor's ear. "Think this is a good time to introduce her to your dad?"

That time she stares at him a little too long and she knows it. When I look at her, her eyes flutter and quickly shy away. I'm tempted to tell her that when Nate and I fuck, sometimes I have to physically force him away because he'd stay inside this body all day if I let him. And I know that's stupid and immature, and bordering on the edge of absurdity, but it's true, and I hate myself for it. I'm probably reading too much into it. I don't know. I don't know *her*, and the thing that bothers me the most is that, despite all this, I still want her to like me.

"Sure," Taylor says, her eyes coming back to me, knees bending in a slight curtsy so she can grab the bottom edge of her train. "Come on. He'll love you."

Sweat rises on the nape of my neck, nervous sweat that's hot and cold at the same time. I force myself to nod. Swallow. Speak. "Okay."

I glance at Nate before my nerves can get the best of me, and he gives me one last look of encouragement as I turn to follow Taylor. I don't expect her to take me by the crook of my arm like a proper escort, and at first it feels oppressive and vaguely performative, some kind of trick, some kind of trap, and I have this immediate urge to snatch free, but then I swallow my apprehension and tell myself to relax. I do expect her to say something to me, though, as we weave our way through the gathering crowds, but she never does.

I clear my throat. "Thanks for doing this. Really appreciate it."

"Don't worry about it. It's the least I can do. Nate is such a sweetie." She doesn't look at me as she speaks. She has her phone in her free hand, texting someone.

I look away and pull my lips in. I feel like I'm drooling.

I still can't figure out why Nate never mentioned he was friends with her. For someone as fond of him as she seems to be, they must have been close, at least at one point.

We wind through the crowd in silence before I'm compelled to ask, "So you two went to Regency Prep together?" I want to hear more about them, their friendship. Anything.

"Yeah," she says. "All four years."

I expect her to keep going, but she doesn't. That's it. That's all she says. I don't know what else to say, if I should say anything at all. Her eyes are still on her phone.

A few people stop her when we cross into the next room. Girls asking for selfies mostly. She smiles down at them like she encounters half-crazed fangirls on the regular and stops for a few pictures.

Taylor leads me out to the terrace, and I can see Simon standing in a small huddle of men. I've only actually seen him twice during the program and I vividly remember him requesting that we interns call him Simon, not Mr. Van Doren, and his subtle rejection of hierarchy made me instantly like him. Even from this distance he is a serious presence, a formidable storm of self-possession. All black suit, no tie—never a tie—his impeccability as consistent as his hairline. He's a tall man with massive hands and a direct gaze, just over fifty but doesn't quite look it. Still wide through the shoulders.

My heart starts to slam against my chest. I'm a fool for even considering this. He's going to laugh at me.

But then I think of Nate, of how much he believes in me, of how he didn't have to do any of this for me. I suck in a breath and try not to think about it too hard because if I do, I'm going to panic and bail. It feels like my whole future is riding on this moment. My feet keep moving, one in front of the other. *He's just a man*, I remind myself, *flesh and blood.* And then there's that moment when I see him seeing me. His eyes meet mine and I feel strange, as if I've been caught doing something I shouldn't, so conscious now of the fact that he's well over six feet, and that I must look tiny to him. And then he smiles at me and it's like sunrise after a thunderstorm, warm and reassuring.

Taylor reaches Simon before I do and slips her arm in his, pulling him away. "Dad, this is Brandi. One of your interns. She wants to go with you to Milan next month."

Her gaze finds me again and she looks smaller somehow, more fragile. Not just physically—something about her expression, the way her eyes seem suddenly drawn to the floor. As if being in her father's presence immediately has this effect on her.

A slow smile eases across his face as he looks at me, eyes sparkling. It's so charming, it's almost sociopathic. "Well, that's a little forward, isn't it?"

My mouth opens. I smile when I realize he's joking. *Of course he's joking.*

I force out a small laugh, hoping it doesn't sound as awkward as I feel. Taylor smiles at me, and I'm sure it was meant to be encouraging, but there's something about it, something off. I can't quite put my finger on it. I think I was more comfortable when she was ignoring me and all over Nate.

"Brandi. I don't think we ever got a chance to meet, did

we?" He extends a hand, and I meet it with mine, my fingers settling between his, too gently. His palm is warm and soft enough for me to immediately feel self-conscious, but his grip is stronger than I expect. "I know you guys are usually pretty busy."

"We shared an elevator once," I say, pulling my hand back. Out of the corner of my eye, I see Taylor stepping away as an Asian girl in a blood-red gown runs up to her, dark tattoos brutal against her deep olive skin. They give each other air kisses. I recognize her from Taylor's Insta feed. Her heavily lined eyes quickly sweep over me with a sort of baffled indifference, and I feel a little humiliated, but I try to ignore it, that nagging pull in my gut. Our eyes lock for a beat, and I immediately notice there's something missing in hers.

Simon's eyes move over me again as if he's trying to place me. "And I didn't notice you? Impossible."

I laugh again, but it sounds as nervous as I'm trying not to feel. "Well, I was transporting a massive rack of samples to the showroom. You probably couldn't see me."

"Ah, I see." He gives me another smile, the lines at his eyes crinkling, and another wave of relief washes over me. He doesn't think I'm an idiot. There's a moment...of something, but I'm not sure what. He's still staring, still smiling. I smile back, nod. Smile again. I don't know what else to do. What else to say. If he keeps looking at me like this, I'm going to start blushing again. I always blush when I get nervous. I was hoping he would have questions for me. I'm not good at small talk, not good at leading conversations.

I swear I can feel Taylor's eyes on me from across the room, watching me, almost scientifically, her staring aggressive in its persistence. I glance over but as soon as I do, she looks away. I can only imagine what she sees, what she thinks of me. I stand up straighter. Now that I've met her in person, I'm still undecided about her and can't help but wonder if she is the kind of white girl who thinks affirmative action is racist while she is of the demographic who has undoubtedly benefited the most from it, who calls cornrows *Bo Derek braids* and enthusiastically belts *nigga* when her favorite trap song bleeds through the speakers, yet habitually slips into black guys' DMs to satisfy her BBD itch.

Simon's voice brings me back. "So, Brandi, there's what, a half dozen of you in the program? Tell me. Why you?"

I immediately freeze at the question, like it's somehow too personal. Also, his gaze feels too intense. I've practiced my elevator pitch with Nate the entire ride out here, but all the words have evaporated into the ether when I part my lips. I take a beat to gather my thoughts and am ready to go for it, but the words stutter to a stop when I lift my eyes back up to meet Simon's. His gaze is still hyper-focused, but it has slipped about a foot, down to the neckline of my dress. I expect him to blush or try to make a joke when he realizes he's been clocked, but Simon Van Doren does not even flinch. He doesn't mind having been caught. He doesn't address his unprofessionalism, as if his blatant admiration of my cleavage is inconsequential, like it is just a little something he was entitled to admire because it was within eyeshot, just like he would any of the lavish floral arrangements around the room.

I smile to keep from saying what I really want to say, then recite my pitch. Halfway through, I feel something else, someone else. Watching me. I flick a glance over Simon's shoulder as he absorbs what I've said and catch the girl in the red dress hawking me like I am vermin scurrying for cover in the black of night.

4

TAYLOR

If I would have known he'd bring this Bratz-faced bitch here, I never would have invited him. He never said she was his *girlfriend*.

I'm so stupid. I should have known. Of course he's moved on by now.

"I'm getting something stiff," Mei says, interrupting my thoughts. "Want one?"

I shake my head. "I'm good."

I'm not. I'm pissed.

Mei slinks away, and I glance down at my phone, checking to see if WWD posted their weekly red carpet roundup yet. Nothing. When I look back up, Nate is heading straight for me. I'm suddenly rooted to the ground like a centennial yew, and then we're eye to eye before I can even think of what to say, him all broad shoulders and white teeth.

"Just wanted to say thanks for being so cool about all of this. Brandi's really psyched about this gig."

As he speaks, I study the symmetry of his face, his wide neck, his pillowy mouth. A new scar cuts across his left eyebrow, and I want to kiss it and ask him if the stitches hurt. He looks bigger than I remember—not just his arms. He seems taller, more confident.

"It's nothing," I say, keeping my tone light, like no time has passed at all.

I planned to say more than that, but what happens instead is this bizarre, out-of-character aversion of my eyes, this immediate internal regression where my brain can't form any other words. And then there's the awkward silence where I'm still staring at him and he's still trying to figure me out because it's so obvious that I'd meant to say more but stopped myself.

Nate nods even though I still haven't said anything, and glances around for a second. "This is dope. Raising a lot tonight, huh?" He says this as if we have no past. As if we're strangers, testing the waters, afraid to say the wrong thing, a pair of socially stilted tweens at their first school dance. But he has seen me cry, he has helped me off the floor when I've fainted, he's seen me at my most vulnerable, so it's odd that he sounds so detached, though I'm happy just to be noticed.

"Yeah," I say. "Thanks for coming. And donating. You look good. You know…like older."

I hate the way I sound. Nervous. Strained. Shy. I'm never a shy bitch.

"Yeah." He pauses, quickly looking me over. "You do too. And thank my dad."

He smiles such a small, earnest smile, and I swear my legs go weak. I can't move or speak.

But I've prepared for this moment. Us being alone together after all this time. I waxed everywhere and I'm not wearing anything underneath this dress. I bought a box of Plan B and a backup one, just in case; they're both under my bed. I haven't eaten anything all day, so there's no chance of any gas or bloating or anything weird. I could say something to him right now. I could be completely honest and tell him how much I miss him, that I think of him all the time, that I'm so happy he reached out. I could tell him that I think we're meant to be together. That no other guy means anything to me, not compared to him. That I love him. I've always loved him.

But I don't. I don't say any of that. The moment passes, and I'm too late.

"Gonna get a drink," Nate says, and I can tell he just needed an excuse to put distance between us, and that shit stings. "Catch you later," he says, leaning in to rub my arm, and it feels like he's rubbed my pussy.

He gives me another one of his perfectly crooked smiles, then strides off without another word.

I don't know what just happened. I don't know why I froze like that. And now I'm staring at him, watching the crowd swallow him whole, wondering why I ever let him get away the first time.

I want to call him back over—I almost do. But some other way-too-buzzed bitch gets his attention before I can. She's all over him. I don't recognize her, have no idea whose plus-one she is, and think about having my father abolish plus-ones. Then another girl shuffles over, one of her falsies hanging off her eye. They take turns stroking his arm, completely fawning over him. One girl angles her phone to take a selfie. Nate has to hunch so low to fit in the frame, it looks like he's doubling over. The world's too small for him. He's so awkward, it's charming. The first girl leans in but stumbles a little in her heels, and Nate reaches out to catch her. She did it on purpose, obviously, but she plays it off like she's theater-trained, laughing like it's the funniest joke in the world. It's pathetic.

"He didn't even look at my tits," I say as Mei slips next to me, sucking on an impaled olive. "They look good, don't they?"

"They look fucking amazing."

I'd know if she was lying. She's not.

Nate's still shuffling through poses, but our eyes catch for the quickest moment, and I can almost feel it. The weight of his body holding mine in place. The hard, steady rhythm of him moving inside me. His breath thrusting into my ear with every stroke. And then he looks away, and it's clear that he'd glanced up not expecting to find me looking.

I blink a few times, then turn to Mei. "Did he look happy with her?"

"Babe, chill. Operation Bag Nate isn't a bust yet." She takes a chug of her drink. "Black guys always leave their girlfriends for white girls when they go pro. He's probably only with her because she's easy. Look at her. She's practically jerking your dad off."

I flick my gaze across the room.

She's right. Brandi's smiling too much. Laughing too hard. She doesn't know my father. His duplicity. She doesn't know how deceiving those crow's feet and smile lines really are.

"I never understand girls who sleep with men for jobs." Mei scoffs. "What am I missing? Working is so overrated."

I laugh. She cackles, a little too loud, and I wonder if she's already high on something.

I wish I was high right now. I want a hit so bad, I can almost feel it, ripping through my veins like lightning.

My eyes find Brandi again. Her braids cascade past her waist and her pink dress looks striking against her warm brown skin. She has the smallest tits I think I've ever seen in my life, and I am being one hundred percent sincere when I say I just don't fucking get it, but somehow her scarcity doesn't make her any less attractive. It only makes her ass seem even bigger. She's sexy in that way guys like: small, cute, easy to pick up. I hate her. I hate the way Nate looks at her, that wistful, almost childish glint in his eyes.

My father is staring at her, trying not to be obvious, but he still is, probably imagining pummeling her right now, and she has no idea. She's so clueless it almost makes me laugh. I should go over and save her. I really should, but I haven't reached that level of maturity yet.

"You think she'd actually fuck him, though?" I ask Mei.

She doesn't seem like the type, but then I don't know her. I could be wrong. Maybe she's not so innocent either. I wouldn't be shocked if she's doing all this just to get close to my father. I've seen other women do worse. Grown women. Mothers.

Mei makes a face like I'm juvenile for even asking the question. "Do you *see* her? She might be sucking up to him now, but trust me, she'll be on her knees sucking the oxygen out of him once they get to Italy."

My phone buzzes in my hand and an email pops up. I go to the link, thumb through the slideshow and growl. "Fuck. That editor at WWD snubbed me."

"The one who still breastfeeds her five-year-old? Didn't you send her a Lady Dior for Christmas?"

"Yeah, the special edition one with the Swarovski crystals. She totally reneged. I'm emailing her boss right now."

"And drop your publicist ASAP," Mei says. "I don't care if she reps the Hadid sisters and that German princess bitch with the forty-inch legs."

I'm too busy typing to respond.

"First your dad is in remission, and now this," Mei says a moment later, typing something on her phone. "Can't believe he beat cancer. Who does that?"

"My mom was a literal angel who rescued pigeons and opossums. She gets stage two cancer and is gone within a year. Dad recklessly fucks some random bitch while she's doing chemo, gets stage four cancer and then *poof*, it's gone. I don't get it."

Mei lifts a shoulder in an irreverent shrug. "So slit his throat."

I stare at her. Her mouth is set in a firm line, but there's laughter in her eyes.

I imagine it anyway, what she says. My father gone, no more reminders of the man who took my best friend from me, my angel. Then I push the thought away and bury it somewhere in the back of my mind where it belongs.

"I would, but I can't do blood," I say. "I get light-headed when I pull out my tampons."

"Gross," a deep voice says from behind me.

For a wild, crazy moment, I think Nate has found his way back over. I whip around with a smile for him.

But it's not Nate. It's Jared.

My eyes fall down the length of him. He looks like the most respectable fuckboy on the planet, as always, dressed in a silver Dior suit, crisp white shirt, no tie, with more than a little chest showing.

"What'd I miss?" He still hasn't looked up from his phone.

A smile creeps across my face. "Let me guess. Six-two, one-eighty, nine inches."

Mei snickers.

His eyes flick up and he flashes a smile, but his fingers are still moving. "I wish. I borrowed the Rolls last night. Forgot to delete the footage from my dad's security system."

Mei leans in. "You can do that on your phone?"

"If I couldn't, I would be disowned by now. My dad would kill me if he knew I've been whipping all the hot boys around in his precious foreigns."

I smile. This is exactly why I like Jared. Badass enough to hack and steal, smart enough to not get caught. I miss the days when he was still in the city full-time, before his dad went all bicoastal on us and bought a 90210 compound in The Flats so

Jared could be close by when he went to USC. Now I only get to spend summers with him. He claims he's not going back this fall, and I'm already planning on dragging him to Paris for fashion week in September.

When he's done, he curls a ripped arm around me, leaning in to kiss both cheeks, then shifts for Mei.

"So who are you sociopaths plotting to kill this time?"

A ghost of a smile finds Mei's lips. "Her dad."

"Again?"

His lack of surprise makes me chuckle.

"He's way out of pocket cutting her off like this." Mei's eyes flick to me. "And don't forget he threatened to ship you off to Arizona last month. Ari-*fucking*-zona."

I roll my eyes. "I'd rather do prison than rehab. At least there's commissary."

"At least your dad's bank isn't going under," Jared says.

I slap him on the arm. "Don't joke like that."

"It's hitting Page Six Monday morning," he says, suddenly solemn in a way he rarely is. "We're headed straight to the poor house."

"Dude." Mei looks concerned, and she never gives a fuck about anything. "What are you gonna do?"

"I don't know. Sodomize the anxiety away?" He runs his hand through his perfect hair, giving total cologne ad vibes. "Apparently, I have to be frugal now. Whatever that means."

I think for a second. "Why don't you just rack up some more DJing gigs now that you're officially a USC dropout? The money's good, right?"

He flicks his eyes around in a quick roll and gives me a look like I should know better. "Working for my money is too stressful."

"Obviously," I say. "What was I thinking?"

There's a brief moment where we're all laughing at that

and it feels nostalgic, like old times, the three of us perfectly in sync.

Then Mei snorts with disdain as her eyes settle across the room again. "Like, what is this? Look at them."

Brandi's leaning over to see something my father is showing her on his phone, her tits pressed into his arm. This is getting obnoxious now. They exchange a few more words, he makes her laugh, then they shake hands for the second time. Their eyes linger in a hold, like their hands. I half expect him to slap her on the ass as she slinks away.

"Who's that?" Jared asks.

Mei jumps in to fill him in.

I tune them out as a woman draped in a silver McQueen gown and cropped fur jacket reaches over and links her arm inside my father's, replacing Brandi. Her long, almost-black hair frames smooth skin that looks retouched.

His new bitch.

I keep my gaze trained on her as she leans in to kiss him, pressing her palm against his chest as she raises to the tips of her toes. I've heard them fucking. I've heard her guttural screams reverberate from his wing of the house. They were raw, desperate, the kind of sounds a woman makes when she's trying to cement herself in a man's future, part performance. I know she isn't pretending to be attracted to him. But that doesn't mean she's not after his money too.

I don't trust her.

I close my eyes, just for a second, and see my mom, her eyes locked open forever, neck bent like the cruelest lie. My insides roil. I force myself to push the image away and swallow down the bile.

My father kisses her back, a real kiss. I want to rip his tongue out of his mouth and strangle him with it.

"Fuck this." I reach over and snatch Mei's glass out of her

hand and swallow it down like medicine, like it can cure all my problems.

There's only so much of this shit I can take.

Jared is staring at me. "At least you're already home."

I wipe my mouth with the back of my hand.

"Calm down, bitch. I have something way better than that." Mei opens her box clutch and tilts it my way so I get a peek of the freshly rolled joint inside. "It's laced with coke," she whispers.

Those are like magic words. I run my tongue over my lips and bite down. "I love you so much right now."

Mei pulls out the joint she flashed at me downstairs and kicks off her mules, giving me an unsolicited flash of her bloodied and bandaged ballerina feet. She flips her hair out of the way, a shiny curtain of black, then lights the joint with a sequined lighter. I watch her, that little fire blooming between two fingers like jasmine in the moonlight.

She inhales hard, then blows out abstract smoke shapes as she passes it to me. "Your dad hasn't updated his will since he found out about the remission thing, right?"

"Whoa," Jared says. "The man fucking beat cancer. Down, girl."

"No," I say, taking a hit and passing it to him.

"So you're still the sole beneficiary?" Mei asks.

I nod.

"Look, we all know you're not gonna be sober by September." She shrugs. "If we got rid of him, you get everything, you know. His entire estate. Fuck five million."

"You're horrible," Jared says, letting the smoke out through his nostrils as he slouches deeper on the tufted couch, and there's something about the way the light from the Murano crystal chandelier above hits his face. He looks boyish and sort of innocent, the way he did before Mei and I corrupted him.

Mei's expression doesn't waver. "Didn't you say he just passed the two billion mark with that new acquisition last month?"

She's looking at me now. I don't say anything.

She's being ridiculous. She gets like this sometimes. Her blinders go up and she can only see her end goal, nothing else, no consequences. She doesn't even stop to consider the collateral damage that getting what she wants could cause. I can't *actually* kill my father. I can't. Even if we did everything right, I'm still the first person the police would suspect. The person who has the most to gain always is.

But then a new thought hits me. "Wait. What if Dad marries this bitch before September?"

It's been two years; it's possible.

I look at Jared as he hands the joint back to Mei, who sighs, bored. "If you don't intercept now, it's over. That bitch is gonna get a custom-cut Lorraine Schwartz and you'll no longer be the heir apparent. You're screwed just like my dad screwed me. His new wife gets control of his estate if something happens to him, not me. It's bullshit, especially now that he's one step away from completely cutting me off."

I heave out a breath. "Fuck."

"You'll have to do a full one-eighty, sober all the way up and you still only get chump change. Total scam."

I snatch the joint, suck it hard and let the smoke out through my nose. "What the hell are tigers going to do with five million dollars anyway?" I say, expecting her to smile, but she doesn't. She's not joking anymore. Maybe she never was.

"Getting clean for that isn't even worth the effort," she says, taking the joint back.

We're quiet awhile. We're both thinking about *him*.

I groan. "You don't have any extra powder on you? This shit is weak."

Mei shrugs. "My delivery's late."

"Fuck," I say, squeezing my eyes shut, craving that sweet floral smell, that burn up my nose before the numbness rolls over my tongue and drips down my throat. That nothing, nowhere feeling. Drowning me. Protecting me.

I open my eyes, the roar from downstairs reduced to a low hum. "Do you think we could actually get away with it?" I ask, serious now.

Jared goes still on the couch. "Hey, this is still a joke, right?"

My face doesn't change.

He looks from me to Mei, but she ignores him too.

"Probably not if you gut him." Her voice is flat and grim. "You could Shakespeare his ass, though."

My nod is slow as I toss that around in my head. "Poison."

My little genius takes another draw and, without skipping a beat, she says, "I know a guy who will definitely know a guy who could get us something to put him to sleep in a few minutes."

She sounds so practical. So sure. I have no doubt she'd be able to get whatever I'd need to kill my father. She can get her hands on anything. Her dealer delivers her blow to her apartment like it's takeout.

Jared studies Mei, then his gaze settles on me. "You guys are scaring me."

I gape at him. "Dude, your dad's bank is *done*. Come on. We'll split my inheritance three ways, even."

He looks away, still not convinced.

I'm not worried, though. I know I can trust him. We've been through too much together for me to not trust him. We met at homecoming freshman year. He was shit-faced and still pretending to be straight. He told me my Taylor Swift–heavy playlist was weak, then introduced me to K-pop and we've been inseparable ever since. He's seen me naked—everybody's seen me naked—and I've seen his dick. It was like seeing your brother's dick. I know all his secrets, what hurts him the most. He will tell no one.

Jared blows out a sigh, and to my surprise, reaches over and takes the joint from Mei's hand, finishing it off with an enormous hit. It makes him choke.

I laugh at his canna-cough until it dies down. "Are we going to have to carry you out of here?"

"Maybe. Fuck." He shakes his head and takes a breath. Then his eyes meet mine, still and pensive. "You really want to kill your dad?"

The indica-pearl blend is starting to turn my thoughts loose inside my head, distancing me further and further away from reality. I close my eyes and rock into the feeling of it.

Mei jumps in for me. "His ass deserves it. Who cheats on their wife while she's doing chemo? He's the reason she put that rope around her neck."

My eyes flick open at the mention of my mom. At those words. It still hurts. It always hurts. I take a deep breath, count the thoughts away. Ten. Twenty.

Suddenly, the air around me seems lighter.

Thirty.

I feel myself float a little higher, and there's a shriek in the room, a scream. And then I realize it's my own laughter.

5

BRANDI

Adrenaline surges through my veins, and I don't know if I'm going to collapse into hysterical laughter or have a full-on nervous breakdown. I want to swing my arms out wide and spin in a ridiculously happy circle. Before I get carried away, I pull out my phone and text Nate.

Where are you? I'm done.

His response is immediate: Over by the bar.

I head back inside to the main room and glance around. My eyes finally find Nate but he's not alone. He's standing between what I'm guessing is an Andy Warhol original and one of Richard Avedon's iconic Beatles portraits, talking with two older men, no doubt fans of his dad's.

I wave slightly, trying to get his attention. Nate's head lifts and he spots me. I can feel the warmth of his smile from here. He quickly poses for a photo, then politely breaks away.

His eyes are about as wide as mine. "How'd it go? What'd he say?"

I can't hold back my excitement. "I have an interview next week!"

"For real?" His entire face lights up. "That's what I'm talking about, girl. Come here."

Nate pulls me into a strong hug. I shriek with laughter when my feet lift off the floor. We're tucked deep enough in the corner that most people don't notice us, but a small part of me hopes Taylor is somewhere in the shadows, watching. She couldn't be more obvious if she hopped into Nate's lap and stuck her hand down his pants.

As soon as my feet hit the floor, Nate pulls me closer and leans for my mouth, but he grabs me a little too hard, too quick, and ends up stepping on the bottom of my dress. A small pink feather floats on the floor between us.

"Hey, be careful," I say as I adjust the train, still smiling. "We have to return this dress tomorrow morning."

"My bad."

His hand finds the back of my head and he kisses me hard. I can taste the champagne on his tongue. It's sweet, intoxicating. I want him. I want him now. All of him. I rock into his body, pressing closer, harder.

His breath hitches and he drops his voice. "B, if we don't stop…"

I can feel the heat of him against my stomach. I bite my lip and look around. "Maybe there's a quiet room upstairs."

I love how cliché this sounds, and it's exactly why I want to do it. I want to be a cliché tonight.

Nate's eyebrows lift, just a bit. A question.

I smile as my eyes slide down to his chest, then back up. "We have to make up for lost time, right?"

"Hell yeah."

He laces his fingers into mine and drags me behind him.

We're heading for the stairs when a guy in a blue suit grabs Nate by the arm, pulling him to a full stop. He smiles warmly at Nate as if he's meeting a hero. The man can barely hold back his excitement.

"You're Reggie Robinson's son, aren't you? My dad's a huge fan. He's out by the pool."

"I am, but I'm..." Nate glances at me, his eyes asking for permission. He doesn't need to ask, but he always does anyway.

I give him a small nod. "It's fine. Go ahead. I'll just look around."

"I'll come find you."

The guy pulls him away, and I watch them for a while. Talking. Laughing. Then I turn for the stairs.

My dress sways as I walk down the long, marble-floored hallway, careful not to make too much noise. The second level is as stunning as the rest of the house, and I haven't even left the hall yet. Once you pass the domed, oak-paneled library and sitting room—complete with a fully stocked wine fridge, because naturally—you reach a guest bathroom, the first of many I'm sure, which is the size of some Manhattan apartments. Inside it's what I can pretty much only describe as perfection. As in, a freestanding clawfoot tub, multiple skylights, marble countertops that must be imported and a ton of Diptyque candles and stylized greenery. The whole place seems ripped straight from the pages of *Architectural Digest*, each room underscored with unique, museum-quality artwork, like the countless full-size Helmut Newtons of naked women posing wide-legged and tugging on cigarettes.

I push in one of the other doors that line the hall, not sure where it leads. The "room" is comically huge, literally bigger than my entire apartment. It's more of a suite, because there's a small hallway lined with a mirror and console table that leads into a bigger space, maybe two thousand square feet. It's set up like a loft—most of the main area has been converted into a closet and a bed is set on the top level, but I'm sure it was originally designed to be the other way around. No doubt this is Taylor's suite. On one side of the lower level is a velveteen, chartreuse couch strewn in a cavalcade of patterned pillows and a fur throw. A vintage, gold-trimmed mirror leans against the wall next to a clothing rack stuffed with glittering dresses, vintage furs and a few basketball jerseys. There's a hot-pink neon sign plugged into the wall next to the mirror that reads *Need Money for Birkin*.

For a moment her whiteness is insufferable. I know the sign is meant to be funny, but it still feels like a slap in the face. I think of all the times I went to bed hungry when I was little, had to ask strangers on the street for money just so I wouldn't pass out in class, and something inside me is on the verge of detonating.

Floor-to-ceiling windows with high arches line the back wall. There's an incredible view of the water, the city a distant glow in the background. I turn away and notice the twelve-foot ladder leading up to her bed. I don't know what possesses me, but I find myself climbing the ladder, sitting on the soft, silky sheets.

From my vantage point, I scan the room again. Aside from a few crystals, flowers and a stack of spiritual books, everything is tucked away, perfectly organized to the point of absurdity. The bedroom-size walk-in is filled with custom-made racks that stretch from wall to wall. I stand there for a moment, taking it all in. Vintage Chanel hangs alongside Tom Ford–era Gucci, Saint Laurent, limited-edition Adidas and impossible-to-find designer pieces that must date back to the late '80s and early '90s. I quickly sift through racks of men's-style blazers, leather fringe jackets, vintage kaftan dresses, delicately embroidered blouses, beaded evening gowns and the occasional tutu. Because of course. And rows and rows of shoes. Clearly, she has a thing for sneakers—she has at least fifty pairs, every color, every style. And the bags. They span from floor to ceiling across two walls lined with glass shelves. Her collection of Olympia Le-Tan clutches, all designed with the covers of classic literature, is truly amazing.

I try hard not to swoon, not to lose my entire mind, but I'm mostly just walking around in straight-up awe. And I know, it's just clothes. This is all trivial, just material things that will all become dust one day like everything else, but it's fun to imagine living this way.

I take a quick look inside her bathroom. Inside, it smells like La Mer and leftover perfume, like flowers and heat. Surprisingly, it's nothing crazy, just a collection of basic hair and skin products set on the counter. I peek inside her shower and there are no washcloths, just coordinating bottles of body wash and shampoo. Underneath the sink, there's a woven basket with cotton swabs, organic tampons, a stack of K-beauty face masks and a small pink vibrator. My eyes linger on the vibrator and for a second I start to feel bad, like I'm violating her. But then I'm wondering how she sounds when she moans. If she's a screamer or one of those psychopathic people who are totally silent except for when they climax. If she's as good in bed as she looks like she would be. If she's better than me.

I have to stop. It's so stupid, so juvenile, what I'm doing, comparing myself to her like this. This isn't me. I'm just... I don't even—

A sound from down the hall makes me almost lurch out of my skin. I pause and strain to listen, but I don't hear anyone approaching. It doesn't matter. I can't be in here. I rush to the door in this heavy-ass dress, hoping it will be Nate.

It's probably Nate.

I peek outside the door before stepping out. No one's here.

I'm heading back toward the staircase when I hear muffled voices. And then I recognize one of them. Taylor.

My feet are moving before I can stop them. A door at the end of the corridor is ajar, just the smallest crack, and as I get closer, their words get louder, clearer. Someone says something I can't make out, then there's an eruption of laughter.

Taylor's laugh echoes through the walls—she has a huge laugh, loud and unrestrained, the laughter of a person without a real care in the world.

A new voice chimes in, gentler than the others. A guy. So there's three of them.

I shouldn't listen.

I listen.

"You seriously want to kill your dad?" the guy asks, his voice deadpan.

I lean closer, my hand pressing flat against the door.

I'm so startled, I forget to listen for a few beats. Then I lean closer, hoping I heard wrong. There's more laughter, then—

"I know someone who did it," the other voice says. I'm assuming the girl in the red dress.

"Did they get away with it?" Taylor.

"Duh. It's clean. No blood. No mess. All you need is a solid alibi and you're good."

Taylor says something else, but it doesn't register. My mind isn't processing any of this quickly enough.

I can't listen anymore.

I knew I was walking into a different world coming here tonight. I knew this might be awkward, a little out of my depth. I didn't expect...this. The hell did I just hear? They can't be seriously plotting to murder Simon. Maybe they're all lightweights, and just drunk and running off at the mouth.

I just want to find Nate and leave. I got my interview. I have what I came for.

I turn for the stairs and my heel gets caught in my train. I press against the door for balance as I try to free it.

The stupid door creaks.

"What the fuck was that?" Taylor.

Heat rushes up my spine. I hold my breath.

No one comes to the door right away. The room is probably huge. Crossing it will take a good minute. Which means I have time to run.

I fly down the stairs, the skirt of my gown balled in the crook of my arm. Once I'm on the main floor, I check back over at the bar, but Nate's not there. When I turn around, Taylor's hustling down the staircase, her dress flying behind her like silk wings. There's something different about her, something off, but I can't put my finger on it. Something about her eyes—something glassy, detached.

I glance back at her before pushing through the crowd, eyes switching left to right, sweeping the room like a hawk. I'm moving as fast as she is, trying to find Nate, but also trying not to be seen. Just as I pull out my phone to text him, Taylor bulldozes past me, stumbling slightly. I follow her gaze.

Shit. Nate.

I head over to him.

Taylor gets his attention a second before I do. Her hand catches his arm. "Nate." It's a snap, a burst of desperation.

I almost fling her bony-ass arm away.

He angles toward her, his demeanor more polite than interested. "Hey. What's up?"

Her head tilts, eyes squint. "Where's your girlfriend?"

"Uh…not sure." He glances around, and I duck behind someone before he catches me. "Last I saw her she was just looking for the bathroom."

Taylor's face hardens, those perfectly full brows crashing together. I see it click on her face. She knows it was me. I thought maybe she and her friends were just talking shit up there, but the serious, almost panicky look on her face makes me think this girl is really planning to murder her father.

Nate frowns. "Why? What's wrong?"

I can't tell if Taylor answers before she flips around and flicks her gaze around the room as she bulldozes the crowd. While her back is to us, I hurry behind Nate and tug on his elbow.

"Hey," he says, looking relieved to see me. "Where you been?"

My head is buzzing too loud to verbalize what happened upstairs. I don't know if I should tell anyone what I heard, even Nate.

"Been trying to find you," I say, playing it as cool as I can. "God, this place is so huge."

He leans in, his lips grazing my ear. "Did you find a spot?"

It takes a few moments for me to process his question, to realize he's asking if I've found a place where we can hook up, and my mouth parts to respond, but before I get any words out, I see her. Hawking me from across the room. And then she's heading back our way, swerving around people like a storm.

I shake my head and blink back into the moment. "What?"

"Upstairs," Nate says, grinning. "Did you find anywhere we could—"

"Let's just get out of here," I say. Taylor is within arm's length, held up by a dramatic five-foot fuchsia train dragging behind a petite girl. "I'm not feeling that well."

That takes away the hungry grin. He morphs into rescue mode and takes my hand. Just as I think he's about to make a beeline for the exit, Taylor hooks her body around us.

"I've been looking for you," she says with a sweet smile. All I can think about is what she said to her friends upstairs.

I look to Nate, hoping he'll save me. Then I remember he has no idea what's going on beneath the surface.

"Oh," I say clumsily, barely able to look Taylor in the eye. "Your dad and I had a nice chat, then I've just been mingling while Nate got mobbed by fans as usual."

"Really?" Taylor asks, her smile not faltering a bit. "You made friends? With who?"

I try to come up with a couple of fake names off the top of my head, but stop myself, figuring she probably knows everyone who was invited. This is a test.

"Was that before or after you went upstairs?" Taylor asks, but it's less of a question and more of an accusation.

Shit. "Yeah, I just felt a little nauseous. Couldn't find the bathroom down here. Sorry. Hope that was okay."

"B isn't feeling well," Nate says, and I'm glad he's finally jumping in. "We're actually about to head out."

"Already?" Taylor says, pouting as if she is actually sad he's leaving.

"Feeling kinda light-headed now. Need to lie down."

I touch my head for effect, but Taylor just stares at me as if waiting for me to say something else. She knows I'm lying. She knows I heard what I heard.

Nate takes my hand, and I feel her staring us down until the crowds swallow us up, and then we're finally outside, the cool night air hitting our faces. I make a big deal out of this, leaning into the feeling-woozy thing so Nate doesn't question how strange I acted back there.

"Sure you good? What do you think it is?" he asks, but there's something in his voice that makes me think he knows I'm lying.

"No idea. Just want to sleep whatever this is off."

Nate gestures for me to rest my head on top of his legs once we're on the road, so whether he's actually fallen for this act or not, he is determined to help me to feel better. He arranges my braids so they're not irritating my neck, which is so sweet,

I start to feel bad for feigning illness. After a few minutes I lift my head and ask our driver to play the radio, anything, because I actually can't stand the silence or the sound of my thoughts. I let down my window, too, even though the AC is on. I need to feel the wind on my face. Nate looks at me, but I pretend to be exhausted and close my eyes.

I still can't stop thinking about it. I've seen some fucked-up shit, *real* fucked-up shit, but hearing the way Taylor talked so casually about killing her own father...it's messing with me. I never knew my dad, or my mom. Not really, not as people. Apparently, only forty percent of hit-and-runs are solved, and I was five when we buried them with no answers, no justice, and there is no god, no cosmic force, no hypothetical explanation, that can make that okay.

People like Taylor don't know what it's truly like to suffer. They create their own problems to offset the perpetual boredom their privilege grants them and then have the gall to pretend we're all equal, like we're all in this fight together. But we're not. All she has to do is present herself and she will be chosen. Shout and she will be saved. And I don't say this because I'm jealous; it's just a fact. She is exceptional by virtue of existing, and I am not.

6

TAYLOR

I let her go.

There's no point in running after her now with Nate by her side. He'll only get in the way. I'll deal with the nosy bitch later.

Jared insisted it was just my paranoia, but I know I heard something. Someone was there on the other side of that door, probably listening to every word.

It was her. I know it.

I watch them walk out the front door, side by side. Brandi looks shaken, withdrawn. Nate moves a hand to her lower back, and I can see that it calms her down, the way candy calms a child.

Something inside me shatters.

I can almost feel the weight of that hand. The warmth. My jaw tightens against my will. I want this night to be over. I want to go back upstairs, disappear in my room, but I know I won't be able to sleep.

I head outside to the bar and a waiter hands me a freshly poured flute. The blow and the weed still have a grip on me, but I don't care.

I glance around, looking for my father. He's nowhere in

sight, and I'm so glad because I can't deal with him right now. I can't deal with anyone right now.

A guy shifts toward me just as I take a sip. "That's an incredible dress."

I ignore him and gulp another mouthful.

His eyes never waver. "You know what? I'm wrong. It's not the dress. *You* look incredible."

I barely glance at him. "I'm not interested."

"But you—"

"Fuck off, okay?"

That amuses him, a dimple forming in one cheek when he smiles. I roll my eyes and swallow down more of the champagne than I should.

He starts to shift away, then changes his mind at the last second and leans in for my ear. "Your loss, baby. I'm hung like a Clydesdale."

My mouth opens.

Our eyes lock for the first time and he holds my gaze, unrepentant. Dark brown eyes, dirty blond hair pulled back into a tight bun. I study him, trying to place his features, but I don't know him. He shrugs and turns to walk away, and it's this, this moment of just total nonchalance, that does me in.

"Wait."

He stops and spins back around to face me. This time there's a certain arrogance in the way that he looks at me, like he just knew I'd stop him. I take a few steps forward and when I stop, my hand settles on his cummerbund.

His eyes drop, then shoot up to meet mine. "What are you doing?"

I smile when he glances over his shoulder to check if anyone is watching us. "Take it out."

His eyes dart from left to right. "You...right here?"

I nod, draining my glass. "Show me."

He snorts out a laugh. He thinks I'm joking, then realizes I'm serious when my expression doesn't change.

"Fine." He glances around one more time. "Here."

I don't know why I'm shocked when he untucks himself from his pants, but I am. It's not just big, it's perfect-looking. Literally the prettiest dick I've ever seen. Long and tan and satiny smooth, a little curved, just the right amount of curve. As I stare, my brain has the urge to intellectualize this moment, because it's obvious that he's a shower not a grower, and I find it weirdly hilarious, but also mildly disturbing because I realize I've never seen a dick like this IRL. And now I'm trying to imagine running or riding a bike with something of this magnitude between my legs, which makes me want to laugh even more, but I don't, and when I glance back up, he has this smile on his face, so completely aware of himself, and it makes me want him that much more. It feels so good—this rush. A different kind of high. Like someone's flipped on a switch.

He shifts closer to me, shielding himself from the crowd, and leans in. "This good enough for you?"

I can't stop staring. I hate that I can't stop staring.

"Go ahead, touch it," he says as if reading my mind, and I want to ask him if he has an OnlyFans because he seems like the type that would. But I don't ask.

I like the way he looks at me, so direct and unafraid, and I wonder what kind of faces he makes when he comes.

I want to touch him so bad. I look him over and notice his body for the first time. He's taller than I realized, maybe six-three. He looks like the kind of guy I could lose my thoughts in, forget every problem. It hurts to remember. And just like that I realize I need him.

As soon as we get upstairs to my room, his hands are all over me, wide and warm, pulling at my dress, at my body. His mouth finds my neck, the tender skin behind my ear.

"Is that your spot?"

He has me against the wall. Soft lips. Tongue velvet against my throat. I let out a breath. "One of them," I say, and then his hand is on my thigh, between my legs.

He trails kisses along my shoulder and collarbone, whispering something else I can't make out, but I don't need foreplay. I'm tired of the talking. I want to tell him to shut up, just shut the fuck up, because every time he says something, it pulls me back into the moment, back to reality, and I don't want to think. I don't want to remember that he's a stranger. That he's not Nate.

I push him down onto the couch and crawl on top of his big body. "Condom?"

"Pocket."

He reaches inside his pants, and I wait for him, pulling off my dress and shoes. Then he sits me down on his dick a little too fast but I don't make a sound because I don't want his sympathy, and for a moment I briefly wonder if this is what it's like to have an out-of-body experience, because I feel myself floating into the air, no hands or feet, and all I can see is a hazy mist of white, of pure glory. My eyes flutter as he pushes deeper. He's desperate, ravenous. I cry out without meaning to, a horrifying, involuntary sound that's more of a shriek than anything else. He chuckles a little, because he's obviously used to this, and I can feel the vibrations inside me. When he asks me if I'm okay, I nod because it's all I can manage at this point. I take the pain. I need it. I grip the headrest with both hands, rocking into him, and he moans. Really, truly moans. At first it's off-putting, undignified, but then I realize I like it, the absurd rawness of it.

"Yeah, like that," I whisper. "Harder. Make me forget."

He pauses beneath me, a train slamming to a stop. "Make you forget what?"

My eyes pop open. "Just fuck me hard," I say, keeping my voice just above a whisper. "Think you can do that?"

I press my lips into his. He opens his mouth and kisses me back just as hard.

I moan when he starts moving again. "Yeah. Like that. Just like that, just like that."

He lets out a shuddering breath. "You look so good."

"You feel so good."

I move his hand to my neck, clamp it hard around my throat, and when I squeeze my eyes tight enough, I can picture Nate inside me, and so I fuck him back, and he comes so fast, so hard. The rest of the world falls away. I can't breathe. I can't think. I hold absolutely still.

And then I peel my eyes open.

Every good feeling inside me dies in an instant, a pebble shattering the mirror-still surface of a lake.

It's not Nate.

It's not Nate.

My breathing sounds so loud. I can hear the blood gorging in my ears, the screaming rush of it, and I have this sudden urge to cry, this weird stream of emotions that I can't comprehend.

"So can I get your number?"

He's staring up at me with that stupid smile again, his face still flushed.

"No." I climb off him and slip inside my closet.

"Just like that? You're not even going to consider it?"

I glance over at him, pulling an oversize sweatshirt. "You're not my type."

He chuckles a little, like I'm joking. "If I'm not your type, why'd you invite me up here?"

"A certain horse-like quality, remember?"

His laugh seems forced as he moves to his feet. "Well, can I at least give you my number? Maybe we can do this again."

His dick swings as he walks over to me, slapping so hard against his leg I hear the sound. I bite down on my tongue without realizing it until the skin starts to break, just the tiniest bit. The taste of iron greets me and I flinch, swallow the pain away.

I hand him my phone. "Just give me your Instagram."

He takes it, and I watch him as he clicks into the app and follows me.

"I won't respond to dick pics in my DMs," I tell him, taking it back.

But he smiles again. He's seen me staring, the look on my face. He thinks I'm being shy. Or playing some kind of game. Or something.

I bend over for his pants and shirt, a small pile on the carpet, and hand them to him.

"You might change your mind," he says, slipping a leg into his pants, and I notice a tattoo on the back of his calf and almost regret the whole thing.

Why is it always guys who try to paint women as the needy, clingy ones when it's *always* the guys who want more?

I sigh and reach for my phone. "Fine. If you go."

He lingers for a moment, staring at me like he doesn't know what to make of me, what to say to that.

"I'll take your number if you leave right now," I say, tossing him my phone.

He catches it with one hand, and I don't know why I'm impressed, like he caught a missile with his bare hands or something. I watch him as he types his number into my phone, counting the seconds. He leans in when he hands it back to me and kisses my mouth, but this time is different than before. Slow and gentle and thoughtful. It feels nice.

I elbow him away. "You said you'd leave."

He throws both hands up. "I'm going."

"You're not."

He chuckles again, shaking his head this time like he still can't believe any of this is happening to him. "Are you always in this good of a mood after sex?"

He has this sort of earnest look in his eyes that pierces right through me. I soften my voice. "Look, it's not you. I just... need to be alone right now." I run my hand over my hair and blow out a breath. "Can you please leave?"

His eyes drift away. "Mind if I use your bathroom first?"

I hesitate, then nod toward the en suite.

He walks away. I watch him, every step. The door clicks shut, a whisper in the dark. I hear him pissing through the door; it gushes from him, drilling into the bowl so hard it sounds like he's going to blow a hole straight through the porcelain. A pause, then it starts up again until it fades to a soft trickle. The same as when he comes. I swallow hard.

The toilet flushes, then the sink hisses, stops and then he's walking toward me again, wiping his hands on his pants.

When we're shoulder to shoulder, he brushes past me. "It's Carter."

I frown. "What?"

"My name," he says, gesturing to my phone.

After he slips out, I slam the door before slumping against it in a sort of small relief. But it doesn't last. My head pounds so hard I can almost hear it. I can feel the high leaving my body, that bliss slipping away a moment at a time. The thoughts are back. Taunting me.

My phone buzzes in my hand. I glance down and see the text from Mei.

Where'd u go? U ok?

Another one pops up from Jared. I'm heading out. Hope ur okay, babes.

I toss my phone on the couch without responding and try to think of happy times, before everything in my world turned so bleak, but when I close my eyes, I see my mom, the colors and lines of her, and think of the last time I saw her. The moment feels too close, like it's happening all over again, and the tears come before I can make sense of them, hot and unstoppable.

They, too, don't last long. They're useless. I wipe my face, hard, angry with myself for letting it get to me again.

I can't cry. I won't. I'm tired of crying because of *him*.

What Mei said is true. My father was the reason she killed herself.

I can still hear her words, like a slice straight across the heart: *Why did you bring me here? You should have left me.*

I shut my eyes as if I can shut off the world, the memories rising like flames.

All I see is blood.

My mom's blood. Dark red streaks on the white walls, rust-colored slashes on the rug, large, viscous pools on the tiled floor. I can still taste it, copper with an undercurrent of something more bitter, a wet penny on my tongue.

There isn't just blood. There's more. Ghastly things. Visceral things. But mostly blood. Vivid and wet and obscene.

Usually, the visions only happen at night. I try to blink them away, but they keep coming in flashes.

I should have been there. I should have saved her.

"Mom, you upstairs?" I call, slipping through the foyer. "I caught a red-eye."

The house is quiet, still. I immediately slow down.

Mom is a force. She brings everyone together with her food, her laughter, her yelling, which isn't aggressive or hostile, just her raw passion. Something she inherited from her Italian mother, my grand-mother, who was as loud and dynamic as she was, even into her sev-enties. And she dances. Mom loves to move, will sway and twirl and gyrate even when the only music playing is in her head. Especially in the kitchen, her happy place. She's infectious and never takes no for an answer. If she wants you to join her, you will flail your arms and swing your hair until you're both sweaty and then she will load you up on carbs, pasta and sauce and bread to replenish your energy and make you want to dance all over again.

That's why this strange calm terrifies me.

I look toward the stairs and remember the last time the house was blanketed by this same eerie hush—the way she'd been sprawled on the bathroom floor, inert, the rug beneath her soaked bright red—and the ground falls away.

"Mom," I shout, taking the stairs two at a time, but there is no answer, only a loud silence that gives my entire body a shudder. I push inside her bedroom, and the door to her en suite is ajar, light peeking through the crack. My stomach sinks, heart pounds. I see blood first—a thin stream growing along the tile, slithering like a viper. Then I smell it, the scent familiar and unkind.

I circle the tub and there she is, on the floor, her emaciated body limp and unmoving. Blood pools under both her hands, so dark it al-most looks black. I glance around the room and see the capless prescrip-tion pill bottles, the small blade next to them on the counter.

"Shit. Mom…"

Last time it had been just the wrists. This time she clearly wanted to make sure it worked.

Panic tries to take over, but I don't let it. I know what to do.

I roll her onto her side, then untie my shoelaces, snatch them out and wrap them around her wrists as tightly as I can. The blood slows down, but doesn't stop completely. I take a breath. The bleeding isn't my biggest concern. The darker the blood, the better. I learned that the first time. I grab a towel and slip it under her head, then sprint into the other room for my phone. I dial 911 and run back to her.

"Come on. Don't do this to me," I whisper, though I know she can't hear me.

I press my ear to her chest and listen for a pulse. It's there, slow and faint, but it's there. I wrap my arms around her flaccid body and hold her close until I hear the sirens.

The ambulance ride is a long, hectic blur. Overlapping voices, sterile smells and sounds I know too well. At the hospital, I sit stiffly under the hum of fluorescent lights and wait, the stench of death and blood and sweat seeping inside my clothes, legs bouncing through the minutes that feel like days until a man in white sidles up next to me. I stand up, and his hand drops down onto my shoulder.

"She's going to be fine," he whispers, and there is something in his voice and in his eyes, something unsaid despite that promise. He looks worried—not for her. For me.

I drift inside her room and stand over her. I search her face, looking for something I'm not sure I can find. She'd given up hope a long time ago, but I still hold on to it, for her, for the both of us. I call her, and she peels open her eyes like that one movement is too painful.

"Where am I?"

I reach and hold her hand. It has never felt more fragile, a dead leaf, a wilted petal.

"The hospital, Mom." I glance down at her fingers, her nails chipped and brittle and stained shades of red. I try to keep my voice even, but it's so hard, seeing her like this. "You lost a lot of blood this time."

Her head turns slowly on the pillow, disappointment filling her eyes. "You said you wouldn't be back until tomorrow."

My heart stops for an instant.

I know what she means. She'd planned to be dead by the time I got home. The thought makes me tremble, and I have to look away from her.

She glances around as if seeing the room for the first time. When she speaks, her voice is weak, but somehow the anger is still there. "Why did you bring me here? You should have left me."

I choke on the words. "Because I love you."

Tears prickle the corners of my eyes, but I move across the room before she can see them fall, my clothes clinging to my body, sopped with her blood.

I stare at my reflection in the window. "How do you feel?"

When she doesn't respond, I turn back, forcing myself to look past the monitor and the tubes.

She turns to look at me, her eyes raw and wet, the skin dark and loose underneath, a shadow of the woman she used to be. "Do you hate me?"

"No. Don't talk like that, Mom. Try to relax." I lean in and press my lips to her cheek. "Try to get some sleep. You're gonna be okay," I say, though some part of me knows this won't be the last time.

I leave the hospital in a rage. I don't have to ask; I already know what happened.

She found out the truth, just like I did.

Before I know what I'm doing or what I'll say, I'm pounding on the door to my father's Tribeca loft—the secret rental he has no idea I know about. The one he bought for his new bitch.

The door swings open, but it isn't my father waiting on the other side. The men's shirt she's wearing swallows her compact little body, and it's clear there is nothing underneath. Her face is bare, her long hair tousled. I stare at her for a long time, like if I stare long enough, she'll somehow vanish.

I look her over and roll my eyes hard enough for them to go around the globe. "So embarrassing."

"Who are…" Her voice trails off, and a glint of recognition flashes in her eyes.

I brush past her hard enough to make her stumble back a step because I don't want to have to make her cry. "Where is he?"

She doesn't answer, just stares at me, maybe in shock, then closes her mouth.

"Where the hell is he?" I snap, snaking from room to room. And then I hear it.

The shower is running.

I push the bathroom door open and the steam warms my face. I hear him mumble something, maybe for her, but the words get lost under the strong downpour. I call him and the water comes to an abrupt stop.

When he steps into the bedroom with me, he's wearing a towel high around his waist. "Taylor..."

The shock on my father's face is unmistakable.

And then he sighs, backed too far into a corner to escape, but there's no forgiveness in my face. "What are you doing here, Taylor?"

Fists clenched at his sides, ropes of veins cording his bare, wet arms, he towers over me, but I'm not afraid. I know he would never touch me. He never has, not once.

"She did it because of you, you asshole," I snap, lit and burning, but he remains impassive.

"What are you talking about?"

I ignore him and catch the bitch fumbling for her clothes out the corner of my eye.

"Mom's fighting for her life, and you're here? With her?" He reaches for my arm, but I push him back. "You're so gross."

"Taylor, calm down." He makes a wall with his arms, keeping me from shoving him again. "Leave Izzy out of this."

That bitch shifts around as her eyes move over my face and pick me apart.

I glare at him. "Was it just about sex? Is that why you cheated on Mom? So you could fuck her whenever you want?"

Something flashes in his eyes, something dark I've never seen before. The sound of damp flesh against my cheek rings in my ear. I stumble back a few steps from the impact, but it takes a second for me to realize it's his palm that has collided with my face. It takes longer for the pain to register. I stare up at him, waiting, but his eyes are unapologetic, and I know it's over between us for good; I'll never be able to look at him the same.

It's not long before Mom takes that blade and tears into her flesh again. About two weeks later.

But this time I'm too late.

7

TAYLOR

I can't believe this bitch actually showed up.

I bite at the inside of my lip, watching Brandi step into Cipriani's from my table near the front. I'm still contemplating how to play this, what to say, how to make my opening gambit.

This girl has no idea who she's messing with.

It was her on the other side of that door last night. I know it was. I'd wager my inheritance on that.

The slim but plain-faced hostess at the entrance greets her with the same effervescence as she did with me, and I resist the urge to chuckle when I hear Brandi give her my father's full name. The hostess motions my way, and then Brandi's head turns.

The sight of me kills her smile. A line appears between her brows.

"Hey," I say, plastering a smile on my face, my fingers twinkling in a little wave.

She smiles back, no wave, her teeth white and perfectly straight, but it falters toward the end. I can see the tension invade her shoulders from here.

She slinks over to the table, wearing tall heels and a midi-length dress with a strong waist and soft, scooped neckline. All her curves are on full display.

"Where's Si…" She stops at the edge of the table, her eyes flicking around the space. "Uh, your dad? Is he here yet?"

When she shifts under the light I can see her skin peeking through her makeup; she's not wearing that much foundation, mainly just highlighter and bronzer.

"He's not coming," I say with no pretense.

"What do you mean? I got an email saying he wanted to meet at ten for a pre-interview."

I don't let go of my smile. "It's just me."

She studies me for several seconds before reaching for the chair opposite me and taking a seat. "Cool. I just didn't realize— I thought it would be just me and Simon."

Of course she did.

"Is he okay?" she asks. "Did something happen?"

She's so determined to keep space between us that she angles her body away from the table when she crosses her legs. I'm about to put her on the spot, but I notice our company out the corner of my eye.

"What can I get for you ladies?"

Brandi looks up at the waitress who's just bounced over. I ignore her.

"Hi. Um, I'll have the…" She picks up the menu from the table. Her eyes move side to side and then something goes wrong. A frown flickers in and out of existence, then Brandi shuts the menu. "I'm actually not that hungry."

I almost laugh, realizing what her problem is. It's all over her face. "It's on me. Go for it."

She glances up at me and manages a smile. Then her eyes are quickly perusing the laminated pages again. It takes her so long to decide, I almost kick her in the shin to nudge her.

"I'll take the penne pasta," she finally says. "No parm, please."

The waitress turns to me, smiling. "And for you?"

I ignore her and scroll on my phone, assuming she'll get the hint.

She doesn't. She's still here. I look up at her. "If you want your twenty percent, I'd leave right now."

She looks at me as if she thinks I'm trying to trick her somehow.

I glance back down at my phone.

She scoffs and walks away.

I can feel Brandi burning a hole through my forehead with her judgmental glare, but I don't acknowledge it. "Losing the last fifteen pounds is always so hard. Skipping the cheese, good start."

That seems to grab her attention, puts a little fire in her eyes. "I don't diet, I just don't eat dairy."

She says the first part like she's proud of that.

I reach between us for my Perrier and take a sip. "Let's just cut to the chase. How much did you hear last night?"

A jolt of panic flashes across her face. But she recovers quickly. "I don't know what you're—"

"We were just joking, you know."

She considers this for a long moment. Finally, her eyes flick up. "Joking about what? I don't…"

She thinks I'm stupid.

I don't know how much she heard, but by the way she seems to pull into herself, I'm guessing it was enough. I reach into my bag. "You lost this before you fled the scene."

Brandi watches as I place the pink feather I found on the floor outside my room on the table between us.

She takes a minute, then runs the tip of her tongue over her lips as her head tilts. "This isn't a pre-interview, is it?"

"You're quick, huh?" I can't help but laugh at the embarrassment disrupting the flawlessness of her face. "What the hell even is a pre-interview? How could that possibly be a thing?"

She opens her mouth to speak, but I cut her off. "So why were you spying on me?" I ask, making sure to keep my voice nonchalant, bored. I have to play this down or she'll stay defensive.

"I wasn't spying."

"Bullshit." I set my jaw.

This isn't a game.

Her eyes lock on to mine. A hint of defiance flickers in them, and this time she doesn't look away. "Like I said, I don't know what you think I—"

"What did you hear before you ran?" My voice is hot now, irritated. I don't have the energy for this. She's wasting my time.

There's a beat, a humming silence, then Brandi pushes herself back, her chair scraping loud enough against the floor to spark a few curious glances from nearby tables.

"I'm looking forward to actually interviewing with your dad next week," she says with just a touch of acidity in her voice, and I want to squeeze her neck until her eyes bulge. "Alone."

Instead, I hold her gaze and smirk. "Yeah, I bet you can't wait to be alone with him."

Her shoulders tense, and from the way she glares at me, I know I'm getting under her skin.

"I just meant that it's really important to me to work for a brand that aligns with my ethics," she says, not missing a beat. "Van Doren is exactly the kind of label I've always wanted to be a part of. I have tons of ideas. I can forward some of them to you. Or your dad. And Milan. I can't even imagine. It'll obviously be amazing for my résumé, but it sounds like a dream. Not that I think it'll be all sipping fancy wine and playing dress-up. I'm a workhorse. I'm ready to roll up my sleeves and do whatever the team needs."

I take another deliberate sip of my water. "Amazing for your résumé...or your bank account?"

Her head cocks to the side, lines of confusion forming down the middle of her forehead. "I thought the position only pays a small stipend."

That makes me smile. "It does."

"I'm not..." Her eyes search mine as if she'll be able to find something there. "I don't understand."

I sigh and force the edge away from my voice. "Look, you can cut the whole innocent act. I get why you're so upset. You were planning on milking my father for what, millions? If he's gone, your whole plan is a bust. But if you stop pretending with all this ethics bullshit, maybe you and I can work something out. Without him."

She scoffs, in disbelief or disgust, I can't tell. She starts to say something, but cuts herself off and glances around the room as if remembering we're in a roomful of dignified people.

"Well, clearly you've made your mind up about me, so there's no point in me being here, is there?" She doesn't wait for a response before jumping to her feet. "Thanks for lunch."

I grab her arm before she steps away from the table. "Wait. You didn't let me finish."

"Don't ever put your hands on me," she snaps, weaseling her arm out of my grasp as if she thinks I might try to hurt her, like I'm that stupid. But she doesn't leave.

I flick my eyes around the room, then lower my voice. "What if we work out a deal? Ten grand and all you have to do is not tell anybody what you heard in there."

She laughs, not like she's amused, but maybe in temporary

shock. Then she lifts a brow, and something mocking eases into her eyes. "Thought you said you were joking?"

I roll my eyes. "Okay, can we just cut the bullshit? You heard what you heard, and I need it to stay between us."

She laughs, and it sounds like she is genuinely amused. "You're going to give me ten thousand dollars to keep quiet about you planning to murder your—"

"Don't say it out loud. Are you stupid?" I snap, and suddenly my heart is racing. I take a breath to steady myself. Check the room one more time.

When I look at Brandi again, she has the same look on her face as I do when I gawk at the homeless people balled up in sleeping bags inside Grand Central, but I'm not the one who's crazy. She's the one out of her mind if she doesn't agree to this deal. This is to protect her as much as it is to protect me.

"Look. It'll take me about a week to get my hands on the cash," I say. "But it's yours if you agree to keep your mouth shut."

Her face breaks into a smile, but there's nothing friendly about it. She stares at me for a moment, rolling her tongue around her mouth as if she's just figured something out. "You really think you can buy your way out of everything, don't you?"

I don't look away. Neither does she.

I lick my lips, taste the bitterness of my lip stain. "Are you saying no? We both know this is the only way someone like you will ever have this much money in your bank account. I mean, unless you want to mooch off Nate for the rest of your life."

Her eyes harden. "Like you mooch off your dad?"

My eyes still. I study her, and then my mouth is moving, but no sound is coming out. I can't decide whether to be impressed or furious. Who turns down ten thousand dollars? Who does this bitch think she is?

Her eyebrows lift just a fraction, still waiting for me to respond, and I can tell she can see I'm flailing, unsure of what to say, how to proceed. I force myself to hold her eyes and stand my ground. "Look, you—"

But she's already on the move, strutting away from the table. I clench my jaw and let her go this time. I don't need her going all angry black girl, fist-in-the-air on me. The click of her heels against the tiled floor rises above all the colliding voices as she heads for the door. I follow her through the glass with my gaze until she turns at the corner, no doubt heading down into that smelly, rat-infested hole in the ground.

I take another sip of my water. The nerve. The fucking *audacity*. I was trying to help her, to keep her out of trouble. She has no idea what she's just tangled herself into.

If this is the way she wants to play it, fine.

Clueless bitch.

I sigh and stare out at the onset of LIE traffic, and, accepting it's going to take forever to get to the other side of the East River, I text Mei. The bitch won't take the money.

It takes her less than a minute to reply. What happened?

I ignore that. I still want to do it.

My phone buzzes as soon as the message shows *delivered*. I lift it to my ear.

"Bitch, how high are you? No paper trail."

"Shit. I wasn't thinking." I slap my forehead, wondering if I really am better high if this is how I function completely sober. "Are you still in class?"

"I have fifteen before rehearsal starts."

"I'm coming over now. Meet me in the back."

★ ★ ★

"Hey, you know I'm down," Mei says, repinning her bun on top of her head.

She's glistening with sweat as we huddle up in the service staircase, the most private space we could find at the NYCB headquarters. I can barely get close enough to whisper because of the stiff pancake tutu she's wearing over her black, halter-back unitard.

"But now it's risky." I sigh. "What if this girl tells someone what we said?"

"Who's she gonna tell? The cops don't even search for black girls when they go missing. You think they'd take anything she says seriously?"

It's a valid point.

I chew my lip, thinking. "What if she tells my father?"

Mei glances at me, but doesn't answer. She's thinking too.

"I just don't want any loose ends if we're gonna do this." I let out a breath, a thousand thoughts running through my head at once. "Has to be done right."

"Then you need to keep her away from the old man."

I pause for a minute. "You really think she's after his money?"

Mei takes a beat, pulling her leg straight up in an extreme stretch that makes me wince, her knee near her ear, then says, "I don't know. Doesn't matter. I don't trust her."

I don't trust her, either.

As much as I try, I can't figure this girl out. Why was she snooping on us in the first place? What did she want?

I pull out my phone and tap on the Instagram icon with my thumb.

"What are you doing?" Mei asks, reconfiguring her body into another stretch that makes my hip flexors scream.

"Hold on a sec," I say.

I open a browser and Mei hovers over me the best she can with that stupid rigid skirt as I search Brandi's name on Instagram. A ton of faces come up, but there are over five hundred results, even with the "i" at the end instead of a "y." Every time I think I've found her, it's some other Brandi with a poorly lit selfie as her avatar.

"Just go to Nate's IG. He's tagged her, for sure."

I smile. "Do those stretches make your IQ stretch too?"

Mei laughs, and I pull up Nate's page. I scroll down until I land on the first snap of them together, a selfie of them at Six Flags last year. Six Flags. How pure. I tap on the square. He's tagged her.

I click through to her page and it's public, but of course she hasn't posted in over a year. I groan. "Shit. She doesn't even post."

I go back to Nate's page and scroll through what are mostly sports pics. There are more cutesy snaps of him and Brandi together, but nothing interesting. Nothing telling.

"I'll try Google," I say to Mei, who's getting impatient, but clearly fighting it.

I search Brandi's full name and location, and it only takes scrolling through the first three pages of results for my eyes to settle on a small shimmering piece of gold. "Oh, my God."

"What you got?" Mei asks, leaning over my shoulder.

I tilt my phone so she can see the photo I found on Google Images of an older white woman hugging Brandi. The woman posted it three years ago and tagged Brandi. I click through to her profile and scroll down.

"Look at where she works," I say, then read from the screen. "Ascend Home for Troubled Teens."

"*Troubled teens?* The fuck?"

"I bet Brandi went there." I type the name of the group home into Google, but after a few moments of skimming the website, there's clearly not much. "Shit. There's nothing up here."

"It's probably one of those reform places where they keep you drugged up with that premium shit," Mei says. "Sounds dreamy."

"Think they'd give us anything if we called them?" I ask, because sometimes it's best to just ignore some of the things that come out of Mei's mouth.

"Probably no specifics, not unless we have some kind of authority." She smirks. "I can do my hoity-toity HR lady voice if you want."

Mei has this incredible ability to sound like a complete condescending asshole, a talent she perfected back in junior high when she used to call it the *headmaster lady voice*. I pop some proverbial popcorn as she dials the home and puts it on speakerphone, then sit back and watch her perform like a trained thespian. The woman on the other end sounds like she has a chronic case of halitosis and hasn't had a decent fuck or night of sleep in decades, but Mei manages to stop her from hanging up on us twice. The woman won't confirm that Brandi attended the home, says something about confidentiality, but she does share something even more interesting: tenants are typically transferred to their facility from a juvenile detention center, but are still considered threats to society and required to board in residences with higher forms of security than a typical group home.

This means Brandi Maxwell is an actual criminal. This is better than gold. This is genius.

I take the reins and google her name with "juvie" and "criminal record" and "mug shot," but nothing comes up. Mei dips out for a cigarette while I make a call to one of my dad's lawyers, the one who handles our family stuff. He's this rich-as-hell sap in his sixties whose wife left him for his nephew decades ago, and he's never recovered. I can see him twisting his index finger around the few thin white hairs still left on his head as I beg him to get his hands on Brandi's rap sheet for me. He's pretty bureaucratic and probably has his house-keeper iron his briefs, but his ex-wife was tall and brunette with light eyes like me, so he predictably caves when I promise him I will come to his country club upstate soon and let him teach me how to hit a hole in one.

Mei slips back into the room as I end the call, and I smirk at her.

"What'd you do?" she asks, sounding greedy.

"Apparently, Brandi could still have a record even if it doesn't come up in a Google search," I tell her. "It could be sealed. Dad's lawyer is going to do some poking around and get back to us if he finds anything."

She smiles. "You're so good at being bad."

I walk her to the backstage area so she can warm up with the other dancers, and when I swing back after her show to scoop her up, Dad's lawyer has already gotten back to me. His email is short and succinct, filled with lawyer jargon, but I skim it, ignoring the words I don't know and his proposed dates to hit the course. Then I open the attachment and my jaw falls open.

"Tell me that's a good jaw-drop and not a bad one," Mei says, reaching for her seat belt as the driver peels away from the curb.

I push the phone so the screen is right in front of Mei's face, so she can see the slightly grainy photo. Brandi against a white brick wall, holding a white sign with her name on it in black, in front of her chest. A mug shot.

Mei's eyes narrow into a squint. "Holy shit."

Brandi looks no more than fifteen in the picture. Her hair is short and curly, and her face looks fuller, but she has the same eyes and nose, the same last name. I don't know how he got his hands on this, and I'm sure this isn't kosher, which means he's truly going to expect me to let him ogle my ass as I try to pretend to know what to do with a golf club, but I'll deal with that later.

I take the phone back and scoff. "The bitch is a legit ex-con."

Mei smiles. "Priceless."

"What do you think she did?" I ask, lowering my voice to a whisper.

"He didn't say?"

"He says her record is sealed."

"Can't he get his hands on it?"

"Maybe, but he's a little creepy and I already have to figure out how to get out of golf." I think it over. "Let's just take this to my dad."

I kiss Mei on her damp, salty forehead and wish her luck on her performance tonight, mainly because I know how much she detests well wishes. She slaps me on the ass and blows a kiss with her hand, and I seriously contemplate whether we were separated at birth because she is my twin, my soul sister straight to the core.

I pass my father's study, the door ajar just enough for me to catch a glimpse of him bent over a pile of proofs, but he doesn't hear me when I backtrack and appear under the threshold because he's too busy barking orders to his cringey assistant through the phone.

He looks up at the tap on the door frame, peers at me over the chic black rim of his glasses.

"Need a minute with you," I mouth.

He gestures for me to wait with an index finger and mouths back, "Give me a second."

I ignore him, march in and shove my phone into his hand. He takes it and nonchalantly glances at the image on the screen, then away, then back at it, a true double take, and stares at it for the longest time, like it'll morph into something less shocking if he burrows his gaze into it long enough. When he looks up, I expect to catch surprise or anger or some flash of emotion on his face, but his expression is full of resignation.

"I need a few minutes. Call me back in five," he says into the phone, then drops the line. He carefully slides his frames down his temples, and the way he glowers at me is almost as if he is more bothered that I've interrupted him than he is by the picture. "What was it for?"

The question sets my spine on fire, not the words but the shrug in his tone. "Who cares? You can't have *criminals* working for you, Dad. Cancel her interview."

He frowns and stares back down at the picture on the screen, his brows slightly furrowed as if he's sifting through a pile of complicated thoughts, then he shifts away to grab something off his desk. "She seemed so nice at the party. Sharp. Well-rounded…"

"That's because you wouldn't take your eyes off her ass," I mumble, a little too loudly.

He glances up and eyes me with a suspicious lift of his brow. "What was that?"

I spread my arms wide. "You can't find her record online to see what she did. It's sealed. That means it *had* to be bad."

"All the records of minors are sealed. Doesn't matter what the charge was. That means nothing." He continues to look at me with his brow lifted. "How'd you even get this?"

I bypass his question, take my phone back and hold it closer to his face, tilting it so he can look right into her delinquent eyes. "She's from *Newark*, Dad. They're all gangbangers, wannabe rappers and criminals down there. She's no different. You can't bring that to Van Doren."

He's quiet for a moment. I can almost see the wheels turning in his head. Then he rises to his feet and looks down at me.

"Newark is west, hon." He smiles, trying to appear playful, but failing. "You sure do get your sense of direction from your mother."

I clench my teeth. Even in death, this fucker scorns her.

He stops at the edge of the room. "These damn diversity quotas. Well, I tried. If none of them last, there's nothing I can do about it."

My eyes dig a hole in his back as he walks off, so hard I'm surprised he doesn't wince. When I look down, my hand is trembling.

8

BRANDI

The words on the screen taunt me.

It's been five minutes since I've opened it, but I can't bring myself to delete it from my inbox. I keep reading the first paragraph over, hoping I've read it wrong.

I am writing to inform you that Mr. Van Doren no longer requires your presence Friday morning.

The front door opens, a low click above the sounds of blaring horns and traffic outside the window, then closes softly. Nate says something to me, probably his usual *wanna order food?* as he steps through the kitchen, coming into the bedroom. I hear him, but the words don't process.

We have chosen the intern who will accompany Mr. Van Doren in Milan based on your performances throughout the program to date and regret to inform you that you were not selected.

It has to be a mistake.

When we spoke at the party, he seemed genuinely interested in me. We had a connection. A rapport.

But a part of me knows there is no mistake. The only mistake was me thinking I had a chance, getting my hopes up just to have them shot down. Going to that party was stupid. Who the hell did I think I was anyway?

Please accept my sincerest apologies for such short notice and any inconvenience this may have caused.

It was too good to be true. It always is. I have to be real with myself. He was never going to hire me.

"Babe, you okay?" Nate's at the edge of the couch now, but I still don't look up.

I scroll down and read the rest of the email, realizing there's more.

Due to information we've recently been made aware of, we also regret to inform you that your internship with Van Doren will be terminated as of today.

My eyes hold on to those words way longer than it takes me to read them, then fly across the rest.

This decision has been finalized.

If you have questions regarding signed policies or returning of company property, please contact HR.

My heart pounds, a loud hammering in my ears. Not only did I not get the Milan job, but I'm also fired. Officially fired.

Nate sits down on the couch next to me. His hand eases across my back, warm and sincere. "Babe?"

I finally blink and look up to him, feeling like I've just come out of a tunnel. He's fresh from the gym, sweat stains darkening his shirt, clinging to his torso.

I don't know what to say.

"Babe, what—"

"Van Doren canceled my interview." The words blurt out of me. "His assistant says they've already made their decision based on our performance so far." I pause. "And they fired me."

I say the words out loud, but they still don't feel real. It just doesn't make any sense. I haven't been to work since that phone call with the head of HR. They've had nothing new to evaluate. They had no reason to fire me. No reason to cancel my interview with Simon. And what *information* did they just learn? What the hell is happening right now?

"Fired?" Nate looks even more outraged than I feel. "Yo, that's some bullshit. For what?"

I shrug. "I don't know." That's all I can say.

I toss my phone onto the bed and sit on my thoughts for a minute. Nate reaches into his pocket and pulls out his own, then holds it up to his ear. No speakerphone. He always uses the speakerphone.

I watch him. "Who are you calling?"

"Taylor."

"Wait." I sit up straighter. "What are you doing?"

"Finding out what happened."

"No. Don't…"

But I can already hear the phone ringing on his end.

My heart races. I don't want Taylor to get involved with this. I still can't stop thinking about what she said yesterday, the way her eyes held me hostage like a threat. A rush of indignity washes over me, but I'm not sure what I'm feeling ashamed about. Being told I need to lose weight by a stranger? Myself in general? Flirting with Simon?

No—I wasn't *flirting* with him. All I did was reciprocate. He smiled, so I smiled. He laughed, so I laughed. I was being polite. Enthusiastic. And for Taylor to insinuate that I was doing it all just to get his *money…*

God. What the hell is with this girl?

As I wait for her to pick up, my mind replaying that part of the night over and over, I realize it might have actually looked like we were flirting, and it is so unsettling I can barely swallow.

And then I remember what Taylor said right before I left: *Maybe we can work something out without him.* What does that even mean? What is there to *work out*?

I don't know.

I don't know.

I just know what I heard on the other side of that door. She was talking about killing her own father, and she wasn't *joking*. People don't joke about shit like that, I don't care who they are or how much money they have. If she was, then why does it matter if I heard them? Why would she show up here like this?

I still don't know what to do, if I should tell Nate or not. It's none of my business, but I feel like overhearing them *made* it my business. I just want to forget that whole night.

Taylor finally answers the phone, and something inside me shrivels like a piece of fruit left too long in the sun.

Nate shifts. "Taylor, what's up?"

I look away when he starts talking, cringing harder with every word.

"Sorry, just two minutes, I promise... Yeah... Yeah, I just— okay... Know what?"

There's a long silence on Nate's end. I can still hear Taylor on the other line, but her words are mumbled. I strain my ears as hard as I can, trying to understand what she's saying. I don't trust her.

I get nothing.

Nate says a few more things, then hangs up and glances over at me. I don't recognize the look on his face. I'm not sure if I've ever seen it before. It's worse than disappointed, but not quite angry. And there is an air of something else, something like disgust. He can barely meet my eyes.

I open my mouth to speak, but his phone dings and he stares down at the screen for the longest moment.

"Well? What did she say?" I ask, feeling weirdly panicked. Why did he look at me like that and then not say anything?

Nate shakes his head, but doesn't answer. He's still looking down at his phone.

Something happened.

"What's wrong?" I say, hoping he answers me this time.

When he looks up again and shows me his eyes, they're hard and distant. "Taylor just sent—what is this?"

He holds out his phone for me to see and the air between us is suddenly different. There's a tone to his voice that I don't like. I don't know what it is, I just know I don't like it.

I glance down and the picture on the screen steals my breath. My own eyes stare back at me, hard and afraid.

I look up at Nate and he's clearly waiting for me to explain. I don't know where to start. I don't know how Taylor found this photo or why she sent it to him. I don't understand any of this.

And then it hits me hard.

This is the reason why they fired me. They found—*Taylor* found out about my past somehow and told them. *She* got me fired. There's no other explanation.

I wish I could smack her across her pretty little face. The bitch is playing games, but I don't have time for her shit. This is my *life*.

I can feel Nate staring at me still, but I can't look at him. I want to disappear. I want this moment to stop existing. Without warning, my eyes blur. I swipe at my face aggressively and force my tears back to where they belong before they can fall.

"That was a long time ago," I say to Nate, my voice taut, barely above a whisper. It's all I can manage.

He stares at me, eyes unblinking, and a horrible pit opens in my stomach. I can almost feel my heart drop through it. "What happened?"

He doesn't sound as indignant as I expected, but I can taste the distrust in his voice like iron on my tongue. Even though I hate the question, I'm grateful for his curiosity, that he wants to hear my side of the story.

I knew this day would come. I just didn't think it would happen like this. I wanted it to be on my own terms, me offering him another layer of myself. Not on the defense, not like I've betrayed him.

I exhale a long, heavy breath, deciding to be vulnerable, that I have to, though I know it'll hurt. He deserves honesty.

"It wasn't my fault," I start, but there's a tremor in my voice, and I have to stop and start again, and when I do, I'm not sure how to explain it all. I've never had to.

After my parents died, I was quiet.

There was nothing *wrong* with me; I just didn't feel like talking. It was as if nothing or no one was worth the effort anymore. I stuck to myself. I rarely ever spoke. The caseworker I was assigned to didn't know how to deal with me—or didn't *want* to deal with me, so after I got kicked out of the first home, she sent my paperwork to a group home for troubled girls, and they accepted me.

That's what they called me. *Troubled.*

I had to get dropped off at school in a dirty white van, and I just knew the other kids, the ones with parents and families and friends, could smell it on us, on me, that *troubled* stench. And if the stale stink was only in my mind, they definitely *saw* it, that robotic blah-ness a heavy dose of psychotropic meds turns you into.

Just the thought of Nate looking at me that way, like there's something wrong with me, like I am mentally disturbed or unstable, is enough to crush me, but I push through the shame and the guilt and tell him everything.

I tell him about the dilapidated, prison-like group home, a three-story compound topped with coils of razor wire in the middle of nowhere. About the vile, psychopathic, racist people there who made you wear thin, old scrubs instead of your own clothes. About the tranquilizers they forced you to swallow dry in front of your counselor if you wanted to avoid being sent to "Punishment Level," which meant you had to sleep in the basement and do twice as many chores, mostly kitchen duty for two weeks, scrubbing out the slop and grease from the pots and pans, which was beyond revolting.

Then I tell him about that day, the day I wish I could take back more than any other. I'd already learned how to defend myself from the previous home I had been placed in. I'd developed reflexes. Everybody knew about the director and his tendency to pat freshly pubescent girls on the thigh during the weekly check-ins. The rumors had prepared me for my first one, but it wasn't until the third time we met that I had to deploy the elbow-to-the-nose move I'd learned from bingeing self-defense videos on YouTube. I claimed it was an accident. My hand slipped. But he knew what it was and never tried to touch me again. What I wasn't prepared for was getting cornered by Lindsay, one of the counselors, a young, plain-faced, lank-haired girl from Missouri, after refusing to tell her what happened in my meeting with that creep or explain how he ended up with a bandage on his nose for two weeks. She had this sick crush on him, a man twenty years older than she was, which everyone knew about except for me, and was jealous because he was into fifteen-year-old me, and not her. Not anymore. The rumors of him assaulting girls were rampant, and she'd gotten a barrage of written and verbal complaints, which she either shredded or claimed were simple misunderstandings. When I refused to admit to breaking his nose, refused to talk at all, she shoved me headfirst into a brick wall, a nose for a nose kind of retribution, and before the pain took over, I swung back at her as hard as I could, fists clenched, all adrenaline. I'd never actually gotten into a real fight before, not even close, and had to stay in my bunk and miss classes for a week to make sure I didn't have a concussion. After that, she was constantly on my back, barging in on my check-ins to make sure I wasn't *being a slut* or *flashing him my cunt*. I caught her hawking a wad of phlegm in my food once and lost ten pounds I couldn't afford to lose after that. Missed another week of school to recover from severe dehydration.

"They were trying to get me on lithium," I say, feeling a little breathless. "All those kids who were on that shit were like zombies. It causes seizures and everything. One of the counselors, the one I really hated—this white girl—she tried to force me to take it and…I don't know. She wasn't even my counselor. She was just miserable. I snapped. I pushed her off me. She tripped and fell down some stairs, then said I attacked her and—"

I have to stop to keep my voice from shaking. I can't believe I'm saying this right now. It sounds worse than what it is. "I just remember waking up in a cell." I'm whispering now. "It was an accident. I never meant to hurt her, I was just…done with that whole place."

It hurts to say all of this, to feel the weight of my confession slip over my lips, to have it exist in this world, alive and breathing and absolute.

I take a breath, air hissing out of a balloon, and finally look at Nate. I have to. "I ran from the cops because I didn't—I did nothing wrong—I didn't do what they were trying to say I did. They were trying to make me seem like I was crazy." The words tumble as they fall from my mouth, land on their backs, broken and wrong. I pause, feeling winded again, like someone has just punched me in my gut. "Do you believe me?"

I watch Nate, his eyes, his expression, wishing I knew what else to say to get him to stop looking at me like I'm some kind of stranger. Something. Anything. But I have nothing.

Nothing more than the truth.

"Why did you keep this from me?" His voice is quiet, withdrawn. I can't tell if he's angry, hurt or just confused.

My shoulders go up in a limp shrug. "I don't know. It never came up."

But that's not entirely true.

This is why I never told him. This moment exactly.

I didn't want him to look at me differently. Didn't want him to decide the total sum of my character based off my past, off *one* mistake, one attempt to cling to my dignity that was blown way out of proportion and landed me in juvie for six months. I'd thought about telling him before. I'd come close, multiple times. But I just couldn't go through with it. Telling Nate would make it more real than I wanted it to be.

Like it is right now.

His expression wavers slightly. "Is there anything else?"

"What do you mean?" My voice sounds hollow.

"Are you hiding anything else?"

I know it's a fair question but the way he asks it stings. My voice spikes. "I wasn't *hiding* anything." I push a stray curl out of my face, but it falls right back. "I just...I wanted to forget all that stuff."

I wrap my arms around myself, the room suddenly too cold to bear. I can feel the tears wanting to fall again.

To my surprise, Nate eases a hand over my leg. I expect his touch to be harsh and distant, the way his words feel, and I almost recoil in anticipation of our skin coming into contact, but his fingers are warm and so is the look in his eyes. "Hey, don't worry about it," he says, and there's a gentleness in his expression that I don't think I've ever seen before. "I get it."

I meet his gaze and hold it. "You do?"

"Yeah. This is nothing compared to the shit people at Regency Prep got off for." He laughs, and a torrent of relief washes over me. "Especially Taylor and her friends. They broke whatever laws they wanted and not because they had to. Because they *could*."

He says that, and I instantly want to know what kind of things he's talking about. What has Taylor done? Is he talking about the two friends who were in that room with her at the party? But I don't ask. The moment doesn't feel right.

A section of my hair slips loose again, and this time, when I go to swipe it back in place, Nate reaches over and does it for me. His hand lingers, rounding my ear then easing along my jaw to cup my chin. "Look, it's just one job. There'll be other opportunities. Forget about Taylor, all right? You don't need her or her father or any of those fake-ass people."

That makes me smile, but it's grim.

I'm so grateful for Nate's softness in this moment that I don't recognize the anger at first—bubbling at the surface, fighting its way through. That bitch got me fired.

The feel of Nate's lips on mine, soft and warm, snaps me back into the present. I kiss him back, and when he speaks, his voice is low and quiet against my skin. "Yo...I love you."

The words shock me into stillness.

They're just words, but they mean so much in this moment. More than I ever thought they would. Or *could*.

Nate's staring at me, but I feel totally and completely speechless. I want to say something, but there is some synaptic glitch between my brain and my mouth, and I can't get the words out.

Nate strokes his thumb over the curve of my lip and my breath shudders. "I do. For real. I love you. You know that, right?"

I wrap my arms around his neck and squeeze him closer to me. "Same," I whisper, opening his mouth with mine.

Instead of kissing me back, he smiles and smacks me on my ass. "You cheated."

"I love you too," I say, laughing, and it's embarrassing and my chest is pounding and the words are too fast, but I don't care.

He pulls back and gives me the softest peck on my forehead, like he's kissing a kitten. "Seriously, don't let these people get you down."

"I won't." I lean against him, this huge wall of muscle, and listen to the pattern of his breathing, matching it with mine.

Nate sighs, and my head moves with his chest, his hand sliding up my back. "I'm sorry you had to go through all that shit."

I look up at him. The way he gazes at me is so pure, it almost takes my breath away. He leans down and brushes another kiss against my hair.

"Thanks for understanding," I whisper into his neck. I can smell the sweat on his skin, that sweet, feral scent, an extra layer of warmth. "Do you really have to go back to Ohio in two weeks?"

It's a pointless question. I know he does. But he smiles anyway. "Don't worry. I can fly back every other weekend before the season starts."

But that isn't enough. It's never enough.

And when he kisses me again, it's both too little and too much, and in his arms, I'm shy for a moment. Then I feel the tickle of his breath on my skin, his palms warm on my body, and I lean in all the way and it feels so good. Everything about this moment feels good. And then we're both breathing hard. Kissing hard. Gripping hard. I kiss his neck, and he moans into mine, and it melts me completely. I need to feel him, all of him. I want to give him everything inside me, everything I have. I straddle him and find the hem of his shirt and pull it hard, yanking the damp fabric over his shoulders, then reach for the string on his sweatpants.

He laughs softly against my lips and gently moves my hand. "Let me hop in the shower real quick."

He starts to shift from beneath me, but I hold him steady. "No. I ordered tacos right before you got here. It'll be here soon."

His smile widens. "Five minutes. Just let me rinse off."

I let him go, but only because I know he's good for it. He always takes short showers because he hates wasting water. I lie back on the couch, pull a pillow over my face and smile, because that's all I want to do in this moment, and just as my cheeks start to hurt, I reach for Nate's phone and click into the Postmates app. Driver is seven minutes away.

I lean my head back against the couch and the thought hits me like a blow to the gut, reality finding me again. I have to find a job. I can't just sit around on my ass all day for the rest of the summer; it'll drive me crazy. I need to be doing something. Learning. Creating. *Something.*

I'm sitting at my desk in front of my MacBook, searching on LinkedIn for anything remotely related to fashion that has an opening when there is a knock on the door. I glance down at the phone. It says the driver is still two minutes away. But maybe it's a glitch.

When I open the door, my mouth opens.

What the hell is she doing here?

9

TAYLOR

The look on Brandi's face when she opens the door is price-less. I don't know who she was expecting, but it definitely wasn't me.

Her hair is down; her real hair. She's taken out her braids and thick, curly hair hangs to her shoulders, framing her face. Dark nipples poke through a sleeveless white Henley that might as well be nothing. She's barefoot, her pretty white toe-nails the perfect contrast against her brown skin.

"What are you doing here?" she asks, her voice flat, un-interested.

"Where's Nate?" I ask, looking around the place.

She stares at me, her eyes hard and still, like she is trying to decide whether or not to answer. "In the shower. He just came from the gym."

"Oh. He's been already?"

"New season's coming up. He goes every day. Same time. He likes to…" She stops, changing course abruptly as if just realizing something. "If you want to see him—"

"I actually came to see you," I say, meeting her gaze.

She blinks at me. Her mouth opens, but the words never come.

I move closer to her, beyond the threshold, and she takes a

step back, confusion bringing the edges of her brows together. "What do you want?"

She shuts the door behind me and quickly locks it like we're in the ghetto or wherever she's from.

I wait for her gaze to meet mine again before speaking. "You already lost your interview and the internship. Do you want me to keep ruining your life? Because I can."

My words hit her hard. It takes her a moment to recover and then her head moves side to side in disbelief. "I knew it was you."

Her eyes crawl over me like I'm a spider she wants to squash, and then she takes off, heading deeper into the apartment. It's the smallest apartment I've ever been inside. Can't be more than half the size of my *closet*. The cognac leather couch set against the wall takes up most of the living room. There are plants everywhere; it's basically a jungle. And books. Lots of books. Two floor-to-ceiling cases full of books.

"If you want more money," I say, stepping closer to her. "I can—"

She laughs, her fillings dark against the whites of her teeth, but it's forced. "I don't want more money."

"Then just tell me what you want."

She stares at me for the longest moment, and then there is some small derangement about her face, her eyes narrowing, mouth tightening.

"Are you really going to kill him?" she asks, her voice breaking slightly like she actually feels something for him, and my jaw tightens.

I swallow and look away. When I turn back, she's still staring at me. "Look, I can—"

I stop at the sound of a door opening, and both our heads turn at the same time.

"Babe, I was thinking. When I get back to Ohio— Oh. Shit."

Nate stops short when he sees me. My mouth opens. He's completely naked, all wet and hard and glistening, his body lean and lightly spattered with coarse, dark hair, towel draped around his neck.

His eyes shoot over to Brandi as he pulls the towel down and wraps it around his waist. "I didn't know you had—"

She cuts him a sharp look. I'm not sure what it means but right now I don't care. I'm still stuck on seeing his dick. Soft and impractical, and slightly leaning to the left. I feel a flush of warmth creeping up my cheeks and clear my throat.

Nate's eyes come to me for the quickest moment, then back to Brandi. "Um, yeah—I'll just…" Nate stumbles over the rest of his words as he heads back into the bathroom.

Brandi cuts her eyes at me so hard I can almost feel the sharpness of her glare on my skin. She folds her arms across her chest. "Can you leave?"

"I'm pretty sure you being jobless means you don't pay the rent here, so you don't really have veto power, do you?"

She looks like she wants to smack me across the room. I want to do the same to her.

Her phone buzzes on the couch. She leans for it and lifts it to her ear. "Hi. Yes, thank you. I'll be down in a sec."

She hangs up and looks at me, and I speak before she can try to throw me out again. "I'll just wait here until you get back."

She flicks a quick glance toward the bathroom, then her eyes meet mine and it almost seems like a warning. I know what she's thinking. I'm thinking it too.

I give a small nod, and she rushes over to the corner, pulls on chunky sneakers and jogs to the door.

I sit on the couch, trying to figure out my next move and glance down at the coffee table.

She didn't take her phone.

I pick it up and click into her iMessage app. But then I realize it's not Brandi's phone. It's Nate's.

Of course, the most recent conversation in his feed is with her.

Him: Need something while I'm out? On my way back.

Her: Almost out of tampons. Can u grab a box pls?

Him: Light or heavy?

Her: Both. You know how random my vagina is.

Him: Got u.

Her: Thanks :)

I scroll up to read their earlier messages and stop when I see a series of nudes Brandi sent a few days ago. I click the most recent one to get a better look. She's wearing a black lace thong, but she might as well be completely naked since her ass is basically swallowing it whole, leaving nothing but a tiny thread of fabric showing. She's twisted back, staring directly into the camera, a golden glow veiling her face. Not a smile but something close, like she knows exactly what she has. Proud. So comfortable in her own skin.

I swallow hard, trying to get rid of the lump in my throat and quickly swipe to the next one. Another picture from behind. This time I can see the gap between her thighs, which only makes her ass seem even more impossible. The next one is a shot of her from the front, one of her hands covering a nipple, the other down between her legs like she's about to rub her clit for the camera. My mouth opens when I scroll to the last one. It's a shot of her pussy. Just her pussy. Dark and smooth and perfect.

I swipe back to the others, the ones from the back.

The lighting is shitty and they're too grainy, not that cool, slightly grainy way, but I can just see it. Nate stroking her from behind, slapping that heart-shaped ass until it turns red. Tugging on that small waist. Pushing inside her until she feels it in her stomach.

I know it drives him crazy.

Swipe. I bet she knows how to twerk, knows how to shake her ass just like the women in those strip clubs do, even while she's getting fucked. They all do.

Swipe. My mind goes red and I try to tell myself that her body isn't that great, that she's probably had some basement injections because, at this point, who hasn't? But I know that's not true. I know this is her natural body.

It's not fair. If I had an ass like that, I'd rule the entire world.

I scroll back down to read the texts sent right after the photos.

Him: Ur so fucking sexy.

Two minutes later: For real. Damn, B.
Ten minutes later: I just came.

Her: Let me see.

Him: Too late.

Clenching my teeth, I click into Nate's photos app to see if there's any more that he saved from a different time. The first photo I see is of them together. Smiling. His arm around her waist, her head pressed against his broad chest, her body so close to his. From the angle, I can tell it was him who stretched out his arm and took the photo.

Slowly, I slide the screen to the next one. It's another shot from the same day and he's kissing her face, eyes closed, looking goofy and happy.

I've never seen him look like that.

Her smile is light, almost blissful.

I tap the photo so I can see the date it was taken. Almost a month ago. That meant he'd flown in all the way from Ohio just to see her.

My heart is pounding now. I keep swiping. More pictures. Lots of them. They go back for months. Almost every one is of her or them together, as if he has no life outside her. But I know that's not true, either. He has a life, one that doesn't involve her for the better part of the year. I chew on that thought, toss it around and savor it.

I go to swipe once again, but my thumb freezes on the screen. I open a new text chain and select all the naked pictures of Brandi. Once I send them to myself, I delete the chain. As soon as they come through to my phone, I hear footsteps on the other side of the front door.

Shit. She's back already.

I drop the phone back on the table exactly where I found it, doing my best to not make a sound. Then I rush to pick up my phone to pretend it's the one I was on all along.

I look up as Brandi shuts the door. She's carrying a bag of takeout. I want to scratch her eyes out.

She looks at me like she wants to tell me to leave again, but I stand and speak before she can. "Look, my father isn't the man everybody thinks he is." I take a breath. "Trust me, he—"

"I'm not the one you need to justify yourself to." She sets

the food down and turns to face me. "I don't want anything to do with this, and I definitely don't want your money."

"It's *ten*—"

"You need to leave right now or I'll tell Nate about all of this."

I pause. "You didn't tell Nate?"

"Do you want me to?"

I drop my eyes down to her waist, then back up and leave without another word.

As I'm heading for the elevator, heat warms my chest. I feel it rising in my gut, something like lava, hot and burning. And just like that, I'm done being nice to her. I'm done trying to reason with her. I'm done negotiating. This could have all been over if she would have just listened to me. I've done my best to be civil with her. I've tried to be fair.

So fuck her and her perfect ass.

10

BRANDI

I don't even believe in karma, but I must have committed a heinous sacrilege in a past life because this week just keeps getting worse.

I'm staring down at the letter I just tore open from FIT that I grabbed from the mailbox on my way back upstairs. Apparently, my tuition just increased by five percent and now I'm in the hole ten thousand dollars and some change. As if it wasn't already expensive enough. I was barely affording it before this spike with my scholarships and loans.

I read it over but the words stay the same.

Amount due: $8,085
Amount due by: June 31

That's only two weeks away. Two. Weeks.

I don't have a job. There is no way I can find one that fast and even if I did, I wouldn't be able to make that much money in time. I can't take out another loan. Tried that last semester when I needed to cover the balance for my books and got rejected. I'm fucked, royally fucked. I might have gotten emails about this earlier this year—actually, I'm pretty sure

I have—but I have this really bad habit of just dumping all my FIT emails straight into the trash since most of them are useless bullshit.

I hear Nate call me and look up, a little shaken, hoping it doesn't show on my face. Normally, he's so on point when he reads me, but when I take in the way he's sitting across from me, staring at me like I'm a puzzle he's trying to solve, he seems lost.

"You're doing it again," he says with the ghost of a smile. "I just called you three times."

"Oh."

"Something wrong?"

"No. I just…"

I keep thinking about the money Taylor offered me. Ten thousand dollars, just like that, as if it was nothing.

That's how I'm rationalizing this. If she could just pay this stupid bill for me—

I shake my head. What am I saying? I can't accept money from her, not like this. She was trying to buy my silence. It was hush money.

I still can't get over how casual she sounded up in that room. That laughter, high and maniacal. Planning to kill her own father. At a party for charity. Everybody focused on giving and there she was, consumed by thoughts of taking.

A girl I knew in high school killed her father. It was no accident. He was a Jehovah's Witness, a venerable elder in the church. He'd been molesting her since she was seven. He attacked her in her bedroom, and she snapped that final time, some primal instinct taking over, clobbered him in the head over and over with the base of her phone until he was down, unconscious, not dead. But she just stood there and watched him bleed out, watched him squirm in pain the way he had forced her to so many times.

This is different. This is calculated. Premeditated.

This is fucking first-degree *murder*. Some white-people, Netflix-limited-series shit.

I don't know if this girl is really going to kill her father. I don't want to know. I meant what I said. I don't want any parts of her shit. I don't know if I even believe her. I know she's an heiress and everything, American royalty and shit, but ten thousand dollars just to keep silent? How do you even give someone that much money without raising red flags?

"What's that?" Nate asks, glancing at the paper in my hand.

I fold it and slip it back into the envelope. "Just a letter from school. It's nothing."

I hate lying to him, but I can't tell Nate about this. He'll insist on covering it. I know him. We've been there before, and it's not worth another fight.

I don't want him paying for my tuition. I told myself from the beginning that I'd always hold myself responsible for my own education, no matter what it took. That way, even if something were to happen between us, if we broke up, I'd still be able to graduate. I can't let my future depend on the success of our relationship. Relationships fail every day. Failure isn't an option for me, not when it comes to school.

I don't know what to do.

Taylor's timing couldn't have been any more on point. But I know it's wrong. It's so wrong. I need a minute to think this over, to clear my head.

I pick up my plate and reach for Nate's. "You done?"

"Yeah. Wait—hold on." He leans over for mine, takes the last few picked-over tortilla chips and stuffs them into his mouth. "Okay."

I laugh at his muffled reply and carry both plates over to the sink and flip the faucet on.

"What did Taylor want?" Nate asks, my back to him. There's a tepid mix of confusion and suspicion in his voice.

I fumble for what to say. I thought I was in the clear. "Nothing. Just...to apologize for getting me dropped from the program."

His eyebrows go up and then he snorts a laugh. *"Apologize? Taylor?* It must have been condescending as fuck, huh?"

Shit. I said the wrong thing. But I couldn't think of anything else off the top of my head.

I glance back at him but avoid his eyes. "No, it was pretty genuine, I think."

"Weird." He shrugs and licks salt from his fingers, and I'm jealous for a second. "Doesn't sound like her at all."

"What do you mean?" I ask drily, trying to not show how much the answer means to me.

"I don't know," Nate says, getting up from the table. "Last time I checked she wasn't exactly the apologetic type."

He drops the drinking glasses we used into the sink. I want to press on, I want to know more of what he means by that, but when I reach for the dish soap, he slips his arms around my waist, his chest hard against my back, and all the tension drains from me in an instant.

"Let me handle these," he whispers in my ear.

My lips curve when I feel his mouth press into the back of my neck. "Really?"

"And as soon as I'm done, we're gonna pick up where we left off." He sounds playful, happy. I love it when he's like this. It makes me feel like everything's going to be okay, even when I know it's only wishful thinking.

"Okay." I smile and turn for the couch, but Nate calls me again.

"Babe, charge my phone?"

"Sure." I grab it from the table and set it in the charging stand on my desk.

Plopping down on the couch, I watch Nate as he washes the dishes for a minute. I flip the TV on, trying to distract myself, but I can't stop thinking about that damn phone. After a few minutes I can't take it anymore. I give in, send Taylor's contact to my phone and then take it with me into the bathroom, shut the door, run the faucet. I'm going to call her. Just to see what she says.

The phone starts to ring, and my heart jumps. I can't believe I am going to ask her for the money, but right now I'm low on options.

She answers right away, but she isn't talking to me when she speaks. "I need to see Dr. Burgess, stat."

I hear the distinct, unobtrusive click of high heels, the sound of some typing on the computer and then she directs her voice to me. "It's Taylor."

My breath gets caught in my throat. "Uh, it's Brandi. Nate's—"

"What do you want?" she asks, the light, airy pitch quickly deflated from her voice.

I take a breath and swallow hard. I don't know what I'm doing. "What did you mean when you said your father isn't who everyone thinks he is?"

It's the best I can come up with. I figure I'll start soft, then go in for the kill. I'm not even sure if I can go through with this.

She grunts, annoyed. "I tried to tell you earlier, but you—"

"I'm listening now."

I actually don't expect her to answer, but she huffs a taut, "Fine," and I can almost hear her rolling her eyes. "You want to know the real reason why twenty percent of Van Doren's profits go to animal charities and why the line doesn't use leather, silk or fur? My mom was a vegan. She wanted to make a difference. Everything Van Doren stands for is because of her. It was her idea. Her vision. Not his. And if it weren't for him, she'd still be alive."

"Wait, you're saying your mom..." I shake my head. "What are you saying?"

Her voice is low and urgent, as if she thinks I won't believe her. "She put nineteen years into that relationship. She was always there for him. Always. She couldn't handle knowing it had all been a lie. When she found out he was cheating on her..."

"Your mom killed herself?" I ask, softly. I shouldn't care, but I do.

Taylor goes quiet. I've offended her. Or something worse. I don't know. I don't know her well enough to interpret her silence.

"Yeah." She lets out a sigh and emotion swells in her voice, heavy and sudden. "Two years ago."

She sniffles, which makes me think she's crying, but I can't imagine it. She seems too...cold. I try to find something to say to fill this weird silence between us, but her voice slithers through as soon as I open my mouth.

"My mom was my best friend." She pauses. "A lot of people say that, but they don't really mean it. I could talk to her about anything. We did everything together. Until she...until she got sick," she says, and this is not even in the ballpark of what I was expecting.

"She was sick? I thought—"

"Breast cancer. We got her the fucking best treatment, the best doctors in the country, but it kept progressing. She would lock herself inside the bathroom and just...sob the whole night. Some days I'd get home from a shoot or whatever and find her lying on the kitchen floor. When she saw me, she'd jump up to her feet, wipe her face and try to be strong. She was al-ways…always trying to be strong. And my father…

"He told her he didn't love her anymore. He'd already been cheating on her, but that piece of shit finally admitted it. Said she'd given up on their relationship. On *him*." Her voice shrinks, then comes back, hard in my ear. "That he wanted to be happy again, that he was moving on." She pauses and when she speaks again, I hear how truly close she is to break-ing. "Do you have any idea what that's like?"

And just like that, my entire perception of Simon morphs in an instant. I can no longer look at him through the same lens. I try to imagine that. How I'd feel if my mom took her own life because my father cheated on her while she was dying. I'd be angry too. I'd want to kill him too.

Taylor sniffles again. "After that, she gave up. She tried—" Her voice breaks. "I saw…I'm the one who found her."

She's definitely crying now. I swallow. My own tears don't feel far away.

"I saw her hanging there…in that bathroom. Just…" She stops, gasping for air, and then tries again. The words come out strangled and I can hear a lifetime's worth of suffering in every syllable. "She had slit her wrists first. She was…"

But she can't finish. She doesn't need to. I know what she's trying to say. And in that moment it becomes clear to me how profoundly alone she is. I press my forehead against the cool tile, her pain gutting me through the wireless connec-tion holding us together, tightening my chest and resurrect-ing my memories of my own mom, what little I can vaguely remember. I try to conjure a discernible picture of her, but the image in my head is nothing but a shapeless, amorphous presence, nothing more than an apparition. I have no memo-ries of being with her beyond quick flashes that feel more like fragments from old dreams than anything else. I'm not sure if any of the things I remember ever actually happened. I don't know what's real and what my brain has tried to fill in the gaps with. I can barely remember the sound of her voice, the scent of her hair. I have no old photos, no clear, trustworthy memories of laughter and love. Sometimes it feels as if I've dreamed her up completely.

I have no recollection of my parents' deaths, only the image of their dead bodies, bruised and disfigured and drenched in blood, barely recognizable from the crash. Doctors and paramedics telling me not to look because it would be too traumatic, but looking anyway. I had to look. I *had* to. I needed to know it was real. That it wasn't just a nightmare, a figment of my imagination.

"I lost my mom too," I say. Maybe because I want Taylor to trust me, maybe because I think it'll make her feel better, I'm not entirely sure, but the words feel right, and then they're gone, lingering in the air like breath in the cold.

Her voice lifts a little. "You did?"

"Yeah. Car accident. I was really young. I barely remember her," I say, thinking it will feel cathartic, but I immediately realize I'm wrong. It only makes me feel worse, that empty abyss inside me opening wider. A tear rolls down my cheek even though these feelings are nothing new and I stopped allowing myself to cry about this a long time ago. I have to swallow a few times before I feel like I can speak again. "But I think about her all the time. I miss her. I wish I... I just miss her."

Taylor sniffs again and an edginess moves into her voice, a stiffness that sounds like defiance. "Do you understand now?" she asks, and I want to say, *Yes. Yes, I do*, but I say nothing.

I hear the sound of a door clicking open, and Taylor says something I can't make out, maybe not meant for me, then comes back on the line. "Look, why are you asking me about this?"

I freeze. The last thing I want is to feel sympathy for the person who got me fired. But hearing her talk about her mom, thinking about *my* mom, I can't help but feel for her. For the first time, I wonder what it must be like to be her, to live with someone you hate, someone that cruel.

I thought she was being too harsh before. Ungrateful. Over-dramatic. I didn't think it could be *this* bad. I don't want to believe her, but I think I do. Everything she's saying sounds so real. Not like she's making it all up on the spot to manipulate me. More like she's surprised I would even question her. And there was genuine hurt in her voice when she spoke about her mom. I know pain, and I know she wasn't pretending.

Taylor is still quiet. I don't know what to say. It's one thing to feel sympathy, another thing to extend it.

I squeeze the back of my neck, my thoughts a chaotic tangle. For a moment I think maybe I have her all wrong. Maybe she isn't as bad as I've made her out to be in my head. Maybe I am just jealous.

Then I remember the way she first looked at me at that ball. Like I was her enemy.

The way she hugged me, as if she was so happy to meet me when we both knew she wasn't. And that strange, manufactured smile that seemed to be hurting her face, stretching her beyond her limits.

The way she hugged Nate, a little too tight and a little too long, and how she gawked at him when he walked into the living room naked earlier. Sure, she was surprised—I was too—but *friends* don't look at friends like that. She was straight-up ogling his dick like it belonged to her. I almost expected her to reach out and stroke it—that is, if she didn't get drool on it first, in which case I'm sure she would have been glad to drop to her knees and suck it.

She's not fooling anyone. Her performance is solid, but I know she's not as innocent as she wants me to believe.

I don't trust her. I can't trust her.

"Because I want to help you out," I finally say, and I barely recognize my own voice. It sounds far away, like a memory.

There is a long pause, then I hear someone speaking, but it's not Taylor. "I could probably get a pinch of fat tissue from your arms, but it's not much," a deep male voice says in a formal tone. "Taylor, I really don't think this is your look."

"With all due respect, Dr. Burgess, you're a plastic surgeon, not a psychologist. I just want to know how much it'll be, ballpark."

Another pause.

"Eight thousand," he says.

I can hear the static of Taylor's agitated sigh on my end.

"Can you give me a minute?" she says to the doctor.

I don't hear a reply, but seconds later the door shuts.

"Keep going," she says in my ear.

"I'm willing to keep my mouth shut, but you're gonna have to do something for me."

There's a pause. "What?"

"I just got this letter from my school. My tuition went up… and I can't cover it. It basically says if I don't make the full payment by the end of the month, I can't return in the fall."

She doesn't hesitate. "How much?"

"Eight thousand." The words leave me, and I all but hold my breath, ready for her to fully go off on me.

"Eight grand?" Her voice is hushed, and for a second I can't tell whether this amuses her or angers her. "What's your Zelle?"

I don't react for a while. It really is that simple for her. "So that's…that's it?"

It feels like there has to be a catch, something she's keeping to herself.

Her voice firms. "As long as you keep your mouth shut."

I go still. Her words, though soft, always seem to carry an element of threat, but this time, in an odd way, it also sounds like she's pleading. Like she needs me. Like I'm the one with the power.

"Yeah," I say. "Of course."

11

TAYLOR

I take one final glance under the table. There she is. My one-of-a-kind, custom Birkin. I've never actually carried her; it's always felt too disrespectful to do anything besides admire her on her shelf. My mom commissioned my favorite artist to hand-paint it for my eighteenth birthday after they met at Art Basel. He signed the inside and even wrote a little note. It's one of the most valuable pieces I own, could probably get fifty grand for it, but I had to take what I could get on such short notice.

I wasn't exaggerating when I told my father I was broke. But I had to find a way to get Brandi her money.

I told Mei and Jared I have it handled. I didn't say anything about me agreeing to pay her tuition; the less they know, the better. All they need to know is that after today she won't be anywhere near my father and she won't be talking to anybody.

When I look up, I see my contact heading over to my table. She's dressed in a cut-off men's Oxford shirt, cropped so short it can basically double as a bra since she's not wearing one, high-waisted biker shorts that barely cover her navel, Celine sunglasses and Balenciaga sneakers. A tiny red purse dangles from her hand, too small to even fit her phone.

She takes off the sunglasses and smiles at me. "Hey."

I don't smile back.

I reach underneath the table and put the bag on top. Her entire face lights up before I even get it out of its dust bag, just like mine did when I first saw it, and a part of me shatters.

I can't believe I'm doing this. It feels wrong. Like selling a piece of my mom. It isn't just a handbag. It's art. It's a piece of history. *Our* history.

The girl picks the bag up and inspects it. I snatch it back before my brain can process what I'm doing.

She frowns. "Didn't you get my payment? I got a confirmation saying it went through."

"I remember when I got her," I say, picturing the moment. "It was the morning after I fell at the end of the Dior runway. The most mortifying moment of my life. I couldn't eat anything that morning. I mean, I never eat in the morning, but it's different when you can't. Anyway, I popped into the boutique before the Balmain show and there she was. I'd been hunting her down for months. London. Vienna. LA. She had just come in twenty minutes before I arrived. It was fate. And then my mom surprised me with the art for my birthday."

I feel her tug on the bag, but I don't let it go. Not yet.

She stares at me, waiting. "Thanks. Can I—"

"It's like a breakup, you know. At least when you split with a guy there's always the chance that you'll have loud, sweaty make-up sex to cushion the blow."

She forces a smile. "Don't worry. I'll treat her well."

She pulls again. I grip harder.

"She likes to be stored on a dark shelf. Cool, not moist."

She nods slowly like she doesn't know if I'm being serious or not, and when she starts to walk away, I'm on my feet without realizing it.

"Wait." I lean over and check the inside pockets of the bag.

"Okay. Sorry. Just wanted to make sure I didn't leave a dime bag in there."

She nods awkwardly and walks off.

I want to chase after her, tell her I've changed my mind and give her money back.

I can't. I dig my heels into the floor and pull out my phone.

A shudder rolls through me when the message pops up.

Transfer completed.

By the time my driver lets me out by the pool, I feel like I'm going to hyperventilate. I push into the garage and open the passenger door of my Audi. I reach under the seat and pull out a small black box. When I open it, it's empty.

Fuck. I need a hit. Just one line. That's it. One.

I don't want to hear myself think. I don't want to sleep.

I flip things around, check the backseat, the glove compartment. Nothing.

I open the trunk again; open the box one more time.

Nothing. Nothing. Nothing.

I must have used it all the other night.

I lift my phone and glance at the time. I won't be able to get to Mei fast enough to slide in that tiny gap she has between rehearsal and her show tonight.

Fuck. Fuck. Fuck. Fuck.

I text her anyway, then throw the box against the door and scream until my throat goes raw.

Upstairs, I fill my tub to the edge, as hot as I can stand. I take off my clothes, but don't get in right away. At first, I just stare at the water, at the stillness of it. I remember when I used to be that calm. Before the nightmares, before—

Before.

When I step in, the water burns my skin, but I need the

pain. I slip inside with a gasp. After it goes lukewarm, my head slips beneath the surface, and I hold my breath. Ten seconds. Thirty seconds. Sixty.

Thoughts of my mom still flicker in my head, a whirlwind of memories clashing together until I can't take it.

Sixty-five. Seventy. Eight—

I pop my head out of the water, gasping, panting for air. I still see her. Hanging there. Lifeless. Limbs swaying into each other like wind chimes, a marionette with loose strings, those big blue eyes locked right on mine. Begging me to do something. Begging me to not leave her.

I'm screaming. I don't know how long I've been screaming, but I can't stop.

Arms close around me from behind, yanking me back, away from her, away from my mom. Strong arms, hard chest at my back. A man. Yelling my name, his voice deep, familiar, telling me to calm down, but I can barely hear the words.

Look at me, Taylor. Look at me!

The man jerks me around with so much force my neck almost snaps back. He shakes me over and over, fingertips digging into my arms, bruising me.

She's gone, he says. *She's gone.*

My father.

He won't let me go. He won't let me hold her.

I shake my head. My head spins. Everything turns upside down and then right side up. I blink. Again. And again.

Suddenly, I'm aware of the water, dripping from my face, cool at my back. My head jerks from side to side. I'm alone. Completely alone. The room is filled with a droning silence. My heart feels like it's going to beat straight through my chest. My hands are in fists, muscles so tense I'm trembling. I swipe a hand across my face, clench my eyes tight and count to ten, fifteen. Twenty. Until the thoughts are gone. I keep counting.

By fifty, I'm angry again.

I need to do something. I need a distraction.

I pull myself out of the water, my hair clinging to my neck, and find my phone on the bed. What did he say his name was? Something with a C.

Carter.

I click into my contacts and start scrolling, looking for Carter. Carter. *Carter.*

I text him. Free right now?

It takes him almost ten minutes to reply. I see you used that number I gave you What u up to?

Me: Why don't you come over and see? Meet me at my place?

There's a long pause, those three dots flickering in and out, and then he finally types back. R u serious???

Me: Just text me when you get here.

He sends another text, but I ignore it and slip into my bathroom. I dry my hair, swipe on a little scented lotion and extra deodorant and pull on a pair of high-waisted jeans and a thin, cropped sweater. When I get back into my room, my phone buzzes.

I'm outside.

When I open the door, he's cuter than I remember. Dark blond hair hangs just past his chin and I can see the geometry of his abs through his T-shirt, the outline of his chest, his jeans low on his hips.

His eyes fall down the front of me. "Thought I was going

to regret taking the subway when I saw this weird guy hawking spit into a pile at his feet, but now I see it was worth it."

He reaches out and pulls me toward him until our bodies slam together. His hand is up my shirt, tongue on my neck before I can stop him.

I push my hand against his chest. "Wait."

"I have one." His breath is warm against my skin, the most gentle fire. He reaches into his back pocket and pulls out a condom.

"No, it's not that. Look." I glance up at him to make sure he's listening. "This is just sex, okay? No sleeping over. No calling me afterward. Just...sex," I say.

I don't need another headache. I don't need any more drama. I just want to feel good. I need to feel good.

He chuckles. "Don't worry. Not gonna fall in love with you."

There is no foreplay this time. No coy, lingering touches or whispered words, only hunger, an overt kind of desperation. Me, dragging him upstairs and pulling his pants down only as far as they need to go. Him, so ready to fuck he pushes me right onto the bed harder than I expect, but I like it.

"What do you want?" he asks, his voice deep, husky. The words drip down my neck like butter, warming me, tickling me. His body is heavy on top of mine and he smells fresh out of the shower.

I bite my lip and snake a hand between his legs. "You know what I want."

"No." He grabs my wrist and pins it down to the mattress, then looks directly into my eyes. "Tell me what you want," he says, pressing into me, soft and hard at the same time.

I want him to fuck me so hard that I can't hear my own thoughts anymore and not stop until I'm a silent, shivering pile of nothingness.

I want him to not care so much about what I want. I'm not his girl. I'm never going to be.

I want this noise inside my head to go away and never come back. I want quiet.

That's what I want.

I don't know how to say any of that. So I tell him he can put it anywhere he wants. He smiles, flips me over and pulls me up to my knees in one fluid motion, like this is all so effortless for him. I sigh when I feel him open me and close my eyes, losing myself in the pain of him, the force of him. The hypnotic rhythm of wet flesh. The low, desperate sounds of his pleasure. A line of sweat drips down my neck, and when I tell him *harder*, I have to press my hand against the headboard to keep from crashing straight into it, and he is so dirty and so into it, and somewhere along the way I think I call him daddy, which is embarrassing and fucking disturbing when I think about it for too long because I never say daddy, never, and then his hand comes down on my ass, hard and fast, no warning or hesitation, just his wide, smooth palm. It makes such a brutal, satisfying sound that I beg him to do it again. My body bucks in shock. The pain is everywhere at once.

He moans, his hand gripping my waist, holding me still. "You like that?"

My voice is barely a rasp of sound. *"Yeah."*

He slaps me again. I squeeze my eyes tight and bite down on one of my pillows and tell him he's about to make me come, and of course this does him in. I feel him shudder and tell him, *don't stop, please don't stop, don't you dare fucking stop*, but then I'm not sure if the words ever actually leave my mouth because I can barely speak, and I'm so close and doing my best to come when he slips an arm around me and rubs three fingers against my pussy, and suddenly it's almost too much. I come so hard, I don't realize it at first. The blood gushing down my face. I taste it on my tongue, the metallic tang of it, then I reach a hand up to touch my nose and my fingers come back bright red.

"That was so hot," Carter says, still moving inside me, slower now, but I barely feel him anymore. I don't know how to stop the blood. It keeps coming, a steady, cruel flow.

Warm lips press into my back, and I almost lurch out of my skin.

"Hey. You okay?" Carter reaches out and gently pulls me toward him.

When he tries to flip me onto my back, I hold still. "I'm fine," I say, my voice a rough croak. My hand flies up to my face again, but I'm not fast enough.

Carter sees the blood and freezes. His mouth opens but no words come out right away, and then he squints down at me with this mild sort of horror in his eyes. "Your um...your..."

"I know."

"Shit. It's a lot. Do you need help?" His voice is soft and compassionate, and I can't stand it.

"No." I grit my teeth, swallow my emotions and push myself off the bed, pulling the sheet with me as if he hasn't already seen everything there is to see. More blood. There's so much blood. A small trickle spills down the front of my neck, an ant crawling on my skin. I violently smear it away.

"Sure you don't need—"

"Can you leave?" I snap, but it's more of a command than a question.

"Leave?" He looks shocked. Offended. "Are you serious?"

I look away to give him privacy, because somehow it feels like the right thing to do in this moment, and also because it's hard to look at him like this all of a sudden, so visible in his vulnerability—skin damp with sweat, body still aroused. It feels wrong, obscene. He doesn't say anything else, just climbs off the bed and starts to tug on his jeans. I run into my bathroom and grab a hand towel. When I glance in the mirror, the blood is bright and ugly, still pouring out. I wet the towel with warm water and clean my face as fast as I can. But the blood won't stop. It clings to my skin, staining every place it touches. I can't look at it; I feel weak, light-headed. I reach over and grab a wad of toilet paper and stuff it in my nose to keep it from dripping.

When I step back into my room, Carter's almost finished getting dressed. His eyes come to me for the briefest second, then he bends over for his shoes, slips them on, and walks away without another word. I follow him down to the lower level.

He stops and looks at me over his shoulder. His eyes are gentle, almost frail. "My kid sister died from an overdose. Last year." He takes a breath. Swallows. "She was only sixteen. *Sixteen.*"

I frown. "Why are you telling me this?"

He stares at me for the longest moment, as if he's trying to figure something out. Then he takes a hard breath like he doesn't want to have to speak his next words. "I saw it in your eyes the other night at your party. I wasn't sure, but—I know those kinds of nosebleeds."

He levels a gaze with me and the pity in his eyes is almost worse than the humiliation.

I hate that he saw right through me.

"Damn. This is your first one, isn't it?" His hand comes up to touch my chin and my breath hitches in my throat. His fingers are soft, his words softer. "Are you sure you're okay?"

My jaw tightens and I snatch his hand away. "Will you just go?"

When I look up, I expect to find anger in his eyes, but there's only surprise. And something else. Something genuine and warm and annoying that tells me I've given too much of myself away, more than he needs to know.

"Look, I know it's none of my business, but you should try to slow down. You might do some serious damage."

I look away, the truth in his eyes like a light too bright to stare at, and I think about those soft, breathless sounds he made while he was inside me; the way he gripped the back of my neck, his hand heavy and inelegant, like who I was, the person inside this body, didn't matter. I want him to be that guy. Not this. I can't handle this.

He takes a breath and his voice is suddenly full of emotion. "I don't know what you're looking for, but you're not going to find it in a line," he says, which only makes me feel shittier.

I find myself blinking back tears, his softness stealing some part of me away. I'm not going to cry. I stomp away from him and snatch open the door. He doesn't know what I'm going through. What I've been through. He doesn't know what the fuck he's talking about.

Carter stares at me like he wants to say something else, then turns to leave, every step slow, unsure.

As soon as he's gone, I grab my phone and block his number. But by then the tears have already begun to fall, the sobs pulling at my throat.

I lean against the door, pressing my forehead against the wood. I should have stayed there in the tub, under the water, waiting for oblivion.

12

BRANDI

"You almost ready?" Nate calls from the other room.

He's a guy, so he's dressed already and has been waiting for me to finish my hair while trying not to get annoyed that I've been stuck on a refrain of *five more minutes* for the past half hour. As I flip through the rest of the clothes in my closet, my mind goes back to Taylor. I've been thinking about her nonstop for the past two days, the deal we made. I still can't believe the money came through. And in less than twenty-four hours. Ten thousand dollars, in my account, just like that. More than I even asked for.

As soon as the transfer was completed, I called the registrar's office at FIT and paid off my balance. They told me it would take a few days to process, but I'm in the clear.

I'm still waiting for the wrecking ball to slam into me. Everything about this feels wrong. Then I remind myself that I really had no choice. Somehow that doesn't make me feel any better, but I almost believe it.

"What's this?"

I flip around and my eyes find the creased letter in his hand and my jaw falls open against my own will.

Shit. I was supposed to toss that.

My mouth is moving but no words are coming out. I can't think of a lie fast enough.

"Why didn't you tell me you needed money?" Nate asks, and I sense his irritation right away.

"I…" Don't know how to explain. Not in a short, sweet way that won't prompt follow-up questions.

"You only have a couple weeks left to get this paid off." He sighs. "B, we talked about this. You know you don't have to figure everything out by yourself, right?"

I pull out a black dress that's snatched at the waist from my closet and start to slip it on. "Nate, chill. It's been taken care of."

He frowns and moves closer to me. "Another loan? Babe, those will ruin your credit. You know it's nothing for me to ask my—"

"I didn't take out a loan. I paid it off."

His brows lift. "What, you been stripping on the side or something?"

My lips press together. I sigh, taking the letter from his hand. "Taylor gave it to me," I say, but my eyes don't meet his.

He pauses. *"Van Doren?"*

I nod and turn away to look for my shoes. "It's a long story."

He steps in front of me, the look in his eyes an unanswered question I still don't have the answer to. "The beginning sounds like a good place to start."

But it isn't really that long of a story, not the way I tell it. My words tumble out of me, crashing into one another. I tell him about overhearing Taylor upstairs in that room at the party, that there were at least two other people who heard the same thing I heard. I tell him what they said, everything I could make out. Then I tell him about Taylor luring me to that little Italian place and how she tried to intimidate me. I try to make it funny. Nate doesn't interrupt me, not once. He doesn't seem shocked or even surprised by anything I'm saying. It's not until that last part, when I mention the money, that I get any kind of reaction from him. But still, he doesn't say anything, just a quick lift of his eyebrows, and that's all I get. When I'm done, he's quiet. Too quiet.

I want to ask what he's thinking as we huddle up on the subway, but I also don't want to know the answer. So I don't say anything, either. A few times I feel the weight of Nate's eyes on me, but as soon as I look up, he glances away and pretends he wasn't watching me.

By the time we make it to the restaurant, I'm already picking at my cuticles, the blood not far away. Nate's never been this quiet for this long. We eat in an almost dead silence. After our waiter refills our glasses and leaves to serve another table, I can't take it anymore.

"Are you okay?"

He doesn't look up. "I'm fine."

I reach over onto his plate with my fork and stab at the last of his pasta.

"I was gonna eat that," he mumbles, before I can even stick the tortellini into my mouth, and I hate the clip in his voice.

"Sorry," I say, though I'm not sure if it's me who should be the one apologizing. "I thought you were done. You still—"

"No. Go ahead." Nate reaches for the bread basket, though there's nothing but broken pieces and crumbs left, and I know it's just to avoid my eyes.

Something flickers inside me, something small, barely noticeable, like the spark of a flame. Tonight was supposed to be low-key, no drama, no worries, just light conversation, good food and that easy, slow sex that makes you tear up a little.

I push it away and sigh. "So how long are you gonna stay mad at me?"

"I'm not mad," he says, too quickly.

It's a lie, and we both know it. Nate always lets me eat the last bite of his food. And it's not just that. It's his eyes, the way they keep averting mine, the abrasion in his voice.

"Then what are you?"

He shakes his head like it's hard for him to even talk to me. "It's just shady. You keeping me in the dark like this."

"I wasn't sure if what I heard was what I heard. Plus, Taylor's your friend. I didn't want to come between—"

"We're not friends, all right?" His eyes snap up to find mine. "We just used to know each other. That's it." He looks away again.

I swallow what he says, but it doesn't go down easy, anger sour at the back of my throat. If they aren't actually friends, then why was Taylor all over him the way she was, so comfortable and entitled? How well did they know each other, then? A million questions bubble at the tip of my tongue, but I don't ask any of them. The moment doesn't seem right, and I'm afraid my words will come out wrong. I don't want a fight. Nate and I don't fight much, and I don't even know if this qualifies as fighting, but we don't do *this*, whatever this is.

My eyes flick around the room as silence stretches between us. I glance down at my plate, but don't touch anything.

A minute passes.

More nothing. We do that thing where we look around the restaurant and try to find something to focus our gazes on, then pretend something has caught our attention and that we're not dying to reach for our phones and drift away.

I know I need to say more. I call his name, and Nate glances up from his plate. It's the first time he's given me real eye contact since we've sat down, and I feel like a small child, like I've been smacked on the wrist in front of the whole class. I sense the tremor in my voice before I speak, and so I swallow the words down and sip my water so I can try again. Normally, I'm not this sensitive, but with Nate it's different. He knows what annoys me, what makes me tick, that I can't stand the sound of gum popping or slurping or metal crashing into teeth. He knows about my irritable bowels and all the weird gurgling sounds my stomach makes hours after I eat anything and that sometimes my condition holds my colon hostage for weeks at a time. He knows how much I hate being ignored, that it's tied to my abandonment issues. He knows my darkest fears, the pieces of me I try to hide from the rest of the world. So with him, I have no choice but to take it personally. He's fully aware of what he's doing; he wants me to hurt and maybe I deserve it, but it's killing me.

My voice is low and unsure. "I didn't tell you because... honestly, it kinda freaked me out. I didn't want to be involved."

His eyes are incredulous. "You taking her money, that's not you getting involved?"

That draws me up short. I flinch. Look away.

He didn't let me finish. I was talking about overhearing them. Which is true. It did freak me out. And I wasn't sure if I'd heard correctly. Not until Taylor showed up at that restaurant the next morning instead of Simon. And then I didn't know how Nate would react, if he'd even believe me. I really wasn't going to get involved, but then I got shoved into a corner with that notice from FIT.

"It's not like I asked for any of this." I pause, keep my voice soft. "She started all this, not me."

Nate doesn't say anything, just finishes off his water, then raises a finger for the check when our waiter saunters by.

"Why are you making such a big deal out of this?" I ask in a hushed but urgent tone.

I shouldn't have, because his voice remains casual and unbothered. "I'm not. Let's just head back."

And then I know he's lying for sure. He's mad, maybe more than that, he just doesn't want to admit it, and I don't know why. I never hold my tongue when I'm mad. I'm verbose and loud and frantic, and he is like a dejected puppy, which makes me want to get even more verbose and loud and frantic.

I watch his Amex go down onto the table, then glance up to his face. His eyes are distant, a mile away. Not sure if we're even still in the same dimension.

I remember the first night we spent together, the first time I realized I had feelings for him. It all happened so fast, faster than I'd ever imagined it would, but there they were. Genuine feelings. It scared the shit out of me. I think that's what I remember most: how truly terrified I was. I'd never been in a relationship before. I'd never met anyone who seemed worth letting my guard down for. I tried to ignore them at first. Those silly, heady, psychedelic feelings. I thought if I pretended they didn't exist, they'd go away and find someone else to torture. But Nate had been so eager to prove himself to me, prove that he was different, that I could trust him.

I never want him to feel that way about me. Uncertain. Unsure. It pains me to think that I've severed his trust, even if it's just a little.

Maybe I made a mistake. Maybe I should have never taken that money from Taylor. I was just trying to avoid a fight, but look where that got me.

There's no point in dwelling on it now. It's done. Just like this date, if you can call it that since it's been more of a stand-off than anything else, and considering the way Nate ignores me for the whole ride home, I'm surprised that when we get back to the apartment he wants to fuck, and when he lies on his stomach and puts his face between my legs, I'm quiet because I'm confused. I thought he'd still be pissed at me. Maybe he still is; I don't know. He's different, not as talkative or playful as he normally is. It's not enough to turn me off, but there's this silent tension that's impossible not to feel despite the heroic strokes of his tongue. When it's over, he gets up and showers for an unusually long time, leaving me alone with my thoughts, and I feel slightly used. But then I realize I kind of like it, and then I feel fucked up for liking it, like what the fuck is wrong with me? And then I'm lying on my back thinking that maybe this was his way of saying we're okay; even though he's upset, we're still okay; we'll always be okay, and before I fall asleep, the dark quiet between us, I'm hoping he wakes me up in the morning before he heads to the gym because the fact that he did that makes me feel so good I want him again already.

13

BRANDI

The next day two weird things happen.

I'm turning out of the apartment, head down as I pull out my MetroCard, when I look up and see a girl staring at me out the window of a parked car. I don't know her, but I recognize her instantly. She was at the ball. The Asian girl in the dress the color of blood. That's how I remember her.

She looks different now. Her face is scrubbed clean and her long black hair is neatly pinned at the back of her head. She's pretty. Rich brown eyes that glint in the sunlight and a tiny gap between her front two teeth, but there's something harsh about her face. Maybe her eyes or the way her mouth curves down on the sides as if she's permanently frowning.

She calls me by my name and waves me over, tossing a cigarette onto the concrete once I meet her gaze.

My feet don't move right away.

She's sitting in the backseat of a blacked-out Denali, her driver up front, waiting with the radio on low. I glance at him, then back at her. I have no idea what this girl could possibly want.

I take a breath and approach the side of the car. I'm probably making a big deal out of nothing. I can at least see what she wants before jumping to conclusions.

Her lips part like she's going to speak, but then her eyes slip down to the bag hooked in the crook of my arm. It's the one I got from T.J. Maxx last summer, which has been surprisingly durable. "That bag is like a sad pit bull at the pound," she says with no hate or judgment, which actually makes it worse, and it's not her words but her unapologetic tone that stuns me.

"What?"

She appraises me over thin, rectangular frames. Her dark, almond-shaped eyes don't blink. "Tay filled me in."

Of course.

I don't say anything. She knows I overheard them. That's why she's here, but I still can't tell if she's on a mission to make a bargain or a threat.

"It's really none of your business, you know," she says. Her eyes are hard and inscrutable. Her voice gives away nothing, either, which immediately makes me think she's the calculating type. Cunning. Strategic. Or maybe that's just the way she talks, monotone and snide. "You're not gonna go around running your mouth, are you?"

"No," I hear myself say, but my voice seems far away.

But she doesn't believe me. I can tell by the way her lips tighten, the way she shifts forward like she knows she needs to try harder.

It's only now that I realize my heart is beating faster. I'm nervous. Maybe even scared. I don't know this girl; I don't know what she's capable of. I just know what I heard in that room. She said she knew a guy who could get her something that would kill Simon. She's obviously got a plug in the city. Who knows what else she's involved in.

She pushes the back door open and scoots over to the opposite side. "Get in. That bag has to go. We'll get you a new one."

She's wearing a black, backless bodysuit tucked into light-washed jeans, the muscles in her shoulders flexing as she shifts to open the door for me. A Gucci bag is sitting on the empty seat next to her, a half-eaten bag of kale chips on the floor.

I stare at her, befuddled. "You...you want to buy me a bag?"

"You look like a Chanel girl."

My eyes flutter. "Chanel?"

"You're not going to talk, right?" she asks, and this time her voice is like a stretched rubber band, the sharpest snap. I almost feel the sting.

I glance at the driver again. He has earphones in and is absentmindedly people watching out his window. He can't hear a word we're saying.

My gaze settles on Taylor's friend again and I realize I still don't know her name. "What's your name?"

She hesitates, like she's weighing the consequences of being cordial and responding to me. "Mei. But not like the month."

That's not what I was expecting. I thought she'd have a more severe name, something with more edge that would match her demeanor. Mei sounds sweet, too sweet.

I want to ask how she found out where I live, how she knew when I'd be leaving, but she speaks before I can. "We'll go to Barneys. On me."

She pats the space she's made for me next to her.

I almost tell her no, shut the door and walk away.

But some part of me can't resist. It's not my fault she, Taylor and that other guy were planning to murder an innocent man loud enough for people to overhear. I didn't ask for any of this. If anything, they are the ones who owe me. And it's not like I'm going to tell anyone anyway. I can't. I already have a ten-thousand-dollar muzzle around my mouth. If she wants to spend her money on me, then who am I to stop her?

As soon as I step into Mei's car, my phone buzzes with a text. The second weird thing. I don't recognize the number.

It's Jared I'm a friend of Taylor's. U free today?

I don't know a Jared. I have no idea how this person got my number.

Then I figure it out. It must be the guy who was in that room upstairs, the third person. They must have all planned this, the three of them, to each come after me with separate bribes to keep me quiet, hoping I'd say yes and forget everything.

I text him back.

He wants to know a good time to pick me up later to *spoil* me, whatever that means. They're all the same, thinking money can solve all their problems. It definitely won't solve mine, but it'll make life a little more fun, at least for now, and as long as they're offering, I don't see the harm in taking. Especially not when it's *their* fault I no longer have a job.

I tell him when I'll be free. At the same time I can't help but wonder what Nate would say.

He wouldn't like it. He wouldn't like any of this.

My phone buzzes again. Jared asking me for my address. Which completely throws me off.

So they didn't plan this together, then? Mei got my address somehow, so why couldn't he have gone to her for it? I guess it doesn't really matter, so I send it to him.

I look over at Mei when I feel her shifting next to me, pulling a pack of Marlboros out of her purse. She lifts one out of the box, slipping the thin stick between pouty pink lips, then flicks her BIC with her thumb and leans forward for the flame. She offers me one, angling the box toward me slightly. I decline with a tight shake of my head and roll my window down when she glances away.

Mei spends most of the ride replaying the same clip of herself on stage in a bride-like costume on her phone, tugging on her cigarette and inspecting her trimmed nails. She doesn't say a word to me in the fifteen minutes of traffic we fight through, and I'm kind of relieved. She doesn't seem like the easy-to-talk-to type. Nothing about her is soft or kind. Not the way she snarls at her driver; not the way she snapped at me before I got in.

We finally pull up in front of what has to be the most pretentious department store in Manhattan, and Mei looks up from her phone. When she steps out of the car, I get a better look at her. She's lean and hard, muscular but thin. I can make out the soft knots of her spine, a column of ellipses, as she steps in front of me, steering us through the tourist-heavy crowds outside the store. Her high-cut jeans fit as though they were made specifically for her body. My eyes pause on her square-toe sandals. They're delicate, thin straps weaving together that could be dental floss, a modest heel, but they still look sexy on her.

As soon as we step inside the store, a couple of sales associates dressed in all black and wearing too much perfume rush over to us. An older woman in her forties and a younger woman, maybe thirty.

At first my heart flutters. I don't understand what's happening. And then I remember who I'm with and it suddenly all clicks. The women can't look any happier; their smiles are practically stretching their faces, eyes wide with excitement, effusive to the point of savagery. They greet Mei by her name and lean in to kiss her cheeks, one at a time.

"She's with me," Mei tells them, and immediately they're

all over me. Asking me how I'm doing. What size I am. If they can help me find anything. I didn't think this kind of thing happened in real life. Or maybe this is just how people treat you when you're rich and are not immediately assumed to be a threat.

The last time I came here with Nate, three security guards followed us from floor to floor, hovered around us and didn't back off until an older fan recognized Nate and asked him about the ESPN show his dad cohosts occasionally. One of them had the nerve to ask Nate for a selfie on our way out. He was willing, but I dragged him away, saying we were late for brunch. We never brunch.

At first, I'm tempted to walk around a little, take in the opulence, but every time I glance at Mei, she looks impatient and forces this weird, tight smile that looks more like a grimace, so I head straight over to the Chanel section. But when one of the sales associates directs me to the bag I want, there's another one right next to it in a different color that calls my name. I can't decide.

Mei's pacing back and forth, still on her phone, thumbs moving so fast I expect smoke soon.

I grab both bags off the shelf and walk over to the mirror, then take turns posing with each one. Either one will be perfect. Every other intern at Van Doren had not only a Chanel, but also a collection of high-end bags they kept on rotation. It's not just a bag, it's an investment, and if I'm going to be a part of this world, this will help me compete.

I glance at Mei again. Now she has a cigarette dangling from her mouth, unlit, checking the time on her phone.

I flick a scrutinizing glance between both bags one last time. Before I can tell Mei which one I've decided to go with, she snatches both bags out my hands and shoves them into the older sales associate's arms.

"Just charge both to my account."

I gape at her. "But I thought you said—"

"I'm late for rehearsal. Don't have time for you to make up your fucking mind."

With that, she turns and heads for the escalator. I watch her the whole way, until she rounds a corner. I glance back at the older sales associate, trying to look as apologetic as I can. "Sorry about that."

I don't know what else to say. I'm still a little thrown. The woman forces a tight smile and leads me to the nearest register.

When I meet Jared two hours later, he is much less hostile. He seems nice, and even gets out of his car to open my door.

He's alone. No driver. Which is odd since we're in the city. Then again, it's a Porsche, and if I had this car I'd drive it whenever I had the chance too.

When he looks at me, his smile actually reaches his eyes. Of course, he, too, is gorgeous. Over six feet tall, at least six-two, but maybe taller. His hair is dyed a ridiculous platinum-blond, the roots much darker than the rest, but somehow he makes it look fashion. He could probably pull anything off; he's that type. His loose-fitting shirt is undone down to the fourth button, showing off a waxed chest, and his jeans are so tight, they strain at the seams. A stack of minimal gold chains is layered around his neck, and multiple rings are stacked on just about every finger. My eyes fall to his shoes, silver-tipped Chelsea boots. I move my gaze back up and this time I take in all the tattoos. His left arm looks like it's completely sleeved and the other stops just before his elbow. I can see the edges of some kind of bird, maybe a dove, spreading its wings on his chest, a date set in Roman numerals peeking from his shoulder.

I smile back at him because I can't think of anything to say. Our gazes meet for the first time and he's looking down at me with these soulful brown eyes that suck you right in, and I realize how long I've been staring.

"Obsessed with your fit. Is that Balenciaga?"

I glance down at the sweatshirt I stole from Nate's side of the closet. It fits me like a dress, so I paired it with some white tube socks and chunky sneakers. The fact that he thinks someone like me could afford a seven-hundred-dollar garment is slightly offensive, but I take it as a compliment.

"Something like that," I tell him, and his expression flickers as he picks up on my sarcasm.

"Ready to do this?"

He looks excited, but I can't help feeling a little skeptical. "What exactly is the plan?"

"No spoilers, love. Jump in."

I hardly know anything about this guy, but I like him already. He has this effortless way of making you feel like the shiniest version of yourself. I duck into the passenger seat and the first thing I notice after I'm swathed in the buttery leather interior is his cologne.

Jared slips on a pair of oversize, white-framed sunglasses and looks over at me. "Comfortable?"

"This is nice."

His shrugs as he peels away from the curb. "The Bentley is better. Has more leg room."

By the time we get settled into traffic, I'm expecting him to bring up the other night or at least mention Taylor again, but he doesn't, and I finally relax in my seat. We both know what this little arrangement is about anyway; we don't need to say it. After plugging in his aux cord and requesting my preference, he pops in a pair of AirPods and FaceTimes a shaggy-haired blond guy who looks slightly older than he does and just as beautiful. I'm nervous because traffic on Park Avenue is so chaotic, but he turns out to be an incredible multitasker.

I try not to listen to their conversation, but once I hear *enema* and *Fendi* in the same sentence, I can't even pretend to be uselessly scrolling through my TikTok feed. Before we arrive at our first destination, he's sweet-talking another guy he tells me he hooked up with last week at a silent party after he ends the call. He says he likes him because he reminds him of a guy he had a crush on in high school right around the time he got close to Taylor. I hold my breath, hoping the conversation isn't going to implode.

But he surprises me and laughs. "I almost gave that bitch my gold star."

"Like..."

"It was before I was out. Luckily, she was highly uninterested, so we caused mayhem in Bergdorf's instead."

"You guys don't really seem..." I don't know how to say this without offending his friend. "When we met she seemed a little..."

"Bitchy?" Jared offers, and I'm grateful because it is exactly what I meant but was trying not to say.

He shifts his gear into Park and releases his seat belt and we head out of the parking garage. "Tay can be a little hardcore, but we balance each other out."

Hardcore isn't what I'd call it, but sure.

Jared leads the way inside an elderly, gut-renovated building and my breath catches once we're inside the palatial spa. The three-story waterfall and subterranean wet lounge has me starting to think we're in some kind of tranquility simulation.

Jared gets a mani-pedi with me and as we sip on custom smoothies from the juice bar, he's full of hyperbolic compliments and reckless flattery, and not just to me, but everyone who services us. I agree to get a lymphatic drainage massage because I assume it is some kind of overpriced facial forty-something actresses get to avoid being subjected to grandmother roles, but once I'm wrapped in a towel and facedown on the heated chaise, I can't stop laughing as the stern Eastern European masseuse allegedly removes toxins and improves circulation with comedically harsh strokes.

I've never gotten a Brazilian because I've never had the desire to have my soul ripped from me via my vagina, but Jared insists it's not as torturous as it seems and when I'm done, I feel both traumatized and horny. I don't have time to text Nate because there is more painful hair removal, brows and upper lip, and a vampire facial, which is exactly what it sounds like except there are no fangs involved and the blood comes from a puncture the facialist makes in your own arm.

When we hit the concrete again, I start to thank him for the ridiculous pampering session, but he grabs my wrist and steers me toward Wooster Street, telling me I can pick out whatever I want from the Balmain flagship store. Unlike Mei, Jared joins me in perusing the racks, and I almost piss myself when I see him ask one of the mannequin-looking sales associates for my size in two items I say I like without even glancing at the price tags. He shops in both the men's and women's departments, so I follow suit and find a couple things from the men's section that ultimately don't work out. Jared makes me model the signature strong-shouldered blazer and monogram mini dress I pick out and provides a shockingly on-point beatbox to strut to.

After about two hours of trying on different pieces and chatting with the manager about Olivier Rousteing's vision for the upcoming fall collection, I finally decide on two mini dresses, a pair of sunglasses and an eau de parfum that smells like expensive sex. Jared puts everything on his account without even handing over his card, which is what wealthy people do in places like this, apparently. He hands me the bag, and I hesitate for a moment, wondering if I'm going to regret this. But then I remember that I'm jobless and missed out on the opportunity of a lifetime in Milan because of all this, and things seem to square out.

Once we step outside, bags in hand, we're immediately ambushed by a ring of paparazzi. They start snapping right away and even though I'm sure my skin is glowing to perfection, I stay behind him. It's like they knew he'd be here.

Jared turns to me as if he hasn't even noticed the shutter-happy battalion. "Anywhere else?"

I start to say no, but stop when three photographers close in on us, stepping way beyond the invisible barrier of personal space. I'm used to this happening with Nate here and there, but when lenses begin to be aimed at me, every muscle in my body tenses. I don't want photos to be released online of us together. This whole thing was supposed to be low-key, not a photo op.

But Jared is loving this. He comes alive even more, though I can see he's trying to play his excitement down for the cameras.

"Jared, what's up, man? Where you headed?" one guy asks.

Jared keeps steering us toward his parking spot but makes sure they get a good angle of his face, and the one in front of us starts walking backward. "Are you still dating Elliot Hayes?"

Jared ignores that and eases into what seems like a familiar dance to the rhythm of the shutters clicking. But I don't know what to do, how to react, if I should pose, not pose.

Jared glances over as if he can sense my unease. "Act normal, love. It's just the paps."

I stay behind him and try to ignore the cameras, though all I can think about is where these will be tomorrow morning.

"And straighten up," he says. "These will be all over by tonight."

And then I realize I was right. I've read this is what some

social media influencers and low-level celebrities do to make
sure they stay in the press, paparazzi on demand, but watching
it happen right in front of me is bizarre. It's like these people
constantly live in a fantasy world where anything they want
is only a command or swipe away. I'm not sure I could ever
get used to this.

I do as I'm directed. I straighten up. Shift my shoulders
back. Suck in my gut.

One of the guys glances at me, then puts his camera in my
face. "Jared, who's your friend?"

The others shift to stare at me, and it feels wrong. I feel off
balance, awkward, like no matter how much I try, I'm not getting the look right. I don't even know what look I'm going for.

Thankfully, Jared doesn't answer. He leans for my ear.
"We'll ditch them at the corner."

When he drops me off back at my apartment, he tells me
the name of the kind of restaurant that has a six-month wait
list and says that all I have to do is give the hostess his name.

Nate pushes in from the gym, his second workout today,
around six. I'm sitting on the edge of the bed in one of the
dresses Jared bought, slipping my feet into my heels.

"Got a date with a Saudi prince?" Nate asks as soon as he
takes me in, his voice light, teasing.

I smile at him over my shoulder. "No. With you. Hungry?"

"Starving."

I quickly swipe on some eyebrow gel using my handheld
mirror, then stand up from the bed and give him a spin so
he can get a full view of the dress. It's skintight and stops
midthigh, with a gold zipper along the back. Nate's eyes move
over me, but he doesn't say anything. I can barely make out
any reaction on his face.

I panic. "You don't like it?"

"Nah, you look hot," he says, closer now, and I can tell there's something else he wants to say. "I just...I don't get it."

Nate heads for the dresser where he keeps his clothes, pulling his shirt away.

I'm right behind him. "What's there to get?"

He's down to his boxer briefs now. "I've never seen you wear anything like that. That's all I'm saying."

I reach out and flip him around, switching gears, a smile spreading across my face. "Want to show you something."

I take his hand and slip it under my dress.

His eyes meet mine. "You got a baldie?"

I feel myself blushing. "You like it?"

He rubs a little more, and I don't ruin the vibe by telling him that I'm still super sensitive. "I'll let you know later."

"Go get cleaned up," I tell him, shifting away so I can finish doing my makeup. "We're going out."

"Again? We just went out last night."

"I know, but there's a table waiting for us at Rao's."

He pauses at the bathroom door and turns back to face me. "In Harlem? That place is hella expensive. You know I don't like to go all out on places like that."

I glance at him through the mirror hanging on the back of my closet door, then go back to stroking on waterproof mascara. "We're not paying for it."

"Then who is?"

I hesitate. When I tell him that Jared made us the reservations, he sweeps his gaze around the room, taking in the empty shopping bags and popped tags.

"So that's where you got the dress?" His eyes are back on me now. "And all this other shit?"

I pull my lip in. I don't like the tone of his voice, the way it's hardened.

"Yo, B, are you serious right now?" The words rip out of

him, but he stops himself from saying more, running a hand over his head as if he's trying to regain his composure.

I pause. I knew he wouldn't be happy about it, but I didn't expect this. "Why are you yelling?"

He has to take a breath to calm himself, which is something I've never seen him do. He immediately lowers his voice, but the edge is still there. "Forget it."

But I don't want to forget it. I can't forget it when there's a vein bulging in his neck.

I pause when I see him stepping back into his pants. His shirt goes over his head and then he's working on his laces.

I take a breath and fight to keep my voice level. "It's Taylor's fault that I didn't get that job at Van Doren and that I got fired. This is the least she and her friends can do to make it up to me." He doesn't respond. "Where are you going?"

"Need some air," he says, pushing the bedroom door open.

I stand there still in a little shock until I hear the front door open, close. I grab my purse from the bed and follow him out to the elevators. "Will you slow down? I haven't broken in these heels yet."

He slips an arm between the doors and waits for me to step in first, but keeps his eyes straight ahead after hitting the Ground button. "B, you need to check yourself. These guys aren't your friends. You don't even know these people."

He's right. I don't know them. My mind flips back to what Nate said before. About how the things Taylor and her friends used to do in high school were worse than anything I've ever done. I wonder what kind of trouble they got in back then, the laws they broke.

"I don't want friends," I say, my words fierce. "They're the ones who need something from *me*. They offered to pay for my silence, not the other way around."

He sighs and stares at the floor for a moment. "Look, I'm not gonna tell you what to do."

"Sounds like you just did."

The elevator dings.

"I'm just looking out for you. Damn, Brandi." Nate slips through the doors and takes off, stepping through the automatic glass doors at the entrance.

He's walking so fast that they shut in my face by the time I get to them.

That sparks something in me—a kind of anger that I didn't even know existed. I slip through the doors and do my best to keep up with him.

"I grew up in the streets. I had no one but myself. You think I don't know how to look out for myself?"

"These guys are different," Nate says, not slowing down. "In the streets, you have your guard up. You know what to look out for, what to pay attention to. This world is different. Everyone is beautiful. The vultures are hard to see. Trust me, Taylor fucked me over, and I never saw it coming."

That shocks me into silence. We're almost at the corner before I speak again and when I do, my voice has an edge. "Thought she was just someone you used to know?"

"She was." He keeps looking straight ahead. "Until we hooked up at prom."

The words hit me like a knife to the back. I can't speak at first. I'm stuck and still, too busy trying to understand how I missed this. "You slept with her?"

I need to hear him say it. Again.

"Only a few times."

A sick feeling churns in my stomach, a weird mix of relief and disappointment.

"Only?" I spit out, because as far as I'm concerned, one time

is too many when he could have just been honest from the beginning. At least then I could have been prepared.

Now it all makes sense. The way he looked at her at that party. The way she looked at *him*. Their chemistry. Why she agreed to help me out and set me up with her dad in the first place. She wasn't doing me a favor; she was doing *Nate* a favor. Not as a friend, as a...whatever they are. Trying to get closer to him. This whole time.

My breath echoes in my ears. No wonder Taylor thinks I'm an idiot. There I was, smiling in her face when she was already one step ahead of me. Who knows what she said to him that night while we were apart.

I thought she wanted him—but no. She wants him *back*.

Of course she almost lost her shit when he came out of the shower the other day. She'd probably been waiting for that moment for years. *Years*.

I've never checked Nate's phone, I've never even *considered* it, but now I'm wondering how long they've been texting. The thought hits me hard and fast, and I'm not ready for it. My mind races as I imagine them together. Kissing. Touching. His mouth on her long neck. Her hands on his—

I stop before I get too far ahead of myself. It's not like I thought Nate had only been with me; I know he's been with other girls. I just don't understand why he couldn't have been up front with me from the beginning. Why did he feel like he had to hide this from me? Is there more he isn't telling me?

A few times.

Nate glances over at me once we reach the intersection. "She said she was saving herself for, I don't know, until she was in love or whatever."

My heart pounds. "You were in love with her?"

"I said until *she* was in love." He looks away. "It doesn't matter. She never cared about me. I walked in on her and some random dude in the weight room. We were boys. She did that shit with no remorse. After we split, I realized she'd been gaslighting me for months."

I go still, understanding his anger. His frustration. This isn't just about me getting involved. It's about Taylor, what she did to him.

But I'm still stuck on the fact that they've slept together. And not just once. Not just prom. It was serious, more than just a couple of random lonely nights. They were together. She was *in love* with him.

"So you were her first?" I ask just as the light changes.

"Allegedly. Who knows with her?"

He shrugs, like none of this matters to him. But it matters to me.

"Now who's withholding shit?" I snap, the words like weapons from my mouth. A few heads turn to look back at us, but I don't care.

"This is different," Nate says. He finally stops walking. "There was no reason to bring this up."

I roll my eyes. "Bullshit."

That seems to surprise him. He studies me, then inhales to speak.

I take a step closer, cutting him off. "I get it now. You want me to stay away from her because seeing her again is stirring up old feelings in you, isn't it?"

But Nate doesn't reply to that. He makes a frustrated sound and strides away again, faster this time. I still don't know where he's going.

My feet are starting to ache in these heels, but I refuse to stop walking. "What exactly is a *few* times?"

"Less than a lot?"

"Nate."

He stops midstride and whips around, his expression incredulous. "B, if I wanted to fuck Taylor again, I would've done it already." His voice is a harsh whisper. Emotion flickers in his eyes, almost too quick for me to catch it, but I do. It's not anger. It's disappointment. Resignation. "This isn't me having unresolved feelings about my ex. I don't want Taylor. I just know her ways."

Suddenly, he's so much taller than I am, and I'm acutely aware of the fact that I'm almost an entire foot shorter than he is.

I believe him. I know he doesn't want to be with her. At least, a part of me does. The other part can't see why he wouldn't—why *anyone* wouldn't. Especially when they have history. Feelings just don't disappear. They evolve, they dissipate, but they can't ever be truly erased.

I feel like I should say something, but I can't find the right words. It's loud and awkward and my feet are killing me and it's too damn hot out here and then the light changes.

Nate crosses, pausing to look back at me, to see if I'm going to follow.

I don't. I watch him get swallowed up by the sidewalk traffic, but my feet won't move. I can't follow him now. If I do, I'll just say something else I'll regret by the morning and probably end up hurting more than just his feelings. It's better if I take some space, get my thoughts together, sleep this off.

Deep down, I know he's right. I feel it, mixed in the bile and acid and other shit. I know I should stay away from Taylor. I know I should have never gotten involved.

But it's over. My tuition is paid. I won't tell anyone. It's over.

14

TAYLOR

I run through a series of basic tried-and-true poses in a fog, but the small, handsome German photographer pushes me to deliver, which I'm annoyed by at first, then we fall into a rhythm, and I appreciate his refusal to allow me to phone this one in. I contort and work my angles, and we bang out frame after frame, barely needing to stop and communicate verbally. When he takes a break to consult with the lighting person, I check the shots of me in the thick, oversize parkas and nothing else and they look great.

As we prep for my next look—a stunning pink velvet suit—I tilt my head to the side so the on-set hairstylist can tame my flyaways. We're doing a twenty-four-inch, slicked-back pony-tail for the rest of the looks, and I see that the crew is almost ready for me when a horrifying stream of crimson trickles out my left nostril and onto the lapel of the suit.

I can barely process what's happening until the stylist steps back to look me over, noticing the blood as it settles into the fabric like an insult. A few minutes later my agent is on the phone with the designer, trying to figure out if a replacement sample can be rushed over to the studio, and someone asks if I'm okay. I help the photographer come up with a few poses where the damage can't be seen and the architecture of the blazer is still on display for his lens. I also suggest draping a double-breasted trench that belongs to the next mini dress look over my shoulders to cover the sullied lapel. The designer approves via FaceTime and the crisis is averted for the moment, so I don't freak out. At least not while I'm still on set with two wads of toilet paper stuck up my nose as the makeup artist adds dramatic liquid wings to my eyes.

Instead, I pull out my phone and frantically text Mei.

Do u still get nosebleeds?

She texts me right back. My nose bleeds more than my vagina these days.

I wasn't expecting that. She never mentions them.

Me: Wtf. Why didn't u tell me this shit was this bad? I'm on set.

Mei: Calm down, bitch. Ur not dying. It's just a ruptured septum.

Me: I got blood all over my look. Designer is pissed.

Not to mention a stranger saw me with blood gushing down my face while he was fucking me. But I don't tell her that part. I don't want to bring up my tryst with Carter. I don't even want to think about him. I can still hear his words in my head, about slowing down. About what happened to his sister.

When my mom died, it didn't just break my heart, it splintered me from the core. I'm no longer the same person. I don't see things the same; I don't feel things the same. At first, it was like everything in me went numb. I couldn't feel anything for so long. No sadness. No guilt. No pain. Nothing.

Sometimes you just need to remember what it's like to feel

something real, even if it hurts. Even if it makes you ache so much you want to end things. Like my mom ended things. That's when it started. That's when I got high for the first time. It was like flying, soaring through the air and never looking down. Never stopping to doubt, question, think.

And then when I started to feel again, it was all too much. The anger. The pain. The nightmares. I realized it was better to not feel. I started getting so high, I'd lose all the feeling in my entire body. It was better than this, this horrible bottomless feeling.

I can't stop. I won't. I wish I had a couple of lines right now.

My phone buzzes.

Mei: Just lay off for three days. U should be good.

I blow out air as my lip liner and highlighter are touched up simultaneously. Three days. She might as well have said three years.

I glance into the hand mirror I used earlier to help the makeup artist with my brows. There's no trace of blood on my face anymore, but I can still smell it. Taste it.

My phone buzzes again. I shift my gaze from my reflection to my screen.

Mei: Need me to come over later?

I text her back: Not sure how long the shoot will go. I head to the bathroom, and then shoot off another message. Oh, did I tell you I have lunch with my father tomorrow? He supposedly has good news.

Mei: What do you think it's about?

Me: No idea. Didn't decide if I'm going yet.

I shouldn't even go to this bullshit lunch. I don't need this right now. I doubt his "good news" will be good for anyone other than himself.

I'm on my way back to set in my last look when my phone buzzes again.

Mei: Wait. What if he's giving you your money?

Holy shit. That never would have crossed my mind, but she's right. What other good news could he possibly have that would warrant an actual meal at Le Coucou? He barely makes time in his schedule for me. I push through the rest of the shoot with renewed energy and send him a generic *excited for tomorrow* text once I'm in the car.

I see my father before he sees me, tucked into a booth in the back section. A server greets me and starts to usher me over, but I tell her I can find my way.

My father starts to stand when he sees me, but I wave off his performative chivalry. He takes his seat again and I take the one across from him.

"You're late," he says, stating the obvious, and there is no give to his expression. No gleam in his eyes. Nothing. He looks pissed.

"Sorry," I say, doing my best to create an apologetic smile. "My meeting ran over. I got here as fast as I could."

"We've talked about this. Text me when you're running late. You're always on that damn phone anyway." His tone is so cold, I start to feel the need to give him another explanation, but I stop myself.

"I said I was sorry."

He stares back at me, eyes narrow and calculating. He thinks I was getting high. He wants to say it; I know he does—but he doesn't. He looks away, mouth tight.

The waiter sets a bottle of chilled chardonnay on the table between us, then excuses himself.

I reach for my water glass and take a sip. "So what's this big news you have to tell me?"

He motions to the menu. "I thought you'd want to order first."

I stare at him. He's stalling. He knows I know he's stalling. I roll my eyes. "Dad, just tell me."

"Okay. Fine." Something moves in his eyes, something I've never seen before, and I'm not sure if it's good or bad. I all but hold my breath. "Izzy and I are engaged."

His words slam into me, driving me against the back of my chair. I blink a few times and seriously start to double down on my atheism because there is no fucking way a god could be responsible for this even if he is a jealous, sadistic, malevolent thug who cares way too much about who people fuck. I do my best to not react, willing every facial muscle to stay exactly where it is. My father is staring at me, waiting for my reaction, but I can't formulate coherent words. I can't even think.

I don't care who my father sleeps with. I don't care who he chooses to live with. All I care about is my money, and there's no way I'm going to let that broke bitch steal it away from me. Not after all I've been through.

"We're thinking about having the ceremony before the summer's over. Maybe the weekend of the Fourth." Now he's smiling, and I swear I almost jump over the table and slap it right off his face.

I take a breath, forcing my voice to stay neutral. "Of July?"

"That's the one."

I don't say anything.

"So what do you think?"

He doesn't really want to know what I think. He wants me to pat him on the shoulder and encourage this travesty.

I wet my lips, trying to not explode. "Don't you think you're rushing things?"

His expression hardens right up. "It's been two years. I've been given a second chance. Might as well make the most of it."

I stare at him, incredulous. "She's *my* age."

My father sighs a breath of obvious frustration, drawing himself back. "She's not your age, Taylor. She's four years older than you."

It takes everything in me not to hurl my plate at his head. "Dad, what if I was banging a guy who was fifty? How can you be this cliché? You're so embarrassing."

He looks as irritated as I feel.

"We're not *banging*. We're getting married. There will even be a church and a priest." After his failed attempt at a joke, he throws a quick glance around the room, making sure no one is within earshot. "Look, I didn't ask you here for your permission. I wanted you to come so you can share this moment with me. Be happy for me. If you can't do that, then you should leave."

I set my jaw and grab the handle of my bag. My chair screeches loud against the floor as I push it back. Heads turn, but I don't care.

My father's neck snaps up. "What are you doing?"

I don't answer him.

I don't even look back when I snatch away from the table. My phone is already in my hand when I push inside the restroom. I group text Mei and Jared.

Code red, bitches. Need to meet at my house.

Mei: What's up?

Jared: What happened? Are u ok?

I have no idea. I feel like I'm still in shock, like the full impact of it all hasn't sunk in yet.

Me: Just come over.

Mei: Ok, I'm coming. But I'm getting in ur pool.

I tell them to meet me in an hour and don't even glance back at my father's table when I come out of the restroom. I head straight for the door, texting my driver.

A woman bumps into me on her way in. I lift my head, starting to apologize—then stop when our eyes meet.

I should have known he'd invited her too.

I glance down at her left hand and there it is. The ring. Suddenly, it all feels too real. I take a breath but feel my shoulders heave.

She tries a smile and starts to say something, but I brush past her, knocking her bare shoulder with mine.

I want to shove the bitch with both hands, but I don't. Too many eyes. Too many ears.

I hear her scoff behind me and keep walking out the door. My driver texts me back, telling me to give him five minutes, he stepped away for a bathroom break.

I turn down a small side street and find the Audi. Just as I'm about to pull open the door, a strong hand catches my arm and turns me around.

My father pins me against the car, his expression a hard wall of contempt, but I make out a glint of amusement in his eyes.

"What the hell is wrong with you?" His voice is soft, but

not in a kind way, the razor-sharp words cutting straight through the core of me.

I grit my teeth and draw back my arm, but he won't loosen his grip.

"Who the hell do you think you are? You think you can do whatever you want and get away with it, don't you?"

His eyes flicker with anger, and then I realize that bitch must have said something to him and sent him after me.

My jaw clenches. "Let me go."

He doesn't let go. He grips me harder.

"Don't embarrass me," he hisses, each word tight and clipped, a rubber band about to snap, like he's scared someone might hear.

It only makes me want to be louder.

I frown, heat collecting in my chest, thickening my words. "She's more than half your age. You're embarrassing yourself. Let me—"

His free hand flies up to meet my face. The hit throws my head to the side. I feel it in my ear first, a prickly, tingling sensation, spreading slowly, then heat flashes across my cheek like a hot iron against my skin. I go still from the shock of it, the humiliation of it, then stare up at him, refusing to look away. But he doesn't meet my eyes. He's busy glancing around to see if anyone saw.

There's no one here. We're tucked too far away from the main street. But I wish everyone could witness the monster he really is.

I watch his neck and chest flush as if the anger has begun to burn his skin, my fingers digging into my palm.

He releases my arm and leans in a bit, eyes searching mine. "Don't embarrass me," he says again, the words a warning, and then stalks away.

I keep my eyes on him until he turns the corner. Goose

bumps rise on my skin. I swallow and puff out a breath, realizing I've started to hold it in, adrenaline rushing through me. My arm pulses where he gripped me. My jaw stings.

If there was any doubt left in me, any hesitation, any ambivalence at all, he just completely fucking demolished it.

When I get home and walk out past the pergola, Jared's at the front edge of the infinity pool in the smallest pair of swimming trunks I've ever seen, the outline of his dick visible through the fabric, practically winking as he poses for Mei. She's straddling a swan floaty in an equally tiny black bikini, trying to get the best angle of him with her DSLR camera without falling into the water or dropping the half-smoked cigarette between her fingers. Her hair is wet and dripping, a slow trickle down her back.

"All my parents do is go at each other ever since we found out about the bankruptcy," Jared says, flexing the muscles in his arms but trying to make it look like he's not. "I honestly have no idea how people live like this. My level of depression is beyond."

Mei takes a couple shots. "Pretty sure some people are born into it, but I hear you."

"I wake up with zero motivation to do anything."

"So...like always."

She laughs, smoke streaming from her nostrils. Jared joins in, the irony not lost on him. I don't.

"Unless we want to be slaves to paychecks for the rest of our lives," I say, biting back my rising frustration, "we need to expedite the plan. This asshole is talking about a Fourth of July wedding."

They both notice me at the same time and stop what they're doing.

Mei's eyes almost pop out of her head. "Wedding...as in nuptials?"

I walk over to Mei and take the Nikon from her hand. I need to do something with my hands before I lose it. "He's engaged."

My eyes fall down Jared's body.

"Move your..." I gesture to his crotch with my eyes. "IG will flag it."

Jared adjusts himself in the trunks so his bulge is less in-your-face and continues posing, shifting into the light. I snap a few pictures.

"What about Brandi?" Mei asks, shifting closer to me.

I glance at her, then get a few more shots of Jared and delete the ones with too much glare from the sun. "What about her?"

She levels a gaze with me and holds it. "You really think she won't talk?"

I don't know. I still don't trust her. She has the ten grand, but she could still talk. It's risky.

"Don't worry about it," Jared says. "She won't tell."

I frown and hand him the bulky Nikon. "What makes you so sure?"

"You said she didn't take the money, so I showed her a good time."

"Meaning?" I ask, impatient.

"Got her the works at the spa and then snagged some Balmain." He shrugs. "Figured it'd keep her mouth shut."

Mei makes a sour face. "Before or after I bought her *two* fucking Chanel bags?"

My head is already shaking. "Tell me you're joking."

They both stare at me, waiting.

"I ended up giving her the ten thousand dollars to cover her tuition," I tell them.

Jared hands the camera back to me. "Okay, Miss Overachiever. You win. Now, can we do some with me climbing out the water? Got this cool caption about a phoenix I've been dying to use."

Mei laughs. "The phoenix emerges from ashes, not water, you—"

"Will you two focus? I said *code red*." My blood feels so hot in my veins, like burning flames. "That bitch. Who the fuck does she think she is? Do you know what I had to do to get that money?"

"You?" Jared gapes at me. "I went over my limit on all my credit cards and you *know* my situation right now."

No one says anything else for a while.

Mei takes a long drag of her cigarette and lets the smoke out of her nose.

"We could get rid of her, too," she says after a moment, looking directly at me. Her eyes flash with something deliciously dark that makes my heart skip a few beats. "Keeping this chick quiet obviously isn't working."

Jared rolls his eyes. "What are we, serial killers now?"

"You're not a serial killer until you kill three people."

He just stares at her, maybe waiting for a *just kidding* like I am, but it never comes.

"It's true," Mei says with a shrug instead and takes another draw from her smoke. "We need to get her off our backs before this gets out of control and she starts making demands."

"You really think she'd do that, though?" Jared asks. "She was kinda cool."

"This is what people do. They get greedy. We're all milked dry already. What do you think she's gonna do when we don't have anything left to give?"

"Okay, we can't kill her, Mei," I snap, a lick of frustration in my voice.

That would be messy and stupid.

Mei rolls her eyes. "So what are we gonna do?"

I swallow, running my hand through my blowout, mind churning.

Jared studies me. "Can't you get Nate to straighten her out?"

I pause. Then fight to keep my voice level, detached. "It won't work. He's in love with her."

He told me himself when I was on the phone with him, right before I sent him the pictures of Brandi's mug shot. I asked him, point-blank. He didn't even hesitate.

"The only way we'll get away with it is if we pin it on someone else. If the cops have a prime suspect, they won't come after me." I sigh, still shuffling through the jumble of thoughts swarming my brain. "Come on, think. If I'm going to split my money with you guys, you're gonna have to pull your weight."

"Izzy," Mei says, right away. "Easy."

I shake my head. I've already thought of that. "No motive. They're not married yet."

She bites her lip, the cigarette forgotten between her fingers. "Then who do we pin it on?"

I stare at her, mind racing, and then it comes to me, that final piece to the puzzle that makes the image so clear. "Hold your breath. I'm fucking brilliant."

They both stare at me, waiting with their heads cocked in anticipation.

"We kill two birds with one stone. Brandi, the sociopathic, wannabe fashion girl who got turned down for the job of her dreams. She goes down for his murder. I get my payout from the estate because everything is in my name. Nate is mine again. It's beyond genius."

Mei snorts right away. "What have you been bingeing on Netflix? That shit is dripping in melodrama."

"I'm with Mei," Jared says. "Who kills the CEO of a company for not hiring them?"

I roll my eyes and start to pace. It'll work. I know it will. It has to. "Listen. The wannabe fashion girl who got turned down for the job of her dreams *email-stalks* the CEO who she's stupidly in love with, then murders him out of pure jealous rage when she finds out he's engaged."

Jared raises a brow. "Like a crime of passion?"

"You can falsify some emails, right? Make it look like they were fucking. Like it was all planned from the start."

Mei shakes her head, hesitant. "I don't know."

I glance at Jared. He doesn't look sold, either.

I sigh and turn away, pulling my top over my shoulders. I step out of my jeans and lower myself into the pool a few inches at a time, until I'm waist deep.

"Okay," I say, thinking out loud. "Brandi, the poor little black girl from Jersey, wants a bigger, shinier life in the city. She pursues a position at Van Doren not only to be a fashion girl, but also to get close to *Simon Van Doren*, her secret crush. People think my father is hot, right?"

Jared makes a grunting sound. "I'd get on my knees for your dad in a heartbeat."

I frown. "Ew. What the fuck?"

He shrugs, smirking. "Sorry for the visual."

I force that image out of my head and fall back into my train of thought. "So we fabricate emails that make her seem like some obsessed bitch who goes batshit on him when he gets engaged to some other chick."

"Because it was supposed to be her," Mei says, finishing my thought, and the edges of a smile find me.

"Exactly. She threatens him in the last one we write. He ghosts her. Then *boom*, a couple days later his heart stops."

Jared stares at me, and I think I peep a twinkle of awe in his eyes. "I'm impressed. Your coldness is truly unrivaled."

"She has a criminal record." I shrug. "It won't be that much of a stretch."

I slip my head beneath the water for a few moments, then pull myself back up to the surface.

"I still think something's missing," Mei says, thoughtfully.

I frown at her, sweeping hair out of my face. "We have motive. Method. Pattern. What else is there?"

She thinks it over. "I don't know. We need something to really seal the deal if we're gonna go with the obsessed-lover trope. Emails are too basic."

I sigh, realizing she's right. We need something more solid. Undeniable.

We all go quiet. I dip back into the water.

Then I remember.

I break through the surface again. Smooth my hair from my face. "Jared, go get my phone." He stares at me like I've lost my mind. "Just do it. You'll thank me later."

15

TAYLOR

I'm pretending to study a five-foot painting on the wall ahead of me that's allegedly reminiscent of Salvador Dali's work, but all I can think about is the Salvatore Ferragamo ankle booties that I saw earlier at Bergdorf's. Even after three consecutive Art Basels and a personalized Louvre walk-through with my hot French professor, I still don't get visual art, especially the old shit. All I see is random colors and abstract lines that don't make sense. I don't see a story. I don't *feel* anything.

I've been here for over an hour and nothing has moved me yet. Nothing has even stirred me until a shadow looms over me from behind. I shift slightly. Jared gives me a small smile, a breath away.

I turn back to the painting. "So do you think it'll work?"

He speaks close enough to my ear to send a shiver down my spine. "You know the password to your dad's desktop, right?"

"Mom's birthday."

He scoffs. "Bastard. Did you finish the drafts for the emails?"

I reach into my purse and slip him a flash drive, keeping my hand close to my side. "Torch this when you're done sending them."

He lifts my hand to his mouth and kisses me there as he takes the tiny device from me, so smooth, and slips it into his pocket.

I study him for a moment, conscious of how he always manages to make me smile. "How do you even know how to do this?"

He keeps his eye on the wall as he speaks, the same as me. "Was dating this guy a few months back. He thought it was more than it was. They all do. Out of nowhere he shows me screenshots of all these guys I was DMing and whatever. Tells me he installed this key-logger software on my phone that tracked my keystrokes. He used the logs to figure out my passwords and spy on me." He shrugs. "Taught myself that shit in case it ever came in handy."

I glance around at slow-moving people. "So how long will it take?"

"I can install the software remotely tonight. So as soon as she logs into her email…"

I lick my lips, trying to find any holes. Nothing jumps out. Jared pulls a prepaid cell phone from his structured Prada and hands it over. "We only communicate with these until he's in the ground, and everything dies down, got it?"

"Yeah." I take the burner and drop it into my purse.

"Hey," Jared says softly, his hand brushing against mine.

I stop and look at him, but he doesn't say anything. "What?"

He searches my eyes for a moment, then swallows so hard, I hear the sound. "You sure you want to do this? Like, really sure?"

The way he says it, gingerly, like he's afraid that the question will anger me, I know that the finality of all this is finally dawning on him. And I get where he's coming from, but this isn't just about the money or my father. It never has been.

This is about so much more than that.

I have to do this. For my mother.

"I need this," I say, trying to sound firm, but there's a hitch in my voice, and I know I only have so much time before the tears. "You know I need this."

"I know. I know." He looks away, takes a breath, then his eyes meet mine again. "But are you sure you want to go through with it? The whole thing?"

I lift a hand and pat at the corner of my eyes with my finger. "It's not just for me. If he hurt my mother the way he did, the mother of his child...imagine what he'll do to someone else. If we get rid of him, we could be saving someone else."

It takes Jared a beat to nod, then he eases a hand around my waist, kissing me quickly on my cheek before slipping away without another word.

Three hours later the burner phone rings on my bed. I roll over and answer it.

"Got her password," Jared says, and I can almost hear his smile.

"Wow. You always finish so fast?"

We both laugh at that.

"I'm gonna spread the emails out over the next few days, then send the ones where she threatens him back-to-back."

I roll that over in my head. "So that brings us to...Friday."

"We do the hit Sunday night?"

"Sunday won't work. He doesn't drink on Sundays. Jesus or whatever. Has to be during the week. He does the same routine every day. Comes home, does some work, caps it off with a glass of Macallan."

"Okay. Monday, then. We'll line all his glasses with the HCN, so no matter which one he picks, he's a goner."

I bite my lip. "Stop. You're making my nipples hard."

He laughs. "Shut up. Bye."

The flip phone buzzes ten minutes later. I check the screen.

Just sent the first email. Check his computer. Make sure everything looks good.

I head downstairs to my father's office. It's empty, of course. He'll probably be locked into a string of meetings for another few hours. I click into the mail app on his desktop and open the email Jared just sent from Brandi's account.

To: Simon Van Doren
From: Brandi.Maxwell1998@gmail.com
Subject: it's me

I turned down some lame guy at the bar last night. He got mad and asked me if I was a lesbian. I said, "No, I love big fat dicks in my mouth," and he left. I was thinking about you. I miss you. Can I see you tonight?

A jolt of relief moves through me. I can't believe it actually worked. My heart is pounding. I drag the message into the trash, just like my father would have done, and then text Jared back: Everything looks good. I put it in the trash for now. It'll stay there for two weeks. But dial it back some. Big fat dicks? Lol This is supposed to be coming from her, not you. Just copy and paste what I wrote for the rest.

Jared: Ok, gonna send 3 more tomorrow. Then u jump in. When u reply, make sure u reply to the chain. Friday will be the last one.

Me: Got it.

By the time Friday rolls along, all the emails have been sent. Nine messages total. I reread them again, then pick up the burner phone and call Jared.

I'm laughing when he answers. *"'Limp-dick son of a bitch.'"*

I can hear his smile. "Was thinking of you when I added it. That last one wasn't too on the nose, was it?"

"Just right." I can't help but smile. "When the cops find this chain, we're bathing in benjis."

Cindy Crawford walks into the room and jumps onto the bed. I reach over and rub her back as she purrs. "How's Mei doing with the HCN?"

"Haven't heard from her," Jared says. "You?"

"Radio silence."

As if on cue, a text comes through. It's Mei. The dove has flown the coop.

"She just texted me," I say to Jared. "She has the powder."

"Okay, question. How do we get it into Brandi's apartment?"

"We need to get rid of both of them for a while. They have to be gone at the same time or it won't work." I bite my lip, thinking. "Don't worry. I know how. She's desperate for a new job, right?"

"Yeah," he says. "What are you thinking?"

Monday takes forever to come. Maybe it's just the anticipation. By ten thirty, I'm in the car waiting in front of Nate's building, watching as he turns out of the front door, slinging his duffel over his shoulder. He doesn't slip into a waiting car or jog down into the subway. He heads to the gym on foot, AirPods in.

He goes every day. Same time.

Brandi was right. Nate is still as diligent about his training as he was back when we were at Regency. I never understood his overachieving mindset. His father is a football legend. There has to be something in his genes. He's never had to try as hard as he does, but then maybe his commitment has always been about proving himself, about showing the world that he's as good as his father.

Commitment.

I fucked things up. I know I did. But that was so long ago. I couldn't see it then, but Nate was the once-in-a-lifetime kind of boyfriend, like Dean was to Rory. I would never hurt him the way I did back then. Never. I just need him to give me a second chance.

But first things first.

Once I can no longer see Nate, I glance at the time on my phone. Mei should be calling me any—

"Where are you?" I ask, in lieu of a greeting. There is no time for small talk.

"Climbing out of the station now," she says, drily.

"ETA?"

"Calm down. I'm down the street."

"Sorry," I say, glancing in the passenger mirror. "I just always wanted to say that."

I keep the phone to my ear as I step out onto the concrete. I barely have time to fret over the fresh soles of my new Fenty sling backs getting their first scuff marks before I see Mei approaching.

"Is the lobby empty?" she asks.

"It's just one doorman. He was reading something. Should be easy."

She ends the call just as I'm about to run through the plan one more time.

"You just hung up on me," I say, feigning shock as I wave my phone in the air.

"We're face-to-face," she says, stopping a foot in front of me, but that's not the point. "That's kind of how this works."

We're about a half block away from the entrance of Nate's building and huddled up under the awning of a yoga studio with a sign in front that promises sixty-minute classes by the best ganja instructor in the city. We recap the plan, and our run-through is punctuated by simultaneous nods. It's solid. We're good to go.

"Wait. Did you bring it?" I ask her, eyeing her mini handbag, which looks small enough for Barbie, not large enough to carry the one prop we need to pull this off—the most integral part of our plan.

She stops. "Shit, I left it at the studio," she says, dramatically slapping her palm to her forehead in a way that matches the sarcasm in her tone.

I let out a breath. The stakes are too high for mistakes and slip-ups. I was just double-crossing our T's.

Rolling her eyes, Mei dips her hand into the pocket of her oversize gray hoodie that she's wearing over a pair of black stirrup pants and a ridiculous red tutu, and now the mini bag makes sense. It's been so long since I've worn anything with pockets, I've forgotten how convenient they are. She pulls out the vial, holding it so only I can see it. I instinctively clench the muscles in my lower abdomen toward my spine. The deep red liquid looks like actual blood even though I know it's not. She snuck into the costume room at the theater she's dancing at last night and stole some of the stage blood they're using for one of the contemporary ballet performances that involves murder.

I check the time again. It's only been a couple of minutes. I need to chill.

"Okay," I say, flicking a glance toward the entrance of Nate's building. "You ready?"

Mei makes a face. She is fearless. She's also a professional performer, so her confidence seeps into me as I break away and make my way inside the lobby.

It goes even more flawlessly than I could have imagined.

As soon as the doorman lifts his head from the Grisham novel in his hands at my frantic announcement that there's a girl bleeding outside, he springs into action, because he is an idiot.

I've clocked him at midforties after assessing the girth of his belly and the thinning of his hair at the crown of his head. He's basically the type of guy who's been overlooked and underestimated his entire life and is dying for his chance to be a hero. The way he leaps from behind the large wooden desk to help Mei, moving so fast it defies the limitations of a middle-aged, overweight man who spends ninety percent of his day on his ass, reaffirms that we couldn't have had a better adversary. He's perfect. He rushes out to Mei's side, the beautiful ballerina who's taken a nasty fall right outside the building, the damsel in distress who needs a guy like Mr. Doorman to help her to her feet and whatever else a man does after he rescues a woman. The last I see of him before I slip behind the front desk is him on his knees, mouth agape, hopefully too distracted by all that blood to notice that Mei hasn't actually been punctured by anything.

I crouch behind the desk and look for the spare key fob that will let me inside Nate's unit. At first, I freak. I don't immediately see where they're kept and all the worst-case scenarios flash through my head. The doorman seeing me behind his desk. Calling the police. This getting out to the press. I force myself to suck in a breath and finally see them in all their plastic glory, right smack-dab in front of my face.

In the elevator on the way to the fifth floor, I hold it in my palm like it's a rare gem. But it's even more valuable than that. This is literally the fucking key to inheriting my father's entire fortune.

16

BRANDI

Nate and I avoid each other cautiously for a couple of days or so, like we did in the beginning, when things were still provisional, fresh and new and uncertain, and we were afraid of stepping over each other's personal boundaries into that realm of intolerance. There are words that need to be said, but we don't say any of them. We haven't been the same since our fight. Some dynamic has shifted between us—I know he must feel it too. Everything's been off. Forced. Quiet.

I hate when he's quiet. I'm tired of feeling like I'm walking on eggshells. I'm tired of him avoiding me. I want us to go back to normal. I need him to be my best friend again.

But Nate has made no attempts to break our silence, even when we cross paths in the morning or at night before bed, and I don't know how much longer I can endure it, this seething, suffocating thing.

When I get back from my interview, the apartment is empty. Nate's at the gym; he texted me while I was on the train, telling me he wouldn't be home until later.

He didn't say when later, just *later*.

The rest of the day moves past me. I don't do much, just throw in a couple loads of laundry, straighten up the apartment a little. After I'm done cleaning, I look for more jobs on Indeed and Glassdoor, and after feeling like a failure for a while, I switch to watching hair videos on YouTube because even though I want to be productive, I just can't deal right now. I take a quick shower and slip into one of Nate's old football sweatshirts because he loves when I wear his clothes, and lightly line my eyes and lips, then light a few candles in the kitchen.

It's been a while since I've cooked for Nate. It's a small gesture, but I'm hoping this will ease some of the tension between us. Usually, when he's here, he's the one who ends up doing most of the cooking once we get sick of takeout, but he loves when I make dinner for him. I could really go for some spinach-stuffed pesto ravioli and fresh garlic bread, but I am not Padma Lakshmi, and so I decide to take the path of least resistance and make noodles, which isn't as selfish as it sounds since it's Nate's favorite. I go into the kitchen and start chopping the veggies.

My neck snaps up when the front door finally swings open. The sun has already started to slip from the sky and streak the horizon with shades of pink, and I'm just now realizing how late it is.

Nate eases inside, shirtless, in nothing but a pair of black running shorts and sneakers. I stop chopping. Sweat dampens his hair, which tells me he's been at it for hours at the gym, but I can't help but wonder if he's been somewhere else all this time. He's been gone for over six hours.

"Hey," I say, doing my best to sound cheerful.

When he looks over and finds me standing behind the counter in the kitchen, he seems startled that I've broken our silence.

"Hey." The tension on his face doesn't ease once he meets my eyes. His brows lift. "You're cooking?"

I give him a smile, hoping it's enough. "Yeah. Mushroom Pad Thai."

He glances down at the shirt I'm wearing, then back up as if he likes that I'm wearing it but doesn't say anything about me making his favorite meal. He puts his bag down and walks up to the side of the counter. "How'd your interview go?"

"It was a scam," I say. Which I should've known. It was nothing I was particularly excited about, not a job in fashion or industry-adjacent, just an entry-level position at an office downtown. But the pay was decent, there were flexible hours for when classes start up again, an inordinate amount of PTO and health insurance. It came out of nowhere. It was too good to be true. I should have known.

"What?" Nate asks.

"The address wasn't even right. It was their old office."

"Damn, I'm sorry. Everything looked legit."

I don't look at him. "Yeah, well. It definitely wasn't."

A moment passes. "You okay?" Nate asks.

"I'm fine." I pick up the knife again and start slicing the bok choy.

"Okay." Nate glances down at the cutting board, then heads toward the bathroom. "Smells good."

A smile tugs at the corners of my mouth, a tinge of hope building inside. "It's almost done. Go take your shower and it'll be ready by the time you're finished."

"Okay," he says, but he lingers in the doorway.

I don't say anything. I'm hoping he will, but then I hear the water come on in the shower. When I look back, the door is halfway shut.

When Nate's clean and dry, he sits down at the table and starts eating immediately. He doesn't say a word to me, though I feel his eyes watching me, on and off. The air between us feels tense and uncertain. We eat in almost dead silence. Occasionally, I glance up, and when I do, Nate doesn't look away, but there's still something distant in his eyes. Contemplative. This lasts for approximately ten minutes until at some point I ask the obligatory *how is it*, and he mumbles, *it's good*, and then I don't know what to say from there, so I shut up and continue stuffing my face. Even when we're done and I'm washing the dishes, he doesn't say much. Only a few words here and there, which is more like politeness than conversation and it stings.

I put the dishes away, sweep the floor and wipe the counters clean. Nate stays in the living room and turns on ESPN. It's the same routine he's been doing for the past couple of days. The perfect way to ignore me. I roll my eyes and grab my phone. Any hope I felt withers up and dies.

Five minutes later the sound from the TV stops. I glance over and see that Nate's still sitting on the couch, staring at the blank screen, his expression unreadable.

I look away and open the fridge for a bottle of water. Just as I close the door, I feel heat easing around my waist, a grip tightening. "Hey."

I jump and whip around. "God. You scared me." I'm nearly breathless. My eyes flutter. "Yeah?"

He licks his lips and it takes him a minute to look up at me. I can smell him now that he's so close, the scent of clean water and soap still clinging to his skin, and I want to bury my face into the curve of his neck, that cozy, perfect nook.

"I shouldn't have flipped out on you like that the other day," he finally says.

I study him. It's obvious now how much this has been eating him up. "Nate, it's fine. I don't care about—"

"*I* care. I shouldn't have…" He takes a breath, stops himself from getting worked up. "I overreacted. I'm sorry, babe."

And now I understand his quietness. He's been feeling

guilty, which only makes *me* feel guilty. This whole thing is my fault, not his.

I let out a sigh, thinking back to how this all started. "No. I was way out of line. You were right. I should've just come to you for the money. I never should have gotten involved with Taylor." I pause for a moment. "And I shouldn't have lied to you."

The air is heavy with silence when I stop again, and neither of us breaks it. Nate is looking away, and I have no idea what's going on inside his head, but for the first time the tension isn't as palpable between us.

"I'm sorry," I whisper.

Nate finally looks back at me, not with anger, but with something else just as dangerous because it's soft and kind and I've never wanted him more than I do in this moment.

And then the edges of a smile break through. "Thanks for dinner," he says, his voice suddenly husky.

He sweeps my hair to the side, exposing my throat. I don't say anything, just lean for his mouth. I can't take it anymore. He gasps, just a little, not expecting my fire. I kiss him harder. His hands grip my waist as he tries his best to keep up with me.

I pull back, panting. "I hate when we fight."

"Especially over petty shit."

"Fighting over petty shit is for those other couples."

He smiles against my mouth, strokes my chin with the pad of his thumb. "Then let's not fight anymore," he says, and I feel lost, so lost in the rush of blood, of heat that seems to burn away every thought. This time, when our eyes meet, his gaze is as hot as mine. The bottle of water slips from my hand as I collapse into him. He has to hold me up to keep us both from falling over and I feel completely weak against his strength. And then my fingers are in his hair, his hand under my shirt, my skin between his teeth.

Nate's hands slide down my legs and he lifts me up like my weight means absolutely nothing to him. A laugh pops from my mouth when he drops me down onto the bed. He shifts over me, solid and safe, and waits until I meet his eyes.

"Hi," he says, close enough for the word to spill straight into my mouth. And then, a flicker of a smile.

I grin back. "Hi."

"I love you."

"I love you too."

Nate doesn't take the sweatshirt off, just moves inside me and holds on to it like it's the only thing that's keeping him from flying away. But I need it off. I need to feel his skin against mine, the humid heat of it. I push myself up and yank it over my head until there's truly no space between us, no boundaries, no limits. I don't know if it's the whole make-up sex thing or the fact that we both know Nate will be leaving in a few days or something else entirely, but tonight feels more intense than all the other times. Emotions rage through us like fire, hot and burning and unstoppable, and it's like we're fucking on the edge of the world. Nate tucks a hand under the small of my back, pushing farther, deeper, and I'm suddenly overwhelmed by the strength of him, the need in him. My nails dig into the flesh of his back, and he grips the headboard, keeps moving inside me like he's not going to stop until the edges of my soul rise in my eyes, and when I feel him start to tremble and slip away, I reach between us and put him back inside as if it's where he belongs. He moans, a small, tender sound, and it's beautiful. I grip his hair and kiss him slow, still rocking into him, not wanting it to be over. He rests his head against my chest, my sweat becoming his, his becoming mine. We stay like this for a few minutes, listening to each other's heartbeat.

★ ★ ★

In the morning, sunlight pours in through the windows, the sheets twisted around my body. I can feel Nate behind me, a hard mass of warmth at my back. My head moves on the pillow; it's still warm and damp with the smell of us. I start to turn over, but he's awake already and stops me, hand easing around my waist. "What did you dream about?" he whispers, scooting closer.

I smile and reach for my phone to check the time. "Can't remember them. You knocked me out cold."

Nate's hand slides down between my legs.

I bite back a moan and smile. "Dreaming hard, huh?"

We both laugh.

Nate presses his face into my neck. "Want to real quick before I hit the gym?"

"Yeah, but go slow."

I glance at the time as Nate shifts beside me, still working his hand on me, in me. It's only eight. Too early. Before I put my phone back, I click into Twitter, just to see if there's anything interesting trending. Immediately, I see a sea of RIP tweets under one of the hashtags and retweets of a TMZ story that just broke two hours ago. "Oh, my God," I say, grabbing Nate's hand.

He chuckles into my skin. "Already?"

"No," I say, the blood cooling within my body. "Stop."

His arm is slack when I move it away and push up to my elbows, clicking the link that brings me to the full story. "'Breaking news: Fashion titan Simon Van Doren found dead in his Nassau County compound early this morning.'"

"What?" Nate grabs my phone and reads it for himself. "Damn." His eyes flick over to me, but I don't know what to say. I'm still trying to process this.

I take my phone back and skim the rest.

Van Doren was taken to Lenox Hill Hospital, where doctors pronounced him dead on arrival. An official statement has not yet been released by the family.

I don't know what or even how to feel, so many thoughts ricocheting inside my head at once. I knew this was going to happen, but somehow, even after all the anticipation, it still feels so unexpected, like the world has stopped spinning.

Nate's hand touches my leg, and I flinch.

"Hey." He waits until I turn to face him. "Maybe it was the cancer. Don't freak out about this, okay? Not until we know more."

But I already know.

I don't know how, but I know, with unwavering certainty, that Taylor murdered her father, and that absolutely terrifies me.

17

TAYLOR

I don't know how I expected to feel. Happy? Relieved? Triumphant? I don't know. I don't know what I feel. It's a certain kind of numbness that feels almost like nothing, but it's something—something I know I've never felt before, like there's been a hollow space carved in my chest. A void. I don't know if it's a good thing yet. I'm still trying to get used to it.

It feels surreal. I know that vile bastard is dead. I know he'll never hurt me or my mom, or any other woman again, but even after the paramedics wheeled his body out of here, even after the medical examiner made the pronouncement, it doesn't feel as final as I thought it would. Maybe because I wasn't there. I wasn't in that room when he took his last breath. I didn't get to see the shock and fear rise in his eyes as the poison took over, didn't hear his last cry for help. Didn't get to see him struggle in those last few moments the way he deserved to struggle. Hear him scream. Hear him choke on his own breath. I almost feel robbed.

But it's done. It's over.

Every channel is reporting the shocking news. They've already turned him into a saint and it's nauseating.

Simon Van Doren dead at fifty-five, found unconscious in his home by his fiancée at 9:35 p.m.

TMZ was the first to break the story. Of course. Because they don't care about anything except ratings. I saw it on Twitter before that bitch even called me. Izzy. Saying she found him on the floor of his office, unresponsive. Confirming what I already knew.

I did my absolute best to affect genuine surprise—tears and all. I know the cops are going to review the phone records, use the first call she made for evidence once they get her side of the story. They always do.

I played my part. I played it well.

I feel a headache coming on. A real banger, the kind of pounding that makes you feel like your head is going to implode.

I've been crying for so long, I'm starting to believe the tears myself.

There are two cops staring at me, standing only a few feet away, hushed suspicion in their every move. The taller one is a black woman, clearly sharper and more fit than her partner. Officer Glover. She's probably in her thirties but looks older, like life has thrown her against the wall a few too many times.

The man at her side, Detective Bierman, says he's the lead in this case. Close-cropped silver hair sits over clear blue eyes and a broad nose. Just by the way he moves, with an assumed authority, I can tell he's more experienced, but right away something tells me he's not the one I need to be worried about. A badge peeks out from his jacket whenever he gestures for Glover to take a note that she seems to be already jotting down every single time.

I have to swallow to form a word. "I bought him that bottle of scotch." My voice is rough, as if I've been screaming. I shake my head slowly. "It was a gift for entering remission."

I glance up at them, but only for a second, just to gauge their reactions, and heavy tears drop from my eyes, streaking more mascara down my face.

Both officers wait me out, never taking their eyes off me.

I sniff hard and cough so I don't choke on my own saliva. "It's like it's my fault," I say, sinking deeper in my chair like some inexplicable force from within is dragging me closer to hell. The words sound like I'm speaking through water.

Bierman gives me a sympathetic look, his eyes softening just a bit. "Ms. Van Doren, no one thinks it was your fault. This was clearly a premeditated situation." His tone is friendly. If he thinks I'm lying, he doesn't show it.

"Our guys found residue on all of the other glasses," Glover says. "It appears as if someone laced them all. So whoever it was seems to have been inside the office before your father arrived home last night."

"Or they were able to slip into his office while he was here," Bierman clarifies.

I'm already shaking my head. "Dad never let anyone else in the office. It's his...*was* his sacred space."

Bierman studies me. "We found a...a pair of underwear that his fiancée..." He trails off as he glances down at his own blank notepad and struggles. Then he flicks a glance toward the female cop.

"Izzy," she says without consulting her notes.

He nods. "Right. Izzy identified as hers lying near his desk."

Of course that asshole couldn't go one night without touching her.

"We spoke to her earlier," Glover says. "She confirmed there was no one else in the house at the time. The entire

staff had gone home for the day. She was alone with him before he had his drink."

"She didn't do it," I blurt out, a little too quickly.

They exchange a glance. Glover flashes her partner a triumphant look, which says *I told you so* louder than her words
probably could.

Bierman returns his gaze to me and it's clear they are not
on the same page. His eyes are much less probing, much less
skeptical. "Ms. Van Doren, you say that with such conviction. Izzy was the only one here at the time of the incident."
He pauses and raises a thick brow. "Do you know something
we don't?"

He holds my gaze. I refuse to blink or look away.

We've already discussed my alibi. I spent the night at Jared's;
so did Mei. At this stage in their investigation, they have every
reason to suspect it must have been Izzy, especially with no
evidence incriminating either one of us. She was the one to
make the 911 call. She was the last one to see him alive.

I sniffle and blow out a long breath, like all of this is so
devastating for me, and say, "Well, I would think it's obvious that a woman like Izzy was only with my father for his
money." I have to pause to make sure my voice gives nothing
away. "So don't you think she would've waited until *after* the
wedding to kill him?"

Glover shoots Bierman another boastful look.

He clears his throat and now I'm sure Glover's the cleverer
one. "Since you're so sure about it not being your father's fiancée who did this, any idea who it could be?"

I take a deep breath and frown as if I'm truly thinking hard.

"Your father had a current will, correct?" Glover asks. "I
would think so, with his diagnosis."

"I think he drew one up with our lawyer," I say with a
shrug.

She scribbles something. "Had you seen it?"

"He didn't really include me in stuff like that. Why?"

"He wasn't married, and you're his only child. That meant everything went to you, right?"

I shrug again. "My dad was super generous. I'm sure there were a bunch of charities and—"

"But not for long, because your father was engaged, correct?" Before I have a chance to respond, Glover sets down her pen and cocks her head. "How'd you feel about his fiancée? Aside from your suspicions that she was only after his money. You like her?"

"As a person?"

"Sure."

"She was great for my dad," I say about a woman I barely know. "Even if she was only using him, he was finally happy again. It's been so hard ever since my mom…"

I let my words trail off and I stare blankly at the wall in front of me until I feel the prickle of tears in both eyes. When I shut them, they drip down my face. I part my lips, make it look like I'm gasping for breath, chest heaving.

"I'm just trying to—"

"Glover," Bierman cuts in.

I glance up at him and catch him giving her an *ease up* look, and I have to fight against the buzz of victory and keep up the despondent act. His stern expression makes it clear that he's her superior, but when he hands me a tissue, his features have noticeably softened. I see Glover glance at me, her face still hard, not an ounce of sympathy, maybe even resentment for getting called out by her more senior colleague. I've got nothing against her, but the tears worked and now I feel much more confident about plowing through the rest of this third degree.

Bierman takes a step closer to me. "Did your father have any kind of business nemesis that you know of? Think it could have been someone on your staff here? Had he received any digital threats recently?"

"No, none that I know of. And no." I heave a sigh, forcing more tears to fall, then gulp for oxygen and try to breathe. My voice breaks. "He just beat cancer. He was so happy. This is so fucked up."

I start to cry again, louder than even before. My face hurts. My eyes burn. It's almost like these tears are real.

"All right, Ms. Van Doren," Bierman says. "What we'll do is draft a warrant application and affidavit. We'll need to examine the entire house, including your father's computer. Laptop. Phone. See if we can find anything there. We'll also need to check his office. Go through his files and find out who might have reason to hold a grudge."

Glover cuts in, "And that copy of the will I requested should be waiting on my desk when I get there. I'll give that a nice comb-through."

Bierman gives her a strong look. Then he looks back at me, sympathetic.

"Do you have somewhere you can stay for the next couple of days, Ms. Van Doren?"

I almost perk up. Almost. But I will my expression to remain the way it is, somber, sad, hopeless, and jump up to my feet for dramatic effect, sliding my Louis Vuitton into the crook of my arm. "Just do whatever it takes to find out who did this to my father."

18

BRANDI

The doorbell rings and Nate and I both jump. No one ever rings the bell. Not without the doorman alerting us first.

Nate is on his feet first. "Expecting someone?" he asks, glancing back at me.

"No," I say in a hushed voice. I jump up from the bed, slip into the first pair of jeans I find, and then I'm right on his heels as he approaches the door.

He leans close to the door, peering out the peephole, then stops moving completely. He doesn't even blink.

"What?" I whisper under my breath. "Who is it?"

"Looks like a couple of cops," he hisses.

I freeze. Pull my lip in. My heart quickens. "You think it's about… What do I say?"

He stares at me directly in my eyes and firms his voice, still whispering. "You know nothing. You heard nothing."

Two hard knocks sound on the other side of the door. I nod and Nate removes the safety lock, swings it open.

A man and a woman peer in. They're both dressed in plain clothes, but they're definitely cops. It's in their posture, in the way they carry themselves, something subtle, but obvious to me. There's nothing subtle about the guns holstered at their waists. I can see a vague bulge through the black woman's slate-colored blazer, but the man has his on display, one hand on his hip like a warning.

His gaze moves over me, and he smiles like we've met before, but I know better than to trust it. "Are you Brandi Maxwell?"

My throat feels like I've just swallowed hot grease. "Yeah."

He holds out a small, calloused hand. "I'm Detective Bierman. This is Officer Glover."

I shake his hand, but I'm immediately self-conscious about my grip. I don't want it to be too strong and come off as aggressive, but don't want to seem meek, either, like he can just intimidate me, so I struggle to find the balance between the two and pull my hand back before he can feel my sweat.

Glover extends her hand as well, and at first, I am wholly disappointed. Her dark skin and gold badge feel so deeply incongruous, it's almost surreal. When she shakes my hand, she is not aggressive at all.

"I know it's early, but I'm hoping you can help us out. We have a warrant to search this apartment," Bierman says, pulling out a crinkled document and flashing it my way. I barely get a glance before he folds it back up and tucks it into his pocket. "Can we take a look inside and ask you a few questions about your relationship with Simon Van Doren?"

He asks this as if I actually have a choice. Nate steps to the side and they both file in, glancing around the apartment with intense, scrutinizing gazes. I don't know what they're looking for, but they inspect the room for a long time, saying nothing to us, exchanging nothing between each other.

Nate speaks up from beside me, following them through the living room. "What is this about?" he asks, his voice calm, respectful.

I walk slightly behind him, trying my best to keep my cool.

I still don't know why they would need to question me. How do they even know I know Simon?

Bierman looks at Nate and smiles, but there's nothing friendly about it. "You must be the boyfriend. Protective. Cute." But he sounds as though he doesn't think it's cute at all. The way he says the word, it's more of an insult, and immediately I get a distinct vibe from him that is a little too torches and fire, a little too blood and soil.

"It's Nate," he says, unfazed. "And whatever you're looking for isn't here."

Bierman pauses to study him again, his bright eyes hard and unyielding. "How do you know that if you don't know what we're looking for?"

"Bierman," Glover calls, her voice sharp, and a bolt of relief zips up my spine at the interruption. I didn't want Nate to respond to this asshole, who's clearly determined to bulldoze him.

Nate responds to him anyway, his voice risen slightly. "Wouldn't it be a hell of a lot easier if you'd just tell us?"

"Maybe. But I think it's more interesting this way." This time his smile is undeniably mocking. "We spoke to Ms. Van Doren, Simon's daughter," he says, turning to me. "She mentioned you."

I go quiet. I have no idea what Taylor could have said about me, but whatever it was, it has this detective looking at me like a red stain on a white sheet. Nate shoots me a confused glance, but I don't meet his eyes. I don't want it to come off as if we're colluding.

"We're speaking to everyone who was close to the victim," Bierman clarifies. "Everything is important at this stage. I'm sure you understand."

"I do, I'm just confused. I mean, I wasn't close to Simon." His face angles. "You weren't?"

"Not by any stretch of the word," I say, attempting a laugh, but it comes out as a croak.

"Really?" He shoots a baffled look at Glover, but it seems more performative than necessary, and then his eyes are back on mine. "I heard you got fired recently," he says, and I try to be cool, but then he shifts, and I see the shaft of his gun again, dark and vulgar. When you see a gun on TV, it feels casual. Exciting. This does not feel casual. This is not exciting.

My heart thumps, but I shrug to feign nonchalance. I'm not going to give anything away until I know where this is going. I take a breath and try to work out why Taylor would have told the cops about me getting fired. Why it would have even come up. Wouldn't they mainly be concerned with re-hashing Simon's last moments, the last time Taylor saw him, things like that? I should have never come up in the conversation, much less my being fired from the internship. But clearly, Taylor slipped it in somehow.

"I was let go," I say in a horrible, small voice, hyper-aware of Nate tucking his chin and shifting his weight from leg to leg like he is embarrassed. "It was just an internship, but I don't get what that has to do with what happened."

"By Mr. Van Doren himself," he says, steadying a barbed look on me, and I see it now: he's suspicious, not just in that way all cops are suspicious, but in a super-pointed way like he already has his own theory.

My mind flips back to Taylor. What else did she tell him? What ideas did she put in his head?

"What went wrong there?" Bierman asks, taking a small step toward me, and I nearly cower back. "It's not every day an intern gets released in such a personal manner by the CEO. There was an HR department who could have handled that, no?"

"It was…something I wasn't up front about. So I was dismissed."

He raises a brow. "Can you be a little less vague?"

I can't help but glance at Nate this time. He looks almost as nervous as I feel, and I feel a physical wash of relief when he steps closer to me, his large body like a shield. I want to reach for his hand, but I swallow hard and resist.

"I was arrested when I was fifteen," I tell Bierman, my eyes on my feet. "My record was supposed to be sealed, but I guess when you deal with people like this, the rules don't apply."

"People like this..." Glover says, speaking up for the first time in such a while, I forgot she was here. "What do you mean by that?"

I'm about to respond, say how the white and wealthy always seem to find ways around the law when it's an inconvenience to them, but Bierman cuts me off. "Are you sure he didn't let you go because things went wayward between you two?"

I frown. "What do you mean?"

"You know what I mean." His smile is so arrogant, it feels violating. "Things went sour and he didn't want you around anymore."

"I barely knew him," I say, finally able to find my full voice. "I spoke to him *once*."

"Ever email him?"

"Only his assistant."

"That must have been a really intense conversation to give Ms. Van Doren the impression that you two were having an affair."

I have to repeat the words in my head over and over before they sink in.

"Taylor told you that?" I ask with a scoff. "What else did she tell you? Lavender oil cures cancer?"

"She was pretty close to her dad," Bierman insists. "She's all torn up, taking this pretty hard."

"That's bullshit."

I'm relieved when Glover jumps back in. "What is? That you were sleeping with Mr. Van Doren or Ms. Van Doren being torn up over her father's murder?"

"Both. And she wasn't close to her dad."

"Yeah, bro," Nate says, and I'm instantly so relieved for the reminder that he's right next to me, bearing this with me. "She fucking hated his guts."

Glover and Bierman exchange a glance. I try to read where they're at, and they're both inscrutable, but it's obvious what we've just said contradicts whatever Taylor told them. I'm not sure what to say, if I should even speak, but before I come up with something, Bierman brushes past Nate and heads into the bedroom. Glover lingers behind him a moment, and I catch her looking my way, and when our eyes meet, maybe it's wishful thinking but I can't help but feel a small spark of solidarity.

Both cops start searching the apartment. Under the bed, inside drawers, then the closets.

I turn to Nate, and he pulls me close.

"What could they be looking for?" I ask, keeping my voice low.

He keeps his eyes straight ahead, watching them with just as much skepticism as they did us. "No idea."

"Why would they even come here? How'd they get a warrant when they have nothing on me?"

"I don't know. Just stay calm. You didn't do anything. You're good."

Glover steps out of my closet with something in her hand and shoots me a specific glance—disbelief, worry, shock, maybe a blend of all—before begrudgingly calling out. *"Bierman."*

I go hard and still, a concrete wall right before it gets pulverized by a wrecking ball. Something's wrong. I can hear it in her voice. And that look. What was that weird look? It almost felt like she looked at me like I'd betrayed or disappointed her somehow. It was so strange.

Bierman steps out of the bedroom. Glover holds up a small plastic bag filled with white powder. He snatches it from her hand. "Holy shit." His eyes drop as he analyzes the contents, then he looks directly at me. "Don't know what's more shocking. That this was so easy or that you were right for once."

He's clearly talking to her, but his eyes never leave mine. I'm so confused. I've never seen that little bag before. Never.

I feel Nate staring at me, but I can't look at him. I glance back up at Bierman. He looks smug.

"That's not mine." He raises a brow and I snap, "I don't even know what that is."

He takes a few steps toward me, holding the bag up as if I couldn't already see it clearly. "Looks a lot like it's a few grams of potassium cyanide." His expression turns rueful, amused, but he quickly frowns. "The same poison that was found lining Simon Van Doren's drinking glasses in the room where he died."

My heart plunges into my stomach. I can't make sense of any of this.

Then I remember I haven't done anything wrong.

I fold my arms across my body and try to sound as sure as I can. "Well, it's not mine."

Glover moves beside him. "Then whose is it?" The question is sharp, jagged, but there's something in her eyes that tells me she's open to hearing me out.

But I don't say anything. I don't know.

I don't fucking know.

I have no idea what the fuck is happening.

Bierman and Glover both shift their glares to Nate as if commanded by some invisible force.

His eyes widen. "I've never seen that before in my life."

It sounds like a lie. It does. But I know it's just the nerves. I probably sound like I'm lying too.

Bierman turns back to me. "Are you aware that Simon Van Doren was murdered, found dead in his home yesterday evening?"

"Yeah. We— I saw it on Twitter this morning…that he was dead."

"Ms. Maxwell, we're going to need you to accompany us down to the precinct."

Nate steps ahead of me. "She's not going down anywhere unless she's under arrest."

Bierman and Glover exchange a look. Nate spoke with such authority, I'm just as surprised by his bravery as they are.

"All right." Bierman shrugs, his eyes leveling with mine. "You're under arrest."

My mouth opens, but I can't speak. I glance at Nate, for help, something, but he's staring at the detective.

Glover hesitates, then reaches down to her belt and pulls out her cuffs. Before I can process what's happening, her hands are on my wrists and I'm being restrained.

Nate doesn't say anything this time, and I suddenly feel more alone than ever. I shake my head, feeling my knees wanting to buckle. It feels like vertigo, my legs wobbly, head spinning. I can't think. I can barely draw in a breath.

The words echo, blending into each other.

You have the right to remain silent. Anything you say can be used against you in a court of law…

My world goes quiet, nothing left but a distant hum, as if my head is being held under water. As if I'm holding my breath.

Maybe I am. Because this feels like dying. Dying a slow death, knowing what's coming but not being able to stop it.

Like falling off a cliff.
Like drowning.

It's been over five years since I have stepped foot inside a police station, but as I'm taken inside and booked, it feels like yesterday. Just like last time, a pair of uniformed officers take inventory of my personal belongings first. I only have a couple of dollars shoved into the back pocket of my jeans, which they assure me—with zero irony in their voices as if they are legitimately doing me a favor—will be properly secured. I feel fifteen again as they take my photo and fingerprints. All I can think of is Taylor sending Nate my first mug shot, the one I swore would also be my last.

The female officer's hair is stringy and greasy, and she is deliberately too forceful when she's confirming I don't have any weapons, stolen items or contraband on me. I keep my eyes clamped shut until it's over, not wanting to see her seeing me naked. I try not to shake, try to mask my fear like the nonchalant guy I saw being dragged in for booking ahead of me, but I can tell by the satisfaction in her eyes when she orders me out of the tiny, fluorescent room that she picked up on every dimension of my fear. The last time I was forced to wear a pair of too-tight cuffs, I was shaking too, from the pure fury of being wrongfully accused. I didn't attack that counselor. I shoved her *off* me. I defended myself.

This time I have no idea why I'm being accused. And I realize there is something even more terrifying than the fury I felt the last time: blind confusion.

I don't know how long it is from the time I provide them a handwriting sample that Glover retrieves me from the crowded holding cell and escorts me to a small, square room with what is obviously a two-way mirror. It's cold and too bright, the space choked with a gray stillness. The chair I sit in is uncomfortable to the point of being painful. Everything about this room is methodical, deliberate in its cruelty.

Glover leans over and keys open the handcuffs. She's much gentler than the woman who conducted my strip search, but I snatch my wrists back anyway like having them closer to me, in my lap, makes them safely mine forever, as if they can't just snap the cuffs back on at any moment they please. She offers me a glass of water, and when I decline, she steps out of the room for a few minutes, returning with Bierman a step behind her, a silver laptop at his side. She glances over, then takes the seat across from me at the metal table.

Bierman opens his jacket and sits next to Glover, legs wide, taking up as much space as he wants, like he's got a monopoly on the square footage in this room. His suit looks expensive, and suddenly, the smell of his cologne—something rich and leathery—is suffocating.

Glover stands up and shifts to turn on a camera mounted to the ceiling. When she sits back down, she pulls out a tape recorder, flips it on and states the date, time and names of everyone in the room. My heart flutters, and then her eyes come to me. "You understand you're being recorded?"

It takes everything in me to keep my voice even. "Yes."

"Okay." Bierman clasps his hands in front of him. "First things first, Ms. Maxwell. You don't have to answer anything we ask without a lawyer present. Do you understand?"

I blink at him.

I understand, but I see no point in acknowledging his question with anything more.

"This can be as easy or as difficult as you want it to be," he continues, already looking impatient.

I don't say anything right away. My heart is pounding against my chest, and I'm afraid if I open my mouth, they'll hear it.

"I can call a lawyer?"

"It's up to you," Bierman says. "If you would like to reach out to an attorney, you can certainly do so." He waits, perfectly still, the edges of a smile pulling at the corners of his mouth, as if he already knows I don't have one. "Would you like to call an attorney, Ms. Maxwell?"

It's just a question, but it feels as pointed as a threat.

I glance at Glover, then back to him, studying the hard, determined lines of his face. "I'm fine for now. Go ahead and ask your questions."

Glover quickly leans in. "One will be appointed to you if—"

"I just want to get out of here. Let's...just go ahead."

Bierman smiles again. That condescending, vaguely triumphant smile I want to slap right off his face. "We checked out the security system at the Van Doren home. There's roughly ten minutes of camera footage missing, which is enough time for someone to get into the house and lace the glasses."

I wait for him to finish, to turn his statement into a question. But he stops like this is supposed to mean something significant. My lips part to respond, but he cuts me off.

"Interesting, isn't it?" he asks.

I shrug. "Maybe to you."

"Know anything about why it would be gone?"

"I could take a wild guess, but it wouldn't involve me if that's what you're insinuating."

"I'm just asking a simple question."

I don't fall for that. "The only time I've ever been to that house was for a party a few weeks ago."

His expression flickers with something minatory, and I feel like a mouse he's watching head straight for a trap. Instantly regretting that detail I offered, I remind myself to only answer what I'm asked. Talking too much is what got me booked last time.

"So you were familiar with the layout of the house, then?" he asks with a cock of his head.

"No. I was only in the main room."

"But you'd been there, so you knew about the cameras. Knew there weren't many blind spots."

"I was there to meet Simon. I wasn't thinking about any cameras."

"Okay," he says, like he's moving on, but it feels too good to be true, like that was too easy. "I want to show you something."

He opens the laptop and angles it so the screen is facing me. It's an email chain, but not one I'm familiar with. I give him a questioning look, and he says, "You don't recognize these?"

I lean forward and start to skim it, noticing right away that they're messages sent back and forth between two people. Then I realize most of the messages have been sent from one person. All but one. One is from Simon. The others...

My heart stops when my eyes flick up to the sent address. I'm staring at my own email account.

It's a mistake. It has to be.

But there it is. My email address.

I start reading again.

I was thinking about you. I miss you. Can I see you?

My eyes fly across the screen faster.

I'm touching myself as I write this. I want you so bad.

This has to be a joke. I glance up. No one breaks.

You don't want to make a woman go crazy, do you?

Who's this bitch you're gonna marry?

I fucking hate you so much.

I still love you. Please get back to me. Please.

My heart is pounding, but it feels like my lungs have completely shut down. I can't breathe. I don't recognize any of these messages. I didn't send any of this shit.

I glance up again.

They're both waiting.

My mouth opens, but I can't speak. My eyes drop back to the screen, shoot up to the time stamp. Last week. Thursday. 2:02 p.m. I scan the others. They were all sent within a week.

They confiscated my phone—I can't check—I *know* I didn't send these emails. There's no way—

"Can't you track who sent these? I didn't—can't you find out what computer these emails were sent from?"

Glover's expression is flat. "It's a Gmail account."

I wait for more. Nothing. "What does that mean?"

"You can't track emails sent from a Gmail account. There's no IP address."

I just stare at her.

Bierman shifts. "Look, they were all sent from your account—"

"I see that, but I didn't send them." It's all I can say at this point, and I know it's not enough.

Bierman heaves a sigh like I've disappointed him. He's staring at me as if he's already decided that I'm guilty. "What about the photos?"

I pause, because I legitimately don't know what the fuck he's talking about.

I look back at the screen, and this time I see that one of the messages has an attachment icon, that tiny paper clip. I move my hand over the trackpad and click into it, see that three images are attached at the bottom. I double-click on the first one. It begins to load, slowly. I wait. Click on the second. The third. They all finish loading at the same time, popping on the screen in rapid succession.

A chill races up and down my body. I recognize the photos. All of them.

The nudes I sent Nate last month.

My instinct is to reach across the table and cover the screen with my hands, then it hits me that they've already seen these photos.

That's the thing with cops. You never know how much they already have.

My stomach turns, the room shrinking by the minute. I don't understand how they could have gotten these photos and attached them to those emails. Nate is the only person I ever sent those photos to—the only person I ever sent *any* nude photos to.

I feel like I've slipped and fallen down a rabbit hole and landed in an upside-down universe. Everything is wrong. Nothing makes sense.

I want to go back, rewind time, start back at the beginning.

But I'm not Alice. This isn't a fairy tale. And this isn't a dream.

I want to say something. Yell, scream, defend myself. Anything. But words won't leave my mouth. I'm paralyzed. No answer seems safe. Not here. Not like this. All I can think of is what this means, how this all must look to them. They think I sent those messages, that Simon and I were having sex, that I'm some psycho lunatic who threatened to hurt—

I can't breathe. It's like an invisible hand choking me. I feel dizzy. Physically sick.

Time seems to slow. They think I killed Simon. They have a motive. They have evidence. It's only circumstantial, but it's still evidence. It all crashes down onto me now. They can easily convince a DA to prosecute this case even without a confession. If I'm convicted, I'll be facing at least—

No. I can't think about that. Not right now. I won't be convicted because I'm innocent. I know that isn't how this system works, but right now I need to cling to this. It's my only hope.

Bierman leans almost halfway across the table, a sharp glint in his eyes. "Let me guess, you don't recognize those, either?"

My eyes flick up to his face. For a second I imagine him staring at those photos, examining them, and I feel so small.

"No." My voice sounds hollow, unrecognizable, but I speak anyway. "I do."

"Can I assume you have a copy of these photos?" Bierman asks. His words are cryptic.

I stop myself from rolling my eyes. "You can assume whatever you want," I snap, and the words hang between us, hot and dangerous.

Bierman makes an exasperated face, then tries again. "That's you in these photos, correct?"

I cut my eyes at him. "What, do you want me to strip right now so you can compare?"

His face goes flat as he shifts uncomfortably. "You're not helping yourself, Ms. Maxwell."

I glance at Glover for backup, for…anything, but instead of finding concern in her face this time, she looks away like she wants to help me, but knows it isn't her place.

Bierman glances down at the papers he has on the table between us. I squint, but I can't see anything from here. "I see here in your file that you've done time before. Six months in the Administration for Children's Services. Resisting arrest. Aggravated assault."

The words come slowly and from far away. I don't say anything. I think he's going to keep going, but he stops, waiting for my reaction.

I blink and then realize I have to speak. "Is that a question?"

"That's a question."

My head is already shaking. "That was…"

"That was what?"

My leg bounces under the table. I feel tears wanting to fall, but I force them back. "I told you about that. It was an accident."

"Pushing a woman down a flight of stairs doesn't seem like an accident to me," he says, barely trying to conceal his disgust.

"Well, it was. I pushed her off me, but she tripped down the stairs on her own." She didn't die. She was barely even hurt. I didn't do it on purpose. "I didn't push her that hard." I look away, impatient, scared.

"Was poisoning Van Doren's drink also an accident?"

My head snaps up.

Glover throws a look at Bierman and there's a moment of unspoken communication between them.

Bierman clears his throat, eyes back on me. "Listen, we've got a problem here, Ms. Maxwell."

"No, *you've* got a problem. And you're wasting time questioning me when you could be out searching for evidence that can lead you to who really murdered Simon."

"Simon," he parrots. "You call him Simon. I noticed you called him that before."

I say nothing.

He shrugs. "Pretty informal way to address a man of his stature."

"He's the one who asked me to call him Simon. It wasn't just me. He told all the interns to use his first name."

He studies me. "You say you didn't send these emails, but you acknowledge this is you in these photos, which were attached to one of the emails that were sent to Van Doren."

I look him in the eye. "For the last time, I never—"

"If you didn't send them, who did?"

"That's *your* job, isn't it? I don't even have his email address. I was only ever in contact with his assistant during my internship."

There is no give to his expression. "Do you expect me to believe a resourceful girl like you couldn't have figured out how to get your hands on it?"

I don't know what the hell he means by that. I want to scream at him, tell him to go fuck himself. But I can't. I know his type. I know that hungry look in his eyes. I've seen it before. He's just waiting for me to make a scene, waiting for any excuse to paint me as the criminal he so badly wants me to be.

I take a breath and choose my words carefully. I don't want to give him any more control over me than he already has. "The only person I sent those photos to is Nate," I say, determined to remain impassive from now on.

Bierman frowns and shoots a glance over to Glover.

"The boyfriend," she reminds him.

"Right. The protective one." Bierman sits on the thought for a moment, his frown morphing into a less confused, more ironic, variation. "Why would your boyfriend access your email account and send them to Van Doren?"

"That's—that's not what I..." My eyes dart between them. "All I'm saying is I didn't send those emails. I met Simon twice. Once when the program started and then at the party I just told you about."

That sparks something in his eyes. "You two interacted at this party? Well, don't stop there."

I keep thinking I should come right out and say everything I heard Taylor say in that room, that she's the one who did this, but I don't know how I could do it without mentioning the ten thousand dollars she gave me. The deal we made. They'd probably charge me with conspiracy or something if they knew she paid me to keep my mouth shut.

I glance down at the tape recorder, then speak slowly, so that they won't miss a single word. "I talked to him to pitch myself for the summer job in Milan that all the interns were up for. Not to—"

"Ms. Maxwell. I promise this will be a whole lot easier if you—"

"I didn't send those emails." I'm on my feet before my brain tells me to stop. "I didn't murder anybody, either."

He stares up at me. He doesn't blink. "Ms. Maxwell, I need you to sit down."

I look away and close my eyes, a sudden roar filling my ears. All of Nate's warnings echo in my head. I should have stayed away from them. From Taylor. From her world. From it all.

I take a breath. I need to make a decision.

Glover looks at me, her mouth tight, but not quite a frown—something kinder than that. She speaks softly. "If there is anything else that you want to tell us, Brandi, this is the time."

The way she says my name, it's like she's removed a barrier. She's making this personal, and I think she's still on my side. Her fishing for more almost feels like a warning in disguise.

I fold my arms across my chest. "I'm done talking until I get a lawyer."

Visibly frustrated, Bierman pushes himself up from the table. His posture betrays his pride when he stands up, as if the badge and the gun make up for what he lacks in character.

He leans forward, hands pressing into the metal. "Listen, it's understandable what emotions you were feeling. You and Van Doren have this thing going on. Last thing you expect is for him to drop you from the summer program. You're hurt. Confused, maybe. Then—"

"I never—"

"I get it. You caught feelings. He didn't. He moves on to someone else. You think maybe you have a chance to win him back. But then he gets engaged. Now you're furious. He ignores you. You threaten him. He still doesn't respond, so you snap and kill him. After all, you have a history of violence." He straightens, satisfied that he has made his case.

For a second I imagine him at home, watching Fox News before dinner and texting some other woman while in bed with his wife, and then I sneer at him. "Don't you have better things to do?"

He doesn't have anything to say to that.

Glover gets my cuffs back on and steers me toward the door.

I haven't been found guilty of anything yet. I've only been accused. I don't have to talk to them if I don't want to, just like he said.

I *don't* want to. They have their theory, but I don't care. They're wrong. And I refuse to let them try to pressure me into admitting to a crime I didn't commit. That's all they want: a confession. I know how this works. It makes things easier for them, costs them less money. The quicker they solve a case, the better. Especially with a high-profile person like Simon. The public will be demanding justice soon.

They don't care about me.

I keep walking, waiting for Bierman to stop me, but he doesn't.

Then I hear a voice at my back. Bierman. "Ms. Maxwell, please understand. I won't be able to help you once you leave this room."

"I don't need your help," I tell him, and walk through the door, Glover right on my heels. Two guards are waiting, eager to put their hands on me and take me back to my holding cell.

I didn't kill Simon. However hard those cops try to twist the facts and trip me up, they can't change that.

I didn't kill him. Which means someone else did, and I know who.

I'm being framed and I need to figure out how to prove it.

19

BRANDI

By the time the guards call for me, the sun has already gone down. I don't know what time it is, but I know visiting hours are almost over. The announcement was made a few minutes ago.

My heart almost leaps from my chest when I see Nate straddle the stool on the opposite side of the booth. I thought he wasn't going to show up.

I try not to think about what I look like as I stare at him from behind the glass. He's wearing a white T-shirt and sweatpants, his chest stretching the T-shirt. His eyes are harder than they've ever been. Wary. And there's something else, something like betrayal, but slightly worse than that. He looks at me, but avoids my eyes, then picks up the receiver on the counter.

I reach down and pick mine up too.

He holds the handset to his ear, but still won't look at me.

I sigh. "Babe, come on. It's me."

Nate shakes his head, trying to understand. "I don't even know what that means right now." There's an edge to his voice that almost sounds like suspicion.

It's obvious he's been filled in. There is no need to ask. It's all over his face. He knows what they're saying I did. I just hope he doesn't believe them. He can't. He knows me. He knows I'm not capable of murder.

"Nate, you know I don't care about anyone but you."

His head snaps up, as if he's surprised I would even have the gall to say something like that to him right now. "So what, you were just pretending to be into him so he'd change his mind and take you to Milan?"

"No!" I take a breath and wait until the rage inside me cools into something like calm. "Nate. Listen to me. You're the only guy I've ever been with, I swear."

As the words leave my mouth I cringe inside, because I've never told him this, that I was a virgin when we first slept together, and I don't know why it embarrasses me so much, but it does, and I'm trying to hide it, and I know I'm failing, but I hope it's enough.

Nate looks away and it feels like cruel and unusual punishment, like someone is squeezing my heart with an enormous pair of pliers just to see me squirm and cry. It takes him forever to turn back to me. "So what did you do? What the fu— Why did you send those emails?" His voice is hard, but I can feel the worry and uncertainty in each word.

"You really think I'd sacrifice my dignity for a *job*?" I pause, weighing how much to say. "It wasn't like that. I never spoke to Simon after that night. *I didn't send any of those emails.*"

His face twists, like he's caught between believing me and listening to what his brain is telling him, what those cops are saying I did. "Then who sent them? And the pics." His head shakes. "You barely wanted to send them to me, and you just dump them in that dude's inbox?"

I tuck my chin against my chest, my eyes suddenly burning.

I told myself I wouldn't cry. I told myself I wouldn't let any of this get to me. I told myself to be strong. But seeing Nate look at me like I'm a stranger breaks me into a thousand pieces. Nate's never been wary of me. He's never talked to me in this tone. He's never looked at me like...like...*this*.

I get it. I look guilty. Those emails...the photos...the cyanide in the apartment. It looks like I plotted and murdered a man I was obsessed with.

If I were those cops, I'd suspect me too.

If I was Nate, I'd have questions too.

I've done nothing wrong, but guilt and shame slump my shoulders like weight on my back anyway. I wish I could erase the betrayal from Nate's eyes, but it's as alive there as much as it is in his voice.

When I speak, my voice is low, but fierce. "Nate, I didn't kill anybody." My voice breaks, and then I'm crying. "This had to be Taylor. She—"

"Taylor?"

"She said it. At the party. I told you, when I was upstairs, I heard—"

"Did you? Or were you just saying that so I'd cover you if you got caught?"

"What? No." A tear slides down my face. "Nate. I know it's hard to look at me right now, but please. Just listen." I drag a hand across my face. "If this wasn't her plan all along, then why was I able to talk her into paying my tuition?"

That makes Nate take a moment and think. He runs a tense hand over his hair. "I believe you, but...you've been acting different ever since I took you to that party."

"I know, I know. I'm sorry." I blink back hot tears and clear my throat. "But we were together all last night. When would I have laced Simon's glasses?"

Nate just stares at me like he hadn't thought about my obvious alibi. Eventually, some of the fire drains from his eyes and a long breath escapes from his lips. "Babe, I'm sorry," he says, and that takes away the edge all his other words carried. "It's just been a lot today."

"Yeah, because you're the one who had some random woman's finger rammed up your ass, violated like an animal, then locked in a cage with psychos all day."

I didn't mean to say that. It slipped out so fast, I couldn't stop it.

Nate flinches in surprise. "Did they...did they hurt you?"

I drop my eyes. I can't take the look of pity that veils his features, the helplessness that swells in his eyes.

He sighs. "I didn't mean to— Look, I'm gonna call my dad. See if he can wire me enough to bail you out. The hearing is in the morning, right?"

"Yeah. But Nate." I take a breath. "Are you sure you want to ask him?"

"You think I'm just gonna stand back and let you sit in jail? Come on, B. I told you about this pride thing. Just let me help you."

I don't know whether I should thank him or apologize. I should probably do both.

But another thought crosses my mind. I stare at him, still thinking. "How much do you think it'll be?"

I don't know what amount I expected the judge to say, but a million dollars was definitely not it.

The phone shakes in my hand as I tell Nate the amount of my bail. He doesn't seem as shocked as me.

I shake my head. "There's no way your dad will give you that much."

"We only need to get them a deposit to post the bond."

I swallow, wondering why the public defender they assigned me didn't tell me that part earlier. "Nate, I'm scared. This place is..." I choke on my words, unable to finish them.

"Hang in there, babe. Mind over matter. I'm gonna get you home. We'll figure this out."

So many things race through my mind, but all I can say is, "Love you."

It's a tiny murmur and I hate how it doesn't even begin to encapsulate how I feel about him.

I don't even get a chance to say bye before someone else jostles me from behind, demanding I hand over the phone. I roll my eyes and toss it to her. A guard follows me back to my cell.

Barely two hours pass before the guard is back in my face, saying I have a visitor. It feels like magic that Nate got them the money already. I follow the guard to the visiting room, but stop dead in my tracks when I glance at the entrance.

Taylor. In a beige oversize suit, a matching crop top peeking through, so close to the color of her skin it barely looks like she's wearing anything underneath. Her hair is bone straight and tucked behind her ears, giving her face a more severe look than usual. I take in her square-toe Bottega Veneta heels as she struts my way and I can't believe I almost became one of them, the kind of people I hate. It seems impossible that only a few weeks ago I was on track to spend the summer in Milan, shadowing Simon for three weeks, sipping espressos with the VD team in centuries-old cafés, doing exactly what I've dreamed of for so long, and now I might be facing life in prison for something I didn't do. I should have never accepted Taylor's money or those gifts from Mei and Jared. I should have never lied to Nate.

Taylor sees me but when we lock eyes, her expression doesn't change. When she steps closer and slides off her sunglasses, I'm struck by the redness of her eyes, the pallor of her face.

She picks up the handset.

"What do you want?" I snap into my end.

"This is all my fault," she says, looking genuinely remorseful. The receiver seems to shake in her hand.

"I knew it. You did this. You kil—"

"I *trusted* you." Her lower lip trembles and she swallows hard. "I'm to blame for Dad's death just as much as you are."

Her words throw me off. I was expecting her to be... apologetic. To admit it was her. For a moment I can't decide if she's crazy—or if I am.

My mouth drops open in confusion. "What?"

"Nate Cinderella'd you, squeezed you into that Givenchy gown and you managed to con everyone at the ball, including Dad. He felt bad for the poor little black girl from 'the hood' with big dreams."

My jaw tightens at the emphasis she put on *squeeze* and her use of those stupid air quotes. I swallow a growl.

Taylor lowers her head, slumping in her seat, as if she's truly suffering. When she straightens, she's crying. Real tears. Thick, shiny tears. Her shoulders are trembling, but no sound comes from her mouth. She looks innocent, vulnerable. Legitimately in pain.

"I tried to tell him. I warned him that you were nothing but a criminal just like the rest of you people. But that's where I went wrong. If I would've never told him to toss your application and just let him pick you for the Milan gig like he wanted to, you wouldn't have gone bonkers, and he'd still be here."

I am going to strangle this racist, condescending bitch.

Now I understand the bulletproof glass between us.

I unclench my teeth. Breathe in, out. "I didn't kill your father." My hand shakes, just like my voice.

She frowns in disbelief. "Then who did?"

I refuse to answer her. If I do, she'll try to trap me.

She killed him. I know she did.

If she didn't poison him, then she hired someone to do it for her. Or maybe it was Mei. She's the one who said she knew a guy who knew a guy. Of course Taylor wouldn't do it herself. She's not dumb. She probably has a Stonehenge-solid alibi.

My eyes move over her again. Her outfit is much more conservative than usual. She's playing the part. She knows the press will be all over her every action, including coming here. She thinks of everything. She's so good at this I'm wondering if she planned it all from the start, if she immediately saw some weakness inside me that made me the perfect choice right away, or if it was something I said, something I did. I'm wondering about all those things Nate mentioned she got away with, the people she's hurt, lives she's ruined, wishing I'd asked instead of holding my tongue.

Taylor's voice snaps me back into the present. "Bet you wish you invested in an LED ring light, huh?" Her voice is laced with sarcasm.

I frown. "What?" I have no idea what this bitch is talking about.

She glances around the room, her gaze pausing on two of the guards standing only a few feet away. "I'm sure you're the Kim K of the precinct by now," she says, looking back at me.

The thought sends a wash of chills over my entire body. I think back to the way Bierman squirmed in his seat when I got loud on him. He's probably already passed the photos around to every male detective in the station by now, even the guards. That's what men do. They're all the same.

Her gaze goes up and down me, the worst kind of laughter in her eyes. Then she frowns like she really means it. "What, did you think because I said I wanted to kill him that gave you free rein to do it? I told you I was joking."

My voice spikes. "I didn't—"

"What was your brilliant plan? To frame me?" She makes

sure she's loud when she says this. Other people hear her. Some turn their heads. I keep my eyes locked on her.

Taylor sighs, a mix of weariness and sadness, the sound almost getting stuck in her throat, in the wetness there.

I suddenly feel exhausted. "I was with Nate all night and I can prove it," I tell her, my voice flat. "Our building has security cameras in the lobby. They would've caught me going in way before the time Simon…was poisoned."

I expect something in her expression to falter, anticipate her eyes to shift the way they do when you realize you've forgotten something important, at least a flinch. But Taylor serves nothing but poker face. She's good, except I know she doesn't actually believe I killed her father. She wants me to believe that she does, but this is all an act.

It doesn't matter. I didn't kill anyone and I have proof.

She watches me as I set the receiver back in the cradle, then rise from my chair. Her eyes narrow. I can practically see the wheels turning in that pretty little head of hers.

She is fooling no one.

She sent those emails. She sent those photos. She planted that cyanide in my apartment. I don't know how, but I know she did. She wouldn't be here if she hadn't. She needs me to look guilty so the cops don't come after her.

It's the only thing that makes sense.

For a moment I was starting to think those cops were trying to frame me. It wouldn't be that much of a stretch. Detectives are under tons of pressure from the city to not only investigate crimes, but solve them too. Every investigation that goes unsolved leads to political drama at the top of the chain. Bad press. Money lost. Lots of money. Plenty of detectives plant false evidence or manipulate whatever's available to lean in their favor when all their other efforts fail.

I thought that was what was happening.

I thought wrong.

Taylor's selling herself short. She should be in front of film cameras—not just posing for pictures. She should be an actress; it comes so naturally to her.

I don't say anything. I want to threaten her, to tell her that if she doesn't stop this bullshit, she'll have to deal with the consequences. I want to scream at her, but it would be screaming at a brick wall. There's no point. This isn't a normal person I'm dealing with. She's not just selfish. Inconsiderate. Reckless.

She's *cruel*. A monster.

I need evidence. I need that security tape. That will prove that I couldn't have been there that night to poison Simon. I'll have a solid alibi. They'll have to move on to other suspects.

But all I can do now is wait.

20

BRANDI

"Maxwell. You posted bail."

My head snaps up and the bars yank open. For a moment I think I'm dreaming. This isn't really happening. But then the guard shifts, everything about him impatient, shouting my name again, and I'm on my feet immediately.

After I'm handed back my phone and two dollars at the front desk, I walk outside, palms damp, looking around for Nate. I can barely breathe. I'm not sure what the vibe will be between us. If he looks at me the way he did back in that shithole, I don't know if I'll be able to take it.

I spot him right away, on the corner, a silhouette of black against the streetlights, and head his way. He hears me and looks up from his phone, nothing but kindness in his eyes. I'm so relieved that I jog forward to hug him. Nate yanks me into his arms and crushes me against his body. He's so warm and strong and smells like home. I cling to him. I can feel his heartbeat through his T-shirt, the heat of his chest beneath the fabric. He grips me just as tight, holding me up on the tips of my toes, burying his head in my hair.

"You okay?" he says, his soft words gliding into my ear.

My voice cracks. "Yeah."

His hand strokes up and down my back and I sink into his touch. "Don't worry. We'll figure this out," he whispers into my shoulder after a moment. I feel the warmth of his breath through my top and I almost want to stay here, just like this. Just me and him. Us against the world.

When I pull back, I see that he's on the brink of tears. My chest tightens. I've never seen Nate cry. Never.

"What's wrong?" I search his eyes, but they shy away from mine.

He shakes his head. I wait, knowing it has to be *something*. "It's not there," he finally says.

My heart pounds. "What's not there?"

"The security camera…there's no footage of you coming in that night."

I called Nate earlier and told him to talk to one of the doormen, Raul, to ask about getting a copy of the security tape from Monday afternoon. I wanted to show that public defender I hadn't gone back out after I came in and couldn't have been in Long Island at the time of Simon's death.

I frown. "What do you mean there's no footage? It has to be there. I came in—"

He keeps shaking his head. "I had the guy play it back four times." He shrugs like his words aren't breaking me. "It wasn't there."

"That's not poss—"

I'm so stupid. I told Taylor about the footage. But there's no way she could have—

My head shakes. I've underestimated her before. I don't want to do it again.

"Look, we'll figure out a different way," Nate says, but I barely hear him.

There is no different way. That footage was my only hope

of proving my alibi outside of Nate's word that I was with him all night, and now it's gone.

It was her. I know it was her.

I'm too tired for this. I feel drained. Numb.

I look up at Nate, my body heavy and limp like I've been dragged a hundred miles. It's only been three days in there, but it felt ten times as long. "Just take me home."

He flags down a taxi and helps me inside like I'm some battered princess who can't do anything for herself, but in some ways, that's exactly what I feel like. Totally and completely defeated. Nate wraps an arm around me and holds it there the entire ride downtown. I lean my head on his shoulder and close my eyes as silent tears roll down my face.

When we pull up in front of our building, I barely move. I want Nate to pick me up and carry me in his arms, but of course I don't ask. I don't say anything. I can't. My mind is moving too fast. I can't keep up with any of my thoughts.

As soon as we step out of the car, it happens.

Bright lights.

Fifty cameras flashing at once.

A cacophony of shouting people, some screaming, waving microphones, thrusting them in my face.

I don't know where to look.

I feel Nate's hand grip mine and I grip his back. "Ignore them. Keep your head down."

I try to ignore them, but their overlapping words echo inside my head until they sound something like pain.

When we walk inside, all I can think about is getting this stale smell off my skin. "I'm getting a shower," I tell Nate, not pausing to look back at him. He says *okay* and lets me be.

I walk right into the bathroom and start stripping out of my clothes. I avoid the mirror. I can't look at myself like this.

I know I look horrible. Like all the life has been sucked out of me.

I turn on the spray and wait for the water to warm up before stepping in. I stay under the pounding heat for as long as I can, until the heat doesn't feel good anymore, then I grab a bottle of shampoo off the shelf and start to wash my hair.

My head jerks toward the door when I hear footsteps. Nate doesn't say anything as he slides the glass open. I stare at him, but he still doesn't speak. His hands go over his head as he tugs off his shirt. I watch him undress in silence; I can't think of anything to say, either. I feel dazed. I lean my head against the cold tile, and water laps at my feet. When Nate steps into the stall with me, I turn my back to him so the spray can run over my face for a while and wash away the tears.

He grips my stomach, then moves his hands up my body, but there is nothing sexual about his touch. It's raw and nurturing. "I missed you so much."

I turn slightly to watch him for a moment. I've never seen him this vulnerable. It's only been a few days, but I know what he means. With me gone, he was starting to imagine the day that I wouldn't come back. I'd started thinking the same thing.

"Missed you too." I shift to let the warm water run down the front of my body as Nate strokes his fingers through my hair, so soft and tender.

"It's all gonna work out," Nate says. "Promise. I'm gonna call my father's lawyer. He'll get you out of this."

I sigh. "How, Nate? There's no footage. They found that poison in our room. They have those ema—"

"You know all the wild shit he's gotten my dad out of."

"Yeah, but he never murdered anyone."

"You didn't either, remember? This guy's one of the best attorneys in the country. Like Kardashian, Shapiro-level good."

I turn around and press my forehead against his neck and

inhale the warmth of his skin. He sweeps a thumb across my cheek. When I open my mouth, my words rush out of me. I don't know what I'm saying, not really. The words are mostly a blur.

I regurgitate what those cops said to me, the questions they asked, the way they kept looking at me. I tell him the things Taylor said, how she produced those fake white tears right in front of my face.

Then I groan and tell him how scared I am.

I know I didn't kill Simon. And I know Taylor is setting me up. But I can't see a way through this. Not anymore.

All Nate can do is listen. And reassure.

And worry.

I can feel it in his body whenever he presses against me. It's an awkward stiffness, a constant trembling. And every time I look into his eyes it's as if I can see him thinking a thousand things at once. Despite his light words, I can see exhaustion in every line of his face. He looks like he hasn't slept the whole time I've been away. He's taking this just as hard as I am, and that makes me feel a little better. It's like we're in this together, always.

Nate helps me rinse and condition my hair, and it's more intimate than any sex we've ever had. We dry off together, then, with all the lights off, climb into bed. Nate holds me quietly for a moment, but I can still feel the stress in his body like it's my own. We don't say anything for the longest stretch of time. Sometimes there's no need for words when you know someone well enough to know exactly what they're thinking.

Time passes.

Sleep won't find me. My body is exhausted, but my mind won't stop working. For a while I watch Nate sleep, his head on my chest, rising and falling gently with every breath I take, lips parted in a way that makes him seem much younger than he is. It occurs to me that I'm probably viewing him the way his mother will view him forever, and the thought warms some fragile part of me.

Sometime later Nate stirs, like he's fighting to stay on that other side of consciousness, and I look down and see that his eyes are open, but only halfway, his face slack with sleep. I reach down between us and squeeze his hand. He squeezes mine back, the smallest movement, as if to say *I'm here, I'm not leaving*, and that's all I need.

21

TAYLOR

My phone almost drops from my hand. "Released? What do you mean, *released*?"

"She posted bail," Detective Bierman says, his voice resigned. "Listen, I fought the prosecutor not to grant bail, but she did. It is what it is. This doesn't change anything. What we have is concrete. We will—"

I drop the call.

Mei slips in from my bathroom, lighting a cigarette. "What happened?"

I look at her, my eyes on fire. "Nate's helping her."

She frowns, confused. "I thought you—"

"I did."

She takes a long, indulgent drag, then blows a thick cloud of smoke my way. "You need to go handle him."

I put my head in my hands and push out a hard breath. "Fuck."

I fight my way past the huddle of reporters who have been on my heels for three blocks now. Yelling and shouting questions at me, demanding to know things about that asshole, if I knew about the affair, when the funeral will be, and I remind myself to be impassive. I can't smile or I'm guilty. I can't cry or I'm faking it.

I push into the Equinox on the corner, the one Nate has been going to for years, and walk straight past reception into the weightlifting area, passing by a girl taking mirror self-ies of her latest surgical enhancements that she'll accredit to squats, a group of guys trying to out-lift each other. No one says anything to me, but heads turn. People whisper, thinking they're being discreet, but they're not. I keep my head down, looking for Nate.

I'm about to give up when I hear hard metal slam behind me. I turn around and see Nate, standing up from the bench press. He's wearing gray sweatpants and a muscle tee, the sides cut low enough for me to see the edges of what's underneath, those dimples in his rib cage, the planes of lean muscles. Sweat clings to his arms, his neck, dripping down his face like salty-sweet rain. He reaches for his water bottle and throws his head back, taking a few gulps.

I close the distance between us and stand right behind him, breathing in his raw scent. He's still unaware of me, completely in the zone. Just as I start to reach out to touch him, he feels my presence and whips around. He goes still at my smile and swallows hard.

His dark eyes flick over my face as he snatches the AirPods out of his ears. "What are you doing here?" He glares at me, so severely that if I didn't know him, I'd probably back away.

"Was hoping I'd find you here," I say, keeping my voice as light as I can, which is hard considering the circumstances. Also, it's just generally hard to act aloof around a guy whose testicles have been in my mouth. "Just wanted to check in. You know, see how you're handling all of this. I saw the news—"

"Why do you care?" He drags a forearm across his brow, dampness against dampness like it used to be when we fucked, then lifts the bottom of his shirt to wipe away more sweat from his forehead. Slim hips peek from above the low waist of his pants, that perfect V.

I move my eyes, fingers twitching at my side. "Look, I lost my father. But I know this all must be hard for you too. Realizing your girlfriend did something so horrific—" My head shakes.

Nate's jaw tightens, but he says nothing.

"Wait." A pause. "You're not still with her, are you?" I ask, trying to sound surprised.

He still doesn't say anything. He's looking everywhere but my face. I'm trying to keep my eyes on his, but it's hard when all they want to do is drop to the sweat dripping down his bare skin.

"She's not who you think she is," I say, firming my voice.

He glances at me sideways, anger flaring in his eyes. "I think I know her better than you."

With that, he turns away and heads down the hallway to the locker rooms. He pulls his shirt off because I guess there's no point anymore and uses it as a towel, mopping sweat from his eyes. Immediately, I notice the scratches on his back, along the side of his waist. Something drops inside me. I know those kinds of marks. Every woman knows those kinds of marks. They're scabbed over now, dark and ugly against the smooth butterscotch of his skin.

My jaw tightens. I've never hated a girl as much as I hate that bitch in this moment. It's like she did it on purpose, trying to mark her territory. The more I try to get rid of her, the more she shows up.

I stay on Nate's heels. "Oh, yeah? Well, did you know she was a serial cheater?"

He looks back at me. "That's bullshit. She never—"

"You don't have the best track record of realizing when your girlfriend's cheating, you know."

He stops and frowns at my reminder, but I'm right, and he knows it. "That's because I *trusted* you."

"Don't you trust Brandi? You said you love her. Your blinders are up. You can't see what I can see."

He swallows and ignores my question. "Brandi didn't send those emails."

"Or the nudes, right? What, they sent themselves?"

"I don't know how they got them. Maybe…"

I wait for him to finish but he never does.

I sigh. "Why do so many mental gymnastics when it's right in front of your eyes? Brandi isn't like you. She's—"

"She's what?" His eyes flare with something I've never seen before, a level of defensiveness he's never had for me.

I lick my lips. "Look, you grew up in a nice neighborhood, in a nice house, with both of your parents. She was practically raised by wolves and—"

"And that makes her a *murderer*?" His eyes narrow, just a fraction. "Is that what you're trying to say?"

"No, but it's probably made her desperate for love. Any kind of love. She clearly thought she was in love with my father. It's all in the emails. The cops showed them to me. I read them all. It's so fucked up."

He shakes his head as if he's trying to shake the words from his brain, then rubs both hands over his hair. Soft, curly hair I remember digging my fingers into.

I sigh. "Nate, just listen."

He stops walking. When he swings his head around to face me, his expression is brutal. I try to stop what's coming, but he speaks over me. "No, you listen. Brandi told me what she heard you telling your friends at that party. You were planning to kill your dad then. Who says you didn't go through with it? I saw the emails too, all right? Even if Brandi was sleeping with your pops, she didn't poison him. She was in bed with me all night."

That gives me hope. He thinks it's a possibility that she slept with my father. I cling to that and try to not think of them in bed together, touching, holding, fucking.

Nate is closer to me now, waiting for me to react.

"I never planned to kill my father," I say, looking him straight in the eyes.

"Yes, you did. Brandi told me—"

"That's just her clumsy cover-up."

He hesitates. "What?"

"She told you that because she knew you couldn't handle the truth."

His frown deepens. "The truth about what?" he asks, sounding impatient now.

I shake my head and scoff. "You want to know what *really* happened at that party, Nate? When you two split up and she was 'looking around at the house'?" I pause for effect, swallowing hard. "She was having sex with my father."

His eyes bore so deep into mine I think I forget to breathe for a second. "You're lying."

I roll my eyes, like my heart isn't beating out of my chest. "My heel broke, so I went upstairs to change and walked in on them. I was so shocked, I just ran back down the stairs." I take a breath, moving my eyes up and down his frame. "But not as shocked as I was when you showed up at the party with her."

He makes a face. "What does that mean?"

"I recognized her. She was the intern that my father's assistant warned me about. Apparently, they'd been hooking up all over the city. She walked in on Brandi on her knees in his office once. He made her sign an NDA and everything."

I reach into my purse and pull out a folded piece of paper.

Lines appear between his brows. "What's this?"

"Just read it," I say, handing it to him.

He holds my gaze, his eyes challenging mine for a moment, then takes it from my grasp a little too firmly. It's not exactly a snatch, but there's some aggression there. I don't take it personally. I watch him as he unfolds it slowly, like he's afraid of what he might find.

"Did you really come here just to give this to me?" he asks, his voice level, staring at me not in shock or disbelief, but indignance. It's like he's more suspicious of me for showing him this than he is of Brandi for having signed it.

"I've been wanting to show this to you. I just didn't know..." I shake my head, feigning distress, then soften my tone. "I didn't want to see you get hurt again."

I stare at the floor and I'm beaming on the inside, proud of my quick thinking, but Nate scoffs. When his eyes drop back down to the document, they flicker across the top of the page, and then down to the bottom where Jared forged Brandi's signature, copying the one she used to sign her three-month intern contract. A strange mixture of surprise and pain flickers across his face. He struggles for a minute. I watch the slow change in him as the reality of this sinks in, his face now full of anger and betrayal and confusion.

"You're saying Brandi was...the whole time I was in Ohio..."

"Nate, there's no reason for someone to sign an NDA at Van Doren if they're just interning. I used to help my mom out during the summer and we never had any employees sign these." I give him a sympathetic look. "I wanted to tell you about this at the party, but you left too soon."

He shakes his head in disbelief, then meets my eyes. "She said she was sick."

"She wasn't sick, Nate. She got *caught*. I saw them with my own eyes."

Nate licks his lips, thinking that over, then his eyes snap up again. "But you paid her tuition."

I swallow hard. My eyes flutter.

"Why would you give her that money if you didn't need her to stay quiet about your plan to kill him?" His voice is clipped and full of acrimony. He's not an idiot.

I don't hesitate. I don't even blink. "I felt bad for her."

Nate's expression doesn't change. I keep going. I have to.

"After the party I convinced my father not to interview her so he wouldn't have a MeToo issue down the line. The mug shot had nothing to do with him letting her go. I just sent that to you because I didn't know if you knew who your girlfriend really was. I was looking out for you."

"So why—"

"When she found out she got fired, she called me, going ballistic, telling me how she was counting on that job, giving me the whole sob story about being raised in group homes. She got me, Nate. I totally fell for it. I was just looking out for my dad when I made him cancel the interview. I wasn't trying to ruin her life." I shrug. "So I figured giving her the money was the least I could do so she could finish school. Figured it would keep her away from my dad too."

Nate sighs and turns those angry eyes away from me. When they come back, they're softer, but still wary, hard around the edges. "So you were never gonna kill your dad?"

"We'd been getting so close after Mom died. Then the cancer. He'd finally made it into remission." My voice breaks, and I take a breath as my body shudders. "I was so happy. I'd already lost one parent. I couldn't..." I jerk my hand up to fan away the tears from my eyes and take a steadying breath.

"The wedding was gonna be a dual celebration. Not just that he'd found love again. That he'd found *life* again."

Nate inhales. I watch his broad chest expand. His eyes flash with something like rage, but then he lets out a breath and lowers his head, as though all the fight in him has died.

"Look," I say, stepping closer to him. "She's not the girl you thought she was."

"But why would Brandi kill him?" he says, almost to himself, and for the first time his voice isn't harsh, only tired, his expression resigned.

I speak softly. "You saw the emails. She couldn't handle him getting engaged. She wanted him to choose *her.*" Nate looks like he's going to argue, then lets out a harsh breath. His face begins to change, and I hurriedly say, "Maybe she did love you at some point. But she fell for my father, and I guess it…consumed her. I don't think she ever meant to hurt you."

Nate is silent for a while. He leans against the wall and runs a hand over his face.

I move even closer to him. "I never meant to hurt you, either, Nate." I whisper it because I'm terrified to say it louder.

He looks at me, but his expression gives away nothing. "Doesn't change that you did." His voice is so quiet now, I can barely hear him.

"Honestly." Honestly. "I never meant to break your heart. I was just young. And stupid. I was so in love with you that— I don't know—it scared me, I think." I stop and catch my breath. "I was scared, Nate."

He shakes his head, like that makes absolutely no sense to him. "Scared of what?"

"Of you. Of *us.*"

My heart is beating so fast I can feel it hammering against my chest. I know he thinks I'm lying. I know he thinks I slept with a bunch of random guys behind his back and that I never loved him and that everything I'm saying is bullshit. But it's not. It's the truth. I didn't sleep around with a bunch of guys. It was just *one* guy. *One* stupid mistake. I can admit that now. I don't even know why I did it. It's not like the guy was really hot or an amazing fuck or something; he was neither. It was my own shit, my own...issues.

I remember when it happened, that first time, so clearly. I don't even remember how it escalated. I just remember we started texting as soon as we exchanged numbers. And soon he invited me to this party and I went, and we ended up in someone's parents' bedroom and I was way too drunk and Nate was on my mind. I wanted to make him jealous. Not a little jealous. Angry jealous. No one wants what no one wants. I think I wanted Nate to want me so bad that he'd do anything to have me—the same way I wanted him. I needed to see him fight for me. Prove to me that he loved me. He'd never said the words. Not really. The most I'd get was a *me too* and *you know how I feel about you*, but never a simple, straightforward, *I love you*. I wanted that. I craved that.

I still do. Everybody does. It's normal. Human.

So I fucked him, that other guy, and it didn't mean anything. Not the first time, not the second or the third or the fifth. What we had was minor and temporary. I didn't care about him. There were no stakes, nothing to lose. With Nate, I had everything to lose. And I did. I lost everything.

It was dumb, it makes no sense to me now, but I was trying to scare him into telling me he loved me—because *I* was scared. I didn't want to be alone in love; I couldn't stand the thought. I needed to know. I didn't do it because I didn't love him. I've always loved him. That's the most important thing. I need Nate to know that. So we can move past this. So we can start over.

I reach out to touch his hand.

He snatches it away, his eyes straight ahead, then heads off without another word to me.

I let him go.

It's okay. I need to give him his space. He's probably in shock. He just needs a little time. He'll come around, I know it, I can feel it, and then he'll realize how much I fucking love him.

22

BRANDI

I can't remember how long it's been since I've slept. Or eaten. My stomach aches from the emptiness, but I can't hold anything down.

I jerk up in bed when the front door opens. It swings so hard it bounces off the wall, startling me to the point of a gasp. I head over to the door. Nate.

Something's wrong. I can tell right away.

At first, I think something must have happened with the press. Those stupid reporters. They probably followed him on the way to the gym. I told him before he left that he shouldn't leave the apartment, that they'd hound him, wanting a statement, a comment, a reaction, but he insisted on keeping up with his regimen since he's about to leave for training.

But now that I'm looking at him, I know that's not what's going on. His energy is different. Strange. I can feel it all the way from across the room.

I climb off the bed and take slow steps toward the front where Nate's standing, glaring at me. "Where were you? I tried—"

"Do you know what I had to do to convince my dad to loan me that bond money?"

I'm quiet for a moment. His words sound a bit slurred and his tone is so harsh, I don't know how to respond.

"Do you have any fucking idea?"

I jump back from the gravel in his voice. The weight of his gaze is almost painful, but I force myself to hold his eyes.

No, I don't want to know, I want to say. Whatever he had to do, I'd rather him keep to himself. It'll only stress me out more, make me feel like even more of a charity case than I already do.

I glance down at my hands, then look up at him. He's staring at me, but his eyes are out of focus. I've never seen him like this, not even close to this. I don't understand. I thought I knew him better than this. This seems completely out of character for him. His voice. His tone. He never sounds like this, even when he's mad. I don't get it.

And then it clicks.

"Nate," I say carefully, trying to lock eyes with him. "Have you been drinking?"

But I don't need to ask. It's obvious by the way he stumbles as he moves closer to me and I can smell the hard whiff of alcohol from here. I fold my arms across my chest.

"I couldn't tell him you'd gotten locked up for murder," he says, completely ignoring me. "So I told him I wanted to buy you a ring. Told him I loved you." He gives me a sideways glance and I can feel his fury. All of it. "Said I was proposing to you. Figured once this was all cleared up, I'd tell him the truth."

I run my brain through the ramifications of that, my throat going dry. By now his father must know he lied, if it was on the news. This must be why he's flipping out. His father must have called and grilled him.

They've probably shown my picture and Nate's by now. They were snapping photos nonstop as we left the precinct.

"Nate—"

"I told him I loved you, and you've been playing me this whole time."

I stumble back a step. I'm so confused.

His eyes are locked on mine now, the anger there unmistakable, but it's laced with hurt, which unsettles me. He was in such a good mood earlier, considering everything going on, all sweet and understanding and patient, and now...

I don't know who this is.

I don't know what happened.

Nate looks away, like he's trying to collect some part of himself.

I'm still trying to understand. I draw a short breath and try my best to stay calm. "What are you talking about?"

"What the hell was I thinking?" He sounds so far away. "Maybe somebody figured out a way to get inside your account, sent some bullshit emails. But nobody could get their hands on those pics unless you sent them," he says, his words crashing into each other, the slurring making them practically incomprehensible now.

I look away. I don't want to see him like this. "I didn't send—"

"Stop lying," he barks, then lowers his voice to a harsh whisper. "Stop fucking lying."

Before I can get another word in, he takes off, storming past the bed, and snatches open the closet door. "You fucked him at the party, didn't you? You just couldn't help yourself when you saw him. What is it, the power? The money? Or do you just have a thing for old, white motherfuckers? Fucking saggy, wrinkled balls—"

"Will you stop it?" I scream, pulling on his arm. "Where are you getting this?"

He whips around, yanking his arm free. His cheeks are

flushed, his breathing quick. "You mean how'd I find out the *truth*?"

Those words settle into my chest and grip my heart and for a moment I think time has stopped.

"Nate." I need to calm him down. "Just look at me for a second. *Nate?*"

His jaw flexes. "I saw the NDA."

"What NDA? I never signed—"

"Why would you have to sign an NDA if you're just an intern?"

"I don't know what you're..."

My voice trails off as he turns away. He grabs a duffel bag from the closet and starts blindly tossing clothes in. I watch him, not knowing what to say or how to stop this.

"You're not supposed to leave for Ohio until tomorrow. We still have one more day."

He doesn't stop. I don't know if he's even listening to me anymore. My eyes catch some of the balled-up things he pushes into the bag.

"What are you doing? That's not even your stuff."

"I know that." His voice sounds so far away.

My chest tightens. "Nate..."

But nothing I can think of to say seems good enough. He can't mean what I think he means. My eyes fill against my own will and I wipe my face with the back of my hand before the tears can roll down my cheeks.

Nate glances at me, jaw tight. I've never seen him this angry. Or this drunk. I know he's feeling vulnerable. I know he's not thinking straight. I know all of that. It still hurts.

"Nate, you..." I shake my head. None of this is making any sense. I reach over, grab his arm. "Where am I supposed to go?"

He avoids my eyes and shrugs me off without answering me.

I feel something inside me collapse, as if someone has punctured a golf ball–size hole in my lungs. I didn't think—I never thought he could be this brutal. I don't care if he's drunk. This isn't him. This isn't the Nate I know.

I try to keep my voice level, but I'm desperate. "Nate. Please, just talk to me. What NDA are you—"

He snatches away and fills the bag with the rest of my stuff. I can't watch. I go in the front and pace back and forth, trying to come up with a way to rectify this. Whatever this is.

Maybe he spoke to those cops again. Maybe they hunted him down, trying to get to me, and filled his head with all this shit. These lies. That's the only sensible thing I can think of.

My head jerks around when I hear Nate come up behind me. He doesn't say anything, just tosses the bag my way. The bathroom door slams a few seconds later and I feel the hurt of that rejection reverberate through me a thousand times.

If Nate wants me out, I'll leave. I know how to be alone. I don't want to stay here with him while he's like this anyway.

Tears threaten to fall, but I force them to stay where they belong. I need to focus on the things that I can control. I need to figure out how I can get more information about the night Simon was murdered. Any information.

When I throw my bag over my shoulder, a part of me thinks Nate will come out and stop me before I leave.

He doesn't.

Some places are designed for you to look right past them.

This is one of those places. The kind you go to disappear, to be invisible like a flame on a wall.

I stare at the long stretch of building and the weed-choked tarmac surrounding it, a shitty two-story strip of weathered doors masquerading as a motel somewhere in Jersey. The red sign above uneven steps only half blinks in the dark. Ten feet down, an old barefoot man in soiled clothing is asleep in the fetal position on the hard, litter-strewn concrete. I've spent nights in these kinds of places before. If you've been to one, you've been to them all.

As I push into the lobby, the balding man behind the counter looks up from a folded newspaper, and it seems like he's been here as long as the rug in the corner, and just as hard used.

His gaze flicks over my shoulder, into the parking lot, then he glares at me. "What kind of trouble you in?"

My eyes fall down to my clothes, my shoes. "What makes you think I'm in trouble?"

The man darts his eyes to my overstuffed bag. "Easy to tell when someone's running."

My leg bounces. "I need a room," I say.

My card is already in my hand. I put it on the counter. The man glances down, then back up, his gaze lingering longer this time.

"What's a beautiful girl like you doing out in a place like this?" he asks, a sudden gleam in his eyes. His smile makes my skin crawl.

I roll my shoulders. "Can I just have a room, please?"

He glances at something on his computer. "Only have one room left. In the basement. Half the price. You want it?"

I don't have a choice so I nod, tell him that I need the room until Thursday because I only have enough money in my account for three nights. When he's done with my card, he rakes his eyes over me again, then jerks a drawer open and pulls out a key dangling from a silver chain.

I take it, then head down to the basement level, the violent stench of mildew immediately assaulting me. I quickly secure both locks and slip the chain onto the latch before slumping against the door, feeling a small wave of relief wash over me. But it doesn't last. The room itself solidifies around me—walls that seem to tilt in and stale smells I know too well: shit, sweat and piss. Just like all the other places I've stayed in, it holds a listlessness, a sort of anguish that seems to be ingrained into the plaster, which has multiple fist-size holes in it.

Nate's words keep piercing me. I push them away, every hurtful thing he said, try to cling to that quiet space in my brain. I have to stay strong. Solid. Like a boulder. But the tears hit me before I'm done inspecting the paper-thin mattress for bedbugs, and before I know it, my shoulders are shaking, my stomach clenching hard as I try to catch my breath. I sink to the floor and cover my eyes with my hands, crying so hard that I can't even draw in enough breaths to calm myself. Hot tears slide down my cheeks, each one taunting me.

I've never felt so powerless.

I gasp for air and try to stop the sobs, but then it passes. I can breathe. I can survive this. I have to. I push myself up to my feet and drag a sleeve across my face.

Outside the window is a brick wall. I can hear the neighbors in the building next door, their windows still open and less than five feet away from mine. I drag the curtain shut and make my way back over to the bed. The sheets are cool and limp and stained. I flip them back, inspecting between the thin folds, and there are a few holes big enough to stick a finger in, but it's not the worst I've seen. I step inside the bathroom to check the toilet, and when I lift the seat, a cockroach the size of my thumb leaps from the water. I jump back, then flush it down and close the door.

I lie in the dark with my shoes on and it hits me how supremely alone I am. I have no one to call, no one to vent to, no one to help me. When I glance over at the nightstand, there is a phone and a pile of cigarette ashes next to an opened condom wrapper. There is also a pervasive shit smell coming from somewhere in the room, but I don't know where.

I shift and get inside the covers, wondering if I'll even be able to sleep, and what dreams will come if I can. Rolling onto my stomach, I almost cry out, but I should have expected it by now: the cramps. I haven't eaten all day. But food is the last thing on my mind. All I want is sleep, except when I close my eyes, the only thing I feel is the pain.

I jerk awake to my phone vibrating on the nightstand, the abrupt hum piercing through the silence like an iron dagger.

I reach over and glance at the screen. Nate's name in big white letters. I hesitate, holding my finger over that little green button. I don't know what he's going to say. I don't know what he needs to hear. But maybe he's sobered up and is thinking clearly again.

A part of me hates him for what he did, throwing me out like I was worthless to him, the way he looked at me. He's supposed to trust me no matter what. If we don't have trust, we don't have anything. I slide my finger over the screen, answer on the last ring, but as soon as I do, the line drops.

The next time it rings, ten minutes later, I answer right away. There's a long pause and then Nate finally speaks. "You good?"

I'm shocked at the gentle tone of his voice, the simplicity of those words. "Yeah," I say, and my voice sounds as weak as I feel. "I'm—I'm okay."

He doesn't say anything. The silence is absolute, almost oppressive. I listen to him breathe.

My throat feels raw, like I've been screaming in my sleep. "Nate, let me just—"

But he cuts me off right away. "I didn't call to talk. I just needed to know if you were okay. That you have somewhere to stay."

I take a breath and talk as softly as I can. "Nate, yesterday I—"

"I can't do this right now, B." He sounds so tired. I've never heard him sound like this, so many sides of him I've never known until all of this drama. "I just—I don't know who to trust right now."

"Nate—"

Before I can get out another word, the line goes dead in my ear.

I stare at the ceiling, face tight from dried tears. He still cares about me. I know he does. I heard it in his voice, though it doesn't make this hurt any less.

I also know how this all must look to him. He thinks I cheated on him. He thinks I sent those messages, that I was actually having an ongoing relationship behind his back, filling his ears with lies while he was filling me with love, patience and sincerity. Maybe a different guy wouldn't be so sensitive to it, but he's been through this before. Being cheated on. Lied to. Manipulated. I have to keep reminding myself of that. I can't take this personally. Those cops have hard evidence against me. I can see how easy it could be to believe their version of the story. Taylor's version. Who knows what else she said that they're not telling me?

I turn onto my stomach and bury my face in the pillow, forcing my eyelids shut, and do my best to push Nate somewhere in the back of my mind.

When sleep finally comes, hours later, it's as if I'm being pulled under water, being taken completely.

23

BRANDI

I stir awake with a strangled scream in my throat and the residual image of a dead man on the floor, his body still trembling as the life leaves him. My hands are damp, pillow moist beneath my neck, shirt soaked through with cold sweat.

Shifting myself up to my elbows, I shake away the nightmare and glance bleary-eyed around the dim room, no idea where I am or how I got here. The sudden movement makes the room shift and sway. Thin carpet ripples near the legs of a battered chair. The musty air coming from the broken AC vent is stifling, a thick layer of dust on every surface. My eyes find my shoes, my duffel bag in the corner.

Time stops for just a moment. Then I remember why I'm in this hellhole.

Nate. Kicking me out.

My stomach tightens. I close my eyes and feel the heavy ache in my chest. I can't tell whether this is truly physical pain or just a figment of my imagination.

I lift my phone from the pillow and check the time. Five after seven. I slept for three hours, but my body feels heavy, like there are days missing from my memory.

I try to move, pull myself up from the bed, but I'm immediately pulled back down. My head is spinning, all the feeling in my body stalled for a few moments. I close my eyes and take several deep breaths. I can feel the blood rushing to my head, then to my arms, my legs. Once I feel like I can stand without collapsing, I pull back the covers and swing my legs over the edge of the bed, which only makes things worse. My stomach convulses. I drop to my knees on the broken bathroom tile as my chest heaves, but all that comes up is pale, watery bile.

The weak spurting that comes out of the rusted shower-head is the color of whiskey and stinks of sewer water, the smell almost pungent enough to compete with the stench of mildew the proprietors obviously thought they could mask with the copious amounts of mothballs scattered around the tiny space. I twist the handle and stop the water without letting a drop hit my skin.

I wash up the best I can and brush my teeth in the gas station bathroom ten blocks away, then pull on clean underwear. I turn in to the bodega on the corner, grab two packs of Cup Noodles, a bottle of water and order a sandwich at the counter. I hold my breath when I hand over my card, and just when I think I'm in the clear, he looks up at me with a telltale look of pity in his eyes.

"*Mami*, you have another card?"

I shake my head, humiliated. "Can you just take the water off?"

He hits a few buttons on the register and slips the card inside the chip reader again. I keep a ten-dollar bill in my wallet for emergencies, but if I can't get Nate to come around before Thursday, I'll have no way of getting back into the city.

I see that my card has been declined again, but can't bear to hear the words, so I jump in before he meets my gaze again. "Actually, can you just do the water and the noodles? I'm not even that hungry."

He looks at me for a second, then gestures to the sandwich. "I already made it, *Mami*. Let me try it one more time."

We both know how futile this third attempt is, but I stay silent as he inserts my card into the machine again. It doesn't go through.

"Sorry," I tell him, wishing I could evaporate. "That's all I have."

I turn away to leave, but he calls out to me and pushes the bag toward me, insisting I take it anyway. I thank him and keep my eyes averted when I grab the handles of the plastic bag.

My equilibrium is completely off when I turn out of the store. I need something in my stomach right now. I open the bag and hustle with the wrapper to get a bite of my sandwich, but as soon as I bring it to my mouth, I'm thwarted by a massive man running for the bus zooming past. I watch him bang on the back doors hard enough for the driver to brake and then look at my sandwich mingling with the puddle of rainwater from last night's shower. Before I can even consider picking it up and attempting to salvage the bottom half, a pair of pigeons waddle over and claim it as their lunch.

By the time I push back into my room, the urge to cry has subsided, though the feeling of defeat hasn't. It's not just the sandwich. It's everything I've lost in such a short amount of time. My internship. A potential summer gig. My apartment. Nate.

I should have listened to him, should have heeded his warning about Taylor. But I had to be stupid and play her game, accept not only her money, but her friends' bribes too.

I make both cups of noodles using the bottle of water, and wait fifteen minutes for them to soften up, then eat it cold. I sleep through the rest of the day, but at night it's too loud. The walls have more holes in them than this raggedy blanket. I can hear things I shouldn't. There's a man in the room above me who sounds like he's in the middle of a psychotic break and a woman next to me who is clearly stuck in a vindictive custody battle with her son's father. In the middle of the night, I stir awake to the sound of the nightshift guy pushing inside the room. When I jump up, he claims he forgot I paid for three nights, but I see his erection as he apologizes and shuffles out. I get up because there's no way I can go back to sleep now, and am determined to locate the shit smell. When I open the minuscule closet, I see that a dirty diaper has been left on one of the racks. I get back in bed and spend the rest of the night monitoring the room for roaches.

On Wednesday morning I check my phone and there are still no missed texts or calls from Nate. I squeeze my eyes shut and try to travel back to so many worse times in my life, hungrier, colder, sadder times, but the doom of the present keeps tumbling back to the front of my brain. I don't know how I ended up so alone again, and I hate myself for ever getting comfortable, for ever thinking that things could be different, that I could somehow outwit the universe that's clearly got an ax to grind with me. An orphan girl coupled up with the son of a football legend. How fucking silly. I don't know how I ever got so tangled in the fantasy of it all. My thumb hovers over his name in my recent calls log. Before I can talk myself out of it, I put the call through. If he doesn't answer, I won't ever call him again. I get his voice mail after three rings and hang up.

Before I let go of my phone, I click into the Instagram app. I don't know why I'm shocked when I see that I have over three hundred unread DMs. I barely ever post, so I guess it didn't take long for the death threats to pile up under all of my photos from the past year. Apparently, a troll letting everyone know that *my corpse deserves to be raped in every orifice* isn't alone. The comment has been liked by over a hundred people and planted under the last photo I posted with Nate. My stomach tightens at the thought of him getting this kind of hate too. How can this not be illegal? These people don't know me. They don't know what actually happened. They don't know what their poisonous words could make me do. To myself. I almost click through to Nate's profile to check, but stop myself at the last moment.

Instead, I torture myself more and click through to the profile of a user who has posted multiple comments on different photos in my feed. And another. And another. They're all rabid Taylor Van Doren stans. Of course. After mapping a dozen trolls back to Taylor wannabes, I deactivate my profile and drop my phone next to my leg. Everything is shaking. The entire room is blurry no matter how many times I blink.

And then I realize I have to get out of here. I have to do something. There has to be some way to find a crack in Taylor's story, some place to start chipping away at. She must have given the cops her own alibi, or else they would have suspected her too. And if she did actually have an alibi, then who laced his glasses with the poison? Jared? Mei? I think about the only other person who was there the night Simon was murdered. His fiancée. The report on TMZ said that she was the last to see him alive.

Maybe she has insight about what happened that night. Maybe she knows about the drama between Taylor and her dad. Maybe she overheard them arguing—Taylor made it seem like she hated him. Not just the normal way girls sometimes resent their parents. She actually *hated* him, in the darkest way possible. I could hear it in her voice that day I called her and accepted her poisonous bribe. If only I could get proof of how severe her hate for him was. She hated him enough to want him dead. Enough to *kill* him.

Maybe I'm getting way too ahead of myself, but another giant cockroach crawling down the wall next to my head reminds me that sitting here doing nothing won't get me any closer to an answer.

I still have Simon's assistant's number saved in my phone. I go into my contacts and dial her number. Hopefully, she can get me in touch with his fiancée.

The line clicks over after three rings, but it's not his assistant who answers. I don't recognize the voice in my ear.

"Hello? Who's speaking, please?" Her accent is strong.

"Oh. Hi. Uh…this is…sorry, who is this?"

"You called me."

I can already hear the contempt in her voice. Then I realize, this must be her. His fiancée. "Um…Mr. Van Doren…I used to work for the company. As an intern. I—"

"I know who you are." Unbridled malice jumps into her voice. "If you call this number again, I'm going to call the cops—"

"No, don't. I swear, I didn't kill your—I didn't kill anyone. I just…I need to talk to you."

"You want to *talk*? You know, you and your lawyers better try for an insanity plea because you sound real fucking crazy to me."

"I—I just think you might know something. I mean, I'm hoping you might be able to help me."

"*Help* you? Why would I help you?"

"I know what really happened to Simon."

"I know what happened to him too. You killed him because he rejected you."

"It's safer if we talk about this face-to-face."

"If I ever see you, you'll end up just like Simon," she says, her voice trembling.

"Look, I know me asking you to trust me is asking a lot of you—"

"You should be in fucking jail with all the other murderers and rapists instead of calling me."

The line drops dead.

I push out a breath and stare at my call log. Izzy is my last resort. Without her, I have no idea how I can clear my name. I suck in a breath and call her back, not expecting her to answer, but she does, on the last ring.

"You kill my fiancé and now you're harassing me?" she snaps, her wrath down to a simmer, and somehow this feels more vicious than when it was fully aflame.

"Please. I just need to..." I force myself to remain calm; have to pace in order to keep my voice level. "It wasn't me. I didn't poison Simon, but I'm pretty sure I know who did and I'm this close to proving it."

"You're..." There's a hitch in her voice. "You can prove it?"

"I can meet you wherever you are and—"

"What do you have?"

I pause. "I can't say over the phone."

I expect her to cave, to at least react, but there's nothing but a buzzing silence from her end.

"I wouldn't be calling you if what I had wasn't solid," I say.

The longest moment of silence slithers by. Then I hear her breathing. She's still there.

When I click into my Uber app, I realize that I'm still logged into Nate's account, so I call a car and arrive at the house in just over an hour. Before I know what I'm going to say, one of the large iron doors swings open in front of my face.

I've seen her on the news, but she's even more beautiful

in person. Up close, she looks like she can pass for my age. She is wearing towering platform ankle boots, a Victorian lace blouse with a leather harness layered over top, which I instantly recognize as a Van Doren sample from the fall collection that hasn't even been released yet. Her fresh blowout hangs past her shoulders, the darkest brown.

I'm a little taken aback by how well put together she is. I was expecting—I don't know—I thought she'd be much more... disheveled. Considering.

Still, I tell myself not to judge her. People grieve in strange ways. Some people completely shut their emotions down and go numb and pretend everything is normal; it's the only way they can deal with the pain. That's what I did after the crash.

Izzy doesn't say much, just glares at me and then leads me through the main living space and kitchen to Simon's office. I step in behind her and a chill covers me. This is where he died. My eyes flick around the room. This space feels eerily intimate, from the scribbled notes scattered across the desk, to the gallery of photos in black frames on the wall. Frozen family moments from throughout the years, the kind I'll never have.

Izzy turns to face me. "Let's see it," she says, making no question of her impatience. "Where's this proof that exonerates you?"

There's something in her tone, an aggression that says she wants to hear me out but she's not really willing to listen to a word I have to say. Her invitation to give her what I have is hostile at best, but really, it's a challenge. She wants me to fail so she can humiliate me, so she can go berserk like she did on the phone, get some of her fury out. But there's something about her anger that feels angsty, almost like fear. Maybe she's afraid to hear what I have to say because it could derail her grieving process. Her almost-husband is dead. He was senselessly murdered. I can only imagine she is desperate for justice, and pegging me as the murderer is much easier to swallow than the killer still being out there.

"It's about Taylor," I say, and the moment I speak her name, something lights in Izzy's eyes.

"What about Taylor?" First, it's confusion that contorts her face, then I see it morph into disbelief. "You have proof that *Taylor* poisoned Simon? That's absurd."

"She framed me. I can prove it."

"Well, if you can prove it, why did you come here instead of to the cops?"

"Because I need you to help me. I need you to help me prove she did this so I can clear my name."

But she is already shaking her head. "You shouldn't have come here."

"Please. Just—"

"You have nothing. All you're trying to do is pin this on his poor daughter so you can get out of going to prison."

"Look, I know this looks bad. I can't explain the emails or how those photos got attached, but I didn't write them. I didn't—I wasn't sleeping with Simon. I love my boyfriend."

She rolls her eyes. "Don't they all."

"The night at the party was the first time I'd ever even spoken to him."

"If you didn't write them…" She studies me, a veil of confusion twisting her soft features. "What makes you so sure Taylor has something to do with this?"

"I overheard her and her friends at the charity ball. They were talking about killing him…about poisoning him." I pause so she can think about what I'm saying. "I think she'd been planning on doing it for weeks. I just never thought she'd actually go through with it."

"Oh, so you…" Izzy pauses and almost looks relieved, then the attitude is back. "You don't actually have any proof?"

"Not exactly. I mean, I can prove it, but I need your..."

I stop, noticing the way Izzy's face contorts as she rubs her stomach. "Are you okay?"

She looks away, and when she turns back, she's in tears. "Am I okay? Would *you* be okay if the father of your first child was dead? God, this is the fourth time today."

I just stand there, dazed for a moment.

My heart pulls as my mind races back to what Taylor told me about her father over the phone that day. About what he did to his wife, his family. And then I think about Taylor and everything she's done, to this woman, to me, and I don't know who's worse.

"That's why you were getting married?" I ask.

Izzy doesn't confirm or deny, just puts her back to me and wipes her face. Her hand goes back to her belly, more urgently this time, gripping at the skin like she can grip the pain and hurl it away. Before I can ask, she's moving to the door. Upstairs I hear a door open and close, then the sound of violent vomiting.

I wait a few moments, then edge near the door. "Do you need help?"

"I'm fine," she shouts. Another loud hurl. I can hear the wetness from here. "You can let yourself out."

"I can hold your hair if you—"

"Just shut the door on your way out."

I step out of the room and glance back at that iron set of doors, but I can't bring my feet to move through the foyer toward them. My mind won't stop whirring. I slip back into the room and glance around the aggressively wood-filled space. My eyes find the desktop from across the room, then my fingertips are on the keyboard. The screen comes to life with a veil of blue light, immediately prompting a password for access. I was expecting this, but was hoping for a miracle. I have no idea what it could be. I don't know any special dates, birthdays, nothing I could even try.

I pull on the top drawer of his desk and find nothing interesting. I move on to the file cabinet pushed against the wall, and when the heavy top drawer opens, my heart speeds up. There's six drawers total. I flip through dozens and dozens of folders stuffed with documents, not sure what I'm even looking for. Nothing sticks out, just a bunch of paperwork I can't really parse, useless legal and tax documents filled with sophisticated jargon. I circle the desk and make my way around the room, opening and closing every drawer I find. I lift stacks of papers. Check behind books. Under magazines. Nothing remotely interesting sticks out, even on my second round. I go back to Simon's desk, fling open every drawer, sifting through receipts and basic office junk for anything that could lead me to something. I stop myself from slamming the bottom drawer shut in frustration and push my hair from my face.

Then I see it.

The last drawer has a second compartment inside it, a secret compartment under a stack of innocuous paperwork. And there's a tiny keyhole on top of it. Shit.

I test it first to confirm it's locked, and of course it is. But I'm not leaving this room until I get inside it. There has to be something juicy or important in here if it's the only drawer that's locked in this entire room. I check the other drawers for a key, find nothing, then scan the surface of the desk to see if there's something else I've missed, and my eyes settle on a collection of paper clips.

It's not my first time picking a lock; in the last home I stayed in we used to hack our way into each other's rooms all the time whenever someone managed to lift a fork from the kitchen. And paper clips are much more malleable than kitchen utensils. I bend and fold one so it has a forty-five-degree angle and can act as a tension tool. I open another one until it's flat with a loop at the crown, but when I apply pressure, it takes way longer than I expect to lift all the pins in the barrel. The lock is tiny and the tension from the safety pins is barely enough, but I keep trying to rake the pins until I hear Izzy coming, her footsteps heavy and measured as she descends the staircase as if she's still in pain. I consider ducking behind the desk in case she comes in to check to see if I've left, but instead, I slip the paper clips inside my back pocket, ease the drawer shut as quietly as I can and slip behind the door. Izzy crosses the threshold, and I hold my breath, but the second she gets another step into the space, another wave of nausea hits her and she scurries back out with a terrible, guttural sound.

Hoping this wave of sickness is as powerful as the last one, I hustle back over to Simon's desk, stick the hook I made with the paper clips into the lock and concentrate on bumping up all the pins in the barrel. Finally, the mechanism disengages, and I'm in. I'm fucking in and there's…not even much here. A leather-bound portfolio with a stack of personal documents— birth certificate, passport, social security card, the death certificate of his wife. That last one makes me pause. I vaguely remember seeing my parents' death certificates, and then suddenly, time is slowing and my head is filling with hazy, psychedelic images of them. When I blink, it comes into focus. Another legal document.

LAST WILL AND TESTAMENT OF is printed at the top. Then a blank line that has been filled in with "Simon Van Doren."

I have Simon Van Doren's will in my hands for less than five seconds before an audible gasp escapes my throat. My jaw tightens and there is almost an audible click in my head, the satisfying sound of the final pieces shifting into place. It seems so simple to me now, so obvious.

I waste no time before I'm on the move, taking the stairs two at a time. The corridor is long and grand, lots of haughty-looking artwork adorning the wainscoted walls, most notably a Helmut Newton of two naked women smoking in front of a car, things that look different now that all the lights are on and there are no people shouting in the background. One of the two French doors at the crown of the hall is ajar, and the closer I get, the louder and wetter Izzy's vomiting becomes.

When I turn inside the slightly opened door Izzy has disappeared behind, I see that this is Simon's bedroom suite. There's a massive four-poster bed in the middle of the room, covered in silky white sheets and a matching duvet. The door to a walk-in closet is slightly ajar. I can see the wood and perfectly arranged clothes and shoes from here. There's a small sitting area in one corner of the room, and a small bar cart in the other. The door to the en suite is wide-open. Izzy is down on her knees with her head in the porcelain. She looks even worse than she sounds, and apparently, she's given up on holding her hair out of the way.

"Taylor got everything if Simon died," I say, what I just read downstairs reverberating in my head as I slowly make my way across the room.

I, Simon Van Doren, make, publish and declare this to be my Last Will and Testament, revoking all wills and codicils at any time heretofore made by me.

I give all of my property and estate to Taylor Van Doren.

I appoint Taylor Van Doren as Executor of this Will.

Taylor tried to get me on her side, telling me all that shit her father did to her, to her mom, but this is why she killed him. I assumed from the jump that Taylor had a hefty trust fund set up just like all the other heiresses who work at Van Doren, who dominate the general fashion scene, but inheriting his entire estate is wild. It's motive doused in marinade.

And now it's in my hands. My literal Get Out of Jail Free card. Maybe Simon Van Doren truly was a horrible man and is the reason her mother took her own life, but inheriting every penny of his net worth was Taylor's prime benefit from making him disappear.

Izzy gags and heaves a few times, and I glance away to give her privacy. After she catches her breath, her eyes flit around for something. She looks completely disoriented, her eyes watery, so I hand her a towel that I grab from a glass cabinet. She wipes her face, and there's some remnants she misses, but I ignore it, clenching my stomach to bear the awful stench, and step closer to her.

"Did you know this?" I ask, but Izzy doesn't answer me. She pushes up to her feet and eases in front of the marble vanity to appraise herself. I watch her as she runs the tap and cleans her face more thoroughly this time.

"What are you still doing here?" she asks after a moment, but she avoids my eyes, maybe ashamed of the way she looks. "God. Thought this was only supposed to happen in the morning."

She rubs her swollen stomach and moans as she collapses onto the bed, and while I obviously don't know what it's like to be pregnant, she seems to be intentionally pulling out the theatrics. She wants me to leave. She doesn't want to address what I've said about Simon, and I have no idea why.

I follow her into the bedroom and once she sits down on the edge of the bed, I show her the copy of Simon's will I found. Her gaze takes a beat to focus, but when she makes out the large print at the top, her eyes widen and meet mine.

"Where did you get that?" she snaps.

"Found it downstairs."

"Down..." Suddenly, she doesn't look so weak anymore

and jumps to her feet. "That was locked up. How'd you get the key?"

"I didn't. I—"

"I had it locked in Simon's desk. How'd you get in there?"

"I know this trick with a paper clip," I say. "Look, you want to find out who really hurt Simon, right?"

She nods and groans as she sits back down.

I step closer. "Then *this* is all we need."

Her eyes drop down to the document and she struggles to find her next words. It's like she has to force herself to ask, "What are you talking about?"

"This is proof that Taylor had a reason to murder her father. Money. The most obvious motive ever. It's just weird that the cops didn't do anything about this."

She takes the paper from my hand and skims it. "Simon modified it when he found out how far along the cancer was so that Taylor got control of his estate."

I take it back, and briefly look over it again.

IN WITNESS WHEREOF, I, Simon Van Doren, sign, seal, publish and declare this instrument as my Last Will and Testament this seventh day of February.

She's right. It was recently changed. Earlier this year.

"So you got nothing if he died?" I ask, the concept completely absurd to me.

"I didn't want his money," she says, but I find that hard to believe.

I stare at her, waiting for her to give me something more, but she just goes quiet, pensive.

And now the timing makes sense, why she waited until now to kill him. She could have killed her father before, but she waited until after he got engaged. That has to mean something.

I'm right. I can feel it.

"Brandi," Izzy says, sounding drained as she addresses me by my name for the first time. "I know how this must look, but I don't think Simon's will is going to do anything."

I'm about to pop. "Taylor got his full estate. You were about to marry him and change everything. She did this to get his money. How can you not see that?"

"The police have had it this whole time. If they thought Taylor had something to do with Simon being—"

"She killed him." My voice surprises me just as much as it does Izzy, but I don't back down. "And she's trying to frame me for it."

I move a few paces away from her, a bolt of energy buzzing through me as the clarity deepens. Then I hit a wall.

It's not enough. She's right. This will is not enough to clear my name. It would have been one of the first things the cops confiscated when they launched their investigation, yet they still arrested me without ever even seriously considering that Taylor did this.

"What did the cops say about the will when they got a copy?" I ask, scrutinizing her expression.

Izzy stares at me for a second, then cocks her head. "You know, if you're so innocent, you should focus on how to exonerate yourself and let the people who actually cared about Simon grieve in peace."

She rises to her feet and reaches out for the will, but I wave it just out of reach.

"I think you should leave," she says, making her way to the bathroom door again. "And if you burgle into my personal property this time, I'll be calling the cops."

A few beats after she slams the door, she's vomiting again.

I call an Uber once I get outside the gate and then I text Nate. I don't care if he's mad at me; I need to tell him this. I say: Need to talk. Call me. It's an emergency.

I want to say more, but I don't want to put any of it in writing.

The traffic back to Jersey is insane. By the time I head inside the motel, the afternoon is gone. I hastily pace back and forth as my call goes to Nate's voice mail again. Shit. I don't know what to do. I can't go to Bierman yet. I still need more proof if I'm going to exonerate myself. I need to figure out who sent those emails, how this person got the nudes from my phone. And I still don't understand how that bag of cyanide got into my closet, but I know it didn't just walk in and plant itself. Taylor couldn't have done this all herself. I went through and rearranged my closet after I went shopping with Mei and Jared, which was *after* Taylor showed up talking all that shit about how she was going to ruin my life. There was nothing there. And that tape. I need that security footage.

I try calling Nate again. There's no answer, but it rings five full times before I get his voice mail.

His phone is on; he's just not answering.

24

TAYLOR

I know Nate's going to think I'm crazy for doing this. But I'm not crazy. I love him. I'm sorry for what I did. I have to get him to understand that. No matter what it takes, he needs to know how I feel.

That's why I'm here. In Ohio. In his dorm room. Draped across his bed in a flimsy crop top with thin straps and high-waisted jeans that make my ass look perfect. I took the G-5 since there were no more red-eyes left. Rehearsed words sit on my tongue, but I'm still not exactly sure what I'm going to say. I thought about taking off all my clothes and surprising him in one of the poses I've practiced, but this isn't about sex. What we had was so much deeper than that.

I made a mistake, but I'm not the same insecure girl desperate for validation that I was back then. I won't make it again. I want him and him only.

The latch on the door clicks open, and my eyes snap in that direction. I swallow, nerves suddenly crawling up my throat, making it harder to breathe.

Nate steps in, headphones blaring so loud I can hear the beat of the rap song he's bumping his head to from here.

He looks up and stops short, his eyes finding me on his bed right away. "How the hell did you get in here?"

He definitely looks more disturbed than pleasantly surprised, but he doesn't look totally revolted.

"Thought we could talk," I say, ignoring his question.

He studies me for the longest time. "You flew five hundred miles to *talk*?" he says finally, and for a moment I can't tell whether he is angry or amused. His voice sounds like an ambiguous blend of both.

I narrow the gap between us. "Fine. I didn't come here just to talk." My eyes drop to his chest, then back up. "I wanted to see you. Do you...have a sec?"

Nate's eyes don't leave mine. He's still trying to figure this out. He inhales loud enough for me to hear the air invade his nostrils like he's going to refuse, but he changes his mind at the last second.

"Let me rinse off first."

I watch him grab a dark gray towel from a hook on the back of his closet door. He doesn't say anything else before he slips out, doesn't look back at me like I hope he will. The door shuts with a loud click. Not a full slam, but it's a statement.

I blow out a breath. This is going to be harder than I thought. I'm here, though. I'm fucking here. I sit back down on his bed and slip my heels off.

Nate's phone buzzes on the dresser. I ignore it and the call goes to his voice mail.

Two more calls come back-to-back. I get up and check the caller ID. It's an unsaved 212 number. I stare at it, debating whether I should answer, then slide my finger across the screen. "Nate's in the shower. Is this urgent?"

I hear someone breathing. Then a faint click in my ear. "Hello?"

Silence.

I drop his phone back on the dresser. "Asshole."

My eyes float around the room again, mind drifting. Then my feet are drifting, too, and I'm peeking into his closet, smelling his clean clothes, sitting at his desk, flipping through notebooks, smiling at his scraggly handwriting, remembering when he stuck a Post-it note on my locker saying he wanted to take me out after one of his home games. Then I see it. Right in the corner of my periphery: a Polaroid of Brandi. She's smiling and pretty as always, but I don't flinch or recoil. I've got him. I know I do. It's only a matter of time before Nate has a pic of me on his desk. I'm so close.

The door clicks open.

Nate steps in, towel around his waist, hair still dripping, and I ache to be in his arms. I watch him as he slides open the top drawer of his dresser, then ease behind him.

"What happened? You used to be King of the Freeball."

He flips around to face me, no humor in his expression. "Taylor, what do you want?"

He sounds annoyed now, and inside I start to panic.

"Nate, it's been three years. I've changed. Matured." I take a breath. Weigh my words. "I'd never hurt you like that again." He opens his mouth to argue, but I speak over him. "I didn't realize what I had back then, but I know now, and I want it back. I want us back."

I take a step forward and put my hand on his. Some of the tension drains out of his body.

"Look, I won't pretend like I've got it all figured out because I don't, okay? But the one thing I do know is that not having you in my life scares me even more. It's been...so... it's just not the same without you." I pause, digging deeper to find the right words. I need him to understand. "I know I'm going to have to earn your trust back. I'm not asking for you to come around overnight. I'll do the work. I'll do whatever I have to. All I'm asking is…all I want is a second chance. Even if I don't deserve it."

I stop and take a breath. I'm very aware of my breathing in this moment. Of his. I haven't felt him this close to me in so long. I want to feel his lips on mine and his hands rough on my skin as he moves inside me. I want us to go back to the way we used to be, when everything in my world was perfect. Everything.

I can't hold back anymore. I take another step, pushing into him with my hips. He hesitates. Freezes. Long enough for my hand to make it to the tuck of his towel. He catches it just before it drops, holding that terry-cloth barrier between us.

"Nate, remember when we were alone at my father's party? When Brandi was talking to my father?" I pause, thinking about the moment. "What if you never brought her?" I lean in and kiss his neck, feel his throat against my lips.

He jerks back. "Stop."

"Don't tell me this is about her." I stare at him hard. "She *murdered* my father."

He frowns. "I don't believe that shit. She's not a murderer. Maybe she was sleeping with him, but she didn't fucking kill anybody."

He sounds so certain, but I can see the doubt in his eyes.

I sigh. "She did. She's mental. She's got you brainwashed."

He shakes his head so hard, I wouldn't be surprised to stumble across a headline tomorrow morning about a mysterious tectonic shift somewhere on the planet. "We were together that whole night."

I roll my eyes. "She obviously did it before she came back to your place. The glasses were laced. She didn't have to be there at the exact time my father drank from them."

He doesn't even consider it. He steps around me, eyes on the door handle, but I sidestep him, blocking him just in time.

"Taylor, you need to—"

"I can't believe this." Is he really trying to throw me out? "Are you forgetting who she is?"

"I'm not forgetting anything. You're the one who's forgetting. We're not friends. We're not anything."

I sigh. "I know I lied to you, but that was a long time ago. I was just confused, okay? I'm not the one who lied to you about who I am. Brandi has been pretending with you this whole time. You think you know her, but you don't."

"You don't know what you're—"

"She didn't tell you about getting arrested, did she?"

"I lied to her, too, all right? I didn't tell her about us. About our past. That doesn't make me a bad guy, and Brandi's omission doesn't make her a murderer."

Nate reaches for me again, softly but with a clear intention, and I move just out of his reach a second before he makes contact.

"Nate, stop." I catch his eyes, which are as tight as his jaw. "She fucked my father at that party. She's been fucking him since she started working at Van Doren. She doesn't care about you. She was just using you. Or maybe she was using my father. Who knows? But she definitely didn't love you. If she did, if she really cared about you, she wouldn't have cheated on you. She definitely wouldn't have been so careless."

He pauses. "Careless?"

That's it. I have him. Just need to reel him in now. Carefully.

I swallow to give myself a chance to gather my thoughts. "She didn't even cover her tracks."

"What tracks?"

"She barely cared if she got caught. Look what she did with the cyanide." His stare is blank. I go on. "Just chucked the rest of the powder in her purse and threw it in the closet. She was so full of herself, she didn't even try to get rid of the evidence."

And then it stops. Time. Nate's indignance. His loyalty to Brandi. He just stands there unblinking for a moment, trapped in such a deep trance that it seems like his respiratory system has paused.

Nate finally cocks his head. "Fuck."

But there's something odd about the way he looks at me then. His gaze drops down past my chin, to my feet, then back up to lock on to my eyes, a look of realization glowing inside them. And then I know I have him exactly where I need him.

"The cops found the cyanide in her bag..." The rest of his words trail off.

His mind is whirring. He's putting the pieces together. I let him continue.

"The bag was in the closet." He peeks at me, then nods to himself. "It's funny."

He looks at me again, expectantly, and I realize he's waiting for me to say something.

"*Funny* funny? Or ironic funny?"

He shifts. "It just seems weird, you know? Like why would she stash it in there? Careless is one thing, but that's straight-up stupid."

I shrug. "Guess she thought the cops wouldn't check her Chanel."

A veil of something I can't quite put my finger on gently contorts his features. It's obviously confusion, but mixed with something else, something unreadable.

"Looks can be deceiving," I say. "If I saw a brand-new Chanel bag sitting pretty on the top shelf, I probably wouldn't think to search it, either." I shrug again. "Guess she had the same thought. Or maybe she was planning on getting rid of it, but didn't have time. It happened so fast."

"Yeah," he mumbles.

Relief washes over me as he nods like I've just made perfect sense. I don't expect him to laugh, and even though it comes a beat too slow and is clearly a tad contrived, I get it. The whole part of his world that revolved around Brandi is crumbling. This will take time.

I give him a faint smile. "I'm sorry, but she's been fucking you over this whole time."

Nate doesn't say anything immediately, and I can almost hear my heart thrumming as he paces the tight space of his dorm room. I inch closer to him and I'm so relieved when he doesn't push me away.

I look up at him. "Just because it's over between you and her doesn't mean you have to be alone."

That pauses him for a moment, but I remember that glint of betrayal that flashed in his eyes after I cornered him in the gym. He's not going to consider taking her back after this. Fuck that *but I love her* shit.

Nate looks like he's jostling between two thoughts, two sides of himself. But I've hit a nerve. I'm so close, I know it. I feel it.

"Yeah," he finally says. His voice is so low and remote I'm not even sure if he's actually said it out loud or if I'm just imagining it.

I reach out a hand to touch his wrist. "So relax. If you want, we can—"

"Taylor, there's no *we*." He moves my hand from his arm.

I feel a sharp pang of rejection, but I push through it. "Nate."

He starts to step off, but I hold him back. He's huge, so really my grip on his arm is just a suggestion. But he stops. He wants me. Somewhere, deep down, I know it's true. There's just too much going on in his head right now. I tuck a hand around the top edge of his towel again, and he stares down at me with this distant look in his eyes, and I want to tell him that he doesn't have to fight it anymore. He doesn't have to worry; he's the only one I want. No one else matters. No one else ever has.

I tighten my grip to free the towel from his waist, but his hand comes down over mine and pushes it away. I shift back and look up at him. Nate doesn't say anything. He doesn't need to. The look in his eyes says enough. He's sneering at me. I half expect him to burst out laughing.

"Get out, Taylor," he says. His eyes don't blink.

"Are you serious?" I scoff in disbelief. "I came all the way here just to see you."

My eyes search his face, his eyes, for some kind of irony, but there is none. I sigh and look down at my hands. I can't look at him anymore.

He steps past me and leans for the door. I stare at him as he pulls it open for me, holding it there. A clear dismissal.

I balk. Don't move. "Why? Because of her?"

I can't say her name. I won't say her name.

"This has nothing to do with her."

"You're lying." My eyes snap over to his. "You still care about her, don't you? Even after all she—"

"Taylor—"

"*Don't you?*"

Nate still doesn't answer.

My head shakes, and then my lips are trembling and I can barely breathe. I push out of his room, the door slamming into the wall, and before I make it down the stairs, the tears come. I grab on to the railing and my body collapses all at once until I'm on my knees.

Mei was wrong about me flying out to Ohio. She was on

my side even though Jared thought it was a terrible idea. But she was right about something else: I should have killed Brandi when I had the fucking chance.

25

BRANDI

I end the call, slamming the phone on the receiver, a sick feeling fluttering in my gut like battered wings. My thoughts scatter in a dozen different directions.

Once again, I legitimately don't know what is happening. Why the hell is Taylor answering Nate's phone?

I want to scream. I can barely breathe, the anger choking me. My mind whirs into overdrive as I head back down to the basement. And then it hits me, in sections and then all at once, the pieces of a puzzle I didn't know needed to be solved.

There was no way Taylor could have gotten the poison into the apartment that day unless...

Unless Nate knew about it.

Unless Nate left the gym and let her into our apartment.

My stomach drops.

Nate.

My head spins. And then I remember. When I first told him that Taylor was planning to murder her father, he wasn't shocked. He wasn't the least bit surprised. It was as if he'd known all along.

No. He couldn't have. That's stupid. Insane. Not Nate. Not—

I don't know what to think.

He was the only one besides me who had access to those pictures that were attached to those emails. I sent them to him. Only him. Taylor couldn't have gotten her hands on them if he hadn't given them to her.

I let that go. Try to think of some other way to explain this. Nothing comes.

Nothing.

I thought today was a win, but now I realize I've been playing the wrong game. I feel so off balance, like I've looked right at a crosswalk when really, I should have looked left. This whole time I've been so focused on Taylor, trying to figure out how the hell she pulled all this off, when the answer has been right in my face all along, and now it seems impossible that I haven't noticed until now.

I pace in circles, the room moving on an invisible axis. I grip onto the edge of the couch to steady myself and another realization hits. My stomach turns. Nate could have gotten into my email account at any time. He has my password. He has *all* my passwords, just like I have all of his.

And to think he tried to turn this around on me, saying I was the only one who could have sent those photos when *he*—this *whole* time—

He lied about his relationship with Taylor. He's been lying to me for I don't know how long. Asking me to that party... setting me up with Taylor's father...

He's planned this all from the beginning.

I just can't figure out why. Why would he do this? Have they been working together this whole time or did she somehow convince him to help her somewhere along the way? None of this makes sense. This doesn't seem like Nate, not the Nate I know. He isn't this calculated or manipulative. I can tell when he's lying to me because he rarely ever lies. Then again, how well do we ever know one another? Do we ever know our partners as well as we think we do? Can we? I don't know. I feel so disoriented, so confused, a million thoughts crowding my frontal lobe at once.

I run my fingers through my hair. "Okay," I whisper. "Okay, okay, okay..."

There's no other way, I keep thinking. *No other way.*

My phone starts to vibrate in my hand, and I jump. I push out a steadying breath and flip it over.

Nate. Of course it's Nate. *Now* he calls me back. How convenient.

I lift up my phone, my hand trembling, and answer. I don't wait for him to speak. Anger climbs up my throat and I can't stop it. "I get it now."

There's a long pause from his end. "Get what?" His voice is low. Calm. Even.

"You sent the emails. God, I'm so *stupid*. All this time, you were the one helping her out. You sent those emails from my account, didn't you?"

"Whoa. B, calm down."

"Didn't you?"

"What are you talk—"

"I've been trying to make sense of all this. I couldn't figure out how she got the cyanide in our closet. But she didn't. *You* did."

"What?"

"Don't play me like I'm stupid, Nate." My hand is shaking so much I can barely keep a grip on my phone. "You wanted her that night at the ball. I knew it. I *saw* it. That's why you didn't tell me that you two were together in high school. You still have feelings for her. Going to that stupid party was never about getting me that job. You just wanted to see her again. Admit it."

I know he won't. I know he won't admit that he's still got

feelings for her. I keep going. I can't stop. My words come out like vomit, a steady, uncontrollable stream. "And now you're with her. What—was this all part of your plan? To frame me and get me out of your life so you wouldn't have to deal with me? So you could be with her? This was all her plan, and you went along with it, didn't you?"

"Brandi, slow down. Just let me—"

"When did she convince you to help her frame me for murder? Before or after you fucked—"

"Would you listen? I didn't help Taylor do *anything*. The only feelings I have for her is relief that I broke up with her when I did. And I don't know where you're getting your intel, but nobody fucked anybody." Now he sounds angry.

It only fuels me more. "Then why is she in Ohio with you, answering your phone, you asshole?"

His voice drops. "Brandi. Look, I..." He fumbles for the words but can't seem to find them. "I don't know why she was...I didn't—"

I hang up and toss my phone onto the bed, my chest heaving. The tears come fast and all at once. I can't help it. I don't know where to go from here. I don't know what's real anymore. And my head. It's starting to throb again.

My phone vibrates again. I almost hurl it against the wall, but I stop myself, hand still shaking and turn it off instead. Deep breaths. I force myself to take several deep breaths. I have to calm down, keep it together. I'm better than this. Stronger than this. I have to be.

I need to figure this out. Start from the beginning and work my way through.

Just as I'm starting to collect my thoughts, a knock arrives on my door, the pounding hard enough to shake the entire room. It's the bald man from the front desk saying I need to get out or pay for another night. I don't have enough money to spend another night here. I shout out to him, tell him I'll be out in ten minutes, and start collecting my things.

I head outside and this time I don't take Uber. I don't want Nate to know where I'm going, to be able to track me in any way. I stop into the corner store to break the ten and get enough quarters for the bus, then buy a one-way Metro-Card once I'm back in the city. I transfer to the R train and of course there has been an accident on the line so we are stalled for over an hour. I get off and walk the couple blocks to Nate's apartment.

Once I get inside the lobby, I'm exhausted by this three-hour commute and can barely hear myself speaking to Raul, who lets me up after I explain that I misplaced my key. I let out an audible sigh as the elevator doors slide shut, so relieved because if Raul would have given me a hard time I don't know if I would have had any fight left in me. I check my phone and see that I have sixteen missed calls that came through while I was stuck underground. All from Nate. I ignore them. I have nothing to say to him. I'll have to figure something out, but for right now I need to get the rest of my stuff.

I empty my side of the closet and start pulling things from drawers, sorting through everything so that I can take only what I truly need. But then I see one of Nate's old high school sweatshirts he gave me and I am completely destroyed, on the floor reliving all of our best moments. When I make it back to my feet and face the bed, all I can see is our bodies in the sheets, laughing, bingeing the latest Netflix drop, stealing each other's snacks, looking in each other's eyes right before we—

I snap out of it, no idea how long I've been zoned out, and hustle to get my things. My hairline is damp and the sun has dropped far below the horizon by the time I finish squeezing everything into two bags. I'm about to head out when I hear the front door swing open.

I flip around, still in the closet, my breathing a rush in my throat. And then I hear him drop his bag on the floor, the familiar squeak of his sneakers. Nate.

My brain doesn't process this fast enough. Why is he here? *How* is he here? Did he somehow find out that I came back to the apartment? I turn out of the bedroom and open my mouth, not completely sure what's going to come out.

"What are you doing here?" I ask, and it's all I can actually manage.

He stops right in front of me, tall and overpowering, but he doesn't look as angry as I expect. He doesn't look angry at all.

"You wouldn't answer any of my calls," he says.

My heart jumps. I don't know why I'm scared. Nate's never given me a reason to fear him. Even when he was drunk and angry, he didn't threaten me or hit me or manhandle me. But I don't know who he is anymore. I don't know what's real and what's not.

I take a step back and I don't know if it's involuntary or not. I can't keep the anger out of my voice. "And you flew here because you thought I'd rather *see* you?"

"No." His eyes lock on mine. "I flew back because I realized you were telling the truth."

My heartbeat speeds up again. I can feel it pushing against my chest, the most intense drumming. "What?"

"I realized— Listen, I didn't help anyone frame anybody, okay? I'm sorry I didn't believe you before, but I know the truth now. I always fucking knew, I just..."

I stare at him. His eyes are bloodshot. I can see the strain of the past couple days in his face. I want this to make sense, but it's not. Nothing is making any damn sense. This is all happening too fast. Or maybe it's not, but I just can't keep up. I need sleep. Actual sleep. My brain is not working properly. I still don't understand why he's here. If he was helping Taylor frame me, why would he—

I don't know that. I don't. But there's no other explanation. The bag of cyanide. The pictures. The emails. It had to be him. Had to be.

"If you really didn't help her, then why was she in your dorm room? How did that cyanide get in the closet? And how'd she get those photos I sent you?"

"Brandi, look, you were right. She's—she did all of this— that day you went to that job interview…she did this. All of it."

I frown. He's talking too fast. I barely understand what he's saying. "What about the day I went to the interview?"

"That's when she did it. Has to be."

"Did what?"

"When she planted the cyanide in your Chanel bag."

"But—"

"It was the perfect opportunity," Nate insists, getting animated. "She knew you'd be gone."

"That doesn't make sense. I went to that job interview, remember? The one that turned out to be a scam? How could she have known about that?"

"Because she's the one who created it."

I shake my head. "What?"

"It was bogus."

"I know."

"That company never existed. She must have sent that email to you to get you out of the apartment so she could plant that shit in your bag. It's not that hard to make a fake company website."

My head shakes, the words not registering right away.

"She flew out to Ohio on her own," Nate continues. "I didn't invite her. I had no idea she was there until I saw her on my bed."

I scoff. "On your bed?"

"B, don't trip over that. Please. Nothing happened, I promise. Just hear me out. Taylor set you up that day. You were right. She framed you. It all makes sense now."

"Back up. What happened in Ohio?"

He sighs, impatient, then tells me the full story. "Taylor's in my room when I get there after training's over for the day. I tell her to get out, go back to New York. She refuses. Starts telling me how I shouldn't still love you because you were fucking her father, and then you killed him, all this crazy shit. I kept questioning her and then she says this shit that sets off all these mines in my head."

My stomach clenches. "What?"

"She said you were so reckless that you didn't even bother to get rid of the evidence. That's why the cops found out you killed her dad. She was still trying to convince me that you did it." My mouth parts, but no words come out, so he goes on. "She said the cops found the cyanide in your Chanel bag on the top shelf of our closet. How does Taylor know exactly where the cops found the cyanide?"

I don't come up with anything right away.

"And how does she know you keep your bags on the top shelf of the closet?" Nate takes a breath. "When she came by the apartment that one time, you were with her the whole time, right?"

I nod, trying to recall that day when Taylor came by to try and buy my silence. "Yeah. No, wait—"

"What?"

"I went downstairs to grab the food we ordered. Maybe she did go in the back."

"In our room?" He shakes his head. "I had the bathroom door open. She had on heels. I would have heard her come back there." He pauses a minute, thinking deeply.

"Maybe the cops told her they found the cyanide in the closet."

He shakes his head effusively. "She knew it was on the top shelf and exactly what bag it was. The cops ain't tell her that shit."

"So you're saying she created that fake interview so I would leave the apartment and that's when she planted the cyanide?"

He nods. "She's calculating, B. I tried to tell you. This is the way she moves. She planned the whole fucking thing." He pauses. "I don't know how she knew I'd be gone, but maybe it was a gamble."

I think for a beat, then shake my head. "She knew you'd be gone too."

"What do you mean?"

"That time she came over, I told her you go to the gym at the same time every morning. She knew and must have scheduled the interview for the same time."

Nate nods like that makes perfect sense, then pushes out a breath. "The person who sent those emails is the only person who knew about the interview, knew you wouldn't be here, knew they would have a safe window to plant some hard evidence. Taylor hacked into your account and then created that bullshit email chain with Simon." He pauses. "Or knows someone who did."

I think all that over a few times. "What about Simon's emails to me?"

"She could have easily sent them from his account. All she needed was his password. They were living under the same roof. Think about it. She had access to his computer."

"But how did she get into the apartment?" I ask, because even though I know he's right, we still have to prove it or none of it matters.

Nate doesn't have a quick answer to that one, but I can tell by his face that he's been working hard to come up with an answer. "I don't know."

"You can't pick our lock," I say, thinking out loud.

"She had to have a key fob."

"I have mine. You have yours. She didn't swipe it from us."

We both drift away in thought for a while, but neither of us comes up with an answer to that.

"So you really didn't send her the photos of me?" I ask, a moment later.

Nate looks up at me like I should know better than that. "B, those were for me, nobody else. I wouldn't do that to you." He looks me straight in the eyes when he says this, and I know he's being honest. I can feel it. I know that feelings aren't pathways to truth—but I know. He's not lying. He's not pretending. He never was.

I run that over in my head again. *He never was.*

I feel horrible. For not trusting him. For thinking he was capable of doing something like this. Setting me up. Framing me. I wish I could take it all back. There are so many things I want to say to him, so many pieces that still don't seem to fit. Questions I need answers to. Like the photos. Taylor hacked into my email account, but how the hell did she get those photos? Did she hack into my phone too? His phone? Why didn't he just delete them when I asked him to? He said he would. And I still don't understand why he changed his mind so suddenly the other day when he kicked me out. What came over him? How could he actually believe that I cheated on him with Simon? And that security footage. What happened to it? *Was* there even footage from that day, and if there was, how could there not be a clip of me coming into the building on it? And what about the ten minutes Bierman said was missing from the Van Doren home security system?

I have to slow down. I take a breath and rub my hand over

my forehead. This conversation has turned around too quickly. My head is drowning.

"Come here," Nate whispers, his hand warm against my cheek.

I take a long breath, then dump myself in his arms. "I'm so sorry. I didn't mean to—I didn't mean anything I said. I was just so confused—I'm sorry—"

I'm trembling and crying and nothing I'm saying is coherent.

Nate's hands grip my back as I bury myself in his armpit. "It's okay. I get it. Hey. I'm sorry too. It'll be okay. We just have to figure out how to convince that detective."

I sniff loud and pull myself back. He's right. We have the advantage. We have the truth on our side.

"I found Simon's will," I say, heading into the bedroom. I reach over onto the bed, under my pillow, and hand it to him. "Taylor got everything if he died. This is why she did it. It has to be."

His eyes drop. "Holy shit. How'd you get this?"

I ignore his question. "This is motive. But we need more. They already have me. This isn't enough for them to want to start over and actually investigate. All they want are convictions, and I'm the perfect target. Plus, they've seen the will already, but they aren't looking at her, so unless I have proof of an alibi…they won't get off my back." I take a breath, running my hands over my hair, and then I remember. "Wait."

Nate steps closer. "What?"

"The Zelle payment. I can prove that she paid me. The ten grand is proof that she was planning to kill him and needed to shut me up."

Nate goes still. When he blinks his gaze back into focus, I expect him to nod in agreement, but instead he shakes his head. "That's not enough. She twisted it with me, tried to make it seem like she was paying you out of guilt for getting you fired. She can twist it with the cops too."

"Yeah, you're right," I say, blowing out a hard breath. "We need that tape."

I bite my lip, and we're both silent for a while, still thinking.

"Let's go downstairs and talk to Raul," Nate says. "If Taylor was here that day, maybe he remembers."

I nod fast and slip into the closest pair of shoes I can find. Just after the elevator doors slide open, painstakingly slow, Nate reaches for my hand, and I slip my palm into his. The past few weeks have been rocky, emotional, intense. But this, his skin against mine, is so calming. He tightens his grip when our palms touch, but squeezes even harder as he leads me out of the elevator.

Raul is happy to help. Nate pulls up a photo from Taylor's Instagram and angles it so Raul can check it out and see if he remembers her coming into the building recently. It's the most true-to-life one we could find. Most of them are too doctored, whether it's FaceTune or professional airbrushing. He inspects the image with squinted eyes like maybe he should be wearing glasses, then shakes his head. "I can't say. Girls like that are a dime a dozen these days, you know? They all look the same."

Nate and I exchange a quick glance. I reach for the phone and scroll to a photo of Taylor and Mei posing together on a boat, arms around each other. Raul leans closer to the screen, but before his eyes tighten again, he's nodding.

"You've seen her here?" Nate asks, pointing to Mei.

"She fell on some glass or something. She was cut pretty bad. I tried to get her to let me call an ambulance, but she called a car service. Said she didn't want to ride in an ambulance." He shrugs. "It costs five hundred a pop. I get it."

I laugh, a harsh, bitter sound. "That girl has five-star insurance. That's not why she didn't want you calling the ambulance."

Nate leans in closer. "What happened exactly? Was she alone?"

"Yeah. Some girl came in saying she saw this girl outside bleeding. I looked up and saw her on the ground. Blood was everywhere, so I rushed out trying to help her. That's when I offered to get her the ambulance."

I nod. "How long were you outside?"

He shrugs. "I don't know. Few minutes tops."

But a few minutes is all the time Taylor would have needed, especially if she had help.

I run both hands over my hair. "Do you have camera footage of people who came in and out this day?"

"Of course," Raul says. "Want me to show you?"

We both nod and hop on Raul's heels as soon as he starts leading the way to the small back security room. Before we all huddle up, an explosion goes off in my head.

"Oh, my God. The footage."

Nate looks at me, lines of confusion between his brows. "We're getting it."

"Might take a minute," Raul warns. "I have to find—"

"No," I say. "The tape from the night of Simon's murder." I swing around to look Raul in the eyes. "You said there was no footage of me on it, but that can't—that doesn't make sense."

"B, we watched that tape back three or four times," Nate says, shaking his head. "You weren't in it."

"Don't you think Taylor could have had something to do with the footage of me being missing?"

I can't put anything past her. I've learned my lesson.

"She's clearly been here before. If she could figure out how to get into our apartment, she could have figured out how to get into the security room."

"Exactly. It had to be her. I told her about it that day you came to see me. I told her and she had this look on her face, this smug look. She knew she had already ruined my alibi."

Nate nods, then looks to Raul. "Can you get us all the footage from that day you saw the girl bleeding? It's an emergency."

Raul nods, taking this all very seriously, but when he finally pulls up the footage from the day I went to that interview, there's no Taylor caught on the live feed.

There are ten seconds missing from the tape.

26

TAYLOR

Inside my room, I slip on my most conservative black dress. I look into the mirror and practice slow, deeply felt tears, the kind they'll expect, but I still feel unprepared. Even after all the planning, I never imagined this part, the last time I ever have to see his face again.

I can't do this sober. I can't. I open the top drawer of my nightstand, pull out a small bag. Open it. Pour the powder on the counter. Just before I inhale, I hear Carter's voice, what he said about his little sister, and then I say fuck it, fuck his stupid sister, and do a hit. I take a breath. Swallow. Do another. I feel the rush immediately.

Everything is right.

I put the bag back, then take in my reflection in the mirror. I need to finish my makeup. I reach for my liquid eyeliner and lean closer so I can see.

The knock on my door jolts me out of my concentration. The liner slips from my hand as my head whips toward the door. "Who is it?"

"Glover."

Fuck. What is she doing here?

I have to let her in. Anything else will seem suspicious. I take a breath and open the door.

"I'm sorry to interrupt you, Ms. Van Doren," she says, reticent, wearing her best cop face. "I know the funeral is today."

I nod, keep my head down. "Starts in a few minutes," I say, hoping she takes the hint.

"You mind if I ask you a few questions?"

"Sure. No problem." I walk back over to the mirror and start winging my eyes. I draw a line and quickly smudge it away, realizing how much my hand is shaking, then drag it on again, smoother this time.

Glover pulls out a notepad but doesn't look at it. "Ms. Van Doren, what is your relationship with Nate Robinson?"

My stomach tightens. Nate? Why the hell is she asking about Nate? I shrug. "He's a friend. We actually were together for a while, but—"

"When's the last time you saw or spoke to him?"

My hand goes still. "I'm sorry, I don't understand what this has to do with my father."

"I would appreciate it if you would just answer the question, Ms. Van Doren."

I swallow, hating that I don't know where this is going. "Last time I spoke to him was a while ago," I say, the lie coming before I can think it all the way through.

Glover meets my gaze in the mirror, her eyes inscrutable. "I spoke to the doorman that works at Nate's apartment building. Raul Sanchez. He says you came into the lobby around three in the afternoon a couple weeks ago. Can you explain what you were doing there that day?"

Shit. I think very carefully before I speak, realizing right away what day she must be talking about. "I was just going up to see him. You know, talk, chill."

"But you didn't go upstairs. You left a few minutes after you arrived."

"He wasn't there."

Glover gives me a long look, head cocked to the side. "You're a Zoomer. No way you got all the way over there without shooting him a text first to see if he was home."

I turn to face her, only one eye finished. "It was one of those no-panties-no-bra kind of surprises." I drop my eyes down to her waist, then back up. "I'm sure you know what I mean."

She breaks the eye contact and her nod is absent-minded, her gaze trained on her notepad now. "Raul also says he remembers you coming in the day your father was murdered. Around noon. There was some sort of accident outside, and you came in for help."

I shake my head. "Must have been someone else."

Glover says nothing for a long moment, then shifts and pulls out a folded document from the inside pocket of her jacket. She hands it over. I open it, and my body immediately turns to ice. "You get all your father's assets," she says.

Something inside me freezes. It's not a question, but I know I have to say something. She speaks before I get a chance.

"I don't think this is your first time looking that over," Glover says. "I think you very much knew his entire estate would be going to you."

I stare at her, my eyes hard. "Is that some kind of accusation?"

Glover falls silent, but her glare is penetrating.

I flip back around and finish my liner. "All you have is speculation."

"For now."

I pause, take in a breath, focus, then lower my voice. "He called me his lifeline. I took that to heart."

Glover's eyes meet mine in the mirror again. I stare back, refusing to look away. If I do it'll make it look like I have something to hide. I can all but see the debate going on in her head. She thinks I'm lying, at least not being completely honest, I can tell.

I don't know what it is, but she finally breaks and backs off. With another nod, she flips the notepad shut. "Thank you, Ms. Van Doren."

A rush of relief rolls down my back, pure and sweet. I can feel sweat dripping from my neck. Hot, nervous sweat. "Thanks," I say. "Is that it?"

"Yeah." She turns and heads for the door. "We'll keep in touch."

Something about this moment feels off. And there was something weird about her voice. I panic when she turns away. "But what is all of this about? What happened?"

She looks back. "I was hoping you could tell me."

She's testing me. Waiting for me to slip up, say the wrong thing.

I swallow and turn to face her. "I don't know what you mean."

"We're trying to figure out what happened to the security footage from the lobby of Nate Robinson's building from Monday afternoon. We found a couple of glitches in the tape. At first it seems normal, but then we slowed it down. The time skips twice. Seems like someone deliberately cut a few seconds of footage from the tape."

Fuck. I do my best to look confused. "Footage of what?"

"Brandi Maxwell says she couldn't have poisoned your father that night because she was home, in her apartment. She thinks someone deliberately deleted the footage of her walking into the building to destroy proof of her alibi." She stops and studies me, waiting for my reaction. "She's convinced it was you."

I don't give her one. Just shake my head, like this is all too much for me to process. "Well, she has to find some way to take the heat off herself, doesn't she?"

Glover stares at me for a long time before lifting a card from her back pocket. "Here," she says, holding it out for me to take. "If anything sticks out to you, anything out of the ordinary, give me a call, will you?"

I answer with a nod and study it. Two phone numbers and an email address.

"You think of anything, you call me. Hey. *Hey.*" I look up. "Call me. Understand?"

I nod again.

Glover gets to the door, and I wait until the last second. "Actually. Officer Glover? There was one weird thing about that day...now that I'm thinking about it."

Her face lights up a bit. "And what was that?"

I hate that it's come to this. I *hate* what I have to do. I really do. But I have no other choice. I can't let her leave like this. She doesn't believe me. She'll talk to that other detective and he won't believe me, either.

I do what I have to do.

"When I got to the building to see Nate, my friend Jared was outside hailing a cab. He said he was just in the neighborhood for a meeting, but...well, a meeting implies he's going to work, and between you and me, he's really not the working type."

Glover moves in closer, a slight tilt to her head. "What are you saying, Ms. Van Doren?"

"He's super techy too."

She frowns. "Techy? In what way?"

"He borrows his father's cars all the time when he wants to

go out, you know, to impress the guys he dates. The Rolls. The Bentley. His dad is still bitter about him totaling the Benz and won't let Jared borrow any of his cars, so Jared deletes the footage from their home security system on his phone somehow." I pause for the briefest moment. "He's never gotten caught."

"Are you saying Jared might have deleted the security footage?"

I hold my breath for a moment. "*Oh, my God.* His dad's bank is going under...he's been complaining about not having money...and he knew about my father's will. I tell him everything."

Glover steps closer, scribbling something on her notepad now. "Now you're insinuating that Jared could've killed your father so he could get your inheritance money?"

I grip onto a chair by the door and slump into it. "I can't believe this. He's been using me this whole time. He got rid of the footage so Brandi wouldn't have an alibi."

"Ms. Van Doren—"

"I *trusted* him. I brought him around my father. I..." I shake my head, concentrating hard, and then tears fall from my eyes.

Glover softens for once. "Okay, we'll look into it. We'll talk to him. Do you know where I can find him?"

Three hours later the service is over and I'm back at the house. Once I make it downstairs, people crowd around me wherever I step: aunts and uncles and cousins I haven't seen for years. Strangers. I wouldn't recognize most of them if we passed on the street. Asking me if I'm okay.

I try to answer all their questions, but talking is even more exhausting than smiling. I want to scream. I want to get the hell out of here, away from their questions and their kind, concerned faces. It must show on my face. I can see some of them looking at me in confusion. I hear their whispers. *What's up with her? Do you think she's all right?*

The burner phone rings just as I get surrounded by another group of faces I barely recognize. I turn away slightly, check it. Fuck. Jared. I have to answer. I have to.

I make my excuses and peel away from the sea of black, head down, rushing toward the powder room off the kitchen. I pull out the burner phone from my pocket and answer it.

Jared. He's talking too fast. I can't understand anything he's saying.

"Wait. Slow down. What'd they say?"

He huffs a breath in my ear, maybe trying to calm himself, but it doesn't really work. "They know I deleted the security footage. I don't know how, but they do. And they asked about the emails too. They're fucking on to us, Tay."

"Don't panic. Just destroy your hard drive."

"What if that's not enough? Maybe you can survive in prison, but I—"

"Jared, calm down." I drag a hand through my hair, my chest pounding. "What about Mei?"

I never wanted it to come to this. The only person who was supposed to get hurt was my father. Not my friends. Not the people I actually care about. But I have no choice.

Jared pauses. "What about her?"

"Did you tell the detective she's the one who bought the cyanide?"

"Why would I..." He pauses, then I almost hear it click in his head. "You want to snitch on Mei?"

"Would you rather go down for this by yourself?"

27

BRANDI

The charges against me were dropped yesterday. I found out from the lawyer the state appointed me this morning, a phone call that lasted no more than two minutes but felt like forever stuck in time. I have no idea what they could possibly want now.

My heart starts to pound, and I'm not sure why. I know I'm innocent. I know I've done nothing wrong. I know I'm right about Taylor.

I just need this all to be over so I can forget any of it ever happened.

I check the peephole before I open it.

Bierman, his eyes impassive as usual, the light hard on his sunburned face.

"Hi," I say, and then take a step back, motioning for him to come inside.

He takes a few steps, just beyond the threshold. "Good evening, Ms. Maxwell." He shifts and looks at me directly. "As you've been informed, the charges against you have been dropped."

I don't say anything. I let those words hover there in the air between us until they feel solid, sure.

"I've just finished speaking to Mei Kwan and Jared Burke, who both admitted to conspiring to murder Mr. Van Doren," he continues. "We will no longer be pursuing you as a suspect."

I swallow. "So they've been taken into custody? Just them?"

He nods. "About an hour ago. You are no longer in custody of the state," he says, like that's supposed to make this all better. "Sorry about all of this."

With that, Bierman turns to leave, and I almost run after him. "Did they confess? How did this happen?"

He pauses at the door, turning to face me, and nods. "They've confirmed their involvement."

"But—"

"We tracked down the dealer who sold Ms. Kwan the cyanide." Bierman shifts closer to me, and when he speaks again, his voice is resigned. "The doorman confirmed he saw Mr. Burke outside the building the same day the footage was deleted. Burke also admitted to sending the emails."

I can't stop my head from shaking. "Taylor is the one who orchestrated this whole thing. She wanted her father dead because she feels like he's the reason her mother killed herself. She was also the sole recipient of his will, which you didn't want to consider because I'm the easier target. You just couldn't resist going for the low-hanging fruit."

"I don't think that's fair."

"I heard her spelling out their plan the night we met. There was a big party at her house.

"That's why she tried to put this all on me. I knew too much. She wanted to get rid of me. She had to," I say, wishing Nate was here to back me up. "Mei's and Jared's parents will hire some million-dollar lawyer and buy their way out of those cuffs. They'll hardly even do community service, and when it all blows over, they'll have millions from Simon's estate to play with."

"Ms. Max—"

"Someone laced his glass," I snap. "Someone had to actually be there and make sure he drank the scotch. And someone framed me. It was Taylor."

"Ms. Maxwell, listen. Kwan and Burke confirmed their involvement. They told us about Taylor masterminding this, but we don't have enough to bring her in right now. We're working on—"

"That's bullshit. You have to arrest her. She did this."

"There's nothing tying her to the actual crime scene," he says, and I finally understand, but also, this still makes no sense. "Listen, why don't you come down to the—"

I brush past him and snatch the door open for him. "If you don't go after her, I will."

"I would highly advise against that, Ms. Maxwell. It's in your best interest to not involve yourself further. We're on it." He heads out the door and looks back over his shoulder. "Take care, Ms. Maxwell."

I say nothing, just wait for the door to close.

I should feel relief. I thought I would when this day came, when my name was cleared. I didn't do it. They *know* I didn't do it. But there's this part of me that just can't let Taylor get away with this. Not after everything I've been through. Not after everything I know now. She deserves to be punished. Anybody who does what she's done deserves to be punished.

I'm not going to do anything stupid.

I'm just going to talk to her. Talk. That's all I want. To hear her admit what she did.

I find the place easily. I checked Taylor's Instagram and she geotagged a selfie from inside the W Hotel's ballroom an hour ago.

I'm wearing one of the Balmain dresses Jared bought me because I had nothing else that was appropriate. It's riding up my ass and I have to tug it down my thighs every ten steps, but I'll manage.

The news hasn't leaked to the press yet. They don't know about Mei. About Jared. They don't know I'm innocent. But no one recognizes me. No one stops me or rushes over to snap pictures. I have on a full face of makeup, my hair is ridiculously straight and my heels are so tall I'm virtually unrecognizable. The last image they have was of me coming out of the precinct in tangled, four-day-old hair and wrinkled sweats.

When I finally spot Taylor standing by a large window posing for selfies with an Emily Ratajkowski look-alike, a current passes through me. It's the perfect iteration of the night we first met. She's stunning, her long hair slicked back into a high pony, her smile wide and flawless. She's standing tall in a pale blue mini dress and it's obvious she's not wearing anything underneath, but this is clearly her thing.

I head toward her and am immediately surrounded by a sea of people. They're drunk and loud and stupid. I push my way past them, through them. I hear a *bitch*, feel heads turning to look at me, but I don't slow down. The rage I feel in this moment is so powerful it scares and excites me at the same time. My heart starts to race. Palms dampen. Taylor smiles, smiles, smiles into the phone held out in front of her. Her teeth gleam like a new moon.

I'm closer now. She's right there. She's within reach.

I take a few more steps, trying to reconcile the person I'd imagined before that ball with the one in front of me, the person she's shown herself to be, but too much has happened; so many lies and so much confusion, I can barely focus my brain, and before I know what I'm going to say, I see her head turning my way. There is this brief moment when I strongly consider punching her in the face and dragging her into the bathroom by her hair so I can properly beat her ass without all the eyes and cameras, but now that she's looking directly at me, which means other people have also turned to look at me, I realize there is no scenario in which putting my hands on her goes over well.

I hate that this is what it's come down to. I'm bigger than this. I am. But I don't know any other way to deal with her. Sometimes when they go low, you just have to meet them down at their fucking level.

I shift so that I'm standing directly in front of her and make myself speak before she can. "Solid plan. Make your friends turn each other in. Too bad you're still not gonna get away with it."

Her eyes stay on me, but she doesn't lose her smile, not yet. Taylor hands the look-alike her phone and turns to me. The girl is staring, maybe trying to figure out how I fit in here, but I don't acknowledge her. Suddenly, before I realize what's happening, Taylor's arms wrap around me, long and thin. She's hugging me. The same fake hug she gave when we first met.

"Brandi. I'm so glad they released you. That stint in jail must've been awful. I've been meaning to reach out and—"

I shove her off me, and she tries to play it off, but everyone's staring at her now. At me. Waiting.

I'm shaking, but not from fear. I'm so angry. At her. At me. For getting involved. For allowing myself to get caught up in her shit. For not trusting Nate the way I should have. For the way she turned him against me. I'll never forget the way he looked at me when he called me a liar, the way he sounded, so distant and cold. I hate her for that. I want to abolish it all from my memory, mummify it with all those other things that hurt more to remember than forget.

"Don't patronize me," I say. "I know about the money."

She makes a face like she's confused, still performing for

this captive audience, or maybe she's truly confused as to how I know. "What money?"

"I saw your dad's will. You're the sole beneficiary to his two-billion-dollar estate."

"You…"

I lean into her, pushing up on my tiptoes and bringing my lips to her ear. "It's disappointing, really. I mean, to be such a cliché." My words come harsh and reticent.

She laughs against my cheek.

I can smell the rancid bitterness of hard liquor on her breath. I pull back. My eyes flick around the room. More people have gathered. I feel like I'm in a haunted house.

Taylor's blue eyes flare. "You think you know everything, don't you? I had nothing to do with my father's murder. I just trusted the wrong people. Jared and Mei went behind my back. They—"

"Bullshit. You planted that cyanide in my room when I left for my interview."

She scoffs. "What, are you suffering from PTSD after being locked up for a few days? It's not my fault the cops got it wrong. How was I supposed to know the emails weren't actually between you and my father? They looked real."

Taylor struts off. This diabolical bitch thinks I'm going to make this easy for her.

I clench my fists at my sides, so tired of her shit. And then I force myself to take a breath.

I'm not going to do anything stupid.

I'm not going to do anything stupid.

I follow her, my heels slapping against the floor. "Because you wrote them."

She stops. I can't describe the look on her face as she turns to me. It defies all etymology, a mix of determination and terror and psychosis.

"Jared and Mei were nothing but leeches," she declares. "They did all of this behind my back. I had no idea—"

"Don't think just because you were able to gaslight Nate that I'm gonna fall for your bullshit too. This was all you. You wanted your dad's money and you wanted me out of the picture so you could get Nate back."

Taylor's eyes lock on mine like she wants me to know she really means what she's about to say. "Hon. If I wanted Nate back, trust me, he'd be in my bed right now."

She smiles at me again. It's as violent as a slap, a punch to the gut. I feel disoriented, off balance.

Taylor walks off again, faster this time.

I stay on her heels. I have to laugh. "Guess I'd be pissed, too, if I flew all the way to Ohio only to get rejected by my ex. Had to burn."

Once again, she slows down, then flips back around to face me. "You're so cute. You believe everything he says, don't you?" She steps closer. "You can have Nate. Obviously, his tastes have changed since I dumped him." Her eyes drop down to my chest, then back up. "He's into basic bitches now."

I roll my eyes at that, at her weak attempt to humiliate me. "You didn't even dump him. You cheated on him with his teammate, got caught and he dumped you."

Her mouth tightens. "That's his version."

"The truth doesn't have versions." I shake my head and grit my teeth. "You're good, Taylor. But you messed with the wrong person this time. You think you've won, but you're going down for this."

She looks amused, as if my conviction is a joke to her. "Is that some kind of threat?"

A weird, wobbly laugh escapes me, and then I smile. "You white girls always think somebody's threatening you when we refuse to take your bullshit."

She glowers at me, her face flushing red.

I walk off. Her pathetic ass isn't even worth it.

And then I stop, the petty part of me I've tried so hard to control snatching free. "Oh, and you're right. Nate's tastes *did* change. He likes warm-blooded girls with a little ass now."

"Nate never had any complaints," she says, staying on me.

"Well, that was before he experienced all this."

Her nostrils flare. "Fuck you. I had him first."

She backs off, like she's going to box turn and head off.

I laugh. "And I'm having him last, bitch. Tonight while you what, get high, right?"

As soon as I start to put more distance between us, Taylor lunges after me and grabs a handful of my silk press. My brain doesn't process it at first. *Did this bitch really just—*

Her hand tugs hard, yanking my neck sideways.

I stumble back her way and vaguely hear people gasping and instigating. Someone shrieks with obnoxious laughter. The voices grow and grow. More and more people turn to witness our altercation, but I don't care. I can't care anymore. The adrenaline surges, blinds me. I don't think. I just react. I yank her down to the floor with me, some feral instinct taking over. I try to pivot out of her hold, but Taylor won't let go of my hair, and then she's on top of me, and I'm on my back. She swings her tiny purse at me but misses, which throws her off for just long enough. I snake my legs over her neck and squeeze my thighs until she has no choice but to loosen her grip. She falls over and lets out a rough, shrieking sound, not quite a scream but something close. Something dark and ugly and bestial.

I push myself up as fast as I can as phones are angled my way from every direction. I need to get out of here. I don't notice the shoe in Taylor's hand until it's almost too late. She swings it at me, bottom side up, the five-inch stiletto the perfect improvised weapon, but I swerve at the last second. She grunts, doing her best to recover, but stumbles forward. I grab her skinny arms and slam her against the wall, because fuck feminism right now. Fuck this crazy bitch. The impact knocks the wind out of her, her mouth popping open. The shoe drops from her hand and so does her purse.

"Did you really think putting your hands on me would go over well?" I say, knocking her against the wall again.

She heaves. "Get off me, you—"

"Just admit it. You killed him. You killed your own father."

Her eyes dart around the room. She's aware she's being watched, recorded. "You're crazy. I didn't—"

"*You fucking killed him.* You poisoned him. You—"

"*Shut up.* I didn't—"

I shove her one last time, then strut off. Before I get two steps away, a security guard comes out of nowhere, heading straight toward me.

It's over. I know what's going to happen before it does. I'm going to be forced to leave. Taylor's going to get away with murder. Call me fucking clairvoyant.

As Taylor straightens out her dress and hastily collects the little things that have fallen out of her purse, I try to ward the guard off, but of course that only makes him more aggressive. As I'm being accosted by an industrial-size man, I get one last glance at Taylor and I'm quickly reminded of our respective places in society. Hers, to be protected. Mine, to be protected from. Because no one goes after her. No one goes after the girl who attacked me. They only come for me when she was clearly the one who put her hands on me first. Once again, her whiteness is so unbearable, so palpable, it's blinding. I want to scream.

And then I faintly hear her voice, gravelly against the noise in my head, rising above every other sound in the room, though it's so low, it's almost a whisper. "I did win. I got the money, bitch."

And then I almost do.

I almost scream.

Just as this guard starts to reach for me like I'm some fucking criminal, I see an ancient-looking cell phone lying on the ground where Taylor attacked me. The realization is immediate and profound, because this is an old, pay-as-you-go flip phone, a device that may have been a revolutionary shimmer of modern convenience less than my lifetime ago, but nothing anyone attending this fancy-ass event would be carrying. It's not an amalgamation of metal and plastic. It's gold. Pure gold. A burner phone.

Taylor's burner phone.

"Miss."

I nearly jump at the bark, at this guard's hand on my arm.

He's black, at least six-five and bald. I quickly scan the room and see another pair of guards who are on crowd control, ushering away people who had started recording the spectacle. We're practically isolated now.

I have to think fast.

I snatch my earring out of my ear, careful to disguise the motion, and look back at him. "My earring."

He sighs and looks as if he is stifling the urge to roll his eyes before dropping them to the carpet.

"They're my grandmother's," I say. "I have to find it."

He sighs again, but this time something clicks inside him, and there is a small moment of solidarity between us just before he lets go of my arm and sweeps his eyes around the area.

He puts his back to me, and I almost blow out a sigh of relief. While he's down in a squat, I pretend like I'm also looking for my missing earring and slip the cell phone deep inside my cleavage.

Two hours later Nate's in bed, intently watching clips of himself running plays during last season. We've both been doing the same thing on repeat for the last couple of hours. At first, he was as interested as I was in the three numbers in the incoming and outgoing call log of Taylor's burner phone. But after two of the numbers turned out to be disconnected and the third just rings incessantly every time I dial it, he tuned out. I've made thirty-two calls to the number that actually rings, but it looks like this whole thing is a bust.

I finally drag myself to the bed and slip in on my side. Nate finishes watching the clip he's in the middle of, then sets his iPad aside and angles his body toward mine.

His eyes drop to the phone still in my hand. "When was the last incoming call for the two that are disconnected?"

"Few days ago." I sigh. "The day Mei and Jared got arrested."

"Those are their numbers, then. Got to be. They're probably not answering because of the arrest."

"Yeah." I've already thought of that.

"What about the other one? You said there were three numbers, right? And there's no voice mail set up? It has to be going to another burner."

Which would make sense except, as far as I know, no one else was helping Taylor out. Mei and Jared are the only ones who were involved.

I dial the third number again to no avail, but mostly just space out, in deep thought, trying to figure out who the third wheel could be.

"Babe, it's late."

I blink out of my trance at Nate's kind but pleading grumble into his pillow and tap the screen of my iPhone. It's a few minutes past one and Nate has to get up early to train.

"I thought this was a sure bet," I mumble.

"I got excited, too, but don't worry. We'll think of something." Nate pulls the phone from my hand and sets it on the nightstand next to his iPad.

I blow out a long sigh and follow his lead as he gets comfy on his side. He lets out a small groan of pleasure when I wrap my arm around his ribs, and I can hear his smile when he whispers, "I get to be the little spoon tonight?"

I giggle at that, and tonight it's so nice, snuggling up with him, simultaneously feeling the firmness of his stomach under my palm and the softness of his bare shoulder against my cheek. Even with the chaos going on in my head, the rhythm of his breathing soothes me as it slows and deepens.

But the peace doesn't last long.

I almost hurdle over him when the phone rings.

Not my phone. Not Nate's. It's the tinny ring of a cheap, disposable phone.

I don't even click the lamp on. I lean over his body and feel around for the small device. I stare at the glowing number shining bright through the dark, the one I've called nonstop for the past couple of hours, and I don't know if I've truly stopped breathing, but it feels like it.

I have to answer it, but I have a brain fart first. Can't figure out how to answer a phone like this. When it rings for the fifth time, I feel immensely silly, almost hot with nerves. With shaking fingers, I open the phone, not sure what I'm going to say after "hello," but also I need whoever's on the other end to not hang up, and then I freeze again with the phone to my ear because I never say *hello*.

The caller, who is exasperated as soon as the slightly distorted voice transmits, starts speaking before I can get a word in. "Taylor, thank God. Sorry I missed all your calls. Thanks for calling me back. I know you're pissed, but please don't hang up. Please."

I recognize the voice. I've only heard her speak on one occasion, but the faint Spanish lilt is easy to place.

I don't say anything.

The caller goes on, her frantic words coming faster and faster. "Look, I know I fucked up. I shouldn't have had the will out like that. I should have made sure I put it away before I let her come over. And I should have told you about that in the first place. I was going to. I just figured I'd see what she wanted and then I'd fill you in. It all happened so fast. I got nervous. I wasn't thinking straight."

Another pause. My heart screams inside my chest. It's my turn, but once again, I don't know what to say, how to handle this, and now Nate is sitting up and inching closer to me, desperately trying to catch my eye. I glance at him as he's in the middle of mouthing *who is it?* but ignore him and shift my focus back on the fast, desperate words crashing into my ear.

"I'm fucking all torn up about what happened to Mei and Jared. It's not over. We can get them out. We'll figure something out. Just don't be mad."

She pauses, and I try to conjure up something to say, but the words stall as the realization slams into my skull like a wrecking ball.

Izzy was the last person to see Simon alive.

Izzy is the one who had access to Simon's office.

She's the one who gave Simon the poison.

She was there the whole time. Taylor's alibi was legit because the bitch really wasn't there.

My mind is racing, and I've missed a bit of what she's just said, but I calm down and listen because she is still talking, and

I think I heard my name. "I've already thought about how to get her to shut up. I know last time paying her off didn't work, but this time we have so much more money. We'll make her an offer she literally can't turn down. And we'll take it out of my cut. Okay? This was my fuckup. I'll pay for it."

Silence again. This time it is glaring. Izzy is done making her case. I don't speak fast enough.

"Taylor? Did you hear me?" Izzy sounds desperate now. "What's going on?"

Nate tugs on my arm. I'm sure he can see the lines of concentration on my face as I run through the harrowing past few weeks.

It's so unbelievable, but also undeniable.

They set it up together. They killed Simon. They framed me. Both of them.

Izzy's voice pops back into my ear. "*Taylor?* You there?" She is about to lose her shit.

I climb off the bed and look at Nate. "Izzy."

His face contorts into shock, then disbelief. I hold up a finger, telling him to give me one more second.

"Oh," Izzy says, almost breathless. "You're there. Did you—"

"It's not Taylor."

28

TAYLOR

It's surreal when the funds finally transfer into my account. I almost don't believe it, but it's really there. Everything is in my name.

I smile, thinking of the way Brandi got dragged out of the W, of how utterly pathetic she looked, of how she thought she'd win.

I got the money.

I won.

I fucking won.

Still, there is this gnawing sourness festering in the pit of my stomach whenever I think of Mei and Jared, my soul sister, my favorite boy. They were supposed to be here, riding this adrenaline high with me, but thanks to that bitch I had to do the unthinkable and turn them in. I had no other choice. I contemplate not touching their cut out of respect, but it would probably crush them even more to know they're trapped in a psychopath-filled hellhole in vain.

My driver pulls over to the curb steps away from the Met and unlocks my door, letting me know we've arrived. I tell him to stay near, that I won't be long, and then head into the small Greek restaurant on the corner. As soon as the staff spots me, they bring me a plate of moussaka and a single glass of champagne. I look down at the casserole, and then glance around the restaurant, checking the other tables, the front entrance, and lose my appetite. I don't touch the food. I check my phone, and when I glance up again, I see her heading to the table, hair down, heels high, smile wide in anticipation.

"Hey," she says.

I look up, but don't speak. I'm still not used to being cordial to her. It doesn't feel right. It never will.

"So how long will it take?" Izzy asks as she takes the seat across from me, almost whispering now.

I tilt my face. "The food?"

"The money." She pauses, glances over her shoulder and then looks back at me. "You transferred the funds, right? I checked my account and I still don't see the dep—"

"Izzy. There's no transfer." I stare at her hard; there's no give to my expression.

Her mouth opens. Closes. Opens. "What are you talking about? You said you got the deposit yesterday."

"I did. I figured the least I could do was buy you something to splash against your throat. Couldn't have done this without you."

Which is true.

Which is why I lift the champagne flute and hand it to her.

She stares at it, but doesn't take it, doesn't even blink. "I don't understand."

I watch her, the glass still hovering in the air above my moussaka. "You forfeited your cut when you spoon-fed that bitch my motive."

"I told you it was an accident. She was snoop— I didn't say anything. She found the will and—"

I get up from the table and head for the door.

I never should have trusted her, but I had no choice. I

needed someone in that room, someone to make sure my father used the glasses I'd already lined for his drink. I couldn't
be there that night. I had to be far away from the house, in the
city. I needed my alibi to be firm and indestructible.

I needed her.

Izzy does her best to keep up with me as I shuffle across
the street, cutting off an army of yellow cabs in my thigh-
high boots.

Her exasperated voice hits my back. "I didn't tell her about
the will. She snuck into Simon's desk and found it."

I glance back at her but keep moving. "You shouldn't have
had it lying around. What are you, stupid or crazy?"

She lets out a frustrated sound. "I poured the drink. I earned
my cut."

"And you almost imploded the entire plan. I could've gotten arrested."

"But you didn't. It worked out. Why are you doing this?"

I stop once I reach the curb and stare back at her. "You
know, you should be grateful. I saved you from years and years
of heartbreak by getting him in the ground."

I found her on the floor in my father's bedroom. She was
on her knees, makeup smudged, a complete mess, crying because she'd caught him cheating. She told me that she wanted
to leave him and call off the wedding, but she'd just found
out she was six weeks pregnant. I told her I had a way for her
to get what she wanted and get back at him at the same time.

If she did me one little favor.

Once Brandi was in jail and the will was executed, she
would get her cut and she wouldn't be a suspect because her
name wasn't included in the will—therefore, there was no
motive.

She said she would do it. She'd pour him a glass of scotch

in one of the contaminated glasses if I gave her part of my inheritance.

I knew this bitch wanted his money. I fucking knew it.

It was the perfect plan.

Until she went and screwed everything up.

Izzy pauses, blinking over and over like she's a broken doll, because obviously my words are too much to process for her itty-bitty brain. "We killed Simon. You *made* me—"

"Cry me a fucking river. I had to snitch on my two best friends because of your screwup and you think you're still getting a piece of the pie?"

Another long pause. This time her nostrils flare, lips trembling. A tear rolls down her cheek. "You're sick, Taylor."

"No, bitch. I'm a billionaire with a capital B. My shitty father is in the ground where he belongs, and I get to spend his money for the rest of my life."

Finally, my driver texts me, letting me know he's down the street, stuck at a light. I text him back, tell him I'll meet him where he is, then take a back street and head down the empty sidewalk. Izzy follows me.

"You think your father was a monster," she says from behind me. I keep walking. Faster. Harder. "You're even worse. *You're the real fucking monster!*"

The last part was a full-on scream.

I give her nothing. I don't give a shit about her precious little feelings. She killed him. She knew what she was doing. If she regrets it now, that's not my fucking problem.

"Taylor."

Her voice is softer now, but just as urgent.

"What?" I snap, flipping around, ready to maul her if that's what it takes to get her off my back, but the disturbing, close-mouthed smile that is suddenly on her face startles me into momentary paralysis.

The tears are gone. Her smile looks like a slash across her face, like she's The Joker and I'm Batman. She still doesn't get it. I'm the fucking Joker. I will always have the last laugh.

And then I see it, and it's like the laces of the world's most constrictive corset are being yanked around my torso, compressing my lungs so close to my rib cage that I can't breathe. Izzy, the marionette, unbuttoning her top enough to pull out a thin black wire that's been secured to the strap of her nude bra.

I want to strangle her until all the youth and pretty drains from her face. I want to carve her open and drown her organs in fresh piss. There are so many ways I want to hurt this lying bitch.

But I get a chance to do nothing before her eyes land on something over my shoulder. Heavy footsteps stop. Right behind me.

"Ms. Van Doren."

My world goes silent as Officer Glover circles me, a pair of shiny shackles dangling from her hand.

It's too much to process at once. Izzy agreed to kill my father, then she forced me to turn my two best friends in because of her idiotic mistake. Then she fucking double-crosses me. When the fuck did she decide to betray me—or was this her plan all along? So many overlapping thoughts crowd my mind.

When I told Izzy she wouldn't be getting the money, the bitch cried. I watched those pseudo tears roll down her cheeks. But inside she was laughing, because she knew I wouldn't be getting a dime of it, either. She was one step ahead of me.

Izzy's smirk morphs into a full-on smile, and it's the strongest act of violence I've ever experienced.

The last laugh. She stole it from my throat right in front of my face.

When I'm in the back of the squad car, wrists clinking, a

laugh finally slips through my mouth. It finally hits me, why all this is happening.

It had to be her. It had to be Brandi. I have no idea how, but this whole operation reeks of that bitch.

She's almost as fucking good as me.

29

BRANDI

The AC is out of order on the subway for most of my ride downtown, so I hop out a couple stops early and dodge the dense foot traffic for ten blocks. Once I reach the precinct, I hover anxiously near the door for a moment, picking at my cuticles. After I finally push in and talk to someone at the front desk, another uniformed officer leads me through to the back where the air smells like burnt coffee and jelly donuts, then steers me through the bullpen to Glover's desk. The first thing I notice is that she is a very organized upper millennial who not only went to Yale but also has a black belt and a massive Marvel obsession. She's wearing a sweatshirt with NYPD across her chest in bright white letters, and as much as I wish she was not on their team, I couldn't have done any of this without her on the inside.

Glover looks up from her desktop's screen and sees me. I smile, and she smiles back.

"Brandi," she says. "Nice to see you. You good?"

"Yeah, I'm fine," I say, because it's hard to explain how I'm really feeling when so many emotions are fluttering around inside me at once.

Glover swings a chair over to me and offers me a cup of

coffee, and I politely decline as I sit next to her desk and cross my legs. We spoke briefly on the phone last night, so my visit is not a surprise, but I still feel awkward being here. There's something so intimidating and austere about this place, and somehow I can still feel the cuffs around my wrists from when I was being dragged through the maze.

I ask the obvious questions. I ask about Taylor. She reconfirms what we spoke about last night, runs through an abridged version of the arrest and the subsequent interrogation. Izzy did everything according to plan, and once she got Taylor's confession, Taylor was arrested on the spot. The whole time she's saying all of this I'm giddy inside, trying hard to keep a straight face and not laugh, but then she describes the look on Taylor's face when she saw that Izzy was strapped with the wire, and I almost lose it.

You see this kind of shit in movies all the time and you know how it ends. Bad guy gets caught. Life moves on. But this isn't a movie, and justice is promised to no one, especially not to people who look like me. So it's different when it happens to you. I just wish I could have been there to witness it all.

"Did she cry?" I can't help myself.

Glover holds my gaze for a beat, completely understanding the gravity of my question. "Not with me. I think she was too embarrassed to show any emotion."

That surprises me, the former more than the latter. Taylor didn't use the most powerful weapon in her arsenal. She didn't manufacture tears for sympathy. I disagree with Glover, but I hold it in. I think Taylor didn't cry because she didn't have the right audience. She's probably stockpiling her tears for the judge and jury.

"Embarrassed," I repeat, shaking my head. Even with her entire future sucked down into a vortex, Taylor clung to her pride.

"Maybe it hasn't hit her yet." Glover sips her coffee and shrugs.

"Or maybe she thinks she can still get out of this."

"Trust me, it'll hit her by the time she's standing under a lukewarm shower with sanitary napkins stuck to the bottoms of her feet. I mean, can you imagine that girl sandwiched between one woman using the shower as a toilet and another in the corner watching her?"

A laugh slips from me. "What about Bierman? Was he shocked?"

"When he finished listening to the recording from Izzy's wire, I think he tinkled a little."

I chuckle and picture the look that must have hijacked his face. His implicit biases couldn't allow him to see what Glover saw, and even though I made it through, it hits me that I'm one of the lucky ones. I had a Glover on my side. So many other black girls didn't, won't.

Suddenly, the moment feels laden with a guilt I didn't anticipate. To lighten things up, I ask, "How much is her bail?"

Taylor's hearing was this morning.

"The judge flat-out denied her request," Glover tells me, just a tinge of pride modulating her tone as she sips what looks like black coffee. "With that new cash flow, she's a flight risk."

I hold back a grin and squirm in anticipation of calling Nate as soon as I leave. He was convinced she would get something soft, like three years in jail and early release after a year, and maybe a half-million dollars of her inheritance because of her pretty white privilege.

It looks like Glover is stifling a victorious quirk of her lips, too, as she sits back in her chair. This is as big a deal for her as it is for me. She handled a first-degree murder case and got a confession. A promotion is definitely on the horizon for her, and we chew over where she can shop for some new flattering suits while she finishes off her coffee.

When I ask her about Izzy, she tells me she was able to work out a deal with the assistant DA. In exchange for her cooperation in getting the confession from Taylor, Izzy's sentence will be reduced, though she'll still spend a significant chunk of her youth behind bars.

A door closes loudly somewhere and when I look up and see Bierman stepping out, I think of everything that's happened, of all the things I've been waiting to say to his face, which basically boil down to him being a racist and hack detective, but when he gets closer, I suddenly lose the inclination.

He's not worth my words anyway.

Glover looks at me and apologizes again for arresting me as if it was all her fault, and I realize she is kind of like my hero. I thank her for all she's done, for seeing me. For so many years, no one saw me.

When I stand to leave, we don't shake hands. Glover hugs me, and immediately I feel like I might cry. I resist the urge to pump my fist into the air and decide that tonight will be the sixth time I watch *Black Panther* just on principle.

30

BRANDI

Still, I don't sleep through the night for five days. Not until it's Saturday and Nate is back in New York for the weekend and there is at least some sense of normalcy in my world after the fucking whirlwind of Taylor Van Doren.

I still can't believe it worked.

Even though I trusted Glover, there was still some part of me that kept telling me that this plan was impossible to pull off. I just swore this crazy girl would find a way out, just like she's always managed to do.

"Babe, come on," Nate says, slipping into the room behind me. "The car is downstairs and you're not even dressed."

He's right. I'm in a nude bra and a seamless thong because I thought I was going to wear my cream knit dress for dinner, but that was three dresses ago. I step out of another chocolate brown dress I picked up from a charity shop on the Upper East Side for thirty dollars and add it to the heap of clothes covering the bed. I thought a dress would be simple and easy, except now I'm thinking maybe a skirt and blouse would be more appropriate for meeting Nate's parents, but when I shuffle through my hangers to pair something together, nothing works.

"I can't do this," I say.

"My mom already has the lasagna in the oven, Great Grandma's secret recipe. We have no choice now."

"I'm serious, Nate. I don't think I can do the whole meet-your-parents thing right now."

I look at him, and of course he looks good, casual in a thin pullover and suede ankle boots. He just doesn't understand how stressful this is for me. I was fine until this morning when he texted me before he boarded his flight. That's when it set in. I agreed to let him introduce me to his impeccable mother and his superstar father. Me, a nobody from nowhere. They're going to take one look at me and wonder where they went wrong with their only son, and then once I'm gone from their palatial Jersey home, they're going to do everything they can to talk him out of getting any more serious with me.

I abandon my rack and toss on my robe as soon as I get into the bathroom. I move to the mirror but can't even look at myself. I know who I am, but what if it's not enough for his parents?

Nate knocks before pushing in, and I feel absolutely mortified when he sees my tears before I have a chance to brush them away. "Hey, hey. Look at me."

I take a breath and open my eyes to see my makeup is streaked. He holds my gaze and asks so softly, "What's wrong?"

"I don't want to go."

I drop my eyes, unable to look at him. I don't want to hurt his feelings. We've already promised his parents we'd come over this weekend. I don't want him to have to let them down, but I just can't do this anymore.

He watches me for a moment. "You don't want to go...or you scared?"

"What if they don't like me?" I can barely make out my own words. "What if they don't think I'm..."

"What?"

"I don't know," I say, exasperated, frustrated that he's making me spell this out for him. "Good enough for you. I didn't go to fancy prep school. My parents aren't rich. They're not even here. And I have a record."

"They don't care about shit like that."

"Just because you don't doesn't mean they're gonna feel the same."

"Yo, my dad grew up in the streets. He was hustling before he was drafted."

I inhale, make a graceless sound. "I know, but—"

"My mom was homeless when she was a kid. Her and her brothers shelter-hopped for almost a whole year. This is family," he says, his arms tightening around me. "You don't have to impress anybody. You just gotta be you."

I lift my eyes to his again and there's a smile in his eyes right before the edges of his lips curl.

I smile back and whisper, "Okay."

"Yeah? You good?"

"Two minutes." I twist around in his arms. "Let me just fix my mascara and I'll throw something on."

"Two minutes. We gotta get there before the lasagna gets cold." He kisses me quickly on the lips and backs out of the room. "I'll be in the front."

This time when I look in the mirror, I smile, because I still can't believe he's mine, that after everything, we are still here, still alive, still strong.

I do some quick touch-ups where my tears have dripped and reapply a coat of mascara. I go back to Maybe Dress Number Three and am caught in the sleeves thanks to the crisscross detailing in the back when my phone starts vibrating. I put the call on speakerphone, and because I'm generally not great at multitasking and I'm down to the last couple of rings now, I completely forget to check the caller ID, so when the voice on the other end says, "Hi, Brandi. This is Lauren Bosch from Van Doren," in that synthetic cheery voice that makes me want to stab out my eyes, I freeze.

All I can think of is the last time we spoke, when she basically told me I was too black to fit into the "culture" at Van Doren, and, at this point, I'm not so much angry but shocked and bewildered by her caucacity.

Finally, I get the straps on right and manage to open my mouth and form actual words, but all that comes out is a scratchy, "Speaking."

It doesn't land as great in real life as it does in my head because after I confirm it's me there is this unspoken expectation hanging in the air, like *are you done?* I should sound more chipper. I should ask how she's doing. I know this, but I am really not in the mood to shuck and jive right now.

"How are you?" she asks, jumping in before it gets too awkward, and I have to give her credit because her enthusiasm is so close to sounding sincere. "I hope you're doing well."

At this point I just want her to get to why she called me so I can pull my dress down over my hips and find my shoes as I am starting to feel weird about having small talk in my underwear even though she can't see me. I tell her I'm doing okay and still don't ask how she's doing in return. The words don't come.

"Well, that's great to hear," she says, and I literally hold my breath because I can feel it coming. Some bullshit I won't know how to respond to fast enough. "I was just calling to let you know we have an opening in the marketing department and we'd love you to join our team as an assistant if you're still interested."

The words don't compute at first.

Of all the things I was expecting her to say, that was not in the ballpark of any of them.

I am completely silent.

Lauren starts to go into how they are trying to diversify things at Van Doren, and I hold in a sigh because I loathe that word. She goes on to say that they are Listening And Learning and trying to do better, slipping dangerously into the territory of Cringey White Apologies, and I'm silently hoping she doesn't bring up George Floyd or Black Lives Matter because that would seriously push me over the edge right now. I sincerely don't want to have to be mean to her.

As she continues, I pretend to listen to her, and I halfway am, but also I'm low-key trying to imagine going back to work at Van Doren, by which I mean making a mental list of every reason this is a bad idea. At some point I hear her vaguely referencing everything that has happened with Taylor, mainly the fight at the hotel, since of course someone posted the whole thing on TikTok, but because she is white and trying oh so hard to be politically correct and is generally clumsy with these sorts of things, she tap-dances around it instead of coming right out and saying she is sorry that some spoiled rich girl attacked me. There is a quick mention of salary, which I quickly calculate to be a pretty decent hourly rate. I throw in a few *yeahs* and *okays* so I don't seem rude. When she's done, I still don't know what to say. I don't know if I should be angry or insulted. So I tell her I'll think about it and hang up.

"Babe."

I look up at Nate, a rightful look of impatience on his face. Then his eyes drop to my phone and he frowns. "Who was that?"

I pause. I'm still not sure if that phone call was real or a sadistic hallucination.

"Van Doren just called me, asking if I'm available," I say,

my voice faint. "It was the woman who fired me. She apologized and said they have an open slot in marketing. Said that she hopes I consider returning."

He scoffs dismissively, and I fucking love how protective he is of me. "What did you say?"

I shrug and wander over to the shoe section of my closet. "I said I'll think about it."

"So what are you thinking?" he asks, following me inside like a new puppy.

I'm thinking I don't want to think about this right now. I don't want to think about Lauren. I don't want to think about Taylor. I don't want to think about anything that's happened over the past few weeks. Van Doren, and everyone who works there, can kiss my ass. Nate is right. Tonight is going to be a great night with his family and I've already interviewed for a few intern positions for next season. True, none of them are at the assistant level, and there's no dreamy trip to Milan included, but I'll grind my way there eventually. I've climbed much steeper hills.

I choose a pair of strappy sandals and flip around once I finish buckling them on. I pose for Nate and I don't even have to ask but decide to anyway.

"Like this one?"

"Yo, Mom loves light blue."

He leans down for a quick kiss, but I open his mouth, give him a little more than I can tell he was expecting. I want him to know how much that meant to me, when he held me as I cried.

"Whoa, girl," Nate says, pulling back with a chuckle. "What you trying to do?"

I blush and grab a jacket, then follow him to the front of the apartment. "Is the lasagna really that good?" I ask as he pulls the door open for me. "That's a four-generation-long secret we're talking."

"Trust me, every time she makes some for the neighbors, Tupperware's stock skyrockets like GameStop did that one time."

"So how come you haven't learned the recipe?"

I don't expect him to pause and really consider the question; I was just teasing. I turn back for him and watch him ponder for a beat. Then he smiles, gently looking me over.

"Maybe she can teach you soon," he whispers.

I blush a little because I know exactly what he's thinking. He's picturing me in his future, sees me becoming a permanent fixture in his life, a part of his family. He's not just taking me to meet his parents; he's introducing me to his inner world, letting me get a taste of what's to come years from now. He pulls me in for a slow kiss and never in my life have I felt more wanted, more secure, like I am exactly where I am supposed to be.

★ ★ ★ ★ ★

ACKNOWLEDGMENTS

Sharing the stories that haunt us at night is a privilege we don't take lightly. But writing a book takes more than blood, sweat, tears and frequently accumulating a horrifying internet search history. None of this would be possible without the gang who made this dream a reality for us, so pardon us while we get mushy.

First, massive gratitude to our insanely badass agent, Jessica Faust. Thank you so much for taking a chance on us, wholeheartedly championing this book and for being such a fierce advocate throughout this entire process. When we signed with you, we felt we'd make a good team, and now that we're over a year into this, we see that was an understatement. Clicking Send was one of the best decisions we've ever made. *SHTDI* would not have made it here without you and the rest of the amazing people at Bookends Literary: Sabrina Castillo, James McGowan and Jenissa Graham.

Of course, we have to thank our inimitable editing team, Brittany Lavery and Sarah Murphy. Brittany, thank you for your endless congeniality, for your commitment to the true essence of this novel, for never being frustrated with us during any part of this process even though you absolutely should have been. You were always extremely patient and kind with your feedback, and you definitely deserve some kind of award. Not to mention, like, three weeks in the Maldives. Having an editor who truly gets the story you're trying to tell is something writers dream about, and we feel so ridiculously lucky to have had you been a part of this journey with us. Of course, without you, none of this would have ever happened; in other words, thank you for existing.

Sarah, thank you for being so nitpicky and never holding back. Your sharp, thoughtful edits elevated our storytelling and genuinely pushed us to make *SHTDI* so much stronger, though they made us want to rip out each other's hair in the moment. Don't worry, we're fine. Totally fine.

Special thanks to Melanie Fried, Leah Morse, Diane Lavoie, Quinn Banting, Kathleen Mancini and everyone else at Graydon House who worked behind the scenes to get *SHTDI* on the shelves. We are so grateful to have had such an incredible group of talented, supersmart women working on this project with us.

Thanks, Mom, for being our number one from the beginning. Also, for these words of encouragement after hearing the news of our book deal: "This shit is unbelievable! But I knew it was going to happen sooner or later. Y'all worked so hard." If there was one person we could count on to not question why we were *still* writing after eight years of steady, relentless rejection, it was you.

Thanks as well to Sadé Grandberry for encouraging us to join our high school's book club. If it weren't for you deciding to write your own story—which spawned our rampant jealousy that drove us to write our first short stories—we would have never made it to *SHTDI*. Thank you for believing in us even when we didn't and for your endless support. (This includes listening to us rant on and on about how we think we're trash and won't sell any copies of this book.)

Thank you to every boss who fired us, with a special shoutout to the one who fired us both on the same day for "brainstorming ideas" on company time—you only encouraged us to write more. Same goes for everyone who told us to get a "real" job. Appreciate the doubt because it only motivated us further.

To Rance Robeson, for seeing us and encouraging us to hone our craft even more.

To our family, who have always surrounded us in love and unconditional support even if it's from two thousand miles away. Aunt Patty, you'll be in our memories forever.

And of course, lastly, to you. We're assuming you're either here because (1) you wanted more of the story so you turned the page and are currently disappointed, or (2) you're just nosy and wanted to see who we would thank. Either way, you made it this far and we can't wait to see you again for the next one.

THE STORY BEHIND
SOMEONE HAD TO DO IT

It's crazy that *SHTDI* ever came into existence since Amber once vowed we would never write a book together because she didn't want us to fight all day long. But one morning, she popped out of bed and said something like, "What if we wrote a story about this girl who wants to be in fashion, but ends up getting sucked into this crazy world and realizes it's not as glamorous as it seems?" The phrase "deceptively beautiful" was on repeat in our heads as we brainstormed a plot from this concept.

We literally sat on the couch for three hours—no breakfast, no shower—and threw out idea after idea, just building off each other until we both knew we had something solid. Something fresh. The more we realized we were telling a cat-and-mouse story, the more it felt right to tell it from two perspectives—one from Brandi, the outsider, because that's essentially who we were when we worked in fashion, and the other from her polar opposite, Taylor, the almost obnoxiously privileged heiress who, from the outside, is exactly where Brandi wants to be.

By the end of our session on the couch, we essentially had a beat sheet with all the major plot points we knew we wanted to hit. Also, tons of notes on characters and scenes we knew we wanted to explore. Tone was instant too. We knew right away that our goal was to write something fun, sexy and fast-paced that would resonate with our generation—millennials and upper Zoomers—because there aren't a lot of thrillers on the market that actually target our demographic. But it was also important that the book touched on certain themes like privilege and entitlement and the inequality of our justice system because that's the reality of the world we live in. The book is part escapist, but it's also grounded in very genuine critique of the corrosive effects of racism and extreme wealth.

Writing this book together completely from scratch was definitely harder than we anticipated, but also, extremely worth it. We both went into it a little naive; we assumed that because we generally have similar tastes and writing styles, writing this novel would be a breeze, but we found ourselves disagreeing on a lot of small things (that, of course, felt gargantuan in the moment). It doesn't help that we both have very strong opinions about everything and can both be incredibly obstinate when we feel we're right. It took us a few weeks of cursing each other out in a Google Doc before we learned how to communicate our concerns and disagreements in a respectful way and how to truly compromise. It'd be hard to point out any line and one of us to be able to say, "Yes, I wrote that," because that's how collaborative the process was. The voice of the book really came together so well because we both built off each other and, in the end, combining both of our viewpoints and sensibilities elevated the book tremendously.

SOMEONE HAD TO DO IT:
THE PLAYLIST

1. "Twenty One," Khalid

2. "Whole Lotta Money (Remix)," Bia featuring Nicki Minaj

3. "deja vu," Olivia Rodrigo

4. "Tumblr Girls," G-Eazy featuring Christoph Andersson

5. "Modern Loneliness," Lauv

6. "Super Rich Kids," Frank Ocean

7. "I'm a Mess," Bebe Rexha

8. "Rich White Girls," mansionz

9. "happier," Olivia Rodrigo

10. "lovely," Billie Eilish and Khalid

11. "New Normal," Khalid

DISCUSSION QUESTIONS

1. We find out very early on that Brandi is put on probation at her internship because she does not fit in with the "culture" at Van Doren. Discuss why this excuse is a microaggression and what her supervisor actually meant by this statement.

2. Nate is an interesting character in both Brandi's and Taylor's worlds because he is sort of the halfway mark between the two. He, like Taylor, has grown up rich and famous-adjacent, but his parents are from humble beginnings and have raised him with limited access to their wealth. How do his and Taylor's different upbringings impact the decisions they each make throughout the story?

3. Taylor and her friends ultimately decide to frame Brandi for the murder of Simon, saying it'd be like "killing two birds with one stone." Why do you think Brandi was the perfect person to take the "fall" in Taylor's eyes? Do you think race and/or class played a part in their decision? If so, in what ways?

4. Glover seems to be wary of Taylor from the start of the murder investigation, suspecting her as the perpetrator from the beginning. Why do you think she wasn't ini-

tially able to convince Bierman to look into Taylor as a prime suspect or even a person of interest?

5. Who do you think was the true villain(s) of the story?

6. We finally learn that it was actually Izzy who laced Simon's glasses with the poison. Were you surprised by this reveal? Did you think it was an interesting plot twist or were you expecting it?

7. What are your thoughts about the ending? Did you think Taylor would get away with her crimes? Do you think she'll actually go to prison for the murder of Simon, or will she find a way to wield her privilege and work the system in her favor?

8. What did you think of Brandi and Nate's relationship? Did you think it was a positive, tender and compassionate representation of black love?

9. Was there ever a point in the story where you felt like you were starting to understand Taylor's motivations for wanting her father dead? Were you ever on her side, even briefly?

10. As a millennial or a Zoomer, what were some of the themes addressed in the novel that specially resonated with you and why?